Of Art and Air

—BOOK ONE OF THE TANNER TRILOGY—

Michele Venné

*To Nancy J—
Breathe into creating [illegible]
Michele Ven[né]
Mystery Con
NM Scottsdale 2016*

Of Art and Air

Dear Reader,

For as long as humans have procreated, children have been a source of fulfillment in numerous ways. Not all of them loving and humane. Abduction is the quickest way to meet the insatiable demand for labor, warriors, slaves, pawns for blackmail or ransom, to fill a loss, feed insanity, and use in all manners of abuse and exploitation. It's an error to believe that all perpetrators are strangers.

Regardless of the means, there are those who take what they want, driven by the need for money and power. Poaching is viewed as theft, yet legal hunting can be seen as either harvesting, or killing. Numerous species are extinct due to man's lack of conservation and preservation. However, considerable effort has been made in recent years to remove pollution from environments and reintroduce endangered species to appropriate habitats. To reduce the impact on every ecological system, there is the suggestion of "take only pictures, leave only footprints".

Tolerance and acceptance fluctuate greatly in every aspect of human existence. Some believe that we're wonderful in our similarities and differences. Others judge, criticize, and express malice towards those who wander outside society's norms. Though they often cause no harm or infringe upon their neighbors, insensitivity and misunderstanding runs rampant in the mainstream.

As you venture into the Wyoming wilderness in this first story of the Tanner siblings, I invite you to take a deep breath and indulge in creativity. By the end of book three, unexpected connections will be made and perhaps some motivation for change.

Fondly, Michele Venné

Acknowledgements

Thanks Jeri, as always, for your patience in typing my handwritten manuscripts and completing the first edit.

Thank you, Stephanie! Your feedback and encouragement mean a lot to me.

Lil, your artistic talent applied to the cover truly makes my books stand out!
www.TheStudioSkye.com

Billy, I give you much gratitude for the use of your incredible photographs and your knowledge to help me get the facts straight.
https://billyrhoades.see.me

I'm grateful to Kristyna and Brian for your expert insight and sharing with me the tiny details of police work and fires.

Prologue

It was the crispness of the air that allowed the smoke from the end of the barrel to be visible as it wafted up and away. His shot was true, deadly. The man, the recipient of the bullet, had been a nuisance. With him no longer around to impede the project, they should be on schedule, the money deposited with regularity into the bank account. He slowly lowered the rifle from his shoulder, resting the polished wood of the stock under his arm. Glancing at the sky, he grunted at the fast-moving storm clouds. The weather experts predicted a late snow in the Central Rockies. Not much at this latitude. Too bad. Several inches of snow would hide his tracks and hinder the recovery of Bear's body.

Turning to retrace his steps down the hill to where he had parked the truck, his mind began to spin with the next step of the plan. Samantha wouldn't be an issue, tucked away as she was on the ranch in Colorado. Shaun would conduct an investigation, as was his responsibility as the town sheriff. The only obstacle left that might keep the plan from completion was Carli, and she was somewhere in Africa, not scheduled to return to the States for another three weeks. Perhaps the one who controlled the flow of finances would be able to push the case through court in Laramie before she returned. And if they couldn't do that, then she may have to meet with an accident.

That thought was followed by a misstep, his left foot sliding forward on the loose gravel covered with dead pine needles, bringing him down on his right side as the rifle was held up in his left hand.

"Goddamn it!" he cursed, looking at the scrapes on his right palm, feeling the soreness in his hip.

Carefully bringing his knee under him in order to leverage himself from the ground, he peered through the branches of the trees next to the trail, and stared at the eight-point buck who had yet to shed his antlers. Liquid brown eyes gazed at him, unblinking. There was knowing, a wisdom that the human failed to possess. The strong, sleek body, partially hidden in the dappled sunlight, paused in his search for forage. Moving slowly, the man brought the stock to his shoulder, and peered through the see-through mounts of the scope at the iron sites. The buck turned his head toward the northwest and sniffed the air. The crack of a rifle spooked the deer, and it bounded off into the woods.

Glancing in the direction of the sound of the report, he climbed to his feet and continued toward the trailhead and his vehicle. Perhaps the customer of Tanner's Outdoor Adventures was more successful at bringing down a trophy than he had been. An hour later he strode to the driver's side of the truck, placed the rifle inside a case, and set the case behind the seat. As he bumped down the service road back toward the highway, he began to visualize the custom homes that would soon be built on Medicine Bow Preserve, a privately owned big game hunting area within the boundaries of the Medicine Bow National Forest.

«««—»»»

One hand holding the camera, the other on the lens that protruded nearly twelve inches from her face, the only movement, besides her breath, was the slight depression of her index finger releasing the shutter. Frame after frame was taken of the black and white striped beasts under the Jacaranda tree. Their trek through the knee-high brown grasses had taken them to the disappearing watering hole fifty yards from the closest shade. Like clockwork, the giraffes were next, the zebras moving a short distance away as a family of African elephants brought their young to play in the water and use the mud in an attempt to protect themselves from the ever-present insects. Pronghorns and gazelles milled around, becoming nervous as the hungry hyenas began to show interest in the fawns.

Of Art and Air

Tim lowered the binoculars and kept his gaze on the slight movement of the grass as it parted, alerting those who were watching to the approach of the lioness.

"Uh, Carli ... we have a visitor that will very soon disrupt your setting."

As soon as Tim announced her presence, those that were often the sustenance for the predator raised their heads and began to move quickly away from the water. She continued to document their reaction, and even caught the lioness as she darted from the cover of the foliage, her two hunting partners to her left and right, and the near miss of claws to the hindquarters of a pronghorn that proved to be quicker and more agile than the huntress thought. Carli's final shot, before lowering her camera, was of the lioness panting, her burst of energy expended, and those that escaped as they scattered into the distance.

Carli sighed, then rose gracefully from her crouched position to stand next to Tim.

"They should have lunch prepared by the time we return to the tents. Are you hungry?" he asked.

She nodded. "But not nearly as what she is," and indicated the lioness and her two partners as they wandered back towards the area their pride marked as their own.

"They'll have another opportunity at dusk," he said as he turned to cover the short distance to the safari vehicle and their guides.

Tim had been her traveling partner since Carli was awarded the position of Lead Photojournalist at *International Views*, a monthly magazine that featured various environments around the world and those that inhabited them. Tim Moore was assistant extraordinaire. He handled the travel plans, most of the cases that contained her equipment, was fluent in French, German, and Spanish, and knew enough of a dozen other languages to get directions to their hotel, the airport, or a decent restaurant. He was a couple years older than Carli, attractive and fit and homosexual. She loved him like a brother, and he often threatened to marry her. They were as opposite as two people could be, with Tim's roots in a rented apartment in Greenwich Village in New York City. While Carli spent her formative years on the wildlife Preserve her father owned outside Laramie, Wyoming, Tim had been surrounded by various artists, rich culture, and international traveling.

Carli was raised mainly by her father, her mother deciding that six months a year with freezing temperatures and snow was more than she wanted, so she returned to her native California. Hiking, fishing, hunting, tracking, and wilderness survival were Carli's curriculum before and during her formal school years. She left Wyoming to attend art school, landed a handful of jobs at various news sources and magazines, then she found her permanent home at *International Views*. She generally returned home between assignments, but not this time. They got the shots they needed, so after lunch they would head to the city where their next flight would take them to Venezuela, via New Zealand.

Disassembling her camera and lens, and withdrawing the roll of film, she had it all packed away before they arrived at the tent. They ate a hearty meal, loaded the remainder of their gear into the largest van used to transport tourists from town to the safari, and left behind the savannah of Kenya.

Passing few vehicles on their way to the city, one moved slightly off to the side of the dirt road, which was the width of a single vehicle, as the van passed. The small truck continued toward the tents and the safari company that was assisting Carli Tanner, the photographer from the big American magazine that came to document the animals. Inside the pocket of the driver from the city was a telegram for Ms. Tanner. Once the truck arrived at the tents, the driver was informed that Carli and Tim had left early, and that he had probably passed the van on his way there. The one in charge of the safari and the driver conversed in their native language, attempting to decide what they should do about the message. The driver opened the envelope and read the telegram:

Come home.

CHAPTER 1

Fortunately, Carli didn't need her own pillow, or even a bed, to rejuvenate. In chairs at busy airports, in vehicles traveling from a bustling city to a remote village, a tent, under the stars, in the rain, or an airplane seat, if her body told her it needed to rest, she would close her eyes and within minutes drop into the abyss of sleep. She slept soundly, and on the rare occasions that Tim wasn't close, she would set the alarm on her watch. The cell phone she carried wasn't always practical if her assignment took her far from a cell tower and the electricity needed to recharge it. She had one because it was convenient, when she was in a location that it worked.

With Tim beside her, a gentle elbow in the ribs brought her out of her slumber as they made their final descent to Caracas, Venezuela. She rubbed her neck, yawned, and stretched before she opened her eyes and looked out the small window of the commercial airplane. Numerous skyscrapers lined the horizon, then gave way to the green of lush vegetation and steep mountains that surrounded the city. She glanced at her wrist, knowing she would need to reset her watch to local time once they were inside the terminal.

"You must be hungry. The meal served while we were in the air was several hours ago," Tim said as he unbuckled his seatbelt and looked down the aisle as the flight attendant stood to take the microphone and welcome them to South America.

"Maybe they'll have a restaurant inside the airport. You know, our last chance at American food before we spend the next two weeks in the bush," Carli suggested.

She followed Tim out of the row to the aisle, then stretched her 5'10" frame, reached her arms overhead, then twisted to the left and right to loosen her stiff spine. He removed her soft-sided case from the overhead bin and held it for her. She pulled her backpack from under the front of Tim's seat and slipped her arms through the straps, then took the case from Tim and, placing the strap diagonally across her torso, rested one of her cameras and several undeveloped rolls of film against her hip. Her partner took his own pack and slung it over one shoulder, then placed the other case in the opposite hand. Loaded down like the burros they would likely be riding into the jungle, they made their way to the front of the plane, thanked the flight attendant, and stepped into the jet way where they felt the humid heaviness despite the air conditioning being pumped from the terminal.

Customs had an unusually short line. The officer raised his brow at Carli as he stamped the last page in her U.S. passport. She smiled back and handed over documentation identifying her as a journalist, which earned her pursed lips beneath his full, black mustache. He placed them on the counter, marked them with a red X on the upper-right corner, then passed them back to her. She stepped forward, then turned to wait for Tim. Long red hair gathered at his neck, goatee, and blue eyes that flashed at the dark-skinned man in the black uniform, temporarily distracted the employee from checking Tim's paperwork. Usually not displaying his feminine side, he leaned his elbow on the counter, rested his chin in his palm, and smiled flirtatiously at the obviously straight customs officer. The Venezuelan native couldn't return the documents quick enough. She stifled a chuckle as Tim blew the officer a kiss, gathered his papers, and joined her as they left customs in search of an American fast food chain.

"Mmmm," Carli sighed and closed her eyes as the hamburger filled her mouth.

"These fries have nothing on llama eyeball soup," Tim commented, shoving four of them, dripping with ketchup, between his lips.

"That was in the Andes, in Chile," she said. "I think we're in for a treat of deep fried guinea pigs."

"Oh! Please! Let's not ruin this fine cuisine." Tim scrunched up his face at the thought of the little critters perched on the end of a stick.

Finishing their meal, they moved to the front of the terminal to locate their connection that would take them, and all their crates, to the village that they would work out of for the next two weeks. Apparently, the magazine was able to contract with a well-connected company this time, as it was very easy to spy the sign held by the driver. After introductions were made and all their cases were loaded, some in the Hummer, the rest in a nondescript van, Carli climbed into the backseat of the Hummer, and Tim sat in the front passenger seat since he was prone to carsickness. Always wanting to be prepared, by the time they exited the airport she had unpacked and loaded film in her camera so it was ready to catch the sights.

Several pictures were taken of structures, both old and recent, new vehicles, and burned-out remains that marked attacks from guerrilla factions that ventured in from their camps in the trees. Brown faces of children from six to sixteen suspended their football game in the street to allow the Hummer and van to pass. The shutter caught everything from their sandaled or bare feet, to colorful striped shirts, to the chipped stucco walls that denoted the economic status of the neighborhood. She leaned back against the seat and rested her camera in her lap as the tires of their vehicle started down the rutted, poorly paved road into the jungle.

«««—»»»

Shaun leaned against the open front driver's side door, pushed his hat back from his forehead, and rubbed his eyes with his thumb and middle finger. A minute. All he needed was a minute to get his emotions under control, to stop the wetness he felt on his fingers from falling unchecked. The flashing red and blue lights, the squawk of the radio from the dispatcher, all disrupted the serene beauty of the Preserve. He could hear Alyssa, born and raised in town, sobbing into Zach's shirt, one of the seasonal employees of Tanner's Outdoor Adventures that had endeared himself to Bear, and therefore became a permanent fixture of the Preserve. The clients who were at the lodge were seated on the veranda and being questioned by Vince Bogard, one of his deputies. Vince was nearly twice Shaun's age, but had no aspirations to be sheriff and was content to take his orders from the one who had been elected to the position.

The back doors to the ambulance slammed shut, securing Bear's body inside. Shaun took a steadying breath, forced the grief and confusion to a dark corner in his mind where he would peer into later, when he was alone. Now, his job was to discover who murdered his father on Wolf's Ridge, and why. Readjusting his hat, he turned to Stan, the driver of the emergency vehicle that would take Bear Tanner to the hospital in Laramie, where the Medical Examiner would tell Shaun what he already knew regarding the cause of death, which was lodged somewhere in the torso of the victim. He hoped the coroner would give more information, something that would lead to answers instead of the jumble of questions that filled his mind. Perhaps if the incident had taken place closer to the lodge, then the ambulance would deliver to the hospital a man fighting for his life instead of one that lost that life in a pool on the Ridge, and in the saddle and on the horse and employee that retrieved the body that was now zipped inside a bag.

Stan extended his hand and gave Shaun the clipboard with forms on it to sign. "Real sorry about your dad, Shaun," he said, then took the papers and pen from the sheriff.

"Thanks, Stan. Give me a call when you're back in town."

"Will do." Stan turned and crossed the now-crowded driveway to the bus, climbed in, and drove slowly toward Highway 130, and Laramie, Wyoming.

Shaun readjusted his hat and wound his way through cars and people, both employees and clients, some deciding to cut their vacation short. Placing his hands on his hips he sighed again and looked at Alyssa.

"Do you think you're able to help me out, Lys?" he asked.

She nodded, sniffed, then eased away from Zach.

"I need you to contact *International Views*. Find out where Carli is, and get a message to her about what happened today," Shaun paused as it looked as if she might start crying again.

When it seemed she would hold it together, she asked, "Do you want me to call Samantha?"

He shook his head. "I'll take care of that. I need you to stay here. Call home, explain that I requested for you to put in extra hours with some clients leaving early and others not being able to go out on planned excursions."

Alyssa nodded, grateful for a job to do to give her a reprieve from crying. She climbed the steps to the lodge, then disappeared inside.

"Zach, get a count of how many rooms were occupied and pull the files on those clients."

"Yes, Sir," Zach said, and followed Alyssa into the lodge and Bear's office.

Shaun glanced at the darkening sky overhead. It had taken most of the day to bring his father down from the Ridge, and he didn't know how long it would be before he could piece together the evidence, and the story, of the demise of Bear Tanner. He would call Samantha, his younger sister, and she would come as soon as she could. What he needed to know was, where the hell was Carli?

«««—»»»

"Thank you, Agent Brooks. You may step down," Judge Carmen instructed.

Ethan left the witness stand and rejoined his boss, Micah Sloane, Special Agent in Charge of the FBI Field Office in Baltimore, Maryland. Folding his 6'2" height onto the narrow, wooden bench, and placing the yellow legal pad in his lap, he gazed at the defendant. The pencil flipped around his fingers, then eventually gave in to the impulse. As the defense began their closing arguments, the faces of Judge Judith Carmen, defense attorney George Hackman, and those sitting at the prosecutor's table began to appear on the yellow paper. He had no need to depict the defendant, Richard Glassier, as the man's face would never be forgotten as the kidnapper and murderer of seventeen children between the ages of five and eleven abducted from Virginia to Vermont, over a three-year period. The jurors would remain anonymous, as would Tommy Mason, the last child stolen, and the only one returned alive to his family.

Ethan had filled three pages with his sketches, and his boss received twenty messages on his cell phone by the time final arguments were completed, and Judge Carmen called all to rise as the jury left their box, escorted by the bailiff, to their room to begin deliberations. He flipped down the front page to cover what he sketched, placed his pencil in his jacket pocket, and made his way, Micah behind him, out of the courtroom to the elevators at the end of the hall. The media had been denied access to the courtroom during the proceedings due to the nature of the crime and the presentation of photos of the recovered remains of the victims. However, once Micah Sloan was outside the building, there would be the flash of cameras and hovering microphones belonging to news stations along the East Coast demanding comments and knowledge of the outcome of the case. Micah would give the press his attention, allowing Ethan to escape unnoticed, ensuring his face remained out of the papers, and thus protecting his anonymity.

Taking an extra moment to pull on his coat and sunglasses before he left the relative protection of the courthouse lobby, Ethan slipped away from the mass of media standing at the front of the structure, and into the clear, but brisk, March afternoon. He rounded the corner, hailed a cab, and returned to the field office. With the closing of this case, he could turn his attention to the other dozen unsolved files. Staring at the snow piled alongside the road from a spring storm, he wondered if he would be the recipient of six hours of uninterrupted sleep that night, or if nightmares would have him searching the web at two in the morning. He paid the cab driver, mounted the steps to the building, then removed his sunglasses, and the objects from his pockets, before walking through the metal detector.

"How was court, Agent Brooks?" the security guard asked as Ethan gathered his belongings on the other side of the machine.

"I believe we'll have a favorable outcome," Ethan replied.

The guard nodded. "Have a good afternoon, Agent Brooks."

He smiled slightly, then walked past the elevators to the stairwell. Loosening his tie as he climbed the first couple of steps, when he reached the second flight, he took them two at a time, the top button of his shirt undone. Emerging at the eighth floor, he regained his breath as he strode down the carpeted hallway to his desk, partially partitioned off from the other FBI agent nearest him. Sitting heavily in his chair, he opened the bottom desk drawer, withdrew the lockbox that housed his weapon, and tossed in the legal pad where it landed on top of the growing stack, all containing sketches of defendants, judges, and attorneys. He retrieved his keys from the front pocket of his suit pants, unlocked the box, placed his gun and holster at his waist, replaced the box and closed that drawer, only to open the one above it. Taking the file folders that contained his twelve unsolved cases, he closed the drawer, dropped his keys back in his pocket, the files in his case, and turned to leave, when he saw Micah blocking his way.

"Three days?" his boss asked.

"As requested."

"And mine is for you to check in with the company shrink," Micah said and watched his agent closely for signs of denial.

Glancing away and readjusting his coat, Ethan said, "I'll see if Dr. Dyne has an opening tomorrow."

Micah nodded. "I'll let you know when the jury returns." He stepped aside and allowed Ethan to move past him and down the hall.

Ethan Brooks had been with the Bureau for ten years and had pulled some of the hardest, and heartbreaking, cases. He followed procedure, but often danced close to the line. His uncanny ability to get inside the suspect's head was aided by his degrees in Psychology, Sociology, and his training with the Profiling Unit. Though he had the leadership skills to manage a team, Ethan preferred to work alone. The senior partner the Bureau paired him with when he was first hired was shot while apprehending a suspect. Mac Waise died of complications encountered during surgery to remove the bullet. Ethan insisted he be the one to inform Suzanne, Mac's wife of twenty-three years. He then told Micah that he either worked alone, or would walk. Good agents were plenty, but few had Ethan's ability. Micah usually allowed Ethan the room he needed to work a case. This one, involving Tommy Mason, was especially tough. Perhaps three days' vacation wouldn't be enough.

He sighed and returned to his office in an effort to answer the numerous messages already sent to his cell, and those awaiting him on his desk phone. Three hours later, he had either deferred or handled all that could be dealt with at that time. Night had come to Baltimore and found Micah staring out the eighth-floor window, not recognizing the patterns of traffic below. The final message he had yet to deal with was a request from the Regional Director. As a 'personal favor', could Micah send a field agent to Laramie, Wyoming, to assist in the investigation of the suspected murder of Bear Tanner, owner of the outfit where the Regional Director had spent his last vacation. It wasn't a request.

Perhaps that is what Agent Brooks needed. A change of scenery, a different kind of case, an opportunity to work with local law enforcement. Micah snorted. Ethan Brooks specialized in serial cases, had never lived or worked outside of a major metropolis, and didn't want the responsibility of working with, and protecting, another officer. The shadows had begun to crowd into his agent's countenance. Pleased or not, Ethan Brooks would be headed to the wild west of Wyoming in three days.

CHAPTER 2

"It's been raining since we got here. If it doesn't stop, not only will we be washed off this mountain, but this will be a wasted trip." He stood behind Carli and peered past her into the deluge.

"No destination is ever wasted, Tim. What one does when they arrive ... that determines the sense of loss, or achievement."

"Well, maybe I'm feeling so damn depressed because I can't do anything with all this rain!"

She lowered the camera, shifted her gaze to her partner, and raised a brow. "You can fill the generator with gas so we have lights later tonight. The new software program is installed on the laptops, ready for the signal from the portable satellite dish that needs to be erected. There are half a dozen memory cards that can be downloaded. And if none of that interests you, it would be nice if our breakfast dishes were cleaned before dinner."

He scowled, crossed his arms, then gestured outside their tent with a tipping of his head. "Yeah, well, what are you doing? Taking shots of mating inchworms?"

She brought the viewfinder to the space a centimeter from her eyelash. "Already have those cataloged on my flash drive. What we have here, Timmy, is something much more ... exotic. It appears our visit has gained the attention of a few Pemons."

He stepped next to her and peered out into the curtain of rain. "Cannibals? Really?" Squinting, he could detect nothing except how the precipitation muted and obscured the vegetation around them. "Huh. Where did you say those memory cards were?"

19

She smiled and watched as the shutter flickered, capturing the brown face decorated with white stripes before it disappeared behind a rubber plant.

«« —»»

The sheriff tried six ways to Sunday to make sense of the filing system in the office. Bear had his own thoughts on organization and the only one who was ever able to decipher it was Carli. Alyssa entered some stuff in the books, but the licenses, deeds, Bear's will, and other documents that his father was in possession of before the digital age, were temporarily misplaced. Tossing down a file folder elicited a cloud of dust. Apparently, Bear didn't spend much time in his office, or hadn't recently.

Dragging his hand through the dark blonde locks on top of his head, he sighed and looked around, hoping what he was searching for would jump out at him. He left the private office in search of the only other person who had intimate knowledge of Tanner's Outdoor Adventures. Closing the door quietly behind him, he turned the deadbolt and took two steps before pausing in the partially lit hallway.

"Of course they'll pay me for overtime. I promise I'll be home after breakfast. No, I'll stay in an empty cabin. Alone. I know, Daddy."

Shaun cocked his head to the side as he listened to Alyssa. He knew she didn't spend much time at home. Her father was an unemployed ranch hand, handyman, and miner. Jim Lockhart had an unhealthy relationship with alcohol, and as a result, was rarely found to have earned a paycheck. Alyssa's mother had died a few years earlier. She was a sickly woman whose hard life with Lockhart sapped what strength she had. Alyssa was the youngest of three. The oldest brother was serving in the military and currently stationed overseas. Her middle brother was an artist of some recognition in New York. Carli had helped him gain entrance to an art school there, and Shaun was the only one who knew she also paid his tuition.

"Such talent should not be wasted simply because there are no funds for an education," was Carli's explanation.

Alyssa had worked for Bear since she started high school, as much for the needed income as to spend time away from her father and the ramshackle house in which they lived. As he listened to her hang up the phone, he wondered what she would do when she graduated in a couple months. It was one more topic to speak with Carli about, if his gypsy sister ever found her way home. He counted to five, then continued down the hallway, not wanting Alyssa to suspect he had overheard her conversation.

"You wouldn't happen to know about Dad's unique filing system, would you?" he asked.

Alyssa shook her head. "He didn't even want me in his office to clean. Said there wasn't much worth keeping the dust mites from eating."

When it looked as if she might start crying again, he pressed on, "Were you able to reach *International Views* and get Carli's location?"

"Yes. When I informed them that she needed to return home, that Bear had ... well ... they said they would contact her. She's in South America."

He nodded. "It's late. Those that have decided to remain and finish their vacation should be turned in by now."

"There are two who are going out with Ray tomorrow morning."

"Hunting?"

"Fishing. Trout. They were tying new flies yesterday. The three staying in the big cabin are hiking with Donna. The other two plan to check out by noon so they can reach Laramie in time for their flight."

"And you'll stay for breakfast?"

She nodded. "Zach will be here to run the desk. Ray said he had work to do and that he would be around."

"Call me if you hear from Carli. She's likely to contact someone here first. Are you alright getting to the cabin?"

Alyssa had turned off the computer and the lights in the lodge, enhancing the glow of the coals from the fire that had burned earlier in the hearth. She moved to the other side of the check-in counter and stood in front of the sheriff. The door opened and Zach paused in the doorway.

She glanced at him, then back at Shaun. "I have an escort, thanks," she said and smiled weakly.

He began to move towards the door, but Alyssa's hand on his forearm stayed him. "Shaun, who would do this? Why would they kill Bear?"

He gathered her in a hug. They had known each other long enough and since they were only eight years apart, he thought of her as a younger sister. "I don't know, Lys. But we're going to find out."

She stepped away and when her gaze met his, tears again were shining in their depths.

"Come on, Alyssa. I'll walk you to the cabin," Zach said from the doorway, Shaun was sure, in an effort to keep the tears from falling.

Pulling the lodge door shut behind him, he turned to watch them stroll in the direction of the first cabin. Zach's arm was around Alyssa's shoulders, her head was tipped towards him.

Shaun glanced up at the clear night sky, then descended the steps of the veranda. Dropping the spare set of keys in one pocket while he fished his personal keys from the other, he thought about the night ahead. Climbing into the four-wheel drive sheriff's vehicle, one of the perks of his position, he drove down the gravel entrance to the highway. Six miles later, a left turn and another half-mile down a graded dirt road, now rutted and muddy due to the last storm, brought him to his own home.

Turning off the headlights, he sat a moment longer. He purchased the land himself, but had taken a loan from his father to build. The two of them had worked on much of it themselves. The outside was finished, as was most of the interior. There was some cabinetry that needed to be installed and a guest room that required sanding and sealant on the walls and floor. After that, it was a matter of decorating, which he didn't have much interest in besides the basics.

Sighing, he made his way to the dark porch, and even darker foyer, as he pushed open the unlocked front door. Flicking on the dimmer switch, he didn't bother taking off his coat as he took two glasses from the open cupboard and a bottle of whiskey from the counter, then returned to the veranda and the two chairs that rested there.

Sitting, exhaling an exhausted sigh, he placed both glasses on the railing. Unscrewing the cap on the bottle, he poured two fingers worth in each glass. Setting the bottle by his feet with one hand, he picked up a glass with the other.

"To the best damn father," he said, raising the glass to the stars and black silhouettes of trees, then brought it to his lips and swallowed the aged, amber liquid. He welcomed the burn.

Retrieving the bottle from the wooden planks, he filled the glass again. "Wyoming ... hell, the world, just lost one of the good ones," he toasted to the wilderness, then tossed back the contents.

Glass clinked on glass as he tipped the bottle a third time. The whiskey didn't touch the constriction in his chest, nor did it keep the wetness from gathering in his eyes.

"I'll find the bastard, Dad," Shaun promised, acknowledging the pungent flavor as it hit his throat and settled in a near-empty stomach.

For a moment, he closed his eyes, and countless memories flashed like a photo album that had been recorded on a DVD, then set to fast-forward. His sisters, Carli and Samantha, birthdays and holidays, graduations, additions to the lodge ... his father at his most joyous, giving people what they could get nowhere else, the experience of a lifetime. Opening his eyes, he swiped at the tears with the back of his hand. Placing his empty glass on the railing next to the other one, and retaining the bottle, he took himself to his room.

Knowing he would get very little sleep, he traded the chair on the veranda for the one on the balcony off the loft upstairs.

Placing the bottle to his lips, he gazed at the stars and the mountains to the north that couldn't be seen in the darkness. Samantha wanted to fly out immediately from the stock show in Austin, but he convinced her there was nothing she could do for the investigation. Instead, he insisted she take care of ranch business in Durango, and he would pick her up when she arrived at the Laramie Airport. He hoped Carli would make it home for the funeral, then shook his head at his globe-trotting sister. Bringing the bottle up for another swallow, then resting it and his arm on the side of the chair, he gazed at the heavens, willing a message to Carli. A belated thought arose that if someone was determined to rid Wyoming of the Tanners, having them all gather for a funeral was a perfect opportunity. He would increase the security at the lodge. It wasn't as if they were helpless. They were, after all, Bear Tanner's children.

«« — »»

Five days. They had been in the green of the South American jungle for five days, and three of those were soaked with rain. They had finally been able to venture out of the village to begin photographing some of the surrounding area and nearby settlements. So far, most of her rolls of film contained human beings conducting what most would consider mundane jobs. Out of the industrialized world, survival was based on these tasks. *Predator and Prey* was the title of the issue she was here to cover, and they had yet to locate a jaguar, tapir, or anaconda. This day had proved to be just as unproductive as the rainy ones, but only when it came to fulfilling the requirements for the feature. Carli never tired of photography or mingling with the natives, whether observing and recording their daily lives, or engaging in the work and celebrations along with families and tribes.

Climbing down from the vehicle that had taken them on a journey further into the jungle, she noticed an unusual amount of excitement in the village for their return. She turned a puzzled look to Tim, who had stepped around the back of the vehicle to begin unloading their gear. He shrugged and lowered the tailgate.

"Glad we're back for the day? I know my feet are ..." his voice trailed off as an official looking man strode up to Carli.

"Señorita Tanner?"

Carli nodded.

He stretched out his hand, in which he held a white envelope. She glanced from the paper to his face, then took in the uniform. Whether he worked for the Postmaster General or the local law enforcement, he had found her, and the only one who knew where she and Tim where, exactly, was her boss, the editor of *International Views*, Scott Banding. And Scott would only contact her in the case of an extreme emergency.

Eyes flicking back to the brown ones of the officer, she felt the sweat trickle down her back, heard the buzz of myriad insects, felt the steamy heat from the sun, and her breath as it hesitated in her chest. She took the envelope from the man and, instead of leaving, he remained. Swallowing, and with a slight shaking of her hands, she opened the flap of the envelope. Sliding the slip of paper partially out, she glanced at the heading, which named the communications company, complete with their contact information printed in blue and red. The three words typed in the middle of the paper had the air rushing out of her lungs, her knees buckling, and her mind whirling in confusion.

Tim, who was looking over her shoulder, caught her and held her to him as his eyes read, again, the message that would get them out of this goddamn wetness.

Bear is dead.

CHAPTER 3

Resting his head back against the seat, Ethan's eyes gazed out the window. Sitting in front of the wing, he had an unobstructed view of a few white clouds and the central plains of the U.S. as he flew thirty-thousand feet above future wheat and corn fields just recently uncovered from the snow. He attempted to stretch his long legs into the space under the seat in front of him and frowned at being cooped up for so long. They would land at the Denver airport in an hour. From there, he would take a puddle jumper to Laramie, where he would find a rental car, and the promised GPS, in order to arrive at the outfitter's lodge before sundown.

Shifting his gaze to the file folder he stuck in the pocket in front of him, his scowl deepened. There wasn't much information from the autopsy report. A .243 caliber bullet to the heart, between a six and fifteen degree downward trajectory. That meant the shooter aimed high, as he was too far away to keep the target in the crosshairs. Obviously an expert marksman, but then anyone with the funds to afford a stay at the outfitter's wouldn't waste their time unless their skill was above average. Well above.

"Mr. Brooks?"

Ethan followed the voice and smiled at the flight attendant, which set off his dimples. She returned the gesture.

"Can I get you anything?" Her raised, single brow and her lower lip drawn seductively between her teeth alluded that she placed herself on the list of complimentary refreshments available in Business Class.

"A gracious offer, but no, thanks. I'm fine," he glanced at her name badge, "Jennifer."

The pretty brunette continued her trek down the aisle, collecting requests for drinks, pillows, and headphones. He looked again out the small window. *Already a Mile-High Club member, Sweetheart,* he thought, briefly remembering the rather flexible blonde on an international flight. Before his mind traveled too far down the road of past adventures, he removed the folder from the pocket of the seat back in front of him.

Keeping the front of the file folder vertical so it acted as a shield from the person in the aisle seat, he shuffled the pictures of the Tanner family. The local sheriff was Shaun, the youngest, age twenty-six, degree in Criminal Justice. Samantha was in the middle, age twenty-eight, and her winnings in college rodeo helped pay for her business degree that she used to run the ranch in Colorado. The oldest, Carli, at age thirty, was the only one to attend a school on the East Coast. Art. What did one do with an art degree? If one was as sought after as Ms. Tanner, one worked as a premier photojournalist for the most prestigious magazine in the world. Just by viewing the photos, anyone could tell all three were obviously closely related. Different shades of hazel irises stared back at him. Their hair coloring appeared to get progressively lighter with each sibling. Carli's was a shiny, dark blonde-medium brown with red highlights, Samantha's was a dirty blonde, and Shaun's was lighter, but still had shades of red.

All were single, so that ruled out greedy in-laws and probably serious relationships with someone looking to cash in on the family fortune. That was only a guesstimate. The land and business in Wyoming, coupled with the ranch in Colorado, allotted the family almost thirty-thousand acres. Both the ranch and the outfitters were prosperous endeavors. Perhaps one of the siblings became desperate. If they were in personal debt and asked Daddy for a loan, and then were denied, it could be motive. None of their faces resembled what people thought of as criminals. But he knew looks were deceiving. Often criminals used their physical appearance to lure victims. Especially if those victims were children.

He shifted in his seat and settled Carli's picture on top. Recounting her information, he began to click off facts. Her employer, bank account balance, frequent flyer mileage, address of a sub-let apartment in Manhattan. Her hair, slightly longer than shoulder-length, held soft curls and framed a face that, if the parts were taken separately, would not be wanted by any fashion magazine. But, when put together in a way that uniquely created her, they somehow worked. Natural eyebrows that managed to accent large, hazel eyes, a straight nose that ended above a cupid's bow upper lip and full lower lip, that when spread in a smile were slightly too wide and a little lopsided. It could have been her expression, as there seemed to be a hint of impatience in her gaze at the picture taker. Wispy bangs shadowed her forehead and the curls accented her cheeks and rounded chin. The collared shirt she wore left her throat open, and he found himself slightly disappointed that the bottom edge of the photograph was above her bust line.

He closed the file and placed it again in the pocket. Resting his head back on the seat, he shut his eyes. Passing the Rorschach's, what he had come to call the visits to the Department Psychologist, had become rote. Routine. He told them what they wanted to hear, what they needed to list in his file and allow him to continue to do his job. The nightmares, sleepless nights, the few wasted days when he thought binge drinking would wipe away the images, would never come to light. Without his job, what would he do? He was damn good at finding the bad guys and saving the victims. Except for the ones that were casualties, the lives that led him to the perpetrator. It was an old argument he had with himself. His guilt for not stopping the crimes sooner, or somehow preventing them to begin with, and using, needing, the victims to piece together a storyline and find the bastards.

Shifting again in his seat, then crossing his arms over his chest, he listened as Jennifer delivered the desired items to others in Business Class, and thought about the request of the Regional Director. He had vacationed with Tanner's Outdoor Adventures and had developed a bond with Bear Tanner. When word reached the Director that Bear had been killed, he pulled a few strings to have one of his own sent out to assist in the local investigation. And for whatever reason, Micah decided Ethan was the agent. Maybe he had been doing too well on the Rorschach and Micah figured he would need a little extra time after this last case.

"Think of it as a company vacation," Micah had suggested on the day after Ethan appeared in court at the trial of the kidnapping of Tommy Mason.

Ethan had argued that he didn't need an extended vacation beyond his requested three days, but Micah had smiled and tossed the plane ticket on his desk.

"Your other dozen cold cases can wait. It will do you some good to break away from the usual pedophile and kidnapper and serial killer. This is an old-fashioned, single murder. The ME's Office hasn't declared it, only the cause of death. I suppose hunting accidents do happen. The Director wants a personal touch, so take your time."

He sighed and shifted again, realizing he was becoming agitated at this forced, 'working vacation', the seemingly smaller airline seats, and that his destination was one with which he had little experience. Wide open places.

"Good afternoon, Folks. Due to a weather front that has developed over the Central Rockies, we've been asked to land in Billings, Montana. You will receive a complimentary connecting flight to get you to Denver, if you wish to wait at least a day, or however long the Denver Airport authorities believe it will take to reopen the runway. The alternative is the variety of car rental companies available at Logan International Airport. We're sorry for the inconvenience and the delay in arriving at your destination. Any questions can be answered by the ticket agents in Billings. We'll be on the ground in about thirty minutes."

Ethan's mood lightened that he could exit from this cramped space. He sat up in his seat and placed the file inside his carryon that doubled as a briefcase. Deciding that arriving at the Medicine Bow Preserve as soon as possible was important, it meant extra miles in a rental car if he couldn't get flight into Laramie. Perhaps scenery other than concrete and metal might silence, however temporarily, the ghosts that lived in his mind. He looked out the window and watched the Rocky Mountains grow larger.

«« — »»

It wouldn't do any good to speculate with Tim because, as he had told her twice already, they had no information and it was a waste of energy to guess about the circumstances around her father's death. Carli had stared moodily out the window of their transportation back to the city where, hopefully, Tim would work his magic and procure two tickets on the next flight to the U.S. Anywhere in the U.S. The connecting flights would come later. They had no cell reception in the village. The airport, however, afforded them access to the web, so she sent a short e-mail to the lodge, knowing Alyssa, who was usually there and able to communicate with everyone, would open it.

I received the telegram. I'm on my way home.

It was an off-day for planes leaving Venezuela, and the partially filled flight manifest had two seats of their choice available. She felt as if she was surrounded by oil. All physical movements seemed to require a great amount of effort. Her mind was spinning with thoughts, none of which she could latch on to. She had questions and no information. Was it too soon for any of them to be answered at the Preserve? Unsure what to say or ask or demand if one of the employees, or even Shaun, answered the international call, she opted to send the e-mail. The hours that would pass before they arrived in Wyoming would be spent gathering her frayed emotions.

She stared at the screen that dropped down from the overhead bin. The first of two movies was playing. It was a romantic comedy with a couple of popular actors, and though she didn't have headphones, it was obvious that they were in a lover's quarrel. Sighing, she turned her gaze to the colorful cover of the magazine that rested on her lap. Remembering all the arguments that her parents had, before her mother called it quits and left them, she wondered if her mother would regret it now that Bear was ... gone. Would Shaun contact their mother? Did any of them even know where Ms. Tanner called home?

Wiggling in her seat, she rolled up the magazine and shifted her gaze back to the movie. The woman was left outside a house, as the man got into a car and drove away. The close-up of the woman's face showed tears of disbelief and regret. Carli crossed her legs and shifted to the other hip, a scowl beginning between her brows. It deepened when the next shot showed the man's expression, his eyes reflecting sorrow in the rearview mirror, gazing at what he had left behind. *Stupid,* Carli thought. *If you love her, why leave? And if she loves you, how difficult it must be to watch you disappear.*

Snorting at her analysis, she uncrossed her legs, moved to the other hip, then crossed her ankles. What did she know of love? Her parents had it at one time, or must have to create three children, but it wasn't enough to keep her mother in Wyoming, or to have her father leave the wilderness. She'd had a few relationships, but they didn't last. It tended to be that way when she was out of the country, or New York, three-fourths of the year. She hadn't given much thought to marriage and a family. Instead, she relied on her deeply satisfying relationship with her work. And Tim.

Uncrossing her ankles, she turned onto the other hip and drew her legs up under her. Raising her gaze to Tim's, she found a scowl that mirrored her own.

"Did you manage to load your pockets with South American Fire Ants? You haven't remained in the same position for more than a minute since we boarded the plane."

"Sorry. My mind is—"

"I know. I'm sorry, too. Look, there's no one else in our row. Why don't you lift up the arms between the seats, stretch out, and catch some z's. We have about eight hours before we land in L.A."

"I don't think I can sleep," she shook her head, but he had pressed the call button overhead alerting the flight attendant.

"Yes? What can I get for you?" the petite blonde asked, smiling prettily at Tim. She obviously didn't pick up that he wasn't interested in her type, as she tipped her head to the side and flipped her hair behind her shoulder.

"My friend would like a blanket and pillow," Tim said, gesturing to Carli.

"Sure. I'll be right back."

He smiled at her, then reached around Carli to flip up the arm. She sighed, then lifted the other three on the row. Rearranging her legs toward the aisle, her head next to Tim's thigh, she grinned mischievously when the blonde returned. The flight attendant's smile not as bright as she noticed the familiarity between the two passengers as Carli shifted her head onto Tim's thigh. He glanced down at her, then took the pillow and blanket.

Carli shifted her gaze to Tim. "Thanks, Sweetie," she said and earned herself an eye roll.

"You just blew my chance at a free drink before we land," he spoke in a harsh whisper.

"I'll buy a bottle of Kentucky's finest, and we can drink ourselves silly in Wyoming."

Spreading the blanket over her, she placed the pillow under her head next to Tim's thigh, then turned on her side. She stared at the seat back in front of her as he gently stroked her hair.

"We'll drink to your father," he whispered, and Carli squeezed her eyes shut to keep the tears from forming.

CHAPTER 4

"Are you sure you're going to be alright?" Zach's eyes searched her face and, looking for the evidence, he found it. A slightly crooked nose, small scar on the outer edge of her left eyebrow, another on her forehead, right at the hairline. She tried to hide the healing of the marks left by the stitches, but the redness remained.

Gritting his teeth, not wanting to upset Alyssa, he gently took her hand in his. If he moved slowly, it gave her time to realize what he was doing, and she wouldn't flinch. He hated when she did that. He kissed her knuckles, and that elicited a smile.

"I'll be fine. There's chores to finish before I can work on my research paper."

"Need any help with that? I could meet you at the library later," he offered with just the beginnings of excitement at seeing her again.

She shook her head. "I need to be at home. I can type on the laptop Ms. Pylner loaned me. I'll see you tomorrow."

He offered her a half-smile, his excitement not completely deflated, and watched as Alyssa climbed into her antique Honda, and disappeared down the long, gravel drive.

Placing his hands in the pockets of his jacket, he turned toward Cabin 3 and the leaky shower, which was the first on his own list of jobs to complete. After that, he would prepare lunch, then meet the farrier in the barn. Most of the tracking and hunting were done on foot, but there were some clients who preferred horseback, so Bear kept a dozen horses on the property. There were extra precautions when a group headed out on horseback. The guides kept the clients in a particular area, lest another hunter mistake a horse for an elk, which has been known to happen, but never on the Preserve.

Stopping at the supply room, a ten-by-fifteen foot alcove behind a locked door on the north veranda to retrieve the tools he would need to repair the shower, his thoughts wandered to Alyssa. She would be eighteen two weeks before prom, which was about six weeks before her graduation. He had graduated two years earlier from a school in Colorado, and answered an ad in the local paper about a handyman and guide. All the experience he had gained on his uncle's farm in Colorado Springs impressed Bear enough that he gave Zach the job, despite his age. What he didn't know, he learned from Bear and Ray, the lead guide and Bear's best friend.

Since he arrived at the Preserve, and met Alyssa, he had been in love with her. At first, he was convinced it was a crush. Alyssa, with her blonde hair and blue eyes, was tall and shapely. Who wouldn't look twice? But she was only sixteen when he came to work for Tanner's Outdoor Adventures, and to touch her would earn him twenty inside Wyoming's finest accommodations. Instead, he set out to be her friend and realized how much she needed one. He would help her occasionally on an assignment, then he recognized how smart she was and that she was just trying to get him to like her in a more-than-friendly way. Finally giving in to his emotions, he began to take her out on dates on Wednesday nights, as Fridays and the weekends were busy at the lodge. He was careful to not be too friendly in an area where the clients might see them together. About two months ago, Bear had requested that Zach meet him in his office. Since that was where Zach was hired, his first thought was that he would be fired.

"Sit down, Zach," Bear said and gestured towards the only other chair in the crowded and dusty office.

Bear Tanner resembled his nickname, standing tall at 6'6" and weighing in at almost three hundred pounds. His hair was thick and he wore it long enough to keep his neck warm. The full beard matched the deep red color of his hair. The sleeves of his flannel shirt were rolled up, due to the space heater in the small office.

"Do you like your job here?" he asked.

"Yes, I do," Zach replied, barely resisting the urge to wipe his palms on his jeans.

"And you're a fine employee. I didn't ask you in here to fire you." His keen eyes had detected the younger man's nervousness "I just wanted to offer you some advice."

"Advice about what?"

It was his turn to give an audible sigh. "Women. Now, before you get all ruffled," and he held his palm out toward Zach to halt any stammering, "I may have made a mess of my own marriage, but I've raised two incredible daughters and they not only graced me with the liberal gray you see in my hair, but with considerable understanding. A blind man could see you're in love with Alyssa."

He watched as Zach looked everywhere except at him, then leaned back in his chair and waited for the ranch hand to meet his gaze.

"She's not eighteen, and I would never do anything to get her in trouble, or to hurt her," Zach said, his convictions growing stronger with each voiced realization.

"I wouldn't expect that from you, else I wouldn't have hired you. You're a good man, Zach. I've seen the way you care for Alyssa, but no matter how hard you try, you'll eventually do something stupid, at least in her eyes, and you'll hurt her. It's just the way of things between men and women. The fact that the two of you are friends and get along well will help you out in the long run," he paused, then leaned forward, placing his forearms on the desk. "Give her the opportunity to choose what she wants to do with her life. If she wants to attend school, encourage her. E-mail. Text. Keep in touch, but let her see what a big world it is out there. Alyssa was born and raised here. Never experienced anything further than Cheyenne. If she wants to travel, offer to *fill up her gas tank." He shook his head. "You don't, and you tie her down with babies, she'll resent you."*

Leaning back in his chair, he interlaced his fingers and rested them across his belly. Maybe it was Zach's age, which put him six years younger than Shaun and in the realm that he could be a younger brother, or the fact that he liked him and didn't want to see him heartbroken. His next words offered a cautious warning.

"You've a lot to offer a woman. Level head. Hard worker. You steer clear of trouble—"

"I'm not one of the horses in the barn, Bear. You don't need to—"

"Yes, I do. You work for me, so does Alyssa, and I care a great deal for the both of you," he sat up taller in his chair and noticed a slight flush on Zach's cheeks. "If you want Alyssa for good, give her choices, and remain the steady man you are. That son of a bitch she has for a father will find any excuse to fuel his temper, and that includes your relationship with her."

"As soon as Alyssa turns eighteen, she can do as she wants," Zach said, adjusting his straw cowboy hat.

"In the eyes of the law, but not according to Jim Lockhart. Don't cross him, Zach, and don't put Alyssa in the middle."

"I wouldn't—" Zach began, but halted his words at the raised brows of his employer and friend. Shaking his head, he smiled sheepishly, realizing Bear had brought him full circle.

"Understand?" Bear asked.

"Yes, Sir," Zach answered and smiled.

Zach wiped the back of his hand across his eyes, grateful he was alone in the supply room. Having thought a lot about that conversation with Bear, he felt he was balancing on a double-edged sword. By bringing up the possibility of her attending college or traveling or moving out of her father's house, she might begin to consider those options that would take her, in his opinion, away from him. The immense respect he had for Bear forced him to follow the man's advice. He didn't know the whole story as to what had become of Mrs. Tanner, but he knew that his life wouldn't be what he wanted if Alyssa left him, her heart full of resentment.

Determined that he would assure Alyssa that she had plenty of time to apply for college, and if she went, he would send her e-mails and text her. If she wanted to see California or Texas, he would tell her he had been saving money each week to get her where she wanted to go. When she was ready to settle into a home, he would be there. Is this what Bear wished he had done with his wife? He shook his head, grabbed a pipe wrench and plumber's tape, then left the supply room for Cabin 3.

《《—》》

"Don't airlines give special consideration to those trying to attend a funeral?" Carli asked, exhausted from her international flight and frustrated that Tim had been unable to procure them tickets to Denver.

"Yes, we do, but the storm in Colorado has the Denver Airport shut down."

"By the time we take off and fly the two and a half hours, the storm will have passed," she argued.

"One would think," the ticket agent smiled with little humor. "But no one leaves any airport heading for Denver until the storm and runway are cleared. I have you on the list, and I'll page you as soon as we get the go-ahead to board the flight."

Carli sighed loudly. "Are there any flights to—"

"Really, Carli, it's a couple of hours. It would take longer to reroute us than it would to just wait it out." Tim held her gaze, unwilling to be badgered into attempting to connect five other flights in the hopes of arriving in Laramie before tomorrow. "Come on, Sweetie, I'll buy you a drink. Then you can cuss at the weathermen. It will make you feel better," he suggested, taking her carryon in one hand, the other slinging companionably around her shoulders.

"Thank you," he smiled politely over his shoulder at the ticket agent.

A short time later, Tim raised a brow as Carli downed her third shot of tequila, lining the glasses up on the bar as if she had something to prove.

"If you don't slow down, I'm leaving your grieving ass here when the rest of us board the plane to Denver."

"Denver? It might as well be Cairo. Look at the storm, Tim," she gestured with her hand to the colorful screen, which showed a huge, pink, swirling mass where Denver used to be.

"As you can see, Denver and the surrounding Rockies, especially to the south, are really getting pounded by this spring storm. We don't expect the clouds and precipitation to move off towards the east until day after tomorrow. The good news is that behind this front, the skies are clear and sunny, with temperatures ranging from the low seventies in inland California to the fifties in Montana and Wyoming. We should have beautiful weather the rest of the week here in the West. Back to you, Carol," and the grinning, balding, weatherman disappeared to be replaced by a blonde in a yellow pants suit.

She stared a moment longer at the television, then began to pat her cargo shorts for her phone. *International Views* sent her into the bush with the best of equipment, but the gadgets didn't usually work. However, now they were sitting in LAX, and Carli's smile showed her network was up.

Grateful for the few minutes of peace as Carli busied herself with her cell, Tim stared broodingly into his short glass of gin and tonic. Hot, humid places were his least favorite to visit. He was glad to have their trip cut short, but certainly not for this reason. They had been gone for almost a month. He was looking forward to returning to his apartment in the Village in New York, but it would have to wait until their side trip to Laramie was completed. A week, ten days tops, and they would leave the wilderness of the Western U.S. for their civilized East Coast. He hoped Scott would give them at least a week at home before the next assignment came through. There was film to develop, friends to reconnect with, parties to attend ... his plans were interrupted by Carli jostling his arm, directing him to pay their tab.

"Come on. We have forty-five minutes to make the station," she spoke as she grabbed her cases, backpack, and jacket, and began to leave the Tail Wind Cantina.

"What? What are you talking about?" he tossed a couple of twenties on the bar, not waiting for a receipt.

He caught up to Carli just as she flagged one of the chauffeured carts that took the elderly or infirm from one terminal to another. Sitting next to her, he grabbed for the seat's edge as the cart lurched forward.

"Where are we going?" he demanded.

"Laramie. By way of train and rental car and plane," she smiled at him. At Tim's incredulous look, she continued, "Union Station is a short taxi drive from LAX. I've booked us tickets on the portion of the Starlight from L.A. to Sacramento. A rental car takes us to Reno, where a charter airline will fly us to Salt Lake City, then we change planes and take the last flight of the day from Salt Lake to Laramie."

"You forgot something," he said.

"What?" she asked, then glanced at the internet connection on her phone.

"Where's the boat, camel, or rickshaw?"

She shook her head and rewarded him with a half-smile.

"Seriously, Carli, if we waited here, we would probably get there the same time as your convoluted travel plans."

She shrugged, her smile slipping away. "This way I feel like I'm doing something. I can't just sit and wait. Not this time, Tim."

"Alright," he agreed quietly and patted her hand that held onto her case.

The cart pulled up alongside the security station, then stopped as they stepped off the conveyance. Tim tipped the driver, then followed the tall, blonde-haired woman in cargo shorts and hiking boots, past the luggage carousels and outside where she had found the line to wait in as taxis were called into the airport from a lot not far from the property. Less than five minutes later they were settled in the back seat of a cab on their way to Union Station.

"How are we going to find the rest of our luggage?" he asked nonchalantly, his attention on the high-rise buildings.

"I've sent an e-mail to Joe Sneely at the Laramie Airport. We know each other from school. When our original flight lands, he'll claim the crates, put them in the lost luggage area, and contact me," she answered.

He glanced at her and raised a brow. "Is there any city or airport that you don't know someone?"

"Is that a rhetorical question?" she responded, her brows drawn together as she concentrated on sending another e-mail to Alyssa at the lodge.

"Just thought it might be a subject to mention at a cocktail party," he shrugged and looked again out the window, hoping they would arrive at the train station before the churning in his stomach got the better of him.

Sighing, she slipped her phone inside one of the pockets of her shorts. She would wait until she was home before she allowed any tears to fall. Sam would be there. Shaun would tell them the truth, and she would say goodbye to her father.

CHAPTER 5

Ethan placed his bag inside the rear door of the Ford Explorer with 4-wheel drive, then settled himself in the driver's seat, his carryon next to him. Glancing at the GPS unit in the middle of the dash, he reached inside the pocket of the briefcase and extracted the map of Wyoming he brought with him from Baltimore. He unfolded it to get his bearings on the length of the drive from Laramie to Centennial, and the surrounding towns. Glancing out the windshield and side window to locate the setting sun, he then turned his gaze to the southeast corner of the Wyoming map. Refolding it so the county that held Laramie was in the middle, he traced Highway 130, west. He should arrive in Centennial, Wyoming, in an hour. Just to ensure he didn't miss an exit and end up in the wrong mountain range, he programed the GPS for Tanner's Outdoor Adventures.

   Flicking around the radio stations, he wasn't surprised to get only a few from Cheyenne, which were all country-western, and then smiled when a classic rock station came in from Boulder. They were getting precipitation, but not as much as Denver, and the bite to the wind that blew and rocked the Explorer to the side was a spin-off from the storm dumping spring snow on the Rockies to the south. That same weather disturbance forced their plane to land in Billings, Montana, and relegated him to take a puddle jumper to Laramie. Coming in from the north, the sky was clear. When they had announced that Denver was shut down, he was grateful that his flight was close enough to be diverted instead of turned back or not even allowed to take off. The sooner he offered his assistance to the local sheriff, the quicker he could return to the bustle of Baltimore and the twelve cases he had yet to close.

Laramie was a fair-sized town, but as soon as the city limits were passed, the houses became more sparse, giving way to stretches of flat grassland, rolling hills, and finally the peaks within the Medicine Bow National Forest. The sun was quickly setting, and he took the vehicle to just over the speed limit, chasing the sunset. If he was pulled over by the Highway Patrol, it was a matter of professional courtesy to evade a ticket.

As he closed in on the foothills of the Snowy Mountain Range, grasses were overtaken by tall pine trees. The wind subsided somewhat, and he became enthralled by the surrounding wilderness, such that he had nearly missed the change in speed limit as he entered the town of Centennial. Continuing on 2nd Street, the main drag through this populated area, he thought about the lodge where he would spend his forced, 'working vacation'. He had the days accumulated to take time off, but why? There was satisfaction with his job when the perpetrators were arrested and the sentencing matched the crime. What he didn't need was time away. He was city born and raised, and though he had spent time in rural areas, he just felt he could never relax in such unfamiliar territory.

Looking both ways along the road, in a minute, the town was behind him. His headlights landed on a building a block beyond the end of the rest of the structures that made up 2nd Street, and he pulled into a parking space in front. The words 'Centennial Sheriff's Office' on the glass door flashed in his headlights. He saw the shadows of two people inside, so he cut the engine and climbed down from the SUV.

Shaun glanced at the headlights outside the window as he took the fax from the machine. It was official looking, including the FBI seal across the top. Reading the memo, he snorted. Seems the Regional Director on the East Coast, a client of his father's, was taking a personal interest in Bear Tanner's death. So much

44

so, that he deemed it necessary to send some federal help to solve Bear's murder. Shaun looked up from the fax as the door opened.

"I'm looking for Sheriff Tanner," Ethan said to the receptionist, closing the door behind him.

The office consisted of a sitting area that held four chairs, a counter that suggested friends and family stay on one side, while the suspects and officers conducted business on the other. To his left was a map of Wyoming and a more detailed topographical one of Laramie, Carbon, and Albany Counties. To his right was a cork board that served not only as a place to display wanted criminals, but for the locals to post classifieds. There was a water cooler, fax machine, half a dozen filing cabinets, two desks, complete with phones and computer monitors, in front of the open door to what he guessed was the personal office of Sheriff Tanner. A hallway led off to the left, and he figured there were a few holding cells out of sight of the reception area. His eyes came to rest on the man in the uniform.

"You found him. You must be the FBI agent," Shaun said and waved the fax.

"Glad my introduction preceded me," Ethan commented with a nod toward the paper.

"Barely. I can understand the concern of the Regional Director, but this is a small town crime. We've had forensics from Cheyenne out here, and the ME at Ivinson Memorial Hospital believes it could be a deliberate act. Despite the town's size, we're capable of solving our own crimes."

Ethan shrugged, hands in the pockets of his jacket. "No one is saying you're not. Perhaps we could talk privately?" he suggested, his eyes swiveling from Esther to the open door of the office.

"Sure," Shaun agreed, then walked to the counter, pulled open the small gate, and allowed Ethan behind the boundary.

Once they were inside Shaun's office, and the door was closed, Ethan stuck out his hand. "Ethan Brooks, FBI, Baltimore Field Office."

Shaun shook it, then gestured for the agent to sit. Not one to cling to formality, the sheriff settled himself on the edge of his desk.

"I'm here at the request of my boss's boss. I have no intention of taking over the investigation—"

"Glad to hear it," Shaun interrupted.

"Only to offer my assistance. I would like to take a look at the ME's full report, photographs of the scene, list of the evidence, and any interviews you've taken."

"I'll ask Esther for the file. Where will you be staying Agent Brooks?"

"Ethan. And I'm booked at the lodge for at least a week," he said, then observed the expression on the sheriff's face as he realized how difficult it would be to keep anything from the FBI since Ethan would be conveniently close enough to instigate his own interviews, gather his own information.

Shaun's mouth was set in a grim line. "Alyssa failed to mention that to me."

"She probably didn't know, since my reservation is under 'Mister' instead of 'Agent'," Ethan replied, then continued, "You know, to keep the town gossip to a minimum."

Shaun laughed without humor as he stood. "One thing a small town always has plenty of, is speculation. Esther is the best I could come up with to keep it under control." His expression became serious as he glanced out his office window at Esther, then back at Ethan. "Bear Tanner was as much a part of this community as the mountain air and 2nd Street. He gave people jobs when they were down on their luck, donated money to the school and the hospital. Hell, he even served several terms on the Town Council. There isn't anyone who would want him dead."

Ethan watched closely. There was honest conviction for the sheriff's beliefs, and a strong tie to protect the town. He nodded, knowing he was beginning to like Shaun Tanner, but would be careful to not step across the line of whose town, or investigation, this was.

"Sometimes fresh eyes and a different perspective can offer alternatives. I promise to keep you updated on anything I discover," he said as he rose from his chair. "We both want the same thing, Sheriff Tanner—"

"Shaun," he interrupted.

Ethan smiled. "And that is to catch Bear Tanner's killer."

Shaun nodded, then opened the door. "Esther, did you file the reports on my father's case?"

"Top drawer, first cabinet," she answered, fingers tapping on a keyboard.

Shaun moved to the indicated location and pulled what Ethan had requested. Stepping over to the copy machine, he ran the papers through, gathered the sheets from the side, and handed the stack to the FBI agent.

"Thanks," Ethan said, taking the papers. "I'll review these tonight. Should I come here tomorrow to discuss our next steps?"

"I'll be at the airport and then the lodge. I'll catch up with you there," Shaun said as he opened the gate on the counter and followed Ethan to the door.

"I was informed there's Internet access and spotty cell service on the game Preserve," Ethan waited for confirmation from Shaun, "but here's my card and ways to contact me."

Shaun took it. "I'll see you sometime tomorrow."

Ethan nodded and turned towards his parked rental. Another fifteen minutes down the road, and the sign for Tanner's Outdoor Adventures was lit up by his headlights. He parked near the steps leading to the veranda, grabbed his carryon and his case from the back, then opened the solid wood door of the lodge.

«« —»»

Glancing at her watch, she saw the numbers roll to 3:03 a.m. Sighing, she shifted her gaze to Tim who slept awkwardly in the seat next to her on the third part of their journey to Wyoming. He looked boyish with his red curls falling across his forehead, the longer strands still contained in the ponytail. They had made a bet that her suggestion for reaching Laramie would get them there quicker than Tim's original travel plans. The winner would receive bragging rights and a hundred dollars. As much as they were together, the bragging would get more mileage than the cash.

Remembering the countless airports they had been in, the incalculable miles traveled, she grinned. That same hundred dollars had shared time in each of their pockets over the years. Stretching her legs out in front of her and interlacing her fingers, resting them on her belly, she didn't think she would find another to tolerate the number of days she was away from home, or her unusual eating and sleeping habits. Realizing how she was sitting was reminiscent of her father, she shifted in her seat, her eyes wandering from Tim, to the darkness out the window, to the few lights that shined over passengers who, like herself, were wide awake. They had an hour before they landed in Salt Lake. She should try to rest.

Closing her eyes didn't take away the images in her mind. Her father guiding hunters, taking her and Sam and Shaun to the carnival in Laramie, teaching her to drive, fix a toilet, clean a gun, track a bear, to stand up to Sheila Jones, the bully in fifth grade. He was there when she had her heart broken the first time. And the second. It was Bear's insistence that encouraged her to pursue her art degree, and to meet her at the Laramie Airport every time she came home. He would make her dessert on her first night back at the lodge, would view and critique her pictures, and wanted to know the tiny details of the natives she observed, spoke to, and often lived with. Who would do that now? She was a grown woman, so did she even need someone to do those things for her? Did she want someone? Restless dreams took her then, and she welcomed the diversion from her conscious, perpetual thinking.

CHAPTER 6

A fire burned in the fireplace and effectively warmed the lobby of the lodge. Rocks, the smallest the size of a man's head, covered the hearth, which extended three feet from the wall, five feet to either side of the fireplace, and around the grate from floor to ceiling. A metal screen in front of the fire prevented sparks from flying out to land on the bearskin rug, and to keep people and objects from falling in. The mounted heads of several beasts were displayed around the Great Room. Elk, deer, antelope, moose, big horn sheep, and mountain goat shared the wall space with preserved fowl and fish. There was a map of the Preserve, efficiently marking trailheads, game trails, and points of interest such as rivers, ridges, canyons, peaks, and even a waterfall. Beside it was a map of the grounds, with symbols indicating the lodge, parking areas, cabins, barn, and two outbuildings.

Ethan moved from the front door to the small area sectioned off from the Great Room by a counter that had its own roof, much like a cabana. The rest of the lobby was set up with leather-covered chairs and couches arranged to instigate conversation. A few chairs were placed under the windows, along with low tables, if one chose to be alone. Scattered rugs sporadically covered the wood floor, and spotlights, which were dimmed and recessed into the ceiling, completed the feel of an exclusive, yet welcoming, vacation destination.

He smiled slightly as he approached the young man behind the counter. "Hi. Reservation for Ethan Brooks?"

"Hello, Mr. Brooks. I'm Zach," he said, and stretched out his hand. Bear always emphasized being friendly with the clients.

"Ethan," he answered, holding the younger man's hand and gaze. There was an open friendliness, and innocence. Zach was the first to be removed from Ethan's suspect list.

Zach released the client's hand and glanced at the computer screen. Alyssa had booked Cabin 4 for the next week. There was no notation indicating what had brought Ethan to Wyoming, all the way from Baltimore. Raising his gaze to the man on the other side of the counter, he tried to pair what he saw with what was available, and wondered if Bear could have discovered this man's game of choice.

"Alyssa didn't make a note of why you're visiting. Most hiking trails are open, and if you're interested in trout, there's an expedition to Little Shy River tomorrow that leaves at seven in the morning," he paused, waiting to see excitement light the man's eyes.

Ethan lifted his carryon, which housed the file Shaun had given him. "I've got some other ... game I'm after. But I'll definitely be needing a guide to take me around the area."

"Just let us know when and where you would like to go, and we'll get you there."

"Thanks. Did I miss dinner?"

"Just barely. I would be glad to bring something to your cabin. Elk stew, cornbread, and salad, if you're into the green stuff."

Ethan smiled. "Sounds great. Is there a coffee machine in the room?"

"Yes," Zach nodded. "Also a mini-fridge. I can bring you a pot. You can save the packaged stuff for backup." He set a smaller version of the map of the complex that hung by the door, on the counter, drawing with a red marker a path from the lodge to Cabin 4. Turning it around so Ethan could read it, Zach explained how to find his accommodations.

"Breakfast is served from six to eight, and tomorrow Alyssa is making blueberry pancakes. Don't know what she does to them, but they're something special."

The light in Zach's eyes told Ethan that Zach thought Alyssa was the 'something special'.

"Don't remember the last time I had blueberry pancakes," Ethan acknowledged, surprising himself that the prospect of breakfast food could elicit any kind of interest.

"I'll make up a dinner tray for you, bring it by in about fifteen minutes."

Ethan smiled and nodded his thanks, took his map and key, hefted his case and left the lodge. On his way down the veranda steps he passed an older man who was headed inside. Out of habit, he made eye contact and categorized what he saw. Clean-shaven face, piercing blue eyes, skin wrinkled and weathered from a lifetime of exposure to the elements. A jacket over a buttoned-down shirt that was tucked inside his jeans, and a straw cowboy hat and work boots completed the look of the outdoorsman. A smile graced the man's lips, but didn't reach his eyes. Ethan nodded a silent greeting, and when he reached the ground, glanced back at the older man as he made his way to the door of the lodge. A slight hitch in the man's right hip was noticed, then dismissed as a likely product of the man's time on earth.

Directing his attention to locating Cabin 4, Ethan unerringly followed the map to the small veranda at the front of his cabin. He unlocked the door, and feeling the heat inside, was grateful that it had been turned on prior to his arrival. Setting his carryon and case on the floor by the queen-sized bed, he checked out the closet, complete with built-in shelves, and the bathroom, which included a tub with jets. Ethan raised his brows at that and left the door open as he wandered back to the main room of the cabin.

He had just unpacked his clothes and removed his laptop and files from his case when there was a knock at the door. There was no peephole in the wooden door, and the curtains were already drawn over the window. His reaction was the same as if he were in a city, by withdrawing his weapon and placing it next to his thigh. He peeked behind the material, then clicked the safety on his gun and placed it inside the back waistband of his jeans as he opened the door to Zach.

"You can leave the tray until morning. Just don't put any of the dishes outside. We try not to encourage the critters that believe they can get a free meal here."

Ethan took the tray, thanked Zach, and watched briefly as the young man descended the steps and aimed in the direction of the lodge. He closed and locked the door, then took himself and his meal to the small table. With one hand on his utensil and the other turning the pages in the reports, he made quick work of both. Pushing the tray aside, he began to make notes regarding the files. The interviews were thorough, and there appeared to be nothing that connected any of the visitors to Bear at the time of his death, other than a client-proprietor relationship. Without a connection, there was no chance that a motive would be discovered. A hunting accident then, despite the Director's assumption?

Ethan sighed and removed the folder that held the information the FBI had compiled. If clients and vacationers had no issues with Bear Tanner, the next logical group were employees. And he had yet to rule out family members. Perhaps the one who would know the most effective way to cover the evidence was Shaun Tanner. That name was at the top of the list that he began on a clean page in a yellow, legal-size, writing tablet. At the bottom of the page, Zach Murphy. Looking at the open space between the names, he flipped the page, tilted the pad of paper, and with the pencil in his left hand, began rough strokes that soon revealed the raised-brow expression of Sheriff Tanner as he glanced up from his fax. Before he shut off the light, other views of Shaun's face joined the first. Turning back a couple of pages, he looked again at the sketches of Shaun, Zach, the client that sat in front of the fire reading a book, Esther, and the man he passed on the steps of the lodge.

Closing and stowing the files in his briefcase, he shut down his laptop, but left it plugged in, and flicked off the lights. He stood a moment in the complete darkness. It was disconcerting to not have light streaming in the window from a lamppost or hear traffic. The light from the computer cord was a beacon. The more he stared at it, the more anxious he felt. Flicking the light switch on, he moved to the bathroom, turned on that light, then closed the door, except for a crack. This time the darkness didn't steal his breath. As he shucked his jeans and shirt, he wondered if seven days would be long enough to learn how to sleep in the quiet night of rural America.

«« — »»

"Good morning, Folks. We'll be landing soon in clear skies and thirty-nine degrees. Local time is 7:48. You'll be gathering your personal items at 8:30. Thanks for flying with Charter West Air. Welcome to Wyoming."

Carli blinked and sat straighter in her seat. Looking up the aisle in front of her, then behind her, she guessed Tim must be in the lavatory. There were twenty passengers, maybe, on this charter flight. The plane's interior was such that one seat was on the left side of the aisle and two seats on the right. She had shoved her backpack in the tiny overhead bin, and her camera case was tucked mostly under the seat in front of her. Yawning and stretching her long legs into the aisle, she glanced out the window and smiled at the familiar mountaintops.

"Morning, Sunshine," Tim said, stepping around her feet and back into his seat across the aisle from her.

"You're awfully chipper," she commented, becoming suspicious.

"I get that way when I'm given a free hundred dollar bill." His broad grin alluded to what he believed was secret knowledge.

"I'll need to double-check your math."

He rattled off the day and time they left South America, their layover in L.A., then proceeded to assume that Denver was open by midnight and that they could have arrived by 3 AM, taken the prop plane to Laramie, and been at the lodge by now.

"You forgot daylight savings," Carli reminded him.

His smile slipped slightly, but then he rallied. "So that puts us two hours instead of three ahead of our current itinerary."

She raised a brow at Tim's outstretched palm, but reached down and pulled the bill from a zippered pocket in her camera case.

"This is contingent on when Denver opened for business."

He tsked, tucking the bill into his front pocket. "A woman your age—"

"*My* age?" she interrupted.

"With thirty years' experience on this earth—"

"Shhh!" she whispered before her lips moved to a grin.

"I think would have learned some patience," he finished as if she said nothing at all. "Waiting three hours—"

"Six. Six hours at the least."

"Would afford a normal person a chance to catch up on some reading or business or people watching."

"I was too restless to read, half my business had been packed in the crates," she narrowed her gaze at Tim since he had thrown, helter-skelter, their belongings into crates and cases that they shipped ahead, "and I watch people for a living. Why would I want to do that to pass the time?"

He ignored her censure on his packing details. "Because the stories you create about the hoards of people that inhabit an airport are entertaining to those of us whose well of creativity is quite shallow."

"Perhaps you should fill your 'well' with something besides techno music and fruity drinks at all the—" Carli was interrupted by the only flight attendant as he cleared his throat.

"Fascinating as this discussion is between you two, we're approaching the airport, so I need you to buckle in and clear the aisle."

"Of course. Sorry," she said, moving her legs back under her as the flight attendant continued his short journey to the rear of the plane.

She turned her head to watch a moment, then refocused on Tim and lowered her voice. "At all the alternative nightclubs—"

"Gay bars."

"I'm being politically correct."

He rolled his eyes.

"It's all about fun and games with you. So, why not make up your own scenario with someone tall, dark, and handsome in snug jeans and a pink boa—"

She stopped and looked up at the flight attendant. Leaning across the aisle, she had again blocked his path, and by the expression on his face, perhaps her voice wasn't as quiet as she thought. Smiling sheepishly, she straightened in her seat and the flight attendant continued to the front of the plane, but paused and turned at the next seat in front of them.

Bending over and whispering for Tim and Carli's ears only, the flight attendant informed them, "I've witnessed fellatio in first class, and one woman who joined the Club four times on a trans-continental flight. There isn't much that I haven't seen or heard that shocks me after twelve years at an altitude between ten-thousand and thirty-thousand feet." He tipped his head to the side and met Tim's gaze. "Snug jeans and a pink boa? Hmm." Then he straightened and made his way to the front and the retractable seat behind the cockpit.

Carli and Tim nearly bumped heads in the aisle as they both leaned out to watch the retreating backside of the flight attendant.

Once they were on the ground and Carli began to descend the steps outside the plane, Tim hung back to chat with Charlie, the flight attendant.

"I'm in Laramie for a funeral," Tim began.

"I'm sorry to hear that," Charlie said.

"Her father, and somewhat sketchy circumstances," Tim paused as two other passengers squeezed past so they could get off the plane. "I'll be in town for about a week. Would you be interested in grabbing a cup of coffee?"

After all this time, he was still a little nervous when asking to meet someone somewhere. There was always the possibility of rejection, then attempting to pretend it didn't matter.

Charlie smiled. "As a matter of fact, I have one more return flight, then I'll be laid over for two days—" he paused as he realized what he said. "Sorry. Poor choice of words."

"Perhaps not," Tim said with a smile. "Here's my card. I'm hoping I have service where we're going. Call me when you get back."

Charlie took the card and placed it in his shirt pocket, returning Tim's smile. "Sure. Sounds like fun."

Tim disembarked the plane to find Carli with her phone to her ear arranging the delivery of their crates and the pickup from her brother.

She disconnected the call, gathered her two cases and asked, "So, you met a new friend?"

CHAPTER 7

Another log was tossed on the fire, sending sparks dancing up into the cold, night air. Three men sat on foldable, tripod chairs, the fourth was rearranging gear in the bed of his pickup in order to make room for the bear and two deer that they had bagged on this trip.

"When we get back into town, I know just the place to go to get that rack mounted," Jerry said, spreading his fingers wide and stretching out his arms to the width of the antlers on the buck he had shot that morning.

"Yours is nice, but it's hard to beat that 8-point with my bullet in him," bragged Dan.

"But if it weren't for Jerry's buck, and that hunger after a long, winter's nap, we wouldn't have a bear skin to bring back with us," Bob added, shaking his head at their luck.

The four of them had been coming to this part of Wyoming for the past few years because the pickings were so easy. They had all grown up hunting with their fathers and brothers, and remember having a few slim years when no one got a tag, or if their number was drawn, they would leave the hunting trip empty handed. Jerry and Bob were from Montana, Dan lived in Colorado, and Paul resided in Oregon, only because his company transferred him there. They had all met on a hunting expedition in Western Wyoming ten years earlier, and had kept in contact with each other. Trading off hosting a hunt, they would travel to various Western states bagging whatever they could hit, whether it was in season or not. Finding locations where they were sure to walk away with a prize, generated the idea that if they had extra, there were others who were willing to pay, and pay well, for what these friends could bring back.

"How much do you think you'll get for that bear hide?" Bob asked.

"Keeping the head on, and with his thick winter coat, premium. I'd say about forty-five hundred," Paul answered as he rejoined the group, and the heat, by the fire.

Dan rubbed his hands together and held them out towards the flames. He was the youngest of the four, and the thinnest. Not much for drinking, like Bob and Paul, he also didn't have a belly that hung over his belt. His wife didn't mind that he took off a few times a year to 'meet up with his hunting buddies', she called it. She didn't know anything about game, and that pleased them both.

Bob was also married and had three grown kids that had moved out. His wife had her friends and vacations that she went on, usually to a spa, and this was his way of getting out of the suburbs. He pulled the flask from inside his jacket and tipped it into his cup to enhance the flavor of the coffee. Passing the whiskey to Paul, he sipped what he hoped would keep him warm that night.

Taking the whiskey and drinking straight from the flask, Paul enjoyed the burn of the alcohol. *A fucking bear*, he thought. They had always come away with something, but never a big-ticket item like a grizzly. He had an inquiry just last month from someone in California looking for bear meat and a hide. It would be nearly all profit, since it didn't cost him much to get here, just a plane ticket and a donation towards gas for Dan's truck.

Jerry picked up a stick and stirred the coals. His deer was nice, but he would have loved to bag that bear. He had two kids in college and construction jobs were hard to come by, especially in the Montana winters. Most of the meat he would keep, the rest he would sell to his cousin who owned a restaurant in Billings. The economy had affected all of them, but him the most. His eyes roamed to the others around the fire, all similarly dressed in jeans over thermal underwear and flannel shirts under their winter jackets. They all wore hiking boots, and he and Bob, with their thinning hair, wore caps. Dan had grown out his beard. Bob and Paul were imbibing perhaps more than they should.

"What time should we head out tomorrow?" Jerry asked, knowing it would depend on how much celebrating Bob and Paul did that night.

"If we pack up and hit the highway by eight, we can make it to Buckshot Taxidermy and Meat Processing by nine-thirty," Dan answered.

Bob gestured with his cup, "And I'm sure Billy will look forward to the business."

They discovered Buckshot on a previous trip. Billy was willing to ignore the out-of-season kills they brought him, for a slight fee.

"Let me check the weather report. That may have us leaving sooner," offered Dan, and went to his truck to try the Laramie radio stations.

At the top of the hour, they started off with local news.

"The shooting death three days ago of local icon Bear Tanner, owner of Tanner's Outdoor Adventures, has rocked the community of Centennial. Bear Tanner also owns an operation in Colorado. An investigation is ongoing as to the cause of his death, whether it was accidental, or deliberate. It is unclear what will become of Tanner's Outdoor Adventures, located off Highway 130 and Ehlin Road in the Medicine Bow National Forest.

In Laramie ..."

Dan ignored the rest of the broadcast. They had stumbled upon this area a few years back, and knew it to be a game Preserve. Bear Tanner was wealthy enough, they had guessed, that he wouldn't miss a handful of sometimes-stocked game. The funeral would most likely be within the week. If the owner was dead, that would mean no parties into the Preserve, which meant they could return and see what else they could harvest before they all headed back home. He climbed out of the truck and returned to the fire that was now burning low to share his idea.

"You know, we've been lucky this trip, five days in, and we got ourselves three kills. We all still got some time before we're scheduled to return home. How about we make a trip to Buckshot, then come back for another couple of days?" Dan suggested as he stood close to the glowing coals.

"Are you kidding?" Jerry asked incredulously. "They're bound to bring a party through here, and it wouldn't be pleasant to explain our presence."

"I just heard on the radio that the owner was shot. He's dead. With the funeral and everything, no one will be taking out guests."

Three pairs of eyes looked at him, unblinking.

Paul and Bob spoke at the same time.

"Hell, yeah!"

"Sounds good."

"Jerry?" Dan asked.

Jerry shrugged. "Don't see why not. There's plenty here for the taking," and gestured to where both deer were hung in a nearby tree.

With that decided, there were discussions as to which ridge or canyon they would scout, and the latest they could stay, and still hit Buckshot a second time before Paul, Bob, and Jerry had to catch their flights from Laramie. They eventually found themselves in their tents, warmed by kerosene heaters.

«««—»»»

"Shaun is the only one here. Sam will probably arrive tomorrow, and God only knows when Carli will make her appearance."

"I'll come for the funeral. Pay my respects," she spoke into the phone, her voice cultured, smooth, persuasive.

"Are you sure you want to do that? I don't think they'll be thrilled to see you," he said, rubbing his forehead.

"I'm their mother. It will give me the opportunity to catch up with them, then see their faces as they realize their father and I never divorced."

"Bear could have changed his will. He could have left everything to the three of them."

"You mean you haven't found it yet?"

"It's not like I haven't been looking. Bear's filing system isn't understandable to anyone but himself."

She sighed. "Even if he did, as his legal wife, I'm entitled to inherit all of it. It's the least he could do, since he dragged me to that—" she stopped, then took a breath. "Max Stevens is still his attorney, I presume?"

"Yes," he said and looked across his room, the same one he had occupied since he arrived at the Preserve.

"Then I'll be making an appointment with Mr. Stevens. Call me when they have made arrangements for the ceremony, and I'll reserve a flight and a car."

"Darla—" he said to stall her disconnecting their call. "Do you have everything in place with the planners?"

"Of course. The layouts are complete, we have financial backers, a bid from Wilson Construction, and now a clear lane to a very healthy bank account. Don't worry. Our early retirements are secured."

Without another word, there was a click and then silence in his ear. He set the phone on the table and hoped she was right.

«« — »»

Samantha climbed down from the truck, then walked to the back where she lowered the tailgate and pulled out her luggage. Matt came up beside her and closed the gate. Leaving one hand on the truck, he placed the other on her shoulder.

"Everything at Crystal Springs will be fine. Joe and I have our orders, and our usual duties. You just take care of what you need to. Don't worry about rushing back." When her eyes began to glisten, he slid his hand across her shoulders and gave her a sideways hug. "If I don't hear from you saying you're extending your stay, I'll be here to pick you up in two weeks."

"Thanks, Matt," Samantha said, then turned and pushed through the glass doors of the airport building, pulling her luggage behind her.

Once she was seated on the plane, she rested her head back against the cushion and stared out the window to watch the ground crew. She had flown home for the holidays, and wasn't expecting to go back for a while. Then her father had caught a bullet in the chest, and her life had turned upside-down. Bear Tanner was fifty-eight years old and fit enough to guide hunting parties on the Preserve, which proved to be a very lucrative business. His other endeavor, Crystal Springs, a horse and cattle farm in Colorado, was what she spent her time directing.

As the plane sped down the runway, she thought back to her childhood. The middle of the siblings, she never felt forgotten. Except by her mother. But her father filled that gap. He taught her how to take care of her horse, how to shoot a gun, to survive in the wilderness regardless of the season, and most importantly, how to trust again after the incident when she was seventeen. None of them spoke of it, but she knew Carli and Shaun looked for lasting effects. There were a few, but she kept them to herself. She briefly wondered if her father had ever forgiven himself for what had happened to her. It was not his fault, and in the end, everything worked out. She was alive and Carl Rutgers was in prison.

Jerking her thoughts back from that time, she instead focused on what would need to be done. A service, donations, cards and flowers she knew others would send, existing reservations ... and decisions to be made regarding the operations of Tanner's Outdoor Adventures. With a half-smile, she thought of her siblings. Carli was extremely independent, traveled the globe, was a gifted artist, and had a rolodex the government wished she would share. Shaun was the quiet one, the deep thinker. He was always coming up with one scheme or another on what politicians should try in order to deal with government issues.

With Carli and Shaun being dreamers, that left her to be the logical one. She made lists, played by the rules, and followed through with her commitments and obligations. Her business degree was well suited to her personality. And it would be her strengths that would be needed as they said goodbye to their father and figured out what to do next.

CHAPTER 8

Shaun was waiting outside the terminal, allowed to leave his vehicle parked by the only skycap booth, due to the 'sheriff' emblem on the front doors, the lights on the roof. There was the same excitement he always felt when Carli and Sam came home. Relief also flooded him when Carli's voice came through so clear on his cell phone. She was home, safe, and the three of them would do what needed to be done.

His breath was white fog for a brief moment before the breeze whisked it away. The airport wasn't too busy this morning, and he took a few minutes to notice the other cars and passengers and architecture of the terminal. His squint in the early morning sun and serious expression gave way to a full smile as his eyes found the tall, dark-blonde beauty, dressed in shorts, boots, and a long-sleeved shirt. Beside her was her work partner, Tim, more appropriately dressed for this climate. Behind them was one of the few porters employed at the Laramie Airport with a flatbed loaded four feet high with cases.

"Shaun!" Carli yelled, and flung her arms around her brother.

Shaun had just enough time to removed his hands from his jacket pockets to catch Carli. It was awkward to hold her with her backpack over her shoulders, but it felt good to have her home.

"You must be freezing. Let's get your gear loaded and head to the lodge," he said as Carli stepped back.

He shook hands with Tim, who expressed his obligatory condolences, then moved on to load the cases, lest Carli begin to break down. She tipped the porter and tossed her backpack and carryon in the backseat while Tim and Shaun loaded the cases.

"Shouldn't you have sent this stuff to New York?" Shaun asked.

Tim snorted, as Carli responded, "With the weather in Denver, it's a miracle it showed up here at all. We sent it straight from Caracas. Must have arrived on a cargo plane. It's everything we need for a shoot. Some of it is finished, some not. I can't have all the company equipment sitting in an airport."

"And the fact that it was taking up space at this airport is ..." Tim waited.

"Irrelevant. There's work that needs to be done before these cases can return to the City. And Laramie Regional is a far cry from La Guardia."

"You mean you don't know anyone at La Guardia?" Tim asked, not believing that her home airport was the only place she was friendless.

"Actually, I know several," she said as they climbed in and closed out the icy wind, "but it's just easier this way," she said, and gave Tim a smile that only Shaun saw in the rearview mirror.

Shaking his head at Carli and her stack of cases, he exited the airport towards Highway 130 and Centennial. He had to ask how they had gotten from where they were to where they are. It felt good to laugh, something he hadn't done since getting the call from Alyssa. Shaun recognized, not for the first time, the by-play between Carli and Tim. They had been together long enough, in confined quarters, to be married. Except that Tim was homosexual. He wondered if that was what allowed them to be so close.

Tim brandished the hundred-dollar bill. "And this is the reward for my original travel plans."

"Shaun, when did the Denver Airport open?" Carli asked.

He glanced at his watch. "About two hours ago."

Carli did some calculations, then said, "That means our flight would have left three hours ago, a two and a half hour flight to Denver, then to Laramie—" she stopped as she leaned forward and plucked the bill from Tim's fingers, "and we wouldn't have arrived for another—" she glanced at the clock on the dash, "two hours. And, you would have missed meeting Charlie."

"Charlie?" Shaun glanced at Tim.

"If it works out, I suppose I'll be offering you a finder's fee," Tim said.

"I wouldn't accept it. Consider this an attempt at matchmaking," Carli smiled.

"Never needed help before," Tim grumbled.

"Maybe he has a straight brother, and we can double."

That brought chuckles from the front seat.

After a mile of silence, Carli spoke quietly. "Have you learned anything, Shaun, about what happened?"

He glanced in the rearview mirror, and all humor was gone. Worry and grief replaced the normal sparkle in her hazel eyes so much like his own. Taking his gaze to the highway in front of him, he had to admit how little he had discovered.

"We know the caliber, the trajectory of the bullet. It happened on Wolf's Ridge. The shot came from across the Pine Canyon. There were no planned parties in that section of the Preserve, hikers or hunters. The clients he was with had to call back to base. Luckily they were high enough to get a signal and that Alyssa was at the desk to receive it. They didn't know how to get out. We went in with the horses, called in the remaining groups. None of the clients saw anything or know anything. I've interviewed everyone at the lodge, employee and visitor." He paused, glanced at a blue pickup heading towards Laramie, a tarp over the bed of the truck. "A while back, a Regional Director for the FBI spent a week at the lodge. Dad must have made an impression—"

"He usually does. *Did*—" Carli interrupted.

"Because we now have federal assistance."

"The FBI is involved?" she clarified, her brows raised.

Shaun nodded. "The agent's name is Ethan Brooks. He's booked for a week at the lodge. Cabin 4. No one knows besides us. And Esther."

"Then the whole town will know and whoever is responsible will disappear," she said.

"I made it clear to her to keep this quiet. If we need to flush the shooter out, I promised to set her loose."

"Is the FBI taking over the investigation?"

"No. He promised full cooperation. Just here to lend a hand. Another pair of eyes. He came in last night, and I gave him the files," Shaun paused and glanced at the clock on the dash. "Perhaps he'll have something to share when we reach the lodge."

The Snowy Mountains loomed large in front of them. The narrow state highway, with curves and dips had Tim gripping the door.

"You alright?" Shaun asked, noticing the tenseness of his passenger.

"Tim gets carsick. Airsick, trainsick, even donkey sick," Carli spoke, then fished out a hard candy from her pocket and tapped Tim's shoulder.

He mumbled his thanks. "A great cosmic joke, I assure you, to have a job such as mine, and the stomach of a five-year-old ballerina."

"Donkey sick?" Shaun asked.

"It was one time, and I really think it was what I ate, not the strides of my trusty steed."

Shaun slowed further as they drove through town, glanced inside the front window of the sheriff's office out of habit, then continued when he didn't see anyone there besides Esther. The remaining drive was made in silence, except for Tim's comments regarding the snow that clung to the ground on the north side of the trees, where the shadows were.

When they turned down the driveway to Tanner's Outdoor Adventures, Tim said, "Carli, I know you'll be busy with, well, family stuff. You know I'll be glad to help in any way I can. But I don't want to be in the way, either."

She patted his shoulder. "Thanks, Tim. Until we have some idea what to do, and a way to keep you busy and earning your keep," to which they both smiled, "unload the cases and set up a workstation in the room upstairs where you stayed last summer. Send an e-mail to Scott, let him know where we are, and for how long."

"And how long will we be here?"

Shaun pulled up to the steps of the lodge, undid his seatbelt, and turned off the vehicle. He wanted to hear Carli's answer.

She glanced from Shaun to Tim, and back. "As long as it takes. Tell him I'll be in touch."

Tim looked over his shoulder at his friend and colleague. If he had a sister, he didn't think they would be as close as he was to Carli. He gave her a half-smile, then pried his fingers from the door to place his hand over hers.

Shaun watched, and knew that more was transmitted between them than just an agreement to contact the boss in New York City. The moment passed, and they all exited from the vehicle and began hauling cases and luggage upstairs where the employees had rooms, where Bear Tanner had lived, and where his children stayed when they came to visit. Alyssa was in the kitchen, and Zach came out to help haul things, and received a hug from Carli. They had just finished dividing up cases between Carli and Tim's rooms, when Shaun's phone rang.

He held Carli's gaze, smiled, then said he was on his way. Closing the phone, he announced, "Samantha. I'm going back to Laramie. Should be here for lunch."

Carli smiled. "See you then."

《《—》》》

Tim closed the door to his private accommodations and sighed. Setting up his laptop on the table by the door, he connected to the lodge's wireless system and went about checking his e-mail. His personal e-mail account was full of party invitations, requests of "Where in the world is Tim?", a game his friends played that he suspected earned a few of them some spending money, forwarded jokes and inspirational messages, and the inevitable spam advertisements for correcting his credit score and his erectile dysfunction, neither of which were cause for concern. Deleting most of them, and responding to a few others, he logged on to *International Views* to contact Scott.

He sent a two-line message, one that informed Scott where they were, and another telling his boss his thoughts on the lack of tact in the telegram that was sent to Venezuela. Before he finished reading and deleting office memos, Scott sent a reply message.

Tim-

Thanks for the update on your whereabouts. How is Carli? When do you two plan to return to the office? How was the shoot in South America?

Regarding the telegram, new administrative assistant-didn't know what was sent. Give Carli my apologies.

S

He read the message and shook his head. Scott was demanding of his staff, and seemed to change assistants as often as most people change their underwear. If they couldn't keep up with the demands of the job, or Scott, they weren't given a second chance. He sent a reply.

S-

Carli is holding up fine-better now that she's home. I hope to return in a week. Carli, I don't know. South America was wet. Got some shots.

Tim

He waited a few minutes, and his boss didn't disappoint.

Keep me posted on the funeral. I need the work from Africa and whatever you have from South America.

He tapped his reply on the keyboard.

I'll forward the plans as they are made. Africa needs a little work. Have no idea what she got in South America. Give me a couple days.

Scott's reply was almost instant.

Two days, and I need Africa. You personally have a week. I need you and Carli if the November issue will be printed on time.

S

Tim sighed at Scott's final response. The man meant well, and generally was sympathetic when it came to his employees and their personal lives, as long as it fit in with his timeline. Brushing his red curls off his forehead with one hand, the other exited his e-mail and brought up the editing program and the files from Africa. He would have to get the film and memory cards from Carli when he saw her at lunch. She would probably want to develop the film herself. Her father had included a dark room, located at the end of the hall that ran the length of the upstairs portion of the lodge, when he expanded the structure. His hope was to entice Carli to lengthen her visits by ending the excuse of, "I have to return to the office to develop film". It worked in the past and would be essential to her now. He glanced at his watch and knew he could have a solid file started in a couple of hours to send to Scott. Setting his iPod to the latest song selection of jazz greats sent to him by a friend, he placed the buds in his ears and got to work.

CHAPTER 9

"Can I get you anything else, Ethan?"

He smiled at Alyssa and understood the look in Zach's eyes the previous night as the young man described Alyssa's pancakes. They were unusually good, and their creator was unique herself. He could picture himself at Zach's age and being attracted to just this kind of girl. Alyssa was tall, thin, with blonde hair and blue eyes, and her classically pretty face could have landed her a modeling job in a big city. As a print model, the publications could have fixed the photos to hide the scars on her face. Most would not have even noticed, but it was Ethan's job to observe the details in those he met. She was soft-spoken and a little shy, and he wondered if she was accident-prone.

"One of those travel mugs with the Tanner logo on it filled with coffee would be great. Zach was right, your blueberry pancakes are something special."

She ducked her head, her hair falling over her shoulder to shield her expression from his gaze, as she collected his silverware and plate.

"Thanks. I'll have the coffee for you in just a minute. I'll have to add the cup to your room bill," she paused, waiting for his agreement.

"That's fine," he said, and watched as she turned, four plates balanced in one hand, picked up the coffee carafe with the other, and then wove around a chair to push the kitchen door open. He filed away the silence, not a crash, from the other side of the door that would have indicated dropped dishes by a clumsy employee.

Turning his attention to the three men he had shared breakfast
with, he learned they were to meet Donna in the lobby for their
hike further into Deer Valley. They wished him luck on his
fishing expedition, and excused themselves. He smiled at the
secret meaning of his answer when they had asked his reason for
visiting Tanner's. With no interest in hunting animals as a sport,
he remembered enough from his childhood fishing trips with his
father and grandfather that he could hold a conversation should
one of his breakfast companions engage in 'fish talk' with him.
Only one had been trout fishing two days ago with a guide. They
all came to see Wyoming and enjoyed leaving their cubicle jobs
in the city of San Francisco for a week. Ethan flipped the page on
his writing pad and crossed off three names. At the sound of
Alyssa's voice, he turned the page.

"If you decide to schedule a hike or late fishing trip and want
a box lunch, just find me or Zach or Ray and we'll get you one. If
you end up hanging around all day, you can still grab a box, or
wait until four when free appetizers are set out in the lobby.
Dinner will be served at six-thirty. If you need something, there's
almost always someone at the front desk."

He took the cup, thanked her, gathered his pad and pencil and
jacket, then excused himself from the dining room. Wandering
through the lobby, he saw that Zach was on duty at the desk.

"Hi, Ethan," Zach said. "What did you think of the
pancakes?"

"Great, as promised."

Zach smiled. "What can I help you with?"

"Who is Ray?"

"He's one of the guides and a friend of Bear's. He helps run
the place. Don't know what's going to happen now. Maybe Ray
will take over," he shrugged, trying to be nonchalant in an
attempt to keep his emotions under control.

"What does he look like?" Ethan asked.

"Older guy. Usually wears a straw cowboy hat, jeans,
sheepskin jacket. Let's see," Zach looked at a schedule hanging
on a clipboard. "He's with two clients at the river," he said,

glancing at his watch. "They should be back around three. Why?" Zach eyed Ethan.

"Alyssa suggested I seek out one of the three of you if I had questions. And I do, actually. Sheriff Tanner mentioned he would be by the lodge today."

Zach nodded. "You just missed him. Carli's home. She came in this morning, then Shaun, Sheriff Tanner, had to turn around and head back to Laramie to pick up Samantha. Said he would be back by lunch."

To keep his cover, Ethan asked, "Carli and Samantha?"

"Sorry, they're Sheriff Tanner's sisters. Alyssa informed you of the death of the owner of Tanner's Outdoor Adventures?" he paused until Ethan nodded. "Well, they're coming here to make, you know, funeral arrange—" Zach paused to clear his throat, "arrangements. How do you know Sheriff Tanner?"

"We were introduced through a friend of a friend. I'll wait until he returns with Samantha to talk with him." He glanced around the empty lobby, as the clients who had reservations and chose to remain after Bear's death were out enjoying the fresh, Wyoming air. "Any chance I can get a guide to lead me up to Wolf's Ridge?" He watched as Zach's eyes grew bigger with surprise.

"I think you'll have to speak with Shaun about that," Zach began.

Carli had descended the steps on a search for food and had heard Zach's comment. She paused at the front desk area and took in the profile of the man leaning against the counter. He was taller than her, with dark hair that curled slightly over his ears and brushed the bottom of the collar of his jacket. A strong chin and defined, clean-shaven jaw, were the bottom of the profile that included full lips and a nose that may have been broken at one time as evidenced by the small bump in the middle of it. He turned his dark brown eyes in her direction a moment before she spoke.

"Ask Shaun about what?"

"Carli Tanner, Ethan Brooks. He's staying in Cabin 4 and is interested in getting a guide to lead him up to Wolf's Ridge." Zach was quiet, his eyes boring into Carli's, hoping she knew the reason for his hesitation.

She did. Ethan was the FBI agent and she guessed he wanted to see the site where her father had been shot. But Zach didn't know who Ethan really was, and she wondered if Ethan knew that she knew who he was.

She smiled at Zach. "We'll double-check with Shaun when he gets back. It's been some time since I've seen the canyon from Wolf's Ridge," she said, and shifted her gaze to Ethan. "When would you like to go?"

He gave her a small grin, enough to engage his dimples. "Tomorrow or the next day would be fine."

"There's a party going to the waterfall tomorrow, so the Ridge is open," Zach informed them, looking up from the schedule.

Without taking her eyes from the FBI agent, Carli said, "Put me down for the guide to Wolf's Ridge. Tomorrow. We'll leave at seven-thirty. Do you ride, Mr. Brooks?" she asked with a raised brow.

He saw a spark of mischief in her eye, and wondered to what mode of transportation she referred. "Ethan. Ride what?"

She gave him a half-smile. "Horses." She wasn't sure if she recognized relief or disappointment.

"I have. It's been a few years."

"Zach, add Samson and Lady to the schedule."

Zach glanced back and forth between the two as if he were watching a tennis match.

Ethan raised a brow. "Samson? We could hike. I'm in decent shape."

She shook her head. "Hiking will take an extra three hours, and I have other … obligations to attend to. Samson is a good boy. He's used to carrying men of your size," she stated, and resisted allowing her gaze to travel the length of what she guessed was a body as well put together as the man's face.

76

Deepening his grin at her struggle to keep eye contact, Ethan ignored the first three comments that formed in his mind regarding 'men of his size', and instead settled on something benign.

"I'm looking forward to getting back in the saddle. It's been a while," he said, and held back a chuckle as Carli's face glowed with a light pink on her cheeks.

"Zach, is Alyssa still in the kitchen?" she asked, trying desperately to cool her cheeks without waving her hand in front of her face.

"Yes. She's cleaning up from breakfast and making a few box lunches."

"I'm famished and can't wait for lunch. I'll be in my room, or Tim's," she finally turned to look at Zach, "so let me know when Shaun returns."

"Sure," Zach said, then observed, along with Ethan, as Carli stepped around the front desk and disappeared into the dining room, calling out to Alyssa as she pushed open the door to the kitchen.

"Huh," was all Ethan could say. He blinked at where Carli had vanished, and was called back to where he was by Zach's voice.

"Anything else, Ethan?"

"No. Thanks." He raised his travel mug and gestured out the window toward the front of the lodge. "I'll be around, waiting for Shaun."

Zach nodded and watched as Ethan left the lobby. He sat down on the tall chair behind him and marveled at what he had just witnessed. Not sure of everything that passed between Carli and Ethan, he understood that there was more going on than their spoken words. The phone rang, pulling him back to his job.

"Tanner's Outdoor Adventures. This is Zach. How can I help you?"

《《—》》

"Are you sure?" she asked to verify what he was telling her.

"Yes. The paperwork was filed with the court, but when you failed to sign and return the document, there was nothing for them to record. The town of Centennial and Albany County have no record that you and Bear Tanner were divorced. All these years, you've been married to him in the eyes of the State of Wyoming."

"Thank you, Michael. You earned your retainer today," she said and disconnected the call.

It had been four days since she was informed of the sudden death of her estranged husband. She turned toward her closet and pulled out a long-sleeved, black dress. Mourning would be appropriate. Sliding it off the hanger and folding it neatly, then placing it in her suitcase, she played out the scene in her mind. Carli, Samantha, and Shaun would welcome her with open arms. They would be shocked at the reading of the will, but she would reassure them that their father's memory would live on, and her plans for Tanner's Outdoor Adventures would bring them all great wealth.

She looked around the room where she had spent the last three months. The pristine white carpet, the glass figurines, the thunder of the surf outside the wall of sliding glass doors, and knew that this was hers.

Glancing at her watch, she realized she would have to leave now to make the appointment, and then her dinner date. Her flight left at eleven the next morning. She would be sure to get back early enough to get her rest. It wouldn't make the right impression if she arrived in Laramie with dark circles under her eyes. Checking her reflection in the mirror next to the front door, she reapplied her lipstick, patted her hair and adjusted her bangs, then gathered her purse and keys and left the Carmel house.

CHAPTER 10

Ray looked down at the trout in the net. They were still alive, but would be turned into trophies of the three men who waded in the thigh-high water. He didn't feel like being here, didn't want to lead these weekend warriors on a fishing outing. But he had made a deal with Bear, his best friend for thirty years. Bear had the idea, but Ray had the experience, so they had partnered in this business venture. He had sold his share to Bear years ago, not wanting to be part of the collapse should something go wrong. Nothing did, and Tanner's Outdoor Adventures had gained international recognition. He had always been well compensated for his labor, and for many years he was satisfied with the arrangement. When he first spoke to Bear about retiring and moving to someplace like Florida, Bear laughed until he had tears rolling down his cheeks, disappearing into his full, red beard. He didn't understand that his friend and former business partner was tired. His body protested a little more each winter, his hip a little stiffer after his fall into the mineshaft. Bear offered him more money, lighter duties, and he always gave in, admitting that he wouldn't know what to do without Bear giving him orders, and they would laugh, and he would return to work.

The lodge had become Bear's life. He raised three terrific kids, and no matter what befell his business, he always managed to recover. Now that Bear was gone, Ray didn't see how the lodge could continue, and so had made his own plans. Carli, Samantha, and Shaun would make arrangements for the funeral. He would attend, of course, and assist them in squaring away the lodge, cabins, livestock, and land. Then he would leave Wyoming.

He glanced up at the excited voices as one of the clients pulled in another trout. *Thinks he's a lucky bastard,* Ray thought. Little Shy River was stocked last week. It was one of his many duties at the lodge. He offered the obligatory grin and helped to remove the hook, then added the fish to those already inside the net.

After a short discussion, the three clients suggested they return to the lodge. They kept the six largest fish, packed them in the ice chest, and released the others into the river. It was a fifteen-minute drive to the lodge, and by the time they stored their gear and climbed into the van, they would arrive in time for lunch. He was glad that the job of cleaning the fish was the client's, and if they needed help, Zach would be the one to offer it. He tuned out the chatter of the clients, except when they asked him a specific question. Watching the trees flash by, he realized he had traveled this road so many times he might as well have named every one of the tall pines.

When he pulled up at the lodge, he understood how difficult the next few days would be. Shaun's vehicle was parked in front, and Carli and Samantha each glanced at him as they held luggage in their hands. He turned off the engine, gathered his courage, and exited the van to offer his condolences to Bear's kids.

«« — »»

Ethan had spent the morning hours wandering the grounds. There were twelve cabins, a couple of outbuildings, and the barn. J.J. was there cleaning stalls when Ethan explained he would be riding Samson the next day. J.J. introduced the two of them. Ethan stepped back as Samson stuck his head over the barn door in greeting. All two and a half feet of it.

"He's part draft horse, and real sure-footed on the trail. If you haven't ridden for a while he'll take care of you. Here," J.J.

offered Ethan a carrot, then gestured toward Samson. "It will make a good impression."

Ethan held the carrot and was amazed that six inches so easily disappeared between Samson's lips. The horse bit down and snapped the carrot just shy of Ethan's fingers. He reached up with his other hand and stroked the horse's face from forehead to nose. Samson seemed gentle enough as he plucked the remaining carrot part from Ethan's hand. Feeling they had established a bond, Ethan left the barn to scout the perimeter of the immediate area, keeping his eyes open for game trails and locations where one could hide amongst the shadows of the trees and watch the activities of the lodge.

There were more places than he could keep track of, and decided it was a waste of his time to try to link the possible killer to a shot he, or she, might make from inside the lodge or the surrounding area. Since the shade of the surrounding forest was degrees colder than the spring sun, he found a boulder at the edge of the parking area to sit and warm himself in sunshine.

With the pad of paper in his hand, he extracted his pencil from his shirt picket, opened to a fresh page, and let his pencil sketch his thoughts. There was nothing in the current client folders that led him to believe any of them had a grudge against Bear Tanner. The employees he had met so far were also unlikely suspects. Alyssa, just about to graduate from high school, admitted that she doesn't hunt or fish, or know how to hold and shoot a gun. He had already eliminated Zach, and J.J. had eyes only for the residents in the barn. But he hadn't met Ray, Donna, or the seasonal employees. He would ask Shaun about records of past clients and any that seemed unhappy with their experience with Tanner's outfit. Former employees could also hold a grudge. That would be several files and a lot of paperwork to read through. Angry acquaintances may show up at the funeral, and he added procuring an invitation to the event to the growing list in his mind.

He paused and looked across the parking area at the approaching vehicle. Shaun had returned from the airport with the other sister. Carli and Zach came out to meet them. He stood, about ready to make his way toward the gathering, then glanced down at his pad of paper. Flipping back two pages, he found three sketches of Alyssa, another of Zach. The other two pages were filled with pictures of Carli. He managed to capture her spark of mischief, and a full-length drawing depicted the back of her as she had walked away from him, just before she entered the kitchen. Her hair fell in soft curls to the middle of her shoulders. A flannel shirt was tucked into snug jeans that revealed her heart-shaped backside. He flipped the pages so the blank one was on top, and went to join the party.

«‹‹—›»

Dan glanced in the rearview mirror and saw 'Buckshot Taxidermy and Meat Processing' grow smaller. Billy was excited at the prospect of the bear. There would be some extra hide removed from the belly in order to disguise the shots fired that brought down the grizzly. The head was undamaged and they had discussed what the finished product would look like, and the cost of the work. Both deer would be stripped, the meat packaged and shipped to their home addresses, the heads mounted, the hides cured.

On the return drive to Centennial, it was decided that they would split up, one pair heading up to the Ridge, the other taking the bottom of the Pine Canyon. They could stay through Sunday, head back to Laramie, and Buckshot, Saturday morning. The weatherman predicted cold temperatures, in the twenties at night, fifties during the day. If they got anything, the lower temps would help preserve the carcass. Just to make sure, they would load up with ice at the gas station. There was still snow on the ground, and they could use that as well. They would clean their weapons and check their gear tonight, and be ready to set out early in the morning.

By the time they returned to camp, it was late afternoon. A small fire was started to begin heating coals for Dutch ovens and water for coffee. It crossed Dan's mind how far away they were from the lodge, and he hoped none of the clients or employees wandered down the road where they were camped. Poaching was illegal. So was trespassing. He didn't want to contemplate paying the fines, and instead thought of the money he would get for the trophies dropped off at Buckshot.

CHAPTER 11

Lunch was a complicated affair. Shaun wanted to speak with Carli and Samantha, and Ethan wanted Shaun's attention. Shaun informed Sam of who Ethan was on the return trip from the airport. The fishing clients opted for box lunches to eat after they cleaned their catch, so it was only family and employees that crowded into the dining room. Sitting one chair to the right of the head of the long, wooden table, he watched the interplay between Zach and Alyssa, Ray and his sisters, and was a little surprised by the amount of time Ethan spent observing Carli. When they were all in school, he had to hear about what other guys thought of his sisters in the locker room. He knew they were beautiful, and they had dated their share of boys in school. When the locker room talk got too detailed for his liking, he would call a halt to it swearing he would tell Carli and Sam who said which comments. Once they had moved on to college, he didn't have to hear about what happened on dates, or what didn't. Each of his sisters had relationships, some that ended congenially, others that led to tearful calls at odd hours of the day, and him promising to kick someone's ass.

They were all adults now and he figured Sam and Carli could take care of themselves. He would keep an eye on Ethan's interest, and watch to see if Carli returned it. A small grin turned up the corners of his lips at the picture of Carli as love-struck as Alyssa. It was the smile on his face that had Carli commenting.

"Want to share the joke?" she asked.

85

"Later. Maybe. I think," he paused as he glanced at Sam, "that we need to figure out what to do with Dad."

That silenced all conversation. Alyssa began clearing dishes. Zach helped, then mumbled about checking the schedule, while J.J. said he needed to take inventory of feed in the barn. Shaun let them go, then raised his brow in Ray's direction.

"I don't have anything to contribute. He was your father. You do what you want," Ray said to Shaun, then slid his chair back from the table as he prepared to leave.

"Ray Foster, Bear Tanner was your best friend for thirty years. You're as much family as we are. Stay." Shaun would consider the man's response later.

Ray glanced at Carli and Sam, then Ethan, and wondered where this client came from and how come he was seated with the rest of them at what appeared to be an employee-family lunch. He nodded in Ethan's direction.

"What's your interest in the funeral plans?"

Shaun spoke before Ethan. "He's an acquaintance of mine. I've asked him to give his input. As I'm asking you."

"And I'm saying I don't have one. What do I know of flowers and receptions?" Ray lowered his voice. "I'll say farewell to Bear in my own way. Just tell me where and when, and I'll be there." He stood and took his jacket from the back of the chair. All eyes were on him as he pushed his arms into the sleeves. He glanced at the three of them, ignoring Ethan, and said, "I have work to see to. Let me know what you decide to do with," he glanced around the room, "all of this."

When no one said anything, Ray left the dining hall, and a moment later they heard the front door of the lodge close.

Shaun sighed and rubbed his forehead with the heel of his hand, then pushed his fingers through the blonde strands. "Ray being difficult is his way of dealing with Dad's death," he explained as he dropped his hand to his lap and looked at who was left. "Sam, I'm betting you made a list before you left Colorado. Let's have it."

86

She glanced at Ethan, then Shaun. "Does he know that we know?"

"He does now," Ethan answered and looked at Shaun. "It's better if no one knows who I am, or why I'm here."

"Shawn has only told Sam and me. And Tim," Carli said.

Ethan raised a brow at the mention of her coworker.

"Close proximity, but Tim knows to keep quiet."

"If you all treat me different than any other guest, it will only alert other suspects."

"'Other' suspects? You mean you think one of us killed Dad?" Carli asked incredulously.

"When a parent's death is suspicious, the spouse and children are often the culprits," Ethan turned his gaze on Shaun. "We follow procedure to rule out suspects."

Shaun nodded, choosing to ignore the censure, and instead elaborate on the procedure. "Motive. Opportunity. Everyone accounts for their whereabouts, and we exhaust all possible reasons someone would want Dad dead."

"I've been out of the country, Sam is in another state, and Shaun is the sheriff. We all love our father very much. None of us killed him," Carli ended her speech with a slap on the table. Shaun and Sam looked at her. It wasn't her nature to lose her cool, but they were all shaken by recent events.

"You or Sam could have hired someone, maybe an employee, to do it for you. And who knows more about hiding evidence than the local sheriff?" Shaun had locked gazes with Ethan by the third word. "How am I doing Agent Brooks?"

Without a moment's hesitation, Ethan answered. "Brilliantly. There's nothing in the client files of those who were staying here at the time of the incident that indicates any of them having a reason to do your father harm. I'd like to review the files for the past few years or so. Clients and employees."

Shaun gestured toward Carli. "There's other paperwork that Dad has, somewhere, that I've looked for and can't find. Carli is the only one who understands Dad's filing system."

"Despite my best efforts to switch him and the business to electronic files, there was some stuff Dad refused to duplicate on the computer," Sam offered, resting her chin in her hand, her elbow on the table.

"Do you still have a key to Dad's office?" Carli asked Shaun.

"And the basement," he said, removing the keys from his key ring and sliding them across the table towards Carli.

"Besides the most recent clients, who else have you crossed off your list of possible suspects?" Shaun asked Ethan.

"Alyssa and Zach."

Sam inquired, "Why?"

"Alyssa can't bring herself to mention 'Bear' and 'death' in the same sentence. She idolized him, and though I didn't have the pleasure of meeting the man, I would suspect he thought of his employees as family, especially Alyssa and Zach. And Zach isn't hard enough to kill another human being."

"'Hard enough'?" Sam asked, her gaze going to Shaun, then back to Ethan as he answered.

"The ME's report is inconclusive as to murder versus an accidental shooting. To look through a scope, take a calculated shot, requires an edge," he turned toward Shaun, "that Zach doesn't have."

"I agree."

"If the shot was intentional, it was pre-meditated. A crime of passion is personal, up close. There was no GSR on Bear's clothing," Ethan continued.

"So, if Dad was shot on purpose, the person knew what they were doing, knew he would be on Wolf's Ridge," Carli deduced aloud.

Ethan nodded. "Which makes employees near the top of the list. Who makes the schedule, who had time available in their schedule."

"Unless it was someone else who waited at the end of the drive or in the trees and just followed the party," Carli offered.

"Also a possibility," Ethan agreed.

"And with any investigation, the goal is to eliminate possibilities," Shaun said. "Carli, can you show Ethan Dad's office and the basement? Information is key to solving any crime."

"Sure. What are you looking for, Shaun?"

He knew how it would sound to the FBI, but he answered honestly. "The will and the deed for the property."

Carli could see the gears shifting in Ethan's mind. Before she could say something to pull him from his scrutiny of Shaun, Sam shifted the conversation.

"Ethan, you also mentioned a spouse."

He turned to look at her. "Where is Mrs. Bear Tanner?"

Carli answered, "That's a really great question."

Sam shrugged. "She left one day, and came back a couple of times, but," she looked at Carli, then Shaun. "I don't think any of us have seen her since Shaun's graduation from the Police Academy."

"Why did she leave?" Ethan didn't intend for the question to sound calloused. He wondered if he would hear the truth when the three siblings exchanged a look, then refused to meet his gaze.

"The day she left was my second day in kindergarten," Shaun began and shrugged. "Guess she figured her job was done. Darla Tanner hated everything about Wyoming. The wind, snow, trees. The isolation in Centennial. She just decided to pack up and move back to California."

Carli continued with what she knew. "She returned for milestone birthdays, sixteen and eighteen, and for high school graduations. She stayed at a hotel in Laramie. The first couple of times, Dad let her stay at the lodge. Guess he thought to reconcile with her."

"After abandoning him with three young kids," Sam added, "and leaving him to work the business alone, you would think Dad would hate her. He never dated after she left."

"That we know of," Shaun said. "He could have kept a girlfriend in Laramie."

Sam shook her head. "I don't think so. He had his hands full with us and the clients. There was no time for a woman."

"So, they were divorced?" Ethan asked.

All three siblings answered at the same time.

"Yes."

"Of course."

"We don't know."

"If they were divorced, the papers are probably in the same location as the will and the deed to the property," Ethan spoke to Shaun.

"Which is on my list to locate," Sam said.

"And we will," Ethan confirmed and glanced at Carli. "Do you know Darla Tanner's last address?"

"Central California coast. She talked about the beach, small tourist town, big houses," Carli answered, leaning back in her chair and resting her hands, with fingers interlaced, across her belly.

"Did she keep her married name?"

"No reason to change it," Sam responded and shrugged.

"I'll see what I can find." Ethan nodded to Sam. "What else is on your list?"

Samantha leaned forward and rested her forearms on the table. "Shaun placed a brief obituary. We should post another one, more in depth, and send it to several papers in Wyoming and Colorado. Friends, relatives, and repeat clients should be notified and made aware of the services. And where to donate money, such as the Humane Society and 4-H and FFA of Albany and Carbon Counties. Dad wasn't a religious man, but he and Darla did have a minister preside over their wedding."

"How do you know?" Ethan asked.

"We've seen their wedding pictures," Sam began.

"And he would threaten to drag us before Pastor William if we abused our curfew," Carli added.

Ethan tipped up the corner of his mouth as he thought what would keep Carli Tanner from returning home on time. "And I'm guessing the wedding photos are stored in the basement?"

"We'll find out," Carli said, and offered a half-smile of her own, indicating she wouldn't be sharing with Ethan what had kept her out past curfew.

Just as congenially, he asked, "And I'll be shown all correspondence regarding condolences of your father?"

"Why?" Sam asked.

Shaun answered, "Because we need to know if any of the responses are out of character. It could point to a suspect."

"I'll also need to know if any of you have received threats or unusual phone calls, e-mails—"

"First we're suspects, and now you think we may be the next targets?" Carli shifted forward, her palms bracing the seat next to her thighs as she leaned toward the table.

Ethan held her gaze, not letting on that the way she sat enhanced the cleavage shown by her V-shaped neckline. Nestled at the pit of her throat and framed by her collarbones, was a tooth of a predator suspended on a cord. A lion or tiger, perhaps.

"If you have received nasty messages, then that changes the direction of the investigation. Widens the scope. Then the person who fired the shot didn't just have a disagreement with Bear, but a contempt for your entire family."

Everyone was silent.

"Just think about anything that might have been out of the ordinary. A persistent e-mail. Seeing the same person at various locations. A recent argument with someone who might take revenge to the next level." He glanced from Carli to Sam, then rested his gaze on Shaun and recognized the sheriff's knowledge. "You've already considered this and decided to wait until your sisters were here to discuss it with them. You didn't want to create any panic or anxiety or undue worry. But a little worry could pinpoint a pattern, help someone remember a seemingly insignificant detail," Ethan paused and lowered his voice. "And if any of that were true, you had planned to assign extra security and wondered how you were going to keep your two very independent sisters safe from a shooter."

Shaun clenched his jaw, a muscle ticked in his cheek. The man was FBI, and apparently good at his job. He nodded once.

"And what was your plan?" Ethan asked.

"That neither of them go anywhere alone. They stay where other people are, so they won't become isolated, which makes them an easier target."

It was Ethan's turn to agree with Shaun. "I believe Zach and J.J. are clear of any involvement. If Carli or Sam need to move any distance from the lodge, one of those two, or you or me, should be with them."

"Why not Ray?" asked Sam.

"Because Ray is still on the suspect list. As are we," Shaun answered.

"Sam, I think you should be able to work through at least part of your list of funeral arrangements without leaving the lodge, or wandering very far away," Ethan told her.

Sam looked from Ethan to Shaun, who nodded.

"And why do you get to roam wherever you want to?" she asked her brother.

"Kevlar," he answered.

"And we need to keep things as close to a regular routine as possible. As sheriff, Shaun has other duties. It would be expected that the two of you would plan the funeral," Ethan included both sisters in his gesture.

Shaun slid his chair away from the table. "I have to check in at the office. I'll contact the DMV in California and see about a current address for Darla."

"I'll get started on the phone calls and have Alyssa help me with the obituary," Sam offered as she stood and began to collect glasses and silverware.

"That leaves the two of us to search for paperwork, starting in the basement," Carli added, holding up the keys between her thumb and forefinger.

"I'll check in with you this evening," Shaun said as he turned to leave.

"You're not staying?" Sam asked, hands full and on her way to the kitchen door.

Shaun shook his head. "I have work to do at home. Call if you need anything. I'll be by for breakfast." He included Ethan in his comment, then exited the dining room.

Ethan watched him leave, then turned toward Carli and the swinging door that alerted him to Sam's departure.

"Ready?" Carli asked.

"After you," Ethan answered, gesturing for her to precede him to the basement, collecting his pad and pencil before following Carli to a probably dark and cramped space. He glanced out the windows in the lobby as Shaun's vehicle drove down the drive, and wished he could have gone with the sheriff instead.

CHAPTER 12

Once they returned from Laramie, Dan parked the truck behind a line of young trees that hid it from any cursory glances from someone on the road. They were a few miles from the state highway, and about the same distance from the Tanner lodge. They hadn't heard any shots the previous day, nor earlier that morning. Based on the quiet of the Preserve, they guessed that all operations had ceased since the announcement of Tanner's death.

After a late lunch, Dan and Paul gathered their gear and set off in the direction of the path they had found that led to another trail that ran along the crest of Wolf's Ridge. The top fifty or so feet of the Ridge was solid rock with a vertical face. The trail lined the area where rock met the soil that held the vegetation. Parts of the trail were above tree line and had more snow than the lower elevations. They wouldn't be traveling that high, as the deer, elk, and antelope would be where the spring had thawed a majority of the snow. This was a scouting trip, but a hunter rarely left camp unprepared, lest an opportunity to get something worth, in their case, some serious cash, presented itself.

Bob and Jerry were to scout the canyon bottom. They had a better chance to see cat or bear which would be after the deer. Some snow had yet to melt, but the sunshine of late spring was creating a muddy trail and several puddles. Thankful for the lower route that wouldn't require as much effort, Bob carried his gun in one hand and his pack over both shoulders. The pain reliever he had taken for his hangover had finally begun to edge back the discomfort. Jerry followed him, neither man saying much, but keeping their ears and eyes open for bull calls and scat.

It had taken two hours, but Dan and Paul had reached a clearing in the trees. There was about a ten-degree drop in the temperature on Wolf's Ridge, as well as an increase in wind speed. Dan raised his field glasses and peered across the canyon to the other side, which was dense with foliage. Tracking the binoculars back and forth he looked for signs of movement or a break in the vegetation. Dan sighed and lowered the binoculars. Paul was seated on a boulder drinking from his canteen. Dan sat on a lower rock, pulled out his pack of cigarettes, and lit one.

Paul glanced at him when he smelled the scent of burning tobacco. "How can you smoke up here? The air is thin enough already."

Dan exhaled a stream of blue smoke that was whisked away with the wind. "It has nothing to do with breathing, but rather related to being calm, creating a point of focus, of concentration," which he demonstrated by staring intently at the lit end of the cigarette.

"Good thing the ground is wet. Keeps you from starting a forest fire," Paul commented, then took another drink from his canteen.

Dan raised the glasses again and this time scanned the bottom of the canyon, looking for Bob and Jerry. Not locating them, he turned around to view the crest of Wolf's Ridge above him. Sweeping the glasses down and to his right, he spotted something unusual on the ground. Lowering the binoculars and taking another drag on his cigarette, he stood and walked to what had caught his attention.

"What? Did you find something?" Paul asked.

Dan ignored him and inspected the ground, placing the cigarette between his lips. Crouching down and shifting his rifle to his other side, he took the fingers of his right hand and touched the dark spot. The color was different than mud.

Paul hovered over his shoulder. "What is it?"

"Blood. Something was wounded here. Maybe died here," Dan answered, wiping his fingers on his pants and removing the mostly burned cigarette from between his lips.

The dark area was irregularly shaped, yet didn't hold enough blood for an elk. He stood and backed up a step, annoyed that Paul was still so close. Dan moved to stand on the uphill side of the bloodstain, then stepped back. The ground around the stain was tamped down. Boot prints. Lots of them. He glanced up and looked across Pine Canyon. Where they stood was out in the open, and directly opposite was thickly wooded.

Paul, too, had been looking at the ground. He moved a small distance away, still examining the soil.

"Not cat prints, or even bear. Horse. Human," Paul looked at Dan as they both seemed to arrive at a similar conclusion at the same time.

"Someone was shot and killed here," Dan said.

Paul nodded. "I think we should stick to the canyon bottom tomorrow. Nothing up this high, this early in the summer."

Dan took a final drag, then tossed the butt to the ground and stepped on it. He exhaled, and said nothing.

"Let's head back to camp," Paul suggested as he glanced at the sky and noted the sun disappearing over the edge of the Ridge. Twilight comes early in a canyon.

Without a word, they returned to the trail and began their descent.

《《—》》

They took the hallway alongside the stairs to the end of the building. The door was on the right, and despite its lack of use, the key easily fit and turned the deadbolt. Carli pulled the door open and flicked the switch. A single light bulb, covered in a glass globe, illuminated their path down the stairs. The wooden steps were unpainted and not as worn as they could have been for being the age they were. There was a railing on the un-walled side of the staircase. Another light switch was at the bottom of the stairs, which they wouldn't need just yet as the afternoon sun streamed in through the three windows that were at ground level on the south side of the lodge.

Ethan forced himself not to duck, as the ceiling was tall enough, but the knowledge that he was underground, below a structure, just seemed to have his head sinking into his shoulders. He paused at the bottom of the stairs and was relieved that the area wasn't as cramped as he had imagined. There was some furniture under sheets along the wall by the stairs. There were stacks of boxes on two of the other walls, but not beneath the windows. A few four-drawer filing cabinets and a safe lined the fourth wall. The boxes and furniture were lifted off of the concrete floor and placed on wooden slats, presumably to help protect them should the basement become flooded.

She lifted the edge of one sheet, pulled open a drawer, and removed a set of keys. Turning towards the file cabinets, she unlocked each one, then placed the keys in her front pocket. She pulled open the first drawer and groaned.

"Damn it, Dad. You were supposed to have fixed these."

Ethan moved to stand behind her and looked over her shoulder. The file folders were multi-colored, unlabeled, and most had papers protruding from their tops and sides. None were in hanging file folders, so they leaned back on each other, some falling underneath others. She closed the top drawer and opened each one under it, one at a time, and they all revealed the same picture of disorder. There were two drawers in the third cabinet that were neatly labeled and filed.

"Sam," she said, gesturing to the organized drawers.

"What do these contain?" he asked.

"Client files. Mostly."

"Are they at least in chronological order? These drawers that Sam organized, they're labeled 1986-1987," he read the front of the drawer and then pulled a file and double-checked the reservation date.

"Hard to say."

"Shaun said you were the only one who knew Bear's filing system."

"And he's right. Dad and I thought a lot alike when it came to organization."

"That it's nonexistent?" he asked pulling open the first drawer.

Carli sighed, leaned an elbow on the top of the cabinet and cocked her hip to the side. "Funny." She paused as Ethan glanced at her, enough of a smile on his face to set off his dimples. It made him look charming, which in her experience was more dangerous than just attractive.

She turned and looked for the container of office supplies she got him as part of his Christmas gift. Locating it, she removed the lid and then the box of hanging file folders. Taking several, she went to the cabinet where Ethan had withdrawn a few of the files and began flipping through pages. Stacking the hanging files on top of the cabinet, she grabbed several files and removed them, placed the hanger inside, and then dropped the files into the folder.

"You're organizing now?" he asked.

"Just getting the files so they're easier to handle. It would go faster if you lifted the files while I put in the hangers," she suggested.

He did as she asked, and with a little rearranging, he admitted that they were more accessible. The closeness afforded him a chance to catch a whiff of her skin. Clean, like soap. He didn't think of Carli as one for preferring cloying scents, then scoffed at himself for thinking he knew any of her preferences. The thought that he would like to, quickly followed.

As they shuffled files and papers in and out of the drawer, there were occasions when their knuckles brushed against the other's. After the third apology, both dropped the niceties and continued with the task. This type of job was never one of her favorites, but she wouldn't view it that same way again. Her eyes on the files and the drawer gave her ample opportunity to observe Ethan's hands. The palm was broad, his fingers long, with clean, short nails. They were dark, as if he spent time in the sun. Not once did they bend or drop or misplace a file. She wondered if it was indicative of a man who was careful, secure in his purpose. They worked through the remaining drawers, then she gestured toward the one where they had begun, and the few files that were on top.

"The most recent client files will be in that one."

"How do you know?" he asked.

"Because it's the closest one to the stairs. Dad would let them pile up, then make one trip down here with a stack of them. And they'll be in order from the bottom to the top." She paused when Ethan raised a brow in askance. "If you fill the top drawers first, it has a tendency to fall over when you open the drawer with no weight in the bottom. And yes," she said when he smiled and before he could ask, "I know from experience. Organization can be a dangerous job."

He chuckled and shook his head. "Then perhaps he also filed from front to back."

"Not completely. He might start that way, but as the drawer filled, he would shove the files in anywhere."

"Laziness?"

"Convenience," she said, and shrugged.

"What about employee files?"

"The shed."

"Shed?" It hadn't escaped his notice that he was asking a lot of questions, yet not gaining much in the way of answers relevant to the case.

"Dad believed in employee confidentiality. He was the only one who had a key for the shed. Well, and Shaun, but Shaun wouldn't have a reason for going in there."

"And the important documents your father had?"

"His office."

"Why wouldn't he keep them in the safe?" he gestured to the fireproof box behind her.

"Because that's where he would store what he considered valuable. Petty cash and a few guns." She watched as his gaze

100

moved from her to the safe and back again. "Yes. I know the combination. All three of us do."

"I'd like to take a look."

She moved to the front of the safe and spun the dial, stopping at 28 right, 17 left, and 4 right, then lifted the handle and swung the door open. On the top shelf were bills, bound and stacked, with a handwritten note under the pile listing the withdrawals and the dates, and when the amount was replaced. There was a second shelf under the top one that contained two handguns. The large space beneath it held three rifles. He removed the note, then checked the cash. They matched.

She stood with her hand on the top of the safe door, and stared into the bottom portion. Cash wasn't her concern. Her father used it for several things, from paying the farrier to shoe the horses, to getting gas for the snowmobiles that they used in winter for hunting parties. The two handguns on the second shelf were there. One was a German automatic, the other an antique revolver.

He glanced at her when she remained quiet, and saw the confusion on her face. "What is it?"

"There's a rifle missing."

CHAPTER 13

Tim polished up the last photo and sent all of the digital shots from Africa to Scott. Carli had the film canisters and she would want to do the developing. He didn't have any of the material from South America, and wrote that in the e-mail, then sent everything to New York.

He leaned back in the chair and rubbed his tired eyes. Blinking to focus on the table in front of him, he peered into the white cardboard box that Alyssa had brought him for lunch, which was four hours ago. Carli had invited him down to the dining room, but he was on a roll and wanted to get the file to Scott. So, Carli had sent Alyssa with a box lunch, which he had devoured. Four hours ago. He stood and stretched and decided to wander downstairs to see who was around, and how long it was until dinner.

Closing the door behind him, he crossed the hall to Carli's room and knocked. There was no answer so he opened it, poked his head inside the door and called her name. She wasn't there, and with the sun nearly set, the room was in shadows. He flicked the switch on the wall and saw that she hadn't been back since she set her case and backpack on the floor and changed into attire more appropriate for this climate. She and Sam kept a few changes of clothes in their rooms for unexpected visits, or suddenly inclement weather. Leaving the light on, he closed the door and went downstairs.

"Yes. Thank you. Of course. The Humane Society of Wyoming, the 4-H Equine Club of Laramie, Rock River High

School FFA, and the NRA Youth Education Program. I will. Good-bye," Sam hung up the phone, crossed a name off her list, then again grabbed the receiver when she looked up and saw Tim.

"Hey, Sam. I'm sorry about Bear," he said, moving to the opening in the counter of the front desk where Sam was making her calls.

"Thanks. Me, too," she sighed as she replaced the receiver, went to him, and rested her head against his chest in an embrace.

"I'm done working for the day, so if there's anything I can do to help, just ask," he offered, kissing the top of her head before she stepped back.

"I have everything under control for now. The church in Centennial is reserved for Tuesday. Well, pending the release of Dad to the mortuary in Laramie. He wanted to be cremated. I have to ask Shaun to take care of the investigation part of it so they can, you know ..."

Tim nodded and watched as she leaned over the counter to retrieve her list. Carli found solace in working, or on rare occasion, drinking. Sam reached for her lists, her organization, whatever she could control when things became uncontrollable. Shaun isolated himself, withdrawing behind the wall that kept people out. Tim guessed he was the one most affected by Darla leaving. Shaun's adult mind knew he had nothing to do with his parents splitting up, but the child inside took the blame. Tim knew the family long enough, and well enough, that he was friends with each of them and understood, as only an outsider with an objective lens could, what made each of the siblings tick.

"I have thirty or so friends and relatives to call. I've already sent an e-mail to repeat clients, as well as those who have reservations in the next few weeks," Sam told him.

"Do you plan to close the lodge?" He raised his brows and wondered how Bear's spirit would feel about that.

Sam shrugged, a gesture shared by all the siblings. "I don't know what we're going to do. Guess it depends on what Dad has outlined in his will."

"Have you seen Carli?"

"Last I knew, she and Ethan went down to the basement to check the files. I haven't seen them pass the front desk," she answered, glancing from her list to Tim. "You look a little thin. Are you alright?"

"South American cuisine is not as palatable as home cooking."

"Is that Carli's reason as well?"

He chuckled. "She works if off. Hiking miles every day helps her keep her figure."

"Zach is cooking tonight. Cowboy beans, steak, biscuits, and salad. Rabbit food, Zach calls it. And there's chocolate cake for dessert."

"Zach bakes?" Tim's face showed his mind trying to make sense of the young outdoorsman in an apron stirring cake batter.

It was Sam's turn to chuckle, and she realized how little of it she had done the past five days. "No. Alyssa made it before she went home. Zach should be setting everything out in about fifteen minutes."

"I'll see if I can be of assistance," he said, his attention already on the treasures he would find behind the kitchen door as he moved in that direction.

Sam returned to her seat behind the counter and contacted the next person on her list.

«« —»»

"Thanks, Dr. Rolstan," Shaun said to the ME, replaced the receiver, then leaned back in his office chair.

Vince, his only deputy available for duty since Denny was at his sister's wedding in Casper, had gone home a while ago. Esther was rummaging around in the front of the office, he knew, to alert him that she was leaving for the night, and that he should do the same. When he didn't stir from the four walls reserved as his space, she came to the door.

"Shaun. Go home. It's six o'clock on Friday night, that means—"

"You won't be back to make fresh coffee until first light on Monday," he finished for her.

"Exactly. You have a lot going on. Go be with your sisters. Vince is pulling half a shift tomorrow, and is on call for Sunday," she paused and looked at his tired face. "Get some dinner, and non-whiskey-induced sleep. You call me if you need anything," she waited for Shaun's nod, then left the Centennial Sheriff's Office.

He shut down his computer, gathered the files that were on his desk, and stood to take Esther's advice. Glancing at the notepad by the phone, he saw the words in his own his handwriting. *Body to be released to the mortuary.* He swallowed. This is what happens. Those are the steps taken when a loved one dies. He knew them. Had helped families with the process and attended his share of funerals. But it was too soon for Bear Tanner's.

Leaving his office, he plucked his jacket from the coat rack on the way to the reception counter and waiting area. Pausing, he shut off the lights, then locked the door behind him. The sun had set and the streets of Centennial were quiet, except for the diner two blocks down and the bar at the end of 2nd Street. A Friday night meant things might not be as reserved at the Rockin' R Saloon. Perhaps he should drive by and make sure everyone was behaving themselves.

The Rockin' R was a stand-alone building in the middle of nowhere. It sat on the north side of Highway 130 that led to Centennial from I-80 and Laramie. When cowboys and tourists wanted something a little wilder, they would leave Laramie and Cheyenne, and come to the Rockin' R. It was a large wooden building with river rock about four feet up the sides of the structure to give it more support when the wind blew the snow and piled it against anything in its path. It was a place where, if a band was offered a gig, the crowd could make or break the band's career. The bar never ran out of liquor, the kitchen of steaks, or John of pretty girls to carry trays.

He slowed as the lights of the Rockin' R came into view. The parking lot was full with the usual trucks and motorcycles, and the requisite cars with out-of-state license plates. The black Corvette with tinted windows was parked on the side. Sissy was working tonight. He pulled into the parking lot and stopped next to the 'vette. Since he was here, he may as well go in and get something to eat.

«« — »»

Dan and Paul had been quiet throughout dinner. Jerry and Bob had talked of the tracks they had found. There were water holes in the canyon where the snowmelt had collected. In the mud around them they had found more prints than they could name. Some, they argued, that belonged to a good-sized mountain lion. When their descriptions and plans had settled, Bob again inquired about what Dan and Paul had found on Wolf's Ridge.

"No prints worth hunting," Dan said.

Jerry peered across the flames of the campfire. "Something that isn't worth hunting, yet has the two of you not saying a word. What did you find up there?"

"Something—" Paul began.

"Some*one*," Dan corrected.

Paul glared at Dan across the fire. "Whatever it was, died. There was a pool of blood. Not enough for a deer or elk. There were a lot of boot prints and some horse hoof prints."

"Probably why we didn't see much else. Animals tend to stay away from old blood," Dan stated, his gaze on the flames.

"Except scavengers," Jerry said.

"You didn't see any tracks?" Bob asked.

Dan shook his head and remained quiet.

"Who do you think it was? Some client of Tanner's who tripped and his gun went off and shot someone?" Jerry inquired as he poked at the fire.

Paul shrugged. "The only death we've heard about on the radio is—" and he stopped, his eyes moving to Dan's as the news report from the previous evening flashed in his mind.

"Bear Tanner," the two of them spoke simultaneously.

Bob, who had the flask to his lips coughed and choked at the mention of the man whose land they enjoyed. "Son of a bitch. I bet that is where Tanner was shot. If there was as much blood there as you say there was, he probably bled out before help could arrive."

"If you're right, all the more reason to stay at the bottom of the canyon," Jerry said.

Taking another swig of the whiskey, Bob began speculating. "Do you think it was an accident? How horribly ironic if it was. A man who earned his living taking others on hunts, gets accidentally shot on his own property."

Dan remembered the heavily wooded area directly across the canyon from the spot where they had turned around. "Maybe it wasn't an accident. What if someone wanted him out of the way."

"Or revenge," Jerry suggested.

"An unsatisfied client," Paul added.

Dan looked at each of his companions. Had they been doing this too long? They seemed to enjoy creating scenarios that led to the demise of a wealthy and powerful man. Realistically, the suspects would be numerous, but the motives, few. Greed, power, revenge, passion. Dan glanced up at the clear night sky and sighed. It was good that they would be leaving day after tomorrow with whatever they shot. It was time for them to return to their families and jobs, to civilization.

《《—》》

"Thank you, Councilman," Darla responded to Ted Worthington's compliment on her choice of attire for their dinner at the exclusive golf resort.

After pulling out the chair for her, he moved to the other side of the table and took his own seat. Wine was ordered, and since he needed to return home to his wife, eventually, he started in on business.

"What have you learned?" he asked.

"Nothing. The local police are investigating. I'm leaving tomorrow morning to attend the funeral," she stopped when their wine was delivered.

"And the property?" he inquired.

"Will revert back to me, the surviving spouse."

Ted ordered two appetizers, deciding her lack of information didn't warrant a full meal.

"Surely your children will balk at that. May even contest it in court."

"They might try, but my attorney assures me that divorce papers were never filed with the county clerk. It would be a waste of our time and their money." She sipped her wine, contriving a way to ease Ted's concern.

"Since you'll arrive tomorrow, I'll assume the funeral will be within a few days. Any employees can be let go by next week, all future reservations canceled." In keeping with his business-centered, profit-geared mind, he ran through the steps necessary to close down an operation such as Tanner's Outdoor Adventures.

Their appetizers arrived, and as they sampled from each plate, he continued with his thoughts.

"If I contact Wilson Construction in a week, we should be ready for the demolition of the buildings by the middle of April. The damn snow should be melted by then."

"It's that 'damn snow' that allows us to sell twice as many plots. Summer and winter vacation homes," she reminded him, sipping more of her wine. "Don't contact Wilson until I have everything handled in Wyoming." The last thing she needed was a construction crew to arrive before Carli, Samantha, and Shaun returned to their lives, leaving the lodge vacant.

He eyed her a moment as he chewed. Swallowing a mouthful of wine, he nodded. "Alright. But keep me updated on your progress. Every day we postpone the groundbreaking is a day we lose sales. With this being an election year, I'll need that income to fund my campaign."

She smiled. "Why, Ted, darling, who wouldn't vote for you? Your reputation on the city council is exemplary. There is nothing the media could find to turn voters against you. You even have me, a top selling real estate broker in Central California contributing to your campaign and attending your functions. Once the good people of California discover your plans for their future, it will be a landslide." As she sipped from her glass, she thought of the positive influence he would bring to her bank account.

They finished their small meal while discussing gossip and plans regarding the city council and other candidates. He paid the bill, then escorted Darla from the Cup & Club to the parking lot. She had taken the spot next to his Mercedes, on the opposite side of the building from the main parking area, between the lampposts.

With his hand at her back, he steered her to the space between their cars. She rested against the passenger door of Ted's Mercedes and readjusted her wrap around her shoulders. He ran his hands up and down her arms in an attempt to warm her on a cool, moist, California night. It was dark where they were, and he had planned it that way, arriving before Darla at the restaurant, knowing she would park next to his car.

"I think I might miss you, Darla."

"You have your wife," she spoke quietly, and leaned closer to him.

"True, but she's not you. Doesn't have your fire, your drive, your tastes," he said and captured her lips.

She leaned further into Ted, allowing his hands to roam where they wanted, touching and teasing. He broke the kiss to bite her neck.

"What can I do to ease your loneliness, Councilman Worthington?" she asked, clinging to his shoulders, her voice breathless.

"What my wife won't do," he whispered in her ear, then stepped away.

Her answer was in her seductive smile. He opened the car door, closing it after she slid onto the front seat. Rounding the back of the car, he glanced left and right to ensure that no one was in that area of the parking lot, then sat in the driver's seat. She leaned over and kissed him, as her hand unbuckled his belt and slid down his zipper. He rested one arm across the back of the seat, the other on the steering wheel.

"And if you're really good, I'll make sure you have some spending cash for your trip tomorrow."

She purred as she lowered her head to the councilman's lap.

CHAPTER 14

Ethan glanced from Carli to the open safe. He could see three rifles standing barrel up in the dark interior.

"Perhaps Bear had it with him on the hunt," he offered. "Call Shaun. He would know if the rifle was recovered."

Her brows were drawn together in thought. If her father had used it, then Shaun might have it in his sheriff's vehicle. Maybe the forensics people in Cheyenne wanted it to match the gun to the bullet. Perhaps one of the clients had recovered it and given the rifle to one of the employees once they all returned. It would be a simple matter to verify with everyone who was around that day.

"Is there anything else missing?" he asked.

She shook her head, then closed and secured the safe.

"I don't think we need to search back any further than six months in reservations. Employees, a couple of years. Now that we know the state of these files," he said and gestured towards the open drawer, "we should locate the employee files ... in the shed?"

She nodded, then glanced at the darkened sky outside. "There is electricity to the storage unit, but I'm guessing dinner is close to being ready. The one thing that's difficult about visiting villages in the bush is that I miss American cuisine. Today is Friday. That means steak and cowboy beans," she said, and smiled at Ethan.

He returned the expression. "I suppose the treasure hunt can wait until after we've refueled. I'll take this stack with me," he said as he turned to remove the files from the top of the cabinet and close the drawer. He waited as Carli replaced the key beneath the sheet, pressed the lock on each file cabinet, and preceded him up the stairs.

Ethan turned the lights off at the bottom of the staircase, then watched as Carli began the climb. He raised a brow at the sway of her hips, hearing her words, but not registering their meaning. Either he was feeling warm from the closed-in space of the basement, or Carli's physical attributes were beginning to affect him. He didn't feel comfortable with that thought. Wyoming, including Carli, were an assignment, albeit a vacationing job, but he was still on the clock.

She reached the top step and turned to check his progress. Her profile was backlit by the light in the hall. He took a steadying breath as his eyes devoured her figure all at once. Long legs, a rounded hip, flat belly, breasts he knew would fit his palm, and hair as curvy as the rest of her. He couldn't see her eyes, but knew them to be an expressive hazel. Shifting the files to bring himself to what she was saying, he thought he grinned like an idiot as an answer, not hearing her question.

"So, I'll meet you in the dining room?"

"Sure," he agreed, and stepped around her and out into the hall where he took a much needed breath. *Get a grip. It's not like you haven't seen, or slept with, beautiful women before,* he groused silently.

Without looking back, he raised the files in his hand and told her he would put them in his cabin. Once he was outside, he welcomed the slap of cold, late spring air. Scowling all the way to his accommodations, unlocking the door, and tossing the files on the table, he attempted to determine what it was about Carli that had him off balance. Perhaps he wouldn't be so distracted had he taken the flight attendant up on her offer. It had been a couple of months since he entertained a woman. Maybe that was too long. He was here to close a case. There was nothing in the rulebook regarding a relationship between an agent and a ... suspect? Possible victim? Family member of the deceased?

"Shit," he said, dragging his fingers through his hair. Until he knew her involvement, he needed to steer clear. After that? Well, that was after.

«« —»»

Bobby and the Boys were on stage beginning their first set, and it appeared that the patrons of the Rockin' R were starting early and were more rowdy than usual. Shaun stood a moment inside the door, next to the bar, and scanned the crowd for those who might push it a little too far. The bikers had commandeered the pool table, and a few tourists were throwing darts. He recognized some of the regulars who came to have fun and twirl their partner during a two-step.

John yelled at him from behind the bar. "Are you on duty?"

He gave him a half-smile and pointed to the badge on his shirt, which was hidden under his jacket. John nodded, passed him a root beer, and set a glass down on the end of the bar. Shaun took a swallow, wished it was something stronger, then poured the rest into the glass. At John's gesture, he leaned over the wooden counter between the small stack of trays and the container of condiments used for a variety of beverages.

The man had owned the Rockin' R for longer than Shaun had been alive. And through all the years, the clientele rarely changed, and the menu only twice, when John got married and again when he got divorced. The wait staff and kitchen help fluctuated with the seasons and the economy in southeastern Wyoming. Bands rotated through, some splitting up, a few getting invited to Nashville or LA for record deals. Through it all, John had been a friend to the local law enforcement, including the Highway Patrol, as all food and drink were on the house.

Now the proprietor raised a brow, and with a bottle opener in one hand, asked, "The usual?"

Shaun nodded, and before John moved away, he inquired, "Sissy out back or front tonight?"

John rested a forearm on the bar. "Front. And she's been swamped since four. Wish the two of you would decide what you're doing. When you're together, she's happy and works hard. When you're not, we all pay the price," he paused as Kim, a waitress, gave him her drink order. John nodded, then turned back to Shaun. "Are you going to propose tonight?"

He shook his head. "Just looking for a friend."

The older man nodded. "Sure am sorry to hear about Bear."

"Thanks," he said, then gestured that he would take a table between the partitioned area where the pool tables were and the side wall that housed the two electronic dart boards. John would know where to send the food order, and Shaun knew that this was Sissy's section on most weekends.

The bikers at the pool table eyed his uniform. He made sure they were the first to look away. Placing his drink on the table, he sat, then wrapped both hands around the pint glass. He tried not to brood, and was brought out of his dark thoughts first by the scent of her perfume, then by a soft hand on his shoulder. He looked up into chocolate eyes that held sympathy.

Sissy pulled out a chair and sat, her hand sliding from his shoulder to his wrist, where she tugged until he released his glass and interlaced his fingers with hers. Setting her tray on the table and sweeping her long, silky strands over her shoulder, she brought his hand to her lips and kissed his knuckles. Her red lipstick left an impression.

"Shaun, God, I'm so sorry about your Daddy. It must be really hard to conduct this investigation."

He fell into the depths of her eyes, knowing her compassion would be his undoing, and remembering the solace he had always found in her body. Thoughts raced through his mind. He didn't come here for condolences. He came because the pain had become too great. He didn't want her apologies, but needed her.

"Thanks. Carli and Sam came home. They're at the lodge. I'm reviewing reports. The ME's Office called. They're releasing the body to the mortuary."

Goddamn it, he cursed to himself as he looked away from Sissy. Could his conversation be any more inane? He didn't want to tell her any of that. Forget. That is what he wanted, even for just a little while.

"When you get the arrangements made, let us all know. The whole town of Centennial and half of Laramie will show up. John will even close for the day. Well, maybe half a day," she said and offered him a small smile.

She turned at the sound of John's demand, and Shaun guessed it must have been a particular pitch he used with the waitresses, because he never heard the old man's voice. When she turned back towards Shaun, her scowl still marred her pretty face. She picked up her tray and extracted her hand from his.

"I'll bring your dinner out when it's ready," she said and began to turn away.

He reached out and snagged her wrist. "When is your next break?"

"About an hour."

"Meet me by the side door," he said and held her gaze.

She nodded, and he released her wrist. Watching her move off towards the bar, he tamped down the jealousy and protectiveness, knowing that every man in the place eyed her ass in the skintight jeans, her breasts in the low-cut, snug-fitting, black top. She wore them because she could, and because it earned her double the tip money. But he had no claim on Sissy. He loved her, but not in the way a man loves the woman he wants to be his wife. She knew it, and he guessed she hung around, keeping herself available to him in part because she hoped to have him as a husband someday, hoped he would change his mind, and his feelings, towards her.

Every time they broke up, he swore it would be the last. But she knew him, understood him like no other woman had. Of course, they were each other's firsts, both sixteen, in the bed of his truck on a warm summer night by the river. He had substituted a few other women during the times when he and Sissy were apart. But none of them were her.

A short time later, she set a plate in front of him and a fresh glass of root beer. He ate because he was hungry, but he didn't really taste the meal.

Money exchanged hands between a few of the bikers. The tourists abandoned the dart machines for the dance floor, and Bobby, the singer, began taking requests. More patrons thought to release their stress from a long work-week, and the tables filled and people were standing three deep at the bar in a few places. He pushed his plate away, drained his glass, and caught Sissy's attention. She gestured toward the side door, so he relinquished the table to an eager couple.

He pulled on his coat as he made his way to the kitchen door. When Sissy joined him, he pushed it open and followed her through to the busy kitchen. She set her loaded tray on a cart where the dishwashers could clear it, and continued through the area to the outside door. They stepped to the side parking lot, the door not completely closing since there was a brick on the ground to prop it open.

Sissy inhaled and sighed deeply as she tipped her head up and looked for the moon. She didn't grab her coat, and the cool night air felt good to her heated skin.

He stepped up behind her, wrapping his arms around her waist, and bending to the side to kiss her neck. "How have you been, Sissy?"

She turned inside the circle of his arms, placed her hands on the lapel of his coat and searched Shaun's face. "I'm doing alright. Better than you. Honey, you look like hell," she commented, placing her palms on his cheeks.

"Thanks," he snorted.

"I'm serious. I'm worried about you."

"This week hasn't been the best."

She brushed the hair back from his forehead. "Anything I can do?"

He leaned forward and captured her lips in a kiss. She allowed it for a moment, then shifted away.

"Is that why you came by tonight? Hoping for a quickie, Sheriff Tanner?" Her voice took on a note of censure, and she raised a brow with the question.

"I was hoping for a friend."

"I'll be your friend anytime, anywhere. But nothing more than that."

Loosening his hold, he allowed her to step back, his arms falling to his side.

She searched his face and saw the pain and sorrow. Though she ached to give him what he wanted, if she did, she would never hold true to the promise she made herself. As much as she loved Shaun Tanner, she was done playing games. She swore to be his friend, not his lover, until he gave her what she wanted. A ring.

"I need you, Sissy," he told her in a tone that depicted his feelings. They were as real and honest as he was capable of revealing.

She wrapped her arms around her middle to give herself courage, to keep from reaching for him. "I'll talk to you, I'll listen, hold your hand at the service, give you my shoulder to cry on. I'll help with the arrangements, make food for the wake, and use as many days as John will give me to help you through this, Shaun. You need a friend, not to get laid. You know where to find me when you figure out the difference."

She stepped around him and pulled open the kitchen door. The slamming of steel on brick brought Shaun out of his stupor. He glanced over his shoulder, but she was gone.

"Shit," he said, chastising himself as he walked to his vehicle and climbed in.

He stared, not seeing the 'Employees Only' sign mounted on the wall in front of his parking space. Feeling the moisture gather, he rubbed his eyes with the heels of his hands. She was his plan to take the edge off whatever had him wound so tight. If he looked like hell to Sissy, he felt worse for thinking he could use her. The headache that had been with him since morning, the only remnant of his time with the whiskey bottle last night, was increasing in intensity. He had three options remaining.

Deciding the Rockin' R was on their own, he drove home. He paused as he stepped onto the veranda, glanced at the glass of whiskey from four nights ago, then exhaled with a heavy heart and went inside. The liquor cabinet was closer, and easier, but because he didn't want easy, he changed his clothes, put on his sneakers, and went to the small room adjacent to the main living area. Glancing at the acoustic guitar on the stand that occupied one corner of the sparsely furnished room, his thumb traced the callouses on his fingertips. There were too many unacknowledged emotions, too much restless, wild energy for his Takamine. Leaving the lights off so he could look out the picture window at what the moonlight touched, he set the speed for 5.5 mph, the time for thirty minutes, and stepped onto the treadmill. It was programmed to start slow, then increase to the desired speed. He didn't pay attention to the colorful digital readout. Instead, he lost himself in the sound of his shoes on the tread, the rushing of blood in his veins, the feel of sweat as it rolled down his skin. The beep and sudden slowing of the machine forced him to focus on where he was. He turned it off and left the room. There was a bottle on the counter, mostly empty from the night before. Maybe a shot would allow him to get some sleep.

CHAPTER 15

With his libido under control, Ethan joined the others already seated at the table. Tim and Samantha sat on one side, Carli, Zach, and Ray on the other. Ethan took the vacant chair next to Sam, the seat at the head of the table was left empty. Usually, clients joined the employees for meals, but those that occupied cabins decided to try the fare in Centennial. There were place settings, but the meal was served family style, with the platters and bowls down the middle of the table. A coffee carafe, water pitcher, and a bottle of red wine were nearest to Zach.

"What can I offer you to drink?" Zach asked as Ethan settled next to Sam.

"Coffee. It's warm and loaded with caffeine. I have some things left to do tonight."

Ray eyed Ethan. "Why aren't you with Shaun?"

Ethan calmly accepted bowls and plates that were passed to him. "He had to return to the office. I'm staying in Cabin 4."

"Plan on doing any hunting or fishing while you're here?" Ray continued.

Carli answered, "Actually, we're going riding tomorrow."

As if cued in a performance, J.J. entered the dining hall, greeted everyone, then sat next to Ethan.

"Samson and Lady are ready. I'll be here to help you saddle, Carli," he offered.

"Thanks. Zach, is Alyssa scheduled tomorrow at breakfast?" Carli asked.

He nodded. "She should be here at five. Apple crumb coffee cake," he added with a smile.

Ethan wondered if Zach would eat mud pie if Alyssa brought it to him. Ray echoed his thoughts.

"You would eat anything that girl put in front of you."

"Probably. But you have to admit—" and he was cut off by everyone at the table.

"Alyssa can cook," they finished, then laughed.

"We'll need a couple box lunches," Carli continued, gesturing towards Ethan.

"I'll make sure she gets the order," Zach promised.

"Where are you headed? The valley is full of deer. Probably get a cat or bear if you're trying," Ray peered around Zach to address Carli.

Ethan watched Ray as Carli gave a nonchalant answer.

"Wolf's Ridge. It's the best vantage point to see most of the Preserve," she answered, her eyes going to Ethan.

He registered the concern on Ray's face at the mention of the location of Bear's death.

"I'm here to take in the scenery. Do a little office work," Ethan shrugged. "I don't have much interest in killing."

There was a slight shake to Ray's hand as he brought the napkin to his mouth. He recovered quickly, saying, "Well, there's none better for pointing out trees, rocks, and tracks than Carli. You'll see more wildlife in a four-hour ride with her than most would see in a month."

Ethan nodded, then turned his gaze to Carli. "Sounds like I'm in good hands."

She looked up from her plate and saw a hint of the full power of Ethan's intensity. He grinned just enough to deepen his dimples, and his eyes danced with the teasing they had shared earlier. She raised a brow, then lifted her wine glass in a salute.

"I'll show you things you probably didn't know existed."

"I may be a city boy, but that doesn't mean I'm naïve."

"If you were, I wouldn't take you into the bush." She glanced at Zach as he made a strangled cough.

"That's what we call the wilderness. Doesn't matter the terrain. If there are few roads, and more wildlife than humans, it's the bush," Tim filled in, hoping to steer the conversation away from its apparent 'adults only' track. He enjoyed Carli's wit and often off-color topics and banter, but he never had the opportunity to observe someone else giving it back to her.

"Where are you from?" Ray asked.

"Baltimore."

"Then the weather here isn't much of a surprise or discomfort for you."

Ethan shook his head. "I don't mind the snow and cold. Makes one appreciate the heat of summer."

"Storms can be sudden here at times. We get the flow from the Pacific and the North. First of April, and it's not uncommon to get one last storm before spring gives way to summer," Ray said, placing his napkin on the table and pushing back his chair.

"You're leaving before the cake?" Zach looked up from his second helping.

"No. Just thought I would give you a hand with the cleanup," he said, carrying his plate and an empty serving bowl into the kitchen.

J.J. asked for whatever was left on the table. He was a few years older than Zach, but young enough to still put away two full plates at a meal. Ethan handed him the platters and remaining bowls, then watched with mild interest as the stack of empty dishes grew on the other side of J.J., a gifted horseman, according to Carli. Remembering that he was here for an investigation, he began to ask the location of those at the table when Bear was shot.

"J.J., do you ever lead hunts, or are you strictly a barn employee?"

J.J. scooped more beans into his mouth before answering. "No one who was hired by Bear is 'just' anything. We all perform multiple tasks. I'm mainly in charge of the livestock, but I also fill in as a guide for parties, either on foot or horseback. I've taken clients to the river for fishing, watched the front desk when Alyssa or Zach are off doing something else. Even changed the sheets and towels in the cabins once when Alyssa got sick and couldn't come to work."

To Ethan, Bear sounded like a smart businessman. He got the most out of his employees, and no one could complain that 'it wasn't their job'.

He nodded, then asked, "What task occupied your time when Bear was shot?"

J.J.'s eyes darted from Ethan's to Carli's. She sipped her glass of wine, holding his gaze, looking benign.

The cowboy swallowed, then answered, "I was in town. We needed parts for various repairs."

"I was told that one of the clients was able to get a signal on his cell phone and called the lodge. Horses were taken to help Bear off the Ridge. Were you the one who saddled the horses?"

"I'm not sure what business it is of yours—" J.J. said, beginning to feel as if he were answering Shaun's inquiry all over again.

Carli spoke for Ethan. "He's a friend of Shaun's, came when the sheriff called. Ethan has an interest in all sorts of crimes."

"Kind of a mystery buff. I entertain myself by attempting to get pieces to fit in situations, such as this," Ethan explained, following Carli's lead.

J.J. took another bite, then asked, "What do you do for a living, Ethan?"

"I'm a consultant."

"For what?"

"A little of this, some of that," Ethan answered and sipped his coffee.

"Who do you work for?"

"I contract with the government. So, were you back here by the time the call came in?"

J.J. set his fork on his plate. "On the way back from town, I stopped at the north entrance to Wolf's Ridge and Deer Valley. Because of the snow, we close it for winter. I wanted to check on the snowmelt. We've had a problem with poachers in recent years. The gate was locked, but there were tire tracks in the mud. It looked like someone pulled in, found the gate locked, then backed up and went on their way. Alyssa got the call from the panicked client. It was the middle of the day and the lodge was full, so we were all out as guides or doing work somewhere on the Preserve. When she couldn't find anyone on the walkie-talkies, she called me. Knew I would be back anytime, and if I was in town or close enough to the lodge, she would get through. She didn't know what to do, just knew where the party was and that Bear was shot.

"I hightailed it back here, saddled two horses, grabbed the saddlebags with the first aid kit, then took the trail at the back of the barn. It cuts about twenty minutes off the ride to the summit of the Ridge, where the clients said they were. On my way out, I told her to call Shaun. She already had, but Shaun was up Interstate-80 north of Laramie, helping the Highway Patrol with an overturned semi-truck. He left that scene, and arrived here an hour before I returned with Bear." J.J.'s face had paled slightly as he retold the events of that afternoon.

"What did you find when you got there?"

Everyone had remained silent. They hadn't heard the details of the rescue attempt. Ethan heard the *swoosh* of the kitchen door just before he asked the question. Though he didn't look, he knew Ray had returned.

"Two of the clients had taken their shirts and pressed them to Bear's chest," his voice had quieted, his gaze looking into the past. "They were soaked with blood. Samson snorted and balked. He'll pack out game, but he's never been asked to carry a ... wounded human. He loved Bear, and I'm sure he was confused when Bear was laying on the ground, not standing, a treat in his outstretched hand," pausing, J.J. swallowed, then blinked, and refocused on Carli's face. When he continued it was with great apology.

"I had to tie Samson, but left Stevie where I dismounted. I took the kit to Bear. He was unconscious. There was ... a lot of ... I took all the gauze pads in the kit and pressed them to his chest, taped them down. It took a few minutes to calm Samson enough to get him close to Bear. The clients helped me lift him onto Samson's back. I propped him up on the cantle and used the ties on the saddle to keep him as centered as I could. Using the trail takes a little longer, but I could ride next to Samson, my fist in Bear's shirt, helping to keep him astride. When we got back, Shaun was here, and he had called an ambulance."

There was a strangled sound, like that of a wounded animal, coming from the end of the table. Ethan looked towards Carli, who shot out of her seat, squeezed between Ray and the table, and left the dining room. A moment later, the front door of the lodge slammed closed. Looking around the table, everyone registered the shock of hearing J.J.'s story, except Ray. His head was down, his hands thrust into the front pockets of his jeans. Samantha wiped tears from her cheeks and stood.

"That's alright, Tim. I'll get her," she offered as Tim rose at the same time.

Tim sat as Sam left, and turned his gaze to J.J. "You could have eliminated some of the details."

J.J. looked from Tim to Ray to Ethan. "I did. If I was too vague, she would have demanded to know more."

"Probably. But smaller pieces would make it easier to swallow," Tim said, standing and taking a few of the remaining empty dishes into the kitchen.

Ethan hadn't moved, as his attention continued to rest on Ray.

Without raising his eyes, Ray mumbled, "Lost my appetite for cake," and started to leave the hall.

"Ray, were you guiding a party when all this was going on?" Ethan asked, stalling the older man's departure.

Ray glanced from Zach, who had turned around to look over his shoulder at Bear's best friend, then shifted his gaze to Ethan.

"No. I was checking the fence line on the south side of the property. A few ranchers run cattle in the national forest on that side. Makes an easy meal if you're a cat or a bear."

"I don't suppose there were two of you checking the fence line," Ethan hinted at an alibi.

"Haven't needed any help since I was a kid. Doesn't take two sets of eyes to find a downed fence. Excuse me," he said, and left the dining room.

Zach gathered the rest of the plates and silverware, and answered Ethan before he could ask. "I was in town, in Centennial, then went into Laramie."

"Getting supplies?" Ethan queried.

Zach glanced from his stack of dishes to Ethan, and considered sharing with this near stranger, friend of Shaun's or not, what he had spent his day off doing. Ethan didn't change his expression, or his posture. He just waited for Zach to make up his mind to be honest, or not.

"I was searching jewelry stores for a ring for Alyssa," he said and raised his chin in challenge.

"About damn time," J.J. commented.

Zach looked at him and scowled.

"Everyone can tell you're in love with her. Actually, there's a pool going, Donna's got the details and the cash, on when you would get around to giving Alyssa a promise ring."

Zach shifted from one foot to another. "Well, shit," he said, then turned and joined Tim in the kitchen.

J.J. looked at Ethan. "We know how to clear a room." He stood and left the lodge.

A minute later, Ethan heard the clinking of dishes and the rush of water from behind the kitchen door. He leaned back in his chair and considered what he had discovered. The details J.J. shared would be replayed tomorrow, by both Carli and himself, when they arrived at the Ridge. He decided that two men, both with no solid alibis, had just moved themselves to the top of his suspect list. It was then he remembered the missing rifle. He would have to ask J.J. tomorrow if Bear had a firearm when he arrived to rescue his employer, and if so, what happened to it.

CHAPTER 16

Sharp. That best described the air that morning. The weatherman spoke of one final arctic blast moving down from Canada. Temperatures would dip about ten degrees below where they had been, but at this time, no precipitation was expected. The sun peeked above the horizon, but in the shadow of Wolf's Ridge, the sky only lightened. They wouldn't see the sun until it cleared the craggy rocks at the summit. If they were fortunate, they would have the opportunity to make two treks into the canyon today. One in the morning, hopefully tagging something that would make it worth their while to return to camp before heading out for an afternoon foray.

Lady Luck was riding on their shoulder, as Bob, Paul, Jerry, and Dan set out along the canyon floor. Breath puffed out in white clouds, the sunshine, filtered through leaves and pine needles, began to spot the ground. Dan was in the lead, Jerry at drag, Bob and Paul, both nursing a hangover, were plodding along in the middle. Dan paused to check the trail. Fresh elk droppings. Bringing his hands to his mouth, he let out a bellow that resembled that of a female elk, a cow. A moment later, the bull that left the droppings answered.

As one, all four poachers readied their rifles. Dan moved off the trail, Jerry beside him. Paul and Bob took the opposite direction, each stepping a few feet away from the others. They used their eyes and ears to locate the bull elk. About thirty yards to the southwest, he raised his head and sniffed the air. Dan made another call, then signaled he had the clearest shot.

Sighting the animal, the stock of the rifle against his right shoulder, his right forefinger moved from the trigger guard to the trigger. The elk stepped twice more, then the explosion from the rifle spooked him. He only bounded two steps before falling to his side. Dan and the others stepped cautiously through the brush to check the location of the shot. The wound was on the left side, just behind the foreleg. Bob checked the head and rack, and noted that the eyes were open, the tongue resting on the ground as the jaw relaxed in death.

"Damn clean shot," commented Jerry.

"We're not far from camp. No reason we should ruin the hide by cutting it up. The four of us should be able to wrestle it back whole. Probably young since the rack isn't as developed, and he's smaller than the one Jerry got last year. Makes him lighter," Dan said as he gestured toward the elk, then back behind him.

For part of the way, the body of the animal slid on the bed of pine needles beneath the trees. They were on a slight slope, so it was easier to get some momentum going with the four of them pulling at the same time. A hundred yards from their camp, they paused, breathing hard with the exertion.

"Jerry, get the tarp. We can drag him the remainder of the way on that," Dan suggested.

They rested while Jerry retrieved what they needed. It was a short time later that they arrived back at camp and hoisted the elk into a tree. Allowing the blood to drain out helped preserve and cure the meat. After a brief meal, the four of them again took the trail that would lead them along the bottom of the canyon, ever watchful for the opportunity to bring back another trophy.

«‹‹—››»

Ethan had spent most of the night reading the stack of files he had taken from the basement, both before and after dinner. Carli had returned to the lodge, and the dining room, and informed him that they would search the storage area next for the employee files. However, she had work to do, would see him in the

130

morning, then took herself upstairs. Sam, who had been standing behind her sister, let him back into the basement and waited patiently at the top of the steps while he removed more files to review.

At 11:53 p.m., he closed the final file, drained his bottle of water, and grabbed his pad and pencil. It wasn't until 2:47 a.m. that he cracked the bathroom door, stripped out of his clothes, and crawled between the sheets. Lying on his back, one arm behind his head, staring up at the ceiling and willing his eyes to close, he observed his sketches as they flashed through his thoughts. The expressions on faces when certain questions were asked, and when Carli didn't save J.J. or Ray. There wasn't one of them that didn't express appropriate emotions at the description of what J.J. had found. He understood Carli's departure, and Sam's rescue. Though he had already eliminated Zach as a suspect, he would verify the younger man's alibi as insurance. J.J. and Ray, however, hadn't lost their place in the line of suspects, though J.J. would probably be dropped soon. There was nothing unusual in the client files, and his gut was telling him he wouldn't find any answers there. Rolling onto his side, he attempted to let go of the scene they would ride to the next day.

The beep of his watch alarm had him prying open his eyes. Glancing at the time, he groaned and rolled over, placed his feet on the floor, and moved to the bathroom and a shower. Dressed in layers, his pad, pencil, binoculars, and cell phone in a small pack, he grabbed his coat and made his way to the lodge.

A cold front from the north was settling over the area, but at least the sun had cleared the horizon to the east and was beginning to warm the air above thirty-five degrees. The crunching of his boots on the remaining snow was reminiscent of Baltimore. Looking at the trees and blue sky, he was reminded he wasn't in the city. The air here was clearer, cleaner. He could smell the trees, the cold. And wood smoke. At this early morning hour, a cardinal darted from one branch to another, and as he watched for a moment, a squirrel scrambled up the side of a nearby tree. He supposed he could see the same thing if he walked in a park.

The sheriff's vehicle was parked in front of the steps of the lodge. According to J.J., Shaun had an alibi. That, too, would be verified. There were a few clients joining them in the dining room to fill their plates, before taking a chair at one of the small tables in the lobby to enjoy the fire or read a newspaper. Alyssa was in and out of the kitchen. Shaun, Sam, Tim, and Carli were at the table. He greeted Zach at the front desk, where he was introduced to Donna.

A hardy woman in her mid-forties, the texture of the skin on her face was proof of her time outdoors. She was the scheduled guide with six hikers to Miner's Paradise, the name of the peak on the opposite side of Pine Canyon from Bear's location. Yes, she had heard the report of the rifle and had planned to ream the guide who led a hunting party to the same section of the Preserve as her hikers.

"By the time we returned to the lodge, the ambulance had just left. We did a head count, radioed everyone who was out, and once all were accounted for, were more wrapped up in losing Bear than figuring out whether it was an accident or not," Donna told him.

Ethan thanked her for her information, nodded to Zach, then wandered to the dining room.

Carli had two box lunches on the table next to her. She looked up from her plate, eyed him from head to foot, then nodded at his pack. "What do you have in there?"

"A few essentials."

"Got room for the lunches?"

"Sure," he said, unzipping the pack and setting the boxes inside.

Alyssa came through the door, a plate piled high with muffins. As if on cue, Zach appeared in the doorway, snatched one off the top, grinned at Alyssa, then disappeared back into the lobby.

Ethan took the chair next to Carli, then looked up at Shaun. "I have a question for you," he paused as Shaun took a bite of his omelet. "When J.J. arrived here with Bear and the horses, did he also have Bear's rifle?"

Shaun's gaze shifted to Carli, then back to Ethan.

"There's one missing from the safe," she told him.

Shaun shook his head. "There was no firearm on Dad when we loaded him into the ambulance. If J.J. had located one, he would have handed it over to me."

"I read the reports from the three clients who were with Bear that morning. There was no mention of one of them bringing a rifle back down," Ethan held Shaun's gaze. "In all the excitement, could it have been left there?"

"We'll look around today," Carli volunteered, realizing the tension stretching between the two men.

"If it was left, Vince would have found it," Shaun said, pushing away from the table. "Be safe. Anything unusual, stick to the trees and get back here. I'll call later," he told Carli as he stood and left the dining room.

She swiveled to look at Ethan. "What was that about?"

Ethan glanced at her, then began to enjoy one of Alyssa's muffins. "A reminder of how difficult it is to investigate the death of a family member. We tend to forget the details." When she narrowed her gaze at him, he explained, "Shaun knows that Bear usually carries his own rifle. He didn't list the whereabouts of the weapon because he forgot."

"I'm sure he was distraught at seeing—"

"Exactly. Anyone else, and he would have verified if a weapon was taken and its current location. He'll check with the clients, and we'll know more later."

Carli leaned back in her chair and crossed her arms under her chest. "If the clients say Dad had a gun, they would also tell who they gave it to when they returned to the lodge. If it was the one from the safe ..."

"Who knows the combination to the safe in the basement, besides the three of you, and where the keys are hidden for the files?" he asked her, following her thoughts.

"Probably every employee."

"Shaun? Sam?"

"They each have their own copy. As do Ray, Zach, and J.J."

"Not Donna or Alyssa?"

"They would use the copy in the drawer, or ask one of the others to retrieve whatever they needed. Dad didn't think of any of them as employees. They're all family. He wouldn't have hired them if he had to be concerned about them stealing from him."

Ethan chewed thoughtfully, then popped the last bite of muffin into his mouth. Carli watched his jaw, then his lips as he licked the crumbs from his fingers. It took her a moment to realize he was talking and for her to concentrate on his words.

"... any one of them would have returned the rifle if the client had given it to them. Bystanders generally don't keep souvenirs. There would be no reason for an employee to keep the gun, unless ..." his voice faded.

Carli refocused on his eyes, and blushed slightly. She had been caught staring, and moved to stand up when his last word sunk in. *Unless.*

She reached for her coffee cup instead and, attempting to recover, asked, "'Unless', what?"

He watched her sip the hot liquid, observed her fingers around the mug, not the handle, and the green of her eyes as curiosity was sparked.

"One of them used it to kill your father."

She hesitated in the process of lowering her cup to the table. "Never happen. Like I said, they're family."

"And family have been known to eat their own."

"We can solve this simply by asking—"

"And hope for a confession?" Ethan chuckled and shook his head. "We wait to hear from Shaun. And I continue the investigation, which means I get to ask the questions."

"Because I'm still a suspect?"

"Because it's my job."

Carli held his gaze and recognized the seriousness of his request. He was trained in investigations, she was not. And if she said the wrong thing to the right person, they would never discover why her father was shot. She nodded her agreement, then rose from the table. Sam and Tim, who had remained silent throughout the breakfast discussion, gathered their plates and followed Carli to the kitchen door. Pushing it open, she stepped aside as her sister and colleague moved past with dishes stacked in their hands. She told Alyssa they were leaving, but would be back before dinner.

When she turned around, Ethan was waiting for her, his pack over one shoulder. Yes, they would return before dinner, lest she place him on the menu. As she preceded Ethan into the lobby, she chastised herself, then Tim for his unmistakable influence. He flirted continuously and would spend time with his on-again, off-again partner in New York when they got home from a trip. It had obviously been too long since one of her short-term relationships had expired. Men were always eager for her company, but not committed when she was gone for months at a time. She didn't blame them, as she would have done the same. Since she couldn't remember when she had met Nathan, the last man she had spent the night with, except that it had to be at least six months and several thousand miles ago, it was the only plausible explanation for her reaction to Ethan. Busy with her thoughts, she was halfway out the door of the lodge when she noticed Ethan was looking at the map of the Preserve and the surrounding forest.

Placing her finger on the spot that marked the trailhead, she began her commentary of the area. "We'll take this trail up to Wolf's Ridge. According to J.J.'s story, the party was here when … it happened. The elevation climb is about two-thousand feet. We're at the head of the valley, which is close to sixty-five hundred. The valley narrows to this canyon. Most of the flora is pine, with some aspen up here. The ridge itself is exposed, just above the tree-line, mostly because it's an outcropping of solid rock, not due to elevation."

Ethan pointed to the opposite side of the canyon. "What is this called?"

"Miner's Paradise. Densely packed with vegetation. There are a few hiking trails that were cut through the brush, but it's too steep in many places to scout deer and elk. A lot of the mines are still open and tend to be more hazardous for the two-legged variety that wander to that side."

"I want to see it," he said, turning his face in her direction.

Carli looked from the map to Ethan, expecting his profile, but instead found the full force of his dark eyes. She nervously wet her lips with her tongue, and watched as his gaze dropped. It pulled at her, and she leaned a fraction of an inch closer. Her movement had his gaze once more locked with hers. Recognizing all she had observed the first time she saw him, the intelligence, mischief, and something else that made her voice deeper and more quiet than she intended.

"The valley is too wide to cross from one side to the other in the time we have—"

"Tomorrow," he interrupted.

"Storage shed."

"Day after."

The distance between their bodies continued to close and she didn't know if she was the only one moving. "Funeral preparations. Funeral. Wednesday. We'll do it—"

The phone was picked up on the first ring and a curious Zach announced himself to the caller. Carli closed her eyes briefly, and when she opened them, recognized the humor and half-smile that set off Ethan's dimples. She cleared her throat and leaned back. Glancing at Zach sitting behind the counter, she stepped out the partially opened front door, Ethan behind her.

"So, how long has it been since the last time you rode?" Carli asked as she walked next to the FBI agent and struggled to rein in her hormones.

"Too long," he answered, wondering what would have happened if the phone hadn't rung and Zach's voice hadn't reminded them that they weren't alone.

"You don't remember?"

Ethan chuckled. "I remember every ride. She had dark brown hair and large brown eyes. Kitty was powerful with a mind of her own."

Carli glanced at him and was about to comment on his sharing, when Ethan clarified his description.

"She was the most beautiful Quarter Horse, and all mine for the day ride in Lexington, Virginia."

Carli smiled, then laughed. He turned to look at her, struck by the genuine mirth and moment of carefree emotion. She tucked her hair behind her ear, and he became fascinated with every detail. White teeth, pink lips covered in lip balm, smooth skin, shiny hair, and ears and fingers devoid of jewelry. He thought about the necklace she wore last night and wondered if she ever removed it. It was a flash in his mind, then he forced it away. He didn't need to dwell on what Carli would look like with nothing on, except the necklace. Caught up in her throaty chuckle, he smiled.

Lady and Samson were tied to the hitching rail outside the barn. A moment later, J.J. appeared, then tossed saddlebags behind the cantle of the saddle on Lady.

"Samson is no Quarter Horse, but he's a calm boy. Usually," she informed him as they stood on Samson's right side.

Ethan stroked the horse's neck, then raised a brow in her direction. "Usually?"

"He doesn't care for snakes," J.J. answered. "Can't blame him. I don't like them either." Finished with the saddlebags, he took the bridle from around the saddle horn, slipped it on over Lady's halter, and eased the bit between her teeth. "Still have a while yet before they come out of hibernation. The bears, however, will be waking up and probably quite grumpy. There aren't many on the Preserve, so I doubt Samson will have reason to give in to his fear."

J.J. handed Lady's reins to Carli, and put on Samson's bridle. Backing the large horse away from the hitching rail, J.J. eyed Ethan's height and adjusted the stirrups. He glanced at Carli as she swung her leg over Lady's back and settled into the saddle.

"Seems you remember what you're doing," J.J. commented.

She leaned back to stroke Lady's hip. "Like riding a bicycle," Carli responded, then patted the stock of the rifle in the scabbard. "Thanks."

J.J. held her gaze and nodded. "Be careful. Kit is in the bags with some water. Got your lunch?"

"In here," Ethan answered, settling the pack on his back. Remembering their conversation at breakfast, he asked J.J., "When you arrived at the Ridge, did Bear have a rifle?"

The cowboy swallowed, glanced from Ethan to Carli, then back. He shook his head. "Bear usually carried his own weapon when he guided parties out on the Preserve. Protection and to complete the picture of a big game hunter, giving the clients all that they paid for. On occasion, depending on what was being tracked or the nature of the clients, he would only head out with a sidearm. Didn't have one of those, either," he volunteered before Shaun's 'friend' could ask.

Ethan nodded, realizing they would have to wait to hear from the sheriff.

J.J. and Carli watched as Ethan placed the reins over Samson's head, his foot in the stirrup, then sat in the saddle as if he had done it every day of his life. J.J. stepped close, and cupping one hand to his mouth, whispered a secret to be kept from Ethan's steed.

"There's a few carrots in the saddlebags as well. A reward for a good climb."

Ethan nodded. J.J. walked into the darkened interior of the barn, and Carli started toward the trail. Within minutes, they were swallowed from view by the trees and foliage that grew in the valley. Eyes in the shadows watched their progress, then returned to the task at hand.

CHAPTER 17

Shaun let himself into the sheriff's office, turned on the lights, then sighed. Shucking his coat as he walked behind the counter usually manned by Esther, he tossed it on one of the vacant chairs in his private office. Sitting heavily behind his desk, he turned on his computer, then rubbed his forehead. Sex wouldn't have given him a headache, and he would probably feel worse if he had finished the bottle.

He pulled up the information of the clients that were with his father on the Ridge and reached for the phone. Pausing, he shook his head. He knew better. Knew that Bear Tanner rarely led a party without a gun, for protection and the look of a wilderness guide. The FBI agent was right to question the location of the weapon, and it irked him that he had overlooked that detail.

Within thirty minutes, it was confirmed that Bear did have a rifle, and that it was given to Ray, the employee they had first seen upon their return. Where was the rifle, and why hadn't Ray mentioned that he had it?

《《——》》

Darla smiled at the agent that was collecting boarding passes. Readjusting the strap of her designer carryon, she walked down the jet way, onto the plane, then settled into her first class seat from LAX to Denver. Accepting a pre-flight beverage from the flight attendant, she sipped and began to wonder how her homecoming would be received.

It wasn't with open arms that she would expect her offspring to welcome her, but with barely disguised, if she was lucky, distaste. She would do them the favor of staying at a hotel in Laramie, having her own car, and allowing them to continue with the funeral arrangements. After all, she had no interest in burying her husband, only in what he had left behind.

Sinking slightly into the seat as the plane left the tarmac, she made plans. The funeral on Tuesday, the reading of the will on Wednesday or Thursday, the canceling of reservations and letting go of staff by the end of the week. As long as she kept to their time schedule, she would have all the cash she would need to purchase the house in Carmel, and begin to move in higher social circles than Councilman Worthington. She sipped again at her drink, excitement building for the money, and the prestige, this endeavor would bring.

«« —»»

Sam hung up the phone, crossed an item off her list, then rubbed her temples. All friends and relatives had been contacted. Accounts were set up to receive donations, the mortuary had the papers signed to cremate the body, and the florist knew which arrangements to deliver to the church. She was waiting to hear from the funeral director on a drawer in the mausoleum wall that would be embossed with her father's name, though his ashes would be scattered on the Preserve.

Glancing at her list to see what else she needed to complete before she stopped for lunch, and she hoped, a nap. She was accustomed to the physical labor of the ranch, but her near sleepless nights since Shaun had called were beginning to catch up with her. Since cell reception was spotty, she was using the landline in the lodge, and raised a brow when her cell phone sang and danced on the table in front of her. Picking it up, she wasn't surprised to see Matt's number.

"Hi, Matt. Everything alright?"

"It's Branson."

She sat a little straighter in her chair. Cole had been away for years. His family owned the ranch to the west of Crystal Springs, the spread she ran for her father. Cole had left right after graduation to attend an Ivy League school on the East Coast in order to pursue his degree in law. He came home for visits on holidays and sometimes during the summer months, when there was a break between semesters, to help take the cattle out to the north pasture, or bring them back in for market. They had seen each other a few times during their college years, but his time on the ranch had been less since he had landed the position at a nationally known firm in Chicago. In high school, they were ... close, and it had been a while since she had bumped into him in town at the feed store or the diner. Maybe that was why he was in Colorado now. A visit.

"What's going on?" she asked, attempting to be as nonchalant as she could, despite the increased speed of her heart's rhythm.

"He called with an estimate of what it would cost to repair the fence and the loss of part of his summer pasture. I told him where you were, and why. He offered his condolences and requested that you contact him when you return to Crystal Springs." Matt set the pad of paper on the desk in the office. He had written the words verbatim, knowing Sam would want to know exactly why Cole had contacted the Springs looking for her.

Condolences. Yes, she would assume he would offer the words. He was certainly more mature, had practiced the fine art of social etiquette at his mother's side, and she was sure the fancy university and expensive firm polished his good manners. She sighed, trying not to hold him accountable for what had happened. He was barely eighteen, had been accepted at the college of his choice, and had his life in front of him. After the ... situation with Carl Rutgers, Cole just left. It was all her own family could do to keep her together. What she needed at that time was Cole, and he didn't know how to help her.

"Sam, are you there?" Matt expected a few choice words, a suggestion of what to tell Cole Branson, but not the silence. Sam was always active, talking and taking care of what needed to be done, or directing others to do it.

"Yes. Sorry. Verify that our cattle have been brought back to the east side of the fence. There's a thousand dollar credit at Walt's. He should be able to purchase some wire and posts. Pick a day that you have free and offer to help. Express my gratitude for the condolences, and the repair." She would have liked to ask why he was home, but that would mean showing interest, something she had abandoned years ago, despite the fact that her heart and secret thoughts held a different dream.

"Sure. I'll get the message to him. Uh … Sam? Are you curious as to why Cole is in Colorado?" Matt asked.

He didn't know the full story, only what Uncle Joe, the ranch hand that had been with Crystal Springs the longest, had told him, which wasn't much. Apparently Samantha Tanner and Cole Branson were an item way back when, but the old man refused to give any details on the break up. Uncle Joe valued privacy, so he rarely offered information on anyone. Which, to Matt's innate curiosity, was annoying, since Uncle Joe knew so much about so many people.

"Alright. Why is Cole home?" She rolled her eyes and pretended to bite her tongue. Will she always fight with her common sense when it came to Cole?

"His mother took a tumble off the veranda steps. She spent the night in the hospital and is back at the ranch now, but can't do all that she's used to doing."

"Was she badly hurt?" Sam eyed the florist's number.

"A couple of cracked ribs, broken wrist, some bruises—"

"That's more than a fall, Matt."

"Well, that's her story, and she's not straying from it."

A thought had a scowl marring her face. "Matt, make a point of checking the fence before you and Cole do the repair. See if it was pushed, or cut."

It was Matt's turn to be quiet. If the fence was cut, that meant they had trouble.

"I'll see what I can find."

142

"Be careful. Cattle don't carry wire cutters."

"Got it, Boss."

Sam shivered. Cole was home. Alice Branson was hurt. A fence line was down. As she dialed the number for the florist to send a bouquet to the JAR-C Ranch, she decided she would be returning to Crystal Springs sooner than what she had planned.

«« — »»

The identification and names of the plants rolled off Carli's tongue. As they turned the corner on one switchback, they paused as she pointed back the way they had come, where the lodge could be seen. Part of the drive leading from the highway to the lodge, one section of the parking lot, and some of the fencing for the corrals attached to the barn could also be viewed.

Ethan was amazed at the distance they had covered, and the beauty of the valley and hills. On the higher peaks in the distance, the snow was still thick. The area of the Preserve, lower in elevation than the distant Rockies, was more green than white. He settled forward in the saddle and nudged Samson to follow Lady up the trail.

Carli was comfortable with her monologue in which she described the history of the area, including the founding of the Preserve, where Bear Tanner procured his animals, his philosophy, and a few statistics on the business. She felt as if she were reciting her life story, which she supposed was the influence her father and this country had on a young girl. No matter how far she traveled, this Preserve, and Wyoming, would always be home.

"How old were you when you started coming up here alone?" Ethan asked.

"Eleven. It was my birthday, and I wanted to ride through the trees. I had started taking forays into the forest soon after Darla left. Dad was busy with clients, and I usually stuck Sam with watching Shaun, who were usually looked after by whichever employee was anchored to the front desk that day. I rode out on

143

Maggy, and saw the most amazing thing I had ever witnessed in all my eleven years."

She stopped and waited for Ethan to bring Samson alongside Lady. She pointed through a row of trees to a small clearing that now was home to a few dozen saplings. The grass was about ankle high, and a couple of varieties of wildflowers had begun to sprout and send out buds. Now that she wasn't talking loudly over her shoulder to be heard, she quieted her voice and continued with the story.

"It was in the morning, maybe about this time, when I saw the movement. I pulled Maggy to a halt and squinted through the branches. A deer had just given birth, and the fawn was trying to stand. It had taken a few tries, and at least one nosedive, but the spindly legs held its weight. The doe didn't seem to know what to think. She traded her time between cleaning her baby and getting a well-deserved meal." Carli's eyes were still focused on where she had seen the doe and fawn.

Ethan's gaze shifted from the grass that she indicated, to her face. There was a softness to her features and what he could only describe as a wistfulness, either for the young deer or her own tender years, he wasn't sure. The moment was interrupted by the report of a rifle. He saw the recognition on Carli's face, then snaked his left hand under his jacket and withdrew his weapon, clicking off the safety.

"I thought the schedules ensured that two parties weren't in the same area," he directed to Carli.

"That's true. Except that was in the canyon, and everyone knows we're riding to Wolf's Ridge. Parties take advantage of whatever presents itself in front of a bullet."

She turned forward and nudged Lady to continue up the trail. After several feet she glanced back at Ethan and saw that he had replaced his gun in the holster that was at his waist, one that she hadn't noticed before breakfast. Maybe he put it on after they left the barn.

"Sound travels differently here," he explained. At home, he would know which direction and how far away the shot was fired.

She nodded, then said over her shoulder, "You're from the big city of Baltimore. Concrete, steel, and asphalt ricochet sound. Here, where there's a lot of space and natural things that absorb, rather than reflect, sounds travel further. We'll take a different trail on the way back, and I'll show you where the shot was fired from."

His respect for Carli and her knowledge was noted in his thoughts, followed by excitement for adding another point in the 'pro' column for instigating a more personal, if brief, relationship with her after the case was closed.

She had unbuckled the flap on the saddlebag and rummaged to the bottom, her fingers locating the slick fabric of the reflective vests. Pulling them out, she halted Lady and tossed one to Ethan.

"We'll let the horses breath out here. We've climbed the steepest part. There's a couple more switchbacks to reach the top of the Ridge. The trail runs the length of the canyon. We won't ride the whole of it today." She put her arms through the vest and used the hook and loop fasteners to attach it around her.

Ethan raised a brow in her direction. "Fluorescent orange isn't my color."

"I'm sure blood isn't either. Wear the vest."

"Are you concerned about who fired the shot back there?" he asked, donning the orange garment.

"Shots fired are always cause for concern in my opinion." She watched him attach the straps, as she leaned forward, her forearms resting on the saddle horn.

"On that we agree. So, why the vest?"

"A horse looks a lot like an elk through the trees. Not all hunters make a positive ID before they pull the trigger."

He glanced down at Samson and patted the horse's neck. "The guides don't verify the animal?"

"Usually. And even though clients are briefed on the rules, not all follow them. Ready?" She waited for Ethan's nod, then turned to continue up the trail.

She commented on the surrounding foliage, then reported their altitude. He asked about her childhood, her relationship with Sam and Shaun, and her father. Admittedly, the information served two purposes. Not only was he creating a more concise picture of Carli and the Tanner family dynamics, but he also began to consider eliminating them from his list of suspects.

As she related tales of growing up in Wyoming, she thought that a summary of them could be shared at the service on Tuesday. Sam suggested that each of them rehearse a part of the eulogy. She wondered if she would be able to get through her portion without tears.

The trail flattened, trees thinned, and more snow remained piled in the areas that were kept in the shade. It had warmed up with the sun fully over the edge of the Ridge and shining down on the canyon which widened into the valley.

Mesmerized by the sway of Carli's torso, he heard her words and was attentive to what she was saying. Glancing to his right, he could understand her explanation that this was the best vantage point from which to view the Preserve. He lifted the reins and pulled gently until the horse stopped. It seemed as if Samson, too, was interested in the scene, as he lifted his head and pricked his ears, looking in the same direction as his rider.

Pausing when she realized she heard only one set of hoof beats, she turned and looked over her shoulder. Ethan and Samson admired the vista, and she noticed how comfortable he sat in the saddle. She was reminded of the man's height by the length of his legs as they rested astride the steed that was half draft horse. The breeze ruffled his dark hair, and without sunglasses, his slight squint deepened the lines at the corners of his eyes. When he glanced at her, he smiled, and the dimples and lines became endearing.

"You're right. This is an amazing view," he said, and turned back to look down at the valley.

You have no idea, Carli thought. Sighing, she dismounted, removed Lady's bridle, looped it over the saddle horn, unclipped the lead line from the halter that was worn under the leather bridle, then allowed the mare to graze on the leveled area.

"We're stopping here. This is about where ... it happened." She glanced a little further up the trail, then behind her toward the rock outcropping. "Ethan—" she began, then stopped.

It was the tone of her voice that pulled his gaze from the sight of the valley. Turning his attention in her direction, he urged Samson to her side, then dismounted and handed the reins to Carli.

Seeing that Lady was getting some lunch and he wasn't, Samson pulled on the reins, wanting to join his barn mate. She quickly slipped off his bridle, but didn't bother with unsnapping the lead line. Instead, she untied it from the front lacings of the saddle and let the horse trail the six-feet of cotton rope after him. He would stay close to Lady, and she was easy to catch. After placing the bridle around the saddle horn, she stepped next to Ethan.

He was crouched down, examining what had caught Carli's attention. There was an area of ground, ten-feet by ten-feet, that was trampled and darkened. He reached out and touched the soil, then looked at his fingers. Mud only from the morning dew. It had been a few days since Bear Tanner had bled out on this spot. Blood and other fluids had seeped deeper into the earth. There were a few scratches, dig marks in the ground where a wolf, or a scavenger, was drawn to the area because of the scent, and had searched for what had been there.

Carli was quiet. She stood, then began to circumnavigate the churned up soil. It hadn't rained or snowed since her father had been here, so she could read the tracks on the ground, and the story they told.

"Here," she said, and pointed to very large hoof prints, "is where J.J. was able to bring Samson. These smaller prints belong to Stevie, the horse he was riding. There are boot prints, probably J.J.'s. These with the tread would belong to the clients. This set travels here, to the boulders," and she moved in that direction, "to get better cell reception, above the tree tops, in direct line with the tower at the highway a mile from the lodge."

He followed her storyline, walking part of the way with her to the pile of rocks. Turning around, he could see the edge of the clearing where he knew the lodge would be, under the branches of trees. He watched as Carli moved back to the trampled earth, placed her hands on her hips and tipped her head to the side. Stepping around her to stand a few feet away, he looked at the myriad tracks knowing he didn't have the experience to pick them apart. Bear Tanner had taught her well.

"What else do you see?"

"Can you decipher the different prints?" she asked instead.

"Some. Wilderness tracking and survival were extra courses at Quantico. I can read a group of gang members, know by the foot traffic if something has gone down, profile a serial criminal, but distinguishing one print from all the others in this churned-up mess ... I'm at a loss."

She glanced at him, acknowledged his honesty, marveled at how different their lives were, then squatted down and pointed her finger. Ethan joined her.

"Here. These boot prints are new. Maybe a day old. See how exact the tread is? There's no softening of the edges. Time, wind, precipitation, if it's not too much, rounds the corners, fills in the valleys and lowers the hills, eventually erasing them. Whoever left these, was not here when Dad was shot." A gust of wind pushed along something small and white. She refocused her gaze on the object. "A cigarette butt. No one at the lodge smokes, and any client that does is told to stuff those in their pocket."

"Shaun reported that he had closed this section of the Preserve until Vince could take pictures and check for other evidence. Could these be his? Maybe whoever came out from Cheyenne Forensics?"

She shook her head, then raised her eyes to his. "Vince and the forensics team examined this area before these prints, and that cigarette. Whoever belongs to these, isn't supposed to be here."

Ethan held her gaze, then remembered the rifle shot earlier. He stood and looked across the canyon at the opposite ridge. Miner's Paradise. It was heavily wooded, as Carli had described, and where they were now standing was out in the open. Whoever shot Bear wouldn't have had to look hard. Feeling exposed, and not thinking of his action other than getting Carli to the closest cover, he reached out, took her hand, and led her to where the horses grazed.

She followed willingly, caught off guard by his protectiveness. Realizing his intent, she was eager to seek shelter herself. They had already discussed the possibility that she, Sam, and Shaun could be targets. Once under the protection of the trees several yards back down the trail, she slowed her steps.

Glancing at their joined hands forced her to focus on the rising sensations, and not only the ones where his skin was in contact with hers. There was warmth and security and assuredness and strength. He was trained by the FBI and knew how criminals thought and how to keep others safe. All that was very logical and accepted by her rational mind. But the tingling of her nerves and fluttering in her stomach were not related to the scene she just examined or the realization that someone would want to cause her harm. It came from the man attached to the wide-palmed, long-fingered hand that held firmly to hers.

As soon as they stepped behind the line of evergreens, he released Carli's hand. He closed his eyes briefly and forced air into his lungs. Resisting the urge to shake his hand, or curl his fingers in towards his palm, he reached under his coat and withdrew his weapon. This was familiar to him. The heavy metal barrel, composite grip, the protection it offered. He looked at Carli and noticed an expression of confusion, and wondered if his face mirrored the emotion.

"I feel more protected here. If someone is roaming the Preserve, leaving footprints and firing shots where there should be none, I don't want to give them an opportunity to eliminate another family member," Ethan spoke as he removed his vest, then his backpack. He pulled his binoculars from the zippered pouch, moved to stand next to a tree, then peered through the glasses.

They were high enough, and the side of the Ridge steep enough, that he could look over a majority of the vegetation to the other side of the canyon. Tracking the glasses back and forth, shifting them down the opposite slope, he scanned the terrain. Nothing. It was too wooded to see anything smaller than an elephant covered in the same reflective material as his vest.

Replacing his weapon, he returned the binoculars to his backpack, noticed the horses were well covered by the trees, then focused his attention on Carli, who had remained mute while he checked out the area. The look of confusion was replaced by one of concern, her brows drawn together, and he wondered at her thoughts.

"I think we've accomplished what we've set out to do today. And gained a little extra information."

"You're thinking that whoever shot my father was across the canyon." She made it a statement.

He nodded, deciding if she was part of the plot to do away with Bear, he wouldn't gain anything by developing the possible scenarios with her. If she was innocent of any involvement, then she would need the information to help him keep her safe. Unless she was a damn talented liar, and his gut wasn't hedging that way, he could share his conjecture.

"The caliber that was used can travel over a mile. Someone who knows a lot about shooting would need to adjust for the exact distance and wind velocity."

"That would mean someone who was a client or—"

"An employee. Someone who knows the terrain," he finished. "I know you don't want to acknowledge that as a possibility," he said and held out one of the lunches.

"There's another group," she said, accepting the box. Keeping her eyes on his, hoping to discern his thoughts, she added, "Bear Tanner's children."

"Or someone they hired. Perhaps informing the shooter of the area and where to be when Bear exposed himself on this ridge."

She moved to a nearby tree where she sat on the ground, littered with pine needles, and leaned her back against the trunk, grateful for the sun's warming rays on skin that had grown cold.

He followed, taking a tree next to hers. With patience he waited, knowing she was forming a logical reason why one of the siblings couldn't have orchestrated the plan. In the brief silence that followed, he opened his lunch, unwrapped the sandwich and hoped eating would settle some of what the prospect of danger had stirred.

In between bites, she gave her reasons for denying any involvement. "I have been out of the country for almost a month. I've had no contact with family or employees here since the holidays. I don't know of anyone in the business of killing-for-hire, nor where to locate such a person," she spoke with a matter-of-act tone, which had Ethan glancing at her with a raised brow.

"I love my job and have no desire to change careers. I have plenty of money in the bank because I'm very good at what I do. My life is exactly as I want it to be. If anything happened to Dad, all of that would change," she shook her head, not wanting to recognize that her life was forever altered. "There's not enough for me to gain to risk going to prison for the next thirty years."

Ethan made a noise that he had heard her, but guessed she had more to say, so he remained quiet.

"Samantha already has what she wants. Crystal Springs. Dad owns ... *owned* it. We all understood that she would run the ranch for Dad. He had no issues with her decisions. Sam has a queasy stomach. Whenever she has to help a cow or mare give birth, she turns a little green and usually ends up teary-eyed. Sam always brought home strays. She's never hurt anyone, well, except Patrick Cooley. He broke her heart in sixth grade, then humiliated her by returning her Valentine. She got even by kicking him in the groin."

Ethan inhaled part of his sandwich and ended up coughing. Once he caught his breath, he shifted the way he sat against the tree and eyed Carli as if she might do the same if provoked.

She smiled at his expression. "Bear Tanner taught his children to protect themselves. When Shaun was old enough, he took safeguarding on as his life's purpose. He was suspended from school a few times for fighting. If Sam or I got our hearts broken, Shaun believed it was his responsibility to teach the boys a lesson."

"And I'm sure the hazel eyes and blonde hair of the Tanner girls ensured Shaun's knuckles were always at the ready."

She chuckled. "We were kind of cute as kids. Wore our hair in ponytails and figured out early on that a smile and some conversation usually got us what we wanted."

"And you've grown up to be quite beautiful. Do you still get what you want?" Ethan's voice had softened, his lunch temporarily forgotten.

The breeze had blown a tendril of soft, curled hair across her face. She absently tucked it behind her ear, holding Ethan's gaze. He was forthright in his opinion and she guessed he often spoke what was on his mind. There was an intensity in his eyes that both excited and cautioned her. Did she get what she wanted?

She raised a shoulder in a shrug. "I suppose I do, but then my wants are not extravagant. My lifestyle has afforded me to indulge in what I choose to do." Would that include Ethan?

"I can see how your career allows you to do as much of the things you like as you please. So, if your tastes aren't extravagant, does that mean you indulge often?"

His look of mischief was back, so she continued to play along. A tiny thought wandered through her mind that questioned if what she was doing was play, or a prelude to something more.

"When the mood and opportunity arise, I suppose I do. But a girl still has to have her standards."

"Really? What might they be?" He rested against the trunk, one arm balanced on his bent knee, the box lunch resting on his outstretched thigh.

"It has to be entertaining, spontaneous, and perhaps something that's been done before."

"Experience has its benefits, but do you ever try something because there was perhaps more to it, perhaps some permanence, or do you partake in the short-term?"

"I've yet to encounter something that's worth keeping," she raised a brow.

"Would you know it if you saw it?"

Before she could answer, Samson nudged Ethan's shoulder, halting their conversation. Carli laughed as Ethan scrambled to his feet.

"He's formidable enough standing next to him, and quite monstrous to be at knee level," Ethan explained, stroking the horse's large head. "I know what you're looking for," he mumbled as he made his way to the saddlebag and found the carrots J.J. had packed. He broke the treat in half, which caught Lady's attention. A moment later, both horses were nosing around his pockets and hands looking for more.

The sound of a shutter drew his attention from the horse to Carli. She lowered the camera slightly to look at him over the top of it, then shifted to peer though the viewfinder again. He was smiling at the antics of Samson and Lady, and seemed relaxed around the horses. She took several more shots before their steeds realized there were no more treats, and so they wandered back to the grass poking out of the ground.

"Do you always carry it with you?" he asked and gestured to her camera.

"Yes. Some of the best shots are those that are ... spontaneous," she smiled.

He pulled his pad and a pencil from his backpack. He flipped to one of the pages that depicted Zach and handed it to her.

"I agree. People take pictures to remember vacations and special events or places. My sketches help me do that."

She was amazed. It took a certain level of observation, one of deep, penetrating perspective to capture human expression the way Ethan had done. The man had some serious talent.

"Have you had any formal training?"

He took the pad back from her before she could flip through all the pages. "An art class here and there. Nothing serious. It helps me to keep facts straight, gives me the opportunity to capture my impressions of people."

Tipping her head to the side, she gave him her honest opinion. "They are quite good. You have a gift. That doesn't come to everyone. Have you thought about doing something with it?"

He shook his head. "I use it for work."

"There's enough here," she gestured around them, "to play with and see if there's something more. Besides work," she added to clarify, and without her intention, ended up in the same double-meaning conversation they had been in before. "If you're not in a hurry to get back, I'd like to take some pictures of the Ridge."

"I have time," he said, then suggested, "Since those prints were placed here after Vince's visit, get a couple shots and we can give them to Shaun."

His comment was as effective as throwing a bucket of water on a campfire. She frowned slightly, then nodded and moved off in the direction of the stained earth.

He looked toward the horses, located a downed tree near their patch of grass, and sat, his pad on his lap. His gaze shifted from the sun's location, to Carli. Flipping to a clean sheet, his hand moved as if on its own, capturing the intriguing woman with the hazel eyes, blonde hair, spontaneous nature, and artist's heart.

CHAPTER 18

Pulling her fur-edged coat closed and tightening the belt, she placed her oversized sunglasses on her nose and waited for the shuttle to take her from the terminal to the lot for rental cars. At least the clouds had drifted away, taking any precipitation with them. It would have added a layer of discomfort to attend the funeral during a snowstorm. Darla was thankful for the late spring climate, and the handsome van driver who insisted on loading her luggage.

After tipping the driver, she left her bags outside the glass door of the small building that housed the car rental office. She managed to upgrade to the last luxury car they had available for the next seven days. A little flirting had awarded her with assistance in loading her bags into the trunk of the Cadillac.

A portion of her life had been spent in the southeast corner of this desolate state, so finding her way from the airport to the only four-star hotel in Laramie was simple. The town had not changed since she had been here last, which was Shaun's graduation from the Police Academy. She certainly had higher expectations for her only son than being the Sheriff of Centennial, Wyoming. Some of the sidewalks and most of the corners of the parking lots outside storefronts were piled with dirty snow. Attached to every other light post were flags advertising a rodeo. In the next two months, the snow would be gone and families on summer vacation would begin to travel through Wyoming. They would notice that Laramie was a lovely town and decide to buy property. Within six months, most of the parcels would be sold, seventy-five percent of the structures erected, and she would have a steady income.

The Blue Sky Chateau hadn't sold out to a national chain, thus keeping its charm and four-star status. Darla pulled under the portcullis, allowed the single bellboy on duty to unload her luggage, place it on a cart, and then hold the door for her as she entered the hotel. She had reserved a suite which overlooked the gardens at the rear of the building, where they eventually gave way to a golf course, the garden and course being separated by a three-foot high, black iron fence. There was a beautiful view of the mountains to the west, which was unimpeded by trees since she was on the top floor, three stories above the gardens.

Tipping the bellboy for placing her largest bag on the stand next to the dresser, she closed and locked the door behind him. There was time for an afternoon nap, then to freshen up before making her appearance at the lodge and offering her condolences to whoever was there. Draping her coat across the back of one of the cushioned chairs, she stretched out on the bed and dozed.

«« —»»

Sam didn't need any help. All the guides that were scheduled to lead parties were already out on the trails. Alyssa had returned home to take care of her chores, and Zach split his time between the front desk and delivering clean linens to the cabins, having transferred any incoming calls from the Internet telephone system to the landline and the cordless phone that hung from his belt. Next, he would be restocking the boxes that held materials for the fly-tying classes. No, he didn't need any assistance, but thanked Tim for asking.

There had been no new e-mails from Scott, and none from his coworkers since they were already out for their Saturday evening. In New York, it was past eight in the evening. Sighing, he grabbed one of the cameras from Carli's case and decided to wander the grounds. He didn't have the training, or the eye, that she had, but he found it passed the time. Occasionally, there was a shot that he captured that Carli commented on, due to its angle or color or composition. Those he kept. The others he deleted from either the camera card or his file on his hard drive.

He began with the tubs of flowers that lined the steps leading up to the veranda and the front door of the lodge. The water feature in the middle of the parking area resembled a natural river and waterfall, complete with boulders and recently placed green plants. He had seen Ray earlier that morning removing the covers that protected the plants from the nightly spring frost. A few shots at different angles, and he moved on towards the barn. Not much of an animal person, he stayed away from the remaining horses, but ambled down the barn aisle hoping to catch J.J. in one of his many daily chores. As soon as he stepped into the shade of the barn, his phone vibrated in his pocket. The number was unfamiliar to him, and being wary of losing the signal, he stepped back outside the barn before he answered.

"This is Charlie. From your flight to Laramie."

Tim grinned. "Hello. Are you in town?"

"I am, for the next thirty-six hours. Are you busy? Am I interrupting?"

He glanced at the digital camera in his hand, then squinted at the sunlit grounds. "No, you're not interrupting. And it so happens, I'm available."

Charlie smiled. "I would like to take you up on your offer for a cup of coffee. I'm staying at the Laramie Star. They have a quaint cafe adjacent to the lobby."

"That sounds inviting," Tim said, eyeing one of the company trucks. "Give me a few minutes to confirm a ride. I can be there in about an hour."

"You know where it is?"

"Haven't been to town enough to know for sure, but I have a reliable source."

"Well, you have my number. Call if you're lost," Charlie offered.

"Sure. See you soon." Tim disconnected, made his way back to the lodge, climbed the steps to the veranda, and hoped Zach was back at the counter.

He was, and not only did Zach give him the keys to truck #2, he also wrote easy directions on how to find the Laramie Star. Bringing the camera with him, and a sense of excitement, Tim left Tanner's Outdoor Adventures for one of his own.

《《—》》

With all of his paperwork completed and filed, the expense report filled out for the month of March, there was nothing left for Shaun to do at the office. There were no calls coming in, and even the channel he kept on to listen to the Highway Patrol was quiet for a Sunday morning. Vince would be on duty that afternoon. Shutting down his computer, he decided he would do his rounds on the streets of Centennial, then end up at the lodge. There was information to share with Ethan regarding the rifle. Maybe he could have a conversation with Ray and settle that question. He was also interested in hearing what Carli and Ethan found at Wolf's Ridge.

Locking the office door behind him, he glanced both ways on 2nd Street, then climbed into his vehicle to begin his patrol. Few people were out at this day and time. As his eyes tracked the roadways and shoulders, ensuring everyone had arrived safely at home the night before, his mind wandered to what would happen to the lodge.

He had no knowledge as to what his father put in his will. Maybe the Preserve was to be sold, the money divided among the three of them. It wouldn't matter to Sam, as she loved Crystal Springs, though they all thought of the lodge as home. He was content with his position of sheriff, had his own land and house, a life that was separate from his father's business. Whenever Carli chose to return to Wyoming, she could stay with him, as he had built four bedrooms under his roof. As far as he knew, Carli loved the adventure of international travel. She was talented and made good money with her career at the magazine. They had spoken before about her doing freelance work. He had encouraged her to showcase her work in a gallery, but she

158

claimed she didn't have the time. Carli always found the time, and money, though, to appear at charity fund-raisers. She would donate her pictures for auction, which always earned the organization a substantial sum.

While he dwelled on Carli, the least tied down of the three of them, Ethan's comments, and the way he gazed at her, entered his thoughts. His sister was certainly of the age to choose who she wished to be with, but he knew from personal experience that involvement with a lawman was difficult. There was more than one woman that had ended her relationship with him because of the fear that he might be wounded or killed in the line of duty. And when one had chosen the law as their life, those consequences were always a possibility. Whatever happens between the two of them during their time at the lodge, he was sure Ethan would eventually return to Baltimore, and Carli to her gypsy life.

«« —»»

"Were you ever in the Boy Scouts?"

"A couple of years."

"Ever do any camping?"

"Once. We spent the night in our tents at a state park."

"Bet they had public bathrooms."

"Sure. But spiders and shadows inhabited them at night."

"You didn't have a flashlight?"

"Of course, but then everyone would know where I was going."

"So?"

"They would wake up and plan a prank that would ensure I would have to use the facilities."

"Scare the shit out of you?" Carli chuckled.

"Figuratively, but I wasn't taking the chance the literal would present itself." When she continued giggling and shaking her head, he felt compelled to explain. "I was only twelve. Something like that could scar a man for life."

That seemed to make her laugh harder.

"Didn't the three of you ever play jokes on each other?"

To that, she nodded, pretending to wipe tears from her eyes, as she continued to laugh.

"I'll be over here," he gestured behind a particularly thick group of trees several feet off the trail.

She gestured for him to do what he needed while she tried to catch her breath.

"You know, there are other ways I could devise to bring a smile to your face," Ethan called over his shoulder, noting her expression of ... interest? Challenge? He turned his gaze forward to keep from tripping and falling, thus offering her another excuse to laugh at him.

Answering the call of nature, he realized how much he enjoyed his banter with Carli, her laugh and the way that her eyes were quick to tease and understand, showing her thoughts clearly. As he returned to where she and the horses were, he looked again across the canyon. His drawings had always helped him make sense of the cases he had worked. Between the sketches, Carli's pictures, and eliminating a few of the employees and the siblings as possible suspects, he thought he would be able to hone in on the person responsible in a few days. After that, he would be free to investigate if there was anything besides casual interest between him and Carli.

Watching as Ethan disappeared around the cluster of trees, she took herself in the opposite direction to accomplish the same task. Grateful that she finished before the FBI agent, she returned to the lunch boxes they had left on the ground. Gathering them in order to pack them out, she paused on her way to Samson's saddlebags at the site of Ethan's pad on the downed tree where he sat while she photographed the Ridge. She glanced from the sketches she could just make out on the top page, to where Ethan would reappear at any moment. Curiosity won, and she traded the boxes for the pad.

She admired his perspective of the Ridge and the canyon, the lodge and the barn. When she turned back a couple of pages, she stilled her hand. It was her. Ethan had sketched four pages of her laughing, scowling, holding her camera, and on horseback. One in particular he had taken the time to add shadowing, which created more depth. It was a close-up of her face, more than a profile, less than a full-frontal view, with her hair tucked behind her right ear and a quizzical expression on her face.

"That's one of my favorites," was the quiet, deep voice behind her that caused her to jump, slapping the pad to her chest as if she were hiding a great secret.

He reached a hand around her and lowered the pad. Leaving his finger on the corner, he began to explain his thoughts about the drawing.

"You have this expression when something catches your attention. You question, not quite ready to believe. Almost as if you're searching for some kind of proof."

The warmth of his breath against her cheek sent chills dancing down her spine. A breeze ruffled her hair, and before she could move, Ethan's hand left the pad and tucked the loose tendrils behind her ear. Her breath hitched as his fingers caressed the outer edge. Hesitating a moment, he eventually lowered his hand to his side, and she felt ... disappointed. Why would the touch of this man be any different from the others she had allowed to be this close?

"There's a slight crease between your brows, often a moment before you raise one. If it is something amusing or understood, there's a half-smile. Confusion is followed by the crossing of your arms."

She forced her left hand from across her middle to her side. It was disconcerting that he could read her so easily. Looking at the drawings of Zach and Alyssa and J.J., she realized it wasn't just her with which he had noticed the nuances of body language. She turned to face him and was caught in his gaze. The fire that began to build between them during lunch was still present, and she wondered if she would survive the flames.

"What training courses in the FBI taught you how to do this?" she asked.

"Profiling. Behavior observation. Psychology."

"And your eye for art gives you an edge," she added.

"Perhaps," he agreed, reaching to take the pad from her by placing his fingers next to hers.

He wasn't imagining it. There was something there that set his nerves tingling. Instead of taking the paper from her, he shifted his grip to hold her fingers and gently pulled them towards his chest. Rather than straightening her arm, she took a step closer to him. He found himself being drawn into the shades of green and brown in her eyes. There was an overwhelming desire to kiss her, to taste her lips, and confirm or deny that she was fuel for his libido.

He placed his other hand alongside her cheek. Her eyes widened, and the wrinkle appeared between her brows. Keeping his eyes on hers, he slowly lowered his lips. She didn't move away or speak. The moment they touched, he breathed in much needed air, and Carli.

The press of lips lasted long enough for him to realize that it wasn't enough. Her hand on his chest was taken as encouragement to angle his head to the side and offer an open-mouthed kiss. Because so much of her was unexpected, it surprised him, and added a layer of excitement, when she met him with the same intention. Gasoline on a campfire couldn't have been hotter or more explosive. He stepped closer, released his hold on the pad of paper, and placed his hand on her cheek. Pulling back slightly to look into the hazel depths of her eyes, he was rewarded with an answering desire. This time, his kiss had more purpose.

From the first touch of his lips she knew she was in trouble. Handsome, intelligent, mischievous, strong … safe. All this she knew about Ethan and felt that these characteristics were a cornerstone of his being. His kiss reminded her of what she had learned about volcanoes. A few had been the object of her job, and she was easily transported back to the foothills of one just before it erupted. The ground was warm underneath her feet as the lava heated the solid rock. Ash and sparks wafted into the air from the exposed crater a mile above her, a warning of what was to come. Ethan was the same. She could sense the heat of his desire just beneath the surface and the press of his lips was only the beginning. Her first taste of him, as their tongues tangled and caressed, sent her teetering on the edge. This was a dangerous man, and if she intended to keep her heart intact, she would need to tread carefully.

Samson's hot breath on the back of Ethan's neck a moment before the large upper lip of the gelding nuzzled Ethan's shoulder, reminded him where he was. When he was slow to end the kiss, Samson nudged him, pushing him into Carli, who laughed. Reaching past Ethan's shoulder to stroke the horse down his face, Carli's gaze shifted from one set of brown eyes with a white stripe between them, to another pair of dark eyes that glittered with humor.

"I think he's jealous," Ethan chuckled.

"Perhaps," she said, then leaned close to Ethan's shoulder, stood on her toes, and kissed Samson between the nostrils.

Ethan turned his head to watch, and witnessed the subtle communication between human and horse. Samson rested his chin on Ethan's shoulder, as he and Carli exchanged exhales. She blew into his nostril, and with ears pricked forward, he returned the gesture. After the third shared breath, Carli again ran her hand down Samson's face, then pushed slightly so he removed his head from its perch.

"That was interesting," Ethan commented, leaving it open for Carli to interpret which event he referred to.

"An exchange of information," she returned, just as cryptic.

"I think he was looking for something more than a kiss."

Carli smiled. "Boys always are. Since he's had his fun and a treat, he's ready to go home."

"Where he'll get something more substantial to sustain him?"

"There's more, but whether or not he'll be satisfied is hard to tell."

"An equine condition?" Ethan asked.

"A male one," Carli answered.

He raised a brow and wondered at the situation she referred to, where perhaps she was not enough. Did an intimate partner cheat on her? Was her trust betrayed in some way by a friend?

She stepped back from Ethan and handed him his pad, then retrieved the boxes from their lunch and placed them inside the saddlebag behind Samson's saddle. Sliding the bit between Samson's teeth, the headstall behind his ears, she handed the reins to Ethan, then tightened the cinch. She spent the next few minutes readying Lady for the return ride to the lodge.

He removed his coat and replaced it with his backpack.

"You can tie your jacket to the back of the saddle with the strings," Carli suggested as she adjusted the camera strap diagonally across her chest.

Taking one last look around the site, she fought off the heavy sadness knowing this is what her father had seen just before he died. He loved Wyoming, the vast spaciousness of it, and knew the creatures that he stocked on his Preserve. He would have hated it if he had died in bed, too ill or weak to leave his room and enjoy the great outdoors. But he certainly didn't volunteer to be murdered.

Ethan easily mounted Samson and turned the horse toward Carli and Lady. He could tell she was puzzling something out in her mind. She shook her head as if discarding some argument. He watched as she swung herself gracefully onto Lady's back.

"We'll head back down the same trail, then take the left fork. It will bring us to the mouth of the canyon and the gate J.J. said he was checking when he got the call from Alyssa."

He nodded. "Lead the way."

After a few minutes of silence, he remembered her earlier opinions as to why she and Samantha could not have conspired to kill Bear. She had yet to offer her insight regarding Shaun.

"Carli, explain why you believe that Shaun is innocent of any involvement in Bear's death."

CHAPTER 19

Ed's was a tiny dive, dark, with the overpowering odor of cigarettes, marijuana, beer, and in the narrow hallway that housed the restrooms and a pay phone, vomit. Country music streamed from the speakers in the corners unless someone dropped a coin in the jukebox and chose a classic rock song, which was often a topic that riled the patrons seated at the bar. There were two televisions and one electronic dartboard. In his mid-sixties with salt and pepper hair, a clean-shaven face, and always dressed in a white, buttoned-down shirt and jeans, Ed, a veteran and long-time entrepreneur, only served alcohol, and didn't accept credit cards or run tabs for his regulars. His clientele consisted of Alcoholics Anonymous dropouts, the unemployed, and those that were older than fifty years.

Jim Lockhart fit into two of the three categories. Ed's beer was almost as cheap as getting a six-pack at the store, but then he would have to drink alone. He did that often enough. When Lys got her paycheck from Tanner, he figured he was due for some conversation, and so he spent a few hours at Ed's catching up with the other customers.

"Shame about Bear," Ed was saying as Jim settled himself on a barstool.

"You know what's going to happen to the Tanner place?" George asked. He was a man in his sixties, rail thin, with a full gray beard and enough lines on his face to be confused with a roadmap of the Eastern Seaboard where he was raised.

"Alyssa hasn't said. Still goes to work every day. Guess after the funeral on Tuesday and his kids get hold of Bear's will, we'll all know."

"What's Alyssa going to do for work if they sell the place?" Ed asked.

Jim shrugged. "There's other jobs in Centennial. If not here, Laramie offers plenty." A former construction worker, he was just over six feet tall and had retained most of his bulk from his working days, though now his arms and torso were covered with a layer comprised of several years' worth of beer suds. Dark hair and eyes, his once handsome face was marked by lines of time and more than his share of bad luck.

"She isn't going off to school?" Mickey, who sat on the other side of George, inquired. His love of whatever was on tap was shown by his extremely large girth. The dirty jeans and stained white T-shirt signaled he was one of the few that held down a job, or rather several freelance handyman jobs.

"Hell, I don't have any money to send that girl anywhere. Far as I know, she's got no aspirations to do anything other than work at Tanner's," Jim answered, then took several swallows of the pint Ed set in front of him.

"That boy, Zach, who works at Tanner's sure spends a lot of time with her," Mickey continued.

George glanced at Jim. "Think they'll get married?"

"She's too young," Jim said, though now that the seed had been planted in his mind, he didn't answer with as much conviction as he would have liked.

"Weren't you and Carol just out of high school when you two got married?" Ed wiped the bar in front of Jim in an attempt to keep it clean.

"Sure, and look how we ended up. Carol's dead and I'm out of work."

The others grunted in understanding and Ed moved toward the opposite end of the slab of wood that ran the length of the main room to serve Justin and Kevin, two hands that worked one of the local ranches. They did a fair amount of business by selling

166

grass out of Ed's and made a stop every time they came into town. It was early enough on Saturday that they didn't need to worry about Sheriff Tanner making a surprise walk-through. If Justin was caught with the requisite number ounces that a judge deemed he intended to sell, it would be sufficient to lock him away for a few years with the added charge of 'parole violation'. The tall, lanky, cowboy had already done a year in the system for auto theft, which was really just a misunderstanding the way Justin told the story.

Ed glanced at the Coors Light clock on the wall opposite the bar. "Jenny said she would come by about four-thirty. You boys will be here until then?"

Justin shrugged. "We're off the clock until Monday morning."

"How about change for a five? We'll toss some darts to pass the time," Kevin said and patted his shirt pocket before extracting the bill.

Ed glanced at his patrons and decided none would object. He took the five dollars, opened the register, and then set a pile of quarters on the bar in front of the ranch hands.

Justin smiled as he slid from his stool and wandered to the corner where the dart machine blinked. Kevin followed, and after inserting the required coins for a game, pulled the pipe and baggie from his other shirt pocket. Moments later, with flame to the dried leaves, the sweet scent of Mary Jane wafted around them.

"... two incomes," Mickey was saying.

"What do you call it when the Daddy is being taken care of? A Sour Pop!" George said, answering his own joke without waiting for the others to offer their thoughts.

Laughter sounded loud in the doubtful thoughts of Jim Lockhart. What would he do if Alyssa left? If she lost her job at Tanner's? His unemployment wasn't enough to cover the bills or the bank loans. He was satisfied with their arrangement, and would have to make sure that Alyssa saw things the same way. Tossing a few bills on the bar to cover the beers he had consumed, Jim turned to leave, then paused at the sight of who had just entered.

Ray Foster was not a member of Ed's usual clientele, but he knew he would find Jim Lockhart here since it was Alyssa's payday, which meant her father's short supply of cash would be replenished. He shifted his cowboy hat further up on his forehead to get a clear picture of who was inside the bar. Lockhart was just about to leave, so it seemed his timing was correct.

"Jim," Ray nodded to Alyssa's father. "Hi, Ed," he greeted the owner, who nodded in his direction then resumed stacking pint glasses behind the bar.

"Ray," Jim returned. "This isn't your usual haunt. What are you doing here?"

"Looking for you."

"Really? Does it concern the future of Tanner's?"

Ray pursed his lips slightly as he thought of how to answer. "Not really sure what will become of the lodge. That will be for the kids and Bear's will to determine." When Jim remained quiet, he continued, "But I did want you to know that Alyssa will have a job as long as the lodge is around. Bear thought of each of his employees as family. Guess I didn't want you to be ... worried that she would be left without work, or not remembered in the will. I'm sure Bear had something set aside for her."

Jim swayed slightly on his feet. So if Alyssa got something from Bear, that meant more for him. He relaxed, planning a different kind of talk with his daughter.

"Thanks for the information," Jim acknowledged Ray with a nod. "Just so happens, I'm on my way home to chat with Lys now."

Ray judged the other man's inebriation and decided he was mostly fit to drive. Vince would be out on patrol. If the two crossed paths, the deputy would deal with Jim. Ray hoped he had saved Alyssa from a boxing match at the prospect of her becoming unemployed. He turned and exited the bar, and as he climbed up into the company truck, he saw Jim do the same. Squinting at the setting sun, he decided he would make a point of having a conversation with Alyssa tomorrow to see if his talk with her father was enough of a deterrent. With the back of the truck loaded down with bagged feed, Ray returned to the lodge.

«‹‹—›››

Checking her lipstick and bangs in the bathroom mirror, Darla guessed she was ready to see her children. She pulled on her coat, grabbed her purse, and closed the hotel room door behind her. In minutes she was on her way to Centennial. Not much of the highway had changed. A few more vehicles on the road, but, after twenty years, even Wyoming would show growth.

Slowing down to the posted speed, Darla left the highway and wondered if she would see Shaun on his afternoon patrol. Both sides of 2nd Street were lined with shops and businesses, most of which were in a lull this late on a Saturday. Her head pivoted as she passed the sheriff's office. No vehicles in front, no lights on inside. Since she had last been to the lodge, there were three new residences along the stretch of Highway 130 that went through town, and had at one time ended at the Preserve. A few years after Bear had purchased the property, the State of Wyoming decided that the highway should lead back to the Interstate. They constructed a narrow, two-lane road that continued beyond Ehlin Road, Forest Service Route 338, and Tanner's Outdoor Adventures.

She slowed almost to a stop at the juncture of the drive into the Preserve and the paved Ehlin Road. The fencing was as she remembered, at twelve-feet high with three strands of barbed wire across the top. Part of the strategy was to keep the animals Bear imported inside the Preserve, and the other was to keep nonpaying clients out. The fence ran the length of the drive, then cut off into the property so when one sat on the veranda of the lodge, they enjoyed a view of the wilderness instead of something from a prison yard.

Turning into the driveway, she suppressed the fluttering in her stomach. Was she nervous? She had come too far to have second thoughts. There was a lot of money, and lives, that depended on her competent role as a mother. That word felt bitter on her tongue. She never wanted to be one, but at the time was in love enough to marry, and her husband wanted children. Without planning it, she had birthed three, and by the time the third, Shaun, started school, she decided she'd had enough of playing house, enough of winter, so she left. Now her children were grown, her husband dead, but she had a life she thoroughly loved.

She rolled the Cadillac to a stop, with two vehicles between hers and the front steps to the lodge. One was a company van, which either meant the clients were through with their outing for the day, or there were no clients. The other vehicle was an SUV with a sheriff's badge painted on the door. Taking her purse, a designer bag that cost nearly four figures, she climbed out of her rental and resolutely made her way to the front door.

Two clients engaged in a game of chess at one of the tables in the lobby, while three more enjoyed the afternoon snacks and refreshments that were available from a cart wheeled into the Great Room and parked between the fireplace and the low table that sat in front of one of the couches. A young man she didn't recognize was behind the front desk, a phone to his ear. He smiled at her, then turned his attention to the computer screen. She had moved halfway across the lobby, when male laughter from behind her halted her progress toward the counter and the young man on the phone.

Shaun began to remove his coat, his smile a remnant of Ray's joke about a poor cowboy. His eyes tracked from right to left across the room, and he froze as they met those of a woman in her early fifties with platinum-blonde hair. She smiled hesitantly at him, which had the corners of his mouth pulling downward and his hunger for dinner evaporating. Behind him, Ray closed the door, then came to stand as still as the sheriff.

"What the hell are you doing here?" Shaun demanded, then glanced at the clients as they looked his way.

"It's alright, folks. Just an unexpected family reunion," Ray explained to those in the lobby.

Holding Darla's gaze, Shaun crossed to her, grabbed her arm, and pulled her to the dining room, with Ray close behind.

As soon as they were out of sight and earshot of the clients, Shaun released his mother's arm and scowled down at her. "Did you take a wrong turn on I-5?"

"Of course not. I heard about Bear and wanted to express my condolences."

He snorted. "You never gave a damn about the man when he was alive—"

"That's not true!" she interrupted, but kept her voice low. "I was deeply in love with your father."

"But not his kids."

"You're mine, too—" she began.

"No. We're not. You gave up that claim when you left." He stood toe-to-toe with Darla, fists clenching at his side as the childhood hurt, and the usual argument, erupted between them.

"Easy, Shaun," Ray said, placing his hand on the sheriff's shoulder. "Darla," he nodded towards the woman standing in front of Shaun, unwilling to give an inch in the room, or in their disagreement.

She shifted her gaze to a face she knew well. "Hello, Ray. I'm sorry for the loss of your friend."

He nodded again, then stepped around Shaun and between the two of them. "Funeral is on Tuesday," he said.

"Yes, I know. It was published in yesterday's paper with an extensive write up about Bear's life. Samantha?"

"She's organizing everything," Ray answered.

"And I don't believe she called you to extend an invitation," Shaun added.

She raised a brow. "Bitterness is unbecoming of you. I married Bear, lived here with him for ten years. I'm exercising my right to pay respects to a wonderful man."

"What would you know about that?"

"All I have to do is look at you and your sisters. Bear Tanner did a fine job raising three incredible children," she softened her voice, the truth of the statement rolling easily from her lips.

171

Shaun ground his teeth.

"Where are you staying?" Ray asked.

"In Laramie. I thought I would come early, see what I could do to help with the arrangements. There will probably be quite a few people I'll know at the services. It will give me a chance to visit with you," she turned her blue eyes towards Shaun, "Sam, and Carli."

"He wouldn't have left you anything," Shaun said.

When Darla remained quiet and only drew her brows together in confusion, Shaun elaborated, "Dad's will. You've come to see if he mentioned you, perhaps designated a few hundred-thousand to the woman who bore his children."

Now Darla's perfectly sculpted brows inched up on her forehead. "You're mistaken if you believe that is the only reason why I came. Really, Shaun. Isn't it time you found a way to get … by or through or around this dislike you have for me?"

"But since you're never here, it's rarely an issue. Besides, that would mean forgiving you."

"Perhaps. Temporarily. This anger of yours serves no purpose. It is quite clear how you feel. I'm only asking for a little civility." She untied her belt and took off her coat.

"She's right, Shaun. The next several days will be difficult. No reason to add to them," Ray placed his hand on Shaun's shoulder and felt the stiffness.

"Has Carli been notified?" she asked.

Shaun nodded. "She's here, but out with a client. Took him trail riding."

Darla smiled slightly. "She always loved to ride. I'm glad she's here. And Samantha?"

At the *whoosh* of the kitchen door behind her, she turned to see her middle child, dressed in an apron over jeans and a red sweater with the sleeves pushed up, dark blonde hair in a braid over one shoulder, and a stack of dinner plates in her hands. Darla reached for the plates.

"Hello, Samantha."

Hazel eyes widened in recognition. Taking in the hair, make-up, and attractive figure of her fifty-something-year-old mother, Sam could understand how her father lost his heart to this woman. Her quick, but thorough, observation also reminded her that she looked the most like Darla, where Shaun and Carli had more of their father's features.

"Darla. What a … surprise. I don't recall having notified you about Dad. That's probably because I wasn't sure how to contact you, not knowing your address or phone number in California. You are still in California, aren't you?" Sam smiled a little to coat her words.

Darla retracted her hands when Sam didn't relinquish the stack of plates. Shaun's anger was easier to deal with. It was straight forward, in her face. The stinging words of her daughter were more difficult to handle. She should have expected it. Couldn't blame them. Perhaps some sentimental corner of her ego believed that in a time of grief her children wouldn't be so harsh. She was obviously very wrong.

With a weak smile she answered, "Yes. I'm still in California. I saw the first notice in the obituaries a few days ago, then the one yesterday. I guessed you had come here to organize things. You were always good at that."

"It was the only way Bear could keep track of his growing client base," Ray said. "I think Sam was organizing his files by the time she was thirteen."

Sam moved around the table, away from Darla, and set a plate on each placemat.

"He tried to stick to whatever system I designed. But he just never went back to his early files. As I developed better systems for the business in all the ways it was growing, he could keep up, but didn't take the time, or effort, to bring everything under one system." She set the last plate, then placed her hands on her hips. "I suppose you want an invitation to dinner."

"While I'm here, I could spend time with you, Shaun, and Carli. I would be happy to help you, if you need it, with the … funeral plans," Darla offered.

"I'll get another plate, but I don't need any help. I'm not sure anyone I need to contact would know who you are," Sam said, then disappeared into the kitchen.

As soon as the door closed, she didn't know what to do first, cuss, hit something, or scream. Instead, she sighed and rubbed her forehead. The headache she had earlier, that lessened with a nap and some aspirin, returned full-force at the thought of dealing with Darla until, and through, the day of the funeral. Tonight's menu included roasted chicken, seasoned potatoes, steamed vegetables, dinner rolls, salad, and apple pie. The chicken and pie were done, so she busied herself with the rest of it. She would tolerate Darla. Shaun would devise ways to be away from the lodge. Carli might blast Darla with anger or ignore her completely. Whatever happened, Sam would not allow Darla to ruin the arrangements she had planned for honoring their father. Three days. The woman would be here for more hours than at any of her visits through the years. Sam could keep the peace, she hoped, for three days.

CHAPTER 20

She thought for a moment, a little surprised at the change in topic. Leaning back slightly as Lady picked her way down the trail, Carli rested her hand on the back of the saddle and spoke honestly, as she rarely did anything else.

"Shaun, being the youngest, was the one most affected by Darla leaving," she began.

"You refer to your mother by her first name?" Ethan asked, watching as Samson's ears appeared to be lower than his shoulders with the steepness of the trail.

"She lost the title of 'mother' the day she left. Whenever she felt compelled to return for a visit, we all called her Darla."

She laid the right rein against Lady's neck, and the horse took the left fork in the trail, which led to a different part of the Preserve.

"Shaun wanted to be a police officer from the time he was about eight. Dad had instilled in us a very dark line between right and wrong. He was always fair in whatever punishment he deemed was necessary, depending upon our infraction. That influenced Shaun, along with what happened to Sam," she paused, wondering what kind of information Ethan, and the FBI, had on each one of them.

"When she was abducted by Carl Rutgers? The taking of a child forever changes a family."

He had unknowingly answered her silent question. The fact that he knew so much about child kidnapping and what often occurs after the child is taken, brought back his last day in court when he testified in the case of Tommy Mason. Tommy was lucky because they had located him before Richard Glassier could follow through on the grisly details of the ritual that had consumed his life. Ethan scowled, then looked at the surrounding trees. The memory seemed to soil the purity of his current environment, and he pushed the thoughts back into their box in his mind and locked the lid shut.

"I guess all of that is in an FBI file," she said.

"It was reported back then, when the local police called in the Bureau, and now it's in the file with William 'Bear' Tanner's name on it. I can understand the impression such an event would have on Shaun at that age, especially since he had already expressed interest in the justice system and protecting others."

"Growing up, Dad was all we had. Now, each of us has our own home, career, life. There is no motive for Shaun."

"Who will inherit the Preserve?" he asked, knowing that the answer could provide a reason.

"I don't know. I'm sure Sam has contacted Maxwell Stevens."

"Your father's lawyer?"

"Yes. He and Dad have been friends, and clients, for years."

"Surely Bear had a copy of everything. Would it be in the office, or the filing cabinets in the basement, or the storage area?" He was hoping their search in the storage room for employee records was more organized than the basement.

"His office is a tiny room under the staircase. And, yes, we all have keys or access to one. But you'll be disappointed. He didn't even let Sam into his office. Said he knew where everything was. And he did. Fortunately," she added at hearing Ethan groan behind her at the prospect of digging through Dad's system, "being the oldest, I often spent time with him in his office, which is why I can generally locate things easier than Sam or Shaun."

She paused at a turn in the switchback and moved Lady to stand sideways on the slope to rest. Ethan followed her example, but angled Samson the other direction so he could see Carli's face. Looking up, he watched a hawk coast on the wind and disappear further down the valley. When he brought his gaze back to hers he noticed her serious countenance.

"Shaun is working on the premise that someone wanted Dad dead. Murder, not an accident."

He nodded. "The ME and forensics can tell us the caliber, the angle, and we can guess the distance. If nothing points to a malicious act, no motive, no other warnings, it will be ruled an accidental shooting, or inconclusive."

"And then what happens?"

Not sure of her context or what answer she was searching for, he covered all the bases. "The case is pending. It can be picked up at any time as a cold case. I go back to Baltimore. And the three of you move on with your lives the best you can."

"Do you ever go by your gut, Ethan? Or is everything you do by the book?" She had pulled her brows together as she tried to make sense of something that felt wrong to her.

"My gut has been right more times than not," he answered, knowing that kissing her wasn't in the rules.

"There's something going on here. I can't reason it out, and that bothers me."

"What are you thinking?" he asked.

"That someone killed my father. I don't know who, or why, but deciding it was an accident just doesn't … feel right," she responded, sticking to the safer topic.

"But without some kind of evidence, we have no one to arrest."

"I know. I think we'll find something in Dad's papers," she hesitated, then nudged Lady closer to Samson.

Ethan stayed where he was, unsure what she planned. He knew there was something between them, something that was combustible. Watching her sway in the saddle on the way down had played with his thoughts, and as she moved nearer, those ideas that had nothing to do with the case, or the book's rules, arose in his mind.

"I'm wondering ... was the kiss at the Ridge a onetime event? Is it just me, or did you think ... did your gut tell you ... there was something more?" she finished in a whisper.

Each phrase brought her lips closer to Ethan's. She wanted to feel the excitement he had elicited earlier. Was it just a chance kiss, and there was nothing there? Had she made it into something more than it was? He didn't move away, but didn't meet her in the middle either. Maybe she was wrong, and seeing the place where her father died had corrupted her usually trustworthy senses.

Remaining still was more of a battle than he had imagined. Her closeness brought her scent to his nostrils. Gripping the reins to keep from reaching for her, he tried to prepare for another touch, another hint of Carli. The press of her lips was something a lifetime of experiences could not have readied him for. His temperature shot up as the blood zinged in his veins. Unsatisfied with the light touch, he invited her deeper, and she accepted. Unable to keep his hands from her soft skin, he reached out and cupped her jaw, his fingers extending into the dark-blonde curls of her hair.

Lady shifted, forcing them to move apart. He was reluctant to drop his hand, and took advantage of Carli's glazed expression to gently caress her cheek. Shadows began to lengthen as the sun neared the opposite ridge and he saw Carli shiver. He was about to ask how far they were from the south gate, or from the lodge, or if she was unusually cold, anything to derail the direction of his thoughts, when the crack of a rifle less than a quarter of a mile away echoed through the valley, and startled both horses.

He grabbed the reins with one hand and drew his weapon with the other. Peering through the trees in the direction he thought the shot came from, he moved Samson in front of Lady.

"Are you alright?" he asked.

"Fine. A little pissed. No hunting party should be in this section of the Preserve. Everyone knows I was on the schedule and where we were going—" she stopped as she met his gaze and realized that what she was saying reflected his thoughts.

"Does this trail take us to where the shooter is located?" he gestured down the slope in front of them.

"Yes, but the shot originated a bit further up the valley. They would have to exit this way. There's no other trail to reach the lodge, unless they hike up and over Miner's Paradise."

Ethan again scanned the trees further down the trail then shook his head. "It's impossible, especially if they have a carcass to carry with them," he said, hoping it was a misguided customer, and turned back to look at Carli. "This trail is wide enough to ride two abreast. You stay between Samson and the upslope. And take off your vest," he dropped his eyes to the fluorescent orange wrapped around her torso. "We don't want to alert them to where we are." He pulled his out from the strings holding his jacket and handed it to her to stuff inside the saddlebag.

She complied. If it was a client, she would give them hell for shooting in this area and make sure the guide knew how severely they had violated one of her father's most important rules. *What if it wasn't a hunting party?* she asked herself. Could it be that whoever killed Bear Tanner was after the rest of the family? Glancing at Ethan, she noticed that, like Shaun, he wore his job as part of his skin. She imagined it was so with those in the field of placing their lives in harm's way to protect others.

Changing sides as they turned on the next switchback, he did what he could to use Samson and himself as a shield. He hadn't bothered to pack his Kevlar, as he was briefed that this case was more investigatory in nature, and they had no proof that Bear's death was a murder.

"This is the last switchback. We're about half a mile from the valley floor, and a quarter mile from that is the south gate," she said from beside him.

They rode the rest of the way in silence, then Ethan slowed Samson as the horse raised his head and pricked his ears. When he glanced at Lady, she had done the same. As prey animals, horses had a wider field of vision and certainly better hearing than a human. As the trees thinned and the ground leveled, Samson stopped, then snorted.

"Something isn't right. Samson is trained to have his rider shoot from the saddle. He hears the round being loaded and braces himself for the noise. Both horses will carry a fresh kill. If he's reluctant to continue down the trail, it could only be for two reasons," she spoke quietly as she pulled Lady to a halt.

In a tree that was mostly in the shade, snow still piled around its base, hung the carcass of a bull elk. She reached out to grab Ethan's arm.

"Shit. We've got poachers," she whispered, then lifted her hand to point to the elk.

The tone of her voice and the sight of the body hanging in the tree had him clicking off the safety on his weapon. The hind feet were wrapped with a rope, which was thrown over a stout branch, then tied to a lower limb. There was a dark circle under the elk, mostly on the ground, but some blood had splashed onto the patch of snow, creating a gruesome scene. They moved forward slowly, keeping an eye on the reaction of the horses and the clearing beyond the body in the tree for any movement. Samson wanted no part of the elk, and stepped widely around that which had a particularly bad odor to his sensitive equine nostrils.

"I'm guessing game that is not a fresh kill is one of the things that Samson doesn't like—" Ethan stopped as voices could be heard.

He waved for Carli to move back into the trees. In answer, she drew the rifle from the scabbard on her saddle.

"What the hell are you doing? The last thing needed here is another gun, which often puts people on the defensive," he whispered loudly.

"They're trespassing. That," she gestured toward the elk, "is stolen property, as is anything that they have with them. Game thieves aren't murderers. You can show them your badge and—" she didn't finish as four men, all carrying rifles, came into sight.

Two of them were arguing, so Ethan kicked Samson in the direction of Carli and Lady, took her reins and led them further into the forest. She struggled to grab them back without jerking on Lady's bridle. He released them as soon as they were out of sight of the men approaching from the north.

"Four against two isn't the best odds. And flashing my badge generally doesn't grant me the warmest greeting and would likely scatter them amongst the trees. We wait here, allow them to enter fully into their camp, store their rifles, then we announce ourselves. Clear?"

His eyes bore into hers. The same intensity that she had recognized when he had kissed her was present as he took control of the situation. She was angry at the poachers for their kill and everything they represented. Complying with his request only because he had more experience with criminals than her, she nodded.

They watched through the branches as the four men approached two tents and a pickup truck at the south end of the area that appeared to have been occupied by them for several days. She glanced at Ethan as the angry words became audible.

"What the hell were you thinking? The bull had turned away and the does were moving out of range," Jerry yelled at Bob.

"I had an opportunity to bag one before Paul spooked the herd. Clumsy Jackass!" Bob turned to face the taller man in the blue flannel shirt.

Paul shifted his rifle to a threatening position and stopped in front of Bob. "Jackass? If you weren't so damn greedy you would have waited for a clearer shot."

Dan stepped around Paul and Bob, walked to the truck, and lowered the tailgate. Setting his rifle down, he turned to find Jerry standing a short distance away from the two hunters engaged in the argument.

Jerry had removed his rifle from his shoulder and was beginning to undo the pack from around his waist that held extra shells, a knife, binoculars, and gloves. Holding the rifle by the barrel in one hand, his pack and canteen in the other, he kept his gaze on the two men, each determined that they were right, just in case things were taken a step too far and he would need to intervene.

Ethan scanned the area of the camp. One had left his rifle in the bed of the truck, the one close to the two who continued to trade insults would have to do some juggling with his weapon for him to be a threat. Ethan thought he could catch the other two off guard. Pulling his cell phone from the clip at his waist, he handed it to Carli.

"See if you can get through to Shaun. Let him know the situation and that we could use a little help."

She took the phone, saw that the signal was weak, but dialed Shaun's cell anyway. It rang twice, then beeped in her ear and displayed a 'signal was lost' message. She tried again and this time Shaun's voice could be heard among the fading and crackling of the airwaves that tried to link the phones around hills and across the distance.

"... everything ... is here ... where ... coming back?"

"Shaun, I can barely hear you. Can you hear me?"

"Yes, ...ing back? S ..."

"Listen. We're a quarter mile from the south gate. We've got four poachers, a dead elk, and two nervous horses, we could—" she stopped when three beeps sounded. "Shaun? Shaun, are you still there?" Pulling the phone away from her ear, the display read 'call was dropped', then it switched to 'searching for service'.

"Shit," she mumbled and handed the phone back to Ethan.

"Did he get the message?"

"I hope so."

He turned back toward the camp, where the two men nearly came to blows. "I want you behind me and on my right. Train your rifle on the one by the truck. I'll encourage the other three to join their friend. When we get them together, I'll get off and gather their weapons. No matter what happens, you stay on Lady. If they do something stupid, you get back to the lodge. Understand?"

She held his gaze and chose not to ask for clarification on what 'something stupid' would entail that she would leave him here. Taking a steadying breath, she nodded. Annoyed that the poachers had chosen the Preserve to do their stealing, she was less concerned that they might panic and take the confrontation to another level. She took a moment to recognize that she would not have thought twice about approaching the hunters had she been alone, but that Ethan changed the circumstances. He forced her to consider what the game thieves might do, and the chance that something could happen to him. Not sure how she felt about that, she decided she would look at it later. As a signal that she was ready, she loaded a round in her rifle.

He moved Samson out of the trees, and when Carli was in position, he raised his voice to announce their presence.

"Good afternoon, gentlemen. Agent Brooks, FBI. You're trespassing on private property. We'll discuss the prize you've raised in the tree, later."

Dan, who was crouched down outside his tent removing boxes of ammunition and the kit to clean his rifle, stood and turned. The man was on horseback and had a woman with him. He wondered if she was an agent and how they knew he and the others were here. Looking at the handgun the agent had pointed at his three companions, Dan began to get nervous.

"Why don't you move over there with your friend. It will be easier to have a chat with you all together," Ethan gestured with a tip of his head in the direction he wanted the hunters to move.

Without taking his eyes from the poachers as they began walking towards the tent, he called out to Carli, "Everything alright?"

"Fine, but it will be better once these bastards are behind bars."

"This is your unlucky day, boys. Not only have you been caught with the goods, but by the daughter of the man on whose land you're trespassing."

He paused, holding Samson about fifteen-feet from the group of four, and about twenty-feet from the carcass in the tree. Without any warning, Samson spun around and nearly unseated him. While he tried to gain control of the spooked horse, he glanced up and saw the reason for Samson's prey state of mind. The scent of blood had drawn a bear, his fur still dark since he had yet to begin molting. By June, his undercoat would be shed, leaving the bear a lighter brown or blonde coloring.

"Back him up!" she yelled to Ethan, but what he heard was the four poachers scrambling for their guns, directing each other to get a shot at the grizzly the elk had attracted.

Ethan had just reseated himself when the bear, who looked larger than most bears, not that he had much experience to compare it to, stood up on its hind feet. Perhaps the bear was as surprised at finding humans and horses around what he hoped was a free meal, as the poachers were at discovering the FBI had come to crash their party. Samson, apparently feeling he would not be outdone by the bear, reared up on his back legs. Catching him off guard, Ethan didn't have the experience to lean forward or pull Samson's head to the side in an effort to force the horse to return his front feet to the ground. Sliding back and to the right, his view went from the bear, to the blue, late afternoon sky, to nothing.

Carli, being further away from the hungry bear than Ethan, was able to dismount and hold onto Lady's reins. She watched, helpless to prevent it, as Samson reared, dumped Ethan, then ran towards her and Lady. She tried to grab his reins as he sprinted into the cover of the trees, but Samson moved too quickly, stirrups and saddlebags bouncing, encouraging his hasty escape from the predator.

The bear had landed and sniffed the air, but wasn't convinced that it should abandon the camp. Samson, unwilling to completely leave his stable mate, stopped and turned back toward Lady, his head up, snorting his fear and discontent. Lady nickered in response, dancing and turning at the end of her reins. Carli looked from the bear to the poachers, of whom two had raised their guns, and leveled her own in their direction.

"You've taken all you're going to get from this Preserve. Lower your rifles, or I'll be reporting a shooting instead of trespassing."

The four men eyed her, then the bear, then each other. Deciding they didn't want a hospital visit before their tour of the police station, two lowered their rifles to the ground. The third one, who held his gun, but hadn't aimed it at the bear, received her full attention.

"That goes for you, too. On the ground," she paused as he complied. "Now—" she was interrupted by Lady yanking on the reins and spinning around to stand between her and the hunters.

The bear, deciding that his hunger was more immediate than any threat from the humans, had moved under the elk, then stood up to swipe at the carcass. Carli raised her rifle and shot into the air, which sent Lady skittering backward to the safety of the trees and Samson. Ignoring the burn on her hand, she kept her gaze on the bear as it snarled in displeasure once more in her direction, then turned and ambled off toward the south.

Swinging around to look behind her, Carli loaded another round and aimed at the poachers. "In the tent. Now."

They shuffled in that direction, leaving their weapons on the ground. She glanced at the horses, who were keeping track of the bear's location, then turned her attention to where Ethan landed. Sirens could be heard from the highway.

She moved to Ethan's side and, crouching next to him with her rifle in one hand, glanced once more at the progress of the four men. Deciding they were far enough away from their weapons, and that Shaun would arrive any minute, she turned her gaze to the still features of the FBI agent.

Feeling first for a pulse, she exhaled when the strong flow was felt under his skin. She ran her fingers around Ethan's head, then paused when she encountered wetness. Pulling her hand away, she saw the red that indicated he had sustained a serious injury.

"Shit," she mumbled, wiping her fingers on her jeans.

She placed her hand on Ethan's cheek and called his name. When there was no response, she moved his hair back from his forehead and spoke to him again.

"Ethan, can you hear me? You took a fall and hit your head. You need to wake up. Ethan, open your eyes." Glancing up at the sound of a revved engine, she saw the flashing lights as Sheriff Tanner appeared at the south gate.

Parking in front of the poachers' pickup truck, three doors opened, and Shaun, J.J., and Zach piled out of the vehicle. Shaun had his weapon drawn and trained on the men standing outside the tent. When he saw Carli on the ground, his face changed. She raised her hand that still clutched the rifle to show him she was alright. He spoke to J.J. and Zach, and a moment later both were on their way towards her and Ethan.

Taking her attention back to the man lying beside her, she saw that his eyes were open and staring intently at her face. A smile graced her previously worried countenance for a moment, then she drew her brows together.

"Don't move. You've hit your head hard enough to bleed. Do you know what happened?"

"Are you alright?" Zach asked her as he crouched next to Ethan, opposite of Carli.

"I'm fine. Ethan took a fall," she said, and she looked up at J.J. "The horses are over there," she gestured with her head, not realizing that her hand was still on Ethan's cheek.

J.J. nodded and moved in the direction she had indicated to gather Samson and Lady.

"Vince is on his way. Should we call for an ambulance, too?" Zach asked her.

"No. I'm alright," Ethan answered and sat up, despite Carli's scowl.

His hand went to the pain at the back of his head, but his eyes dropped to where Carli rested her hand on his shoulder. He didn't know if she felt compelled to help him stay upright, or if she was steadying herself.

"I'll ... go help J.J.," Zach mumbled, realizing the fallen rider would be alright, and feeling uncomfortable at witnessing the intimate moment between Carli and Ethan. He stood, looked over his shoulder at Shaun, and saw that the sheriff had all four men seated on the ground, about two feet from each other.

Speaking into the radio held in one hand, the other with his gun on the suspects, Shaun glanced to where Carli was crouched to see Ethan sitting up and Zach walking toward the trees at the edge of the clearing where J.J. was approaching two very distraught horses.

"Bring the van," he spoke to Vince, indicating he should call for an ambulance.

The tents, well-blackened fire ring, and trampled grass told him that these men had been here for about a week. His eyes tracked over the truck to the elk hanging in the tree, and he felt a surge of anger. Trespassing, poaching ... he knew he couldn't add stupidity, but these guys deserved an award. This time of year especially, the scent of food would bring in a bear. Perhaps that was their plan. Bear hide was worth more than elk. He paused in returning his full attention to the game thieves as his eyes landed on the rifle set on the tailgate. Moving to the back of the truck to look closer, he recognized that the gun was the same model, according to the lab reports, that shot the bullet that ended his father's life.

His steady eyes shifted to meet those of one of the men seated on the ground. "You know where you are?" Shaun asked.

Dan sighed. They were caught. There was nothing to be gained by lying. Maybe a judge would be lenient if they offered their cooperation.

"Tanner's Outdoor Adventures, located on the private property called Medicine Bow Wildlife Preserve."

Shaun nodded. So, they would be forthright with the information. It would make the interrogation easier.

"Can you explain how this rifle," he gestured towards the one on the tailgate, "happens to be the same model that killed Bear Tanner five days ago?"

CHAPTER 21

"Wilson Contracting," said the gruff voice in her ear.

"I'm looking for Mr. Wilson."

"Just a minute," he said.

Darla glanced out the window. The tops of the trees swayed slightly in the breeze that seemed as much a part of the landscape as the blue sky and the mountains. Sliding her hand into her pocket, she wished she had thought of it. Poachers. What a delicious distraction. It had gotten Shaun and two of the employees out of the lodge. Sam was busying herself in the kitchen in order to avoid her company, and Ray volunteered to watch the front desk as the others went to aide Carli and the client. This gave her the time and access she needed.

"Wilson."

"Hello, Mr. Wilson, it's Darla Tanner."

"I thought I was going to be hearing from the councilman. You calling to tell me we're pushing up the groundbreaking?"

"Not exactly. You see, Mr. Wilson, I believe the councilman is involved in, well ... a bit of a compromising situation."

"What do you mean?" There was skepticism in the deep voice, whether for the news that Councilman Worthington may not be a trustworthy client, or that he had to deal with a woman, she didn't know.

"Worthington will be announcing his candidacy soon. That will feed the media and they'll want to investigate every aspect of his life. And ... well, everyone has a skeleton or two, Mr. Wilson. Therefore, I'm suggesting that in order to keep this project on our timeline, and for you to get paid, I would advise you to accept me as the lead contact in this endeavor."

She glanced around the room, the one Carli usually stayed in when she visited Bear. There was nothing unusual, just the requisite luggage and cases containing her equipment. The laptop on the desk against the wall didn't offer anything interesting since the whole system was password protected and she didn't have much technology experience. The clothes hanging in the closet and folded in the dresser were worn, drab, and certainly not in fashion. Her attention was drawn back to the change in plans she had instigated by the voice on the phone.

"Look. I'll take direction from whoever signs the checks. Are we still scheduled for surveying in two weeks?"

"Yes. I'll call and give you an update by the middle of next week. And, Mr. Wilson, since the councilman will be busy with his campaign, let's keep this conversation between us. Alright?"

"Sure," Wilson agreed, then hung up.

She smiled. It felt good to take control. By situating herself as the one in charge, Ted will have to defer to her. She closed the door quietly behind her, excited for her impending importance in Councilman Worthington's life.

«« — »»

Jim pulled his truck into the driveway in front of the house he had bought as a newlywed, when the future with his young wife and the construction business in this part of Wyoming, was promising. The roof over the front porch sagged, the support beams were in need of paint, the bushes that his wife had planted and tended, and that Alyssa had tried to salvage, were dried twigs. In the past, they would have had green leaves and budding flowers by this time of the year, but with the diminished bank account, he had to cut back on everything, which included pouring water into the ground for something that gave nothing in return. Alyssa tried to explain that it would make the front of the house more appealing, and he had argued that no one cared. The tires on the utility trailer that housed the tools of his once-prosperous trade, were flat from disuse. He had tried to sell off what he could, then gave up as there were few buyers in Centennial, since the residents had already accumulated what they needed.

Alyssa's Honda was parked by the side of the house. She had saved up the money and was given a good deal by the only car lot in town. It allowed her to get to school without depending on the bus, or him waking up in time to get her there. It also gave her the independence to arrive at Tanner's whenever they needed her, and over the past months, that demand had grown. She was still home often enough to do her chores, and the increase in her paycheck was welcome.

He climbed out of the truck and up the two steps of the porch. Through the screen, as the front door was propped open, he could smell what Alyssa made for dinner. She had a way with food and seemed to be able to create something edible, and a lot of it, with few ingredients. He thought that sometimes she pilfered from the lodge, but never questioned her about it.

Allowing the screen to slam behind him in order to warn her he was home, he tossed his keys in the dish on the table next to the door, and wandered into the kitchen. His boots crunched on the cracked linoleum, but Alyssa was involved in removing a roasting pan from the oven, so didn't turn around right away. She took after her mother with her youthful beauty and place on the honor roll. Neither he nor Carol had a college education, and he didn't think that most people in Centennial had graduated with anything besides a high school diploma, if that. He hadn't saved money for any type of school fund for his daughter, and now that she would be graduating in a couple months, he wondered what her plans were. A scholarship was an option, but what would he do without her here?

He cleared his throat, and Alyssa spun around to face him.

"Dinner smells good," he said as a greeting.

She gave her heart a moment to return to its normal rhythm, and then the thought entered her mind that it usually beat a little faster when her father was around.

"Roasted chicken, potatoes, and broccoli. There's chocolate cake for dessert."

He pulled out a chair at the kitchen table and sat, his eyes watching as Alyssa moved around the kitchen, then set a plate and silverware on the faded placemat in front of him.

"You're graduating from Rock River High School soon," he began.

"Uh-huh," she answered.

"What are your plans after you're through with school? Do you think you'll find a job in Centennial or Laramie?"

She scooped potatoes into a serving bowl. "No one knows what will happen at the lodge. We're all hoping that Shaun, Sam, and Carli will keep the business open. There is a steady stream of clients, and the Preserve has built up a reputation." She placed the bowl and the platter of chicken in the middle of the table.

"What if they decide to sell the place?"

She shrugged, set the broccoli next to the plate of chicken, then sat across from her father.

He spooned up some potatoes and stabbed a piece of chicken. "You don't want to go to UW?" he raised his brows.

Again she shrugged. "We don't have the money."

He reached out towards the saltshaker and saw Alyssa flinch. It was important to him that she be a well-behaved child, and therefore he employed strict discipline. Deciding that his daughter had no immediate plans for the future, and mentioned that things would be kept as they were, the rest of the meal was consumed in silence.

When he was done, he rose from the table and retrieved a beer from the refrigerator, then moved to the living room where he reclined back on the couch and turned on the TV.

She cleaned up the kitchen, then took another beer from the fridge. Glancing around to ensure all was in order, to preclude her father from getting upset, she flicked off the light. Walking through the living room, she placed the bottle of beer on the end table by her father's right hand and continued down the hall to her bedroom.

Once inside, with the door closed, she sighed in relief. He was drunk, as he was every night, but he didn't start an argument or find fault with the cleanliness of the house today. Sitting heavily on her bed, she pulled her borrowed laptop from her backpack. As she waited for the system to boot up, she glanced at the door to ensure her father was still in the living room, and withdrew the pamphlet she had taken from the counselor's office containing information on the University of Wyoming. The front showed college students with broad smiles, carrying books and walking across the campus, green grass beneath their feet and blue sky above. The buildings were faded brick, the words emblazoned across the top read, "Invest in Your Future". She didn't open it, but turned it over to view the list of colleges and the Bachelor's degrees that the University awarded.

She had hoped to keep her job at the lodge, and didn't have plans to attend college. The counselor had encouraged her to complete the scholarship and grant applications, but she knew from a lifetime of experience that her expectations often led to disappointments. It was better to not plan for a future away from Centennial, as the odds were it wouldn't happen.

The laptop beeped, and she stuffed the brochure into her backpack. Sighing, she opened the file that contained her essay, but her thoughts were drawn to Zach. She met him when he came to work at the lodge almost two years ago. They had formed a friendship, and from that blossomed an innocent, delicate love for each other. She had shared her feelings with him, and Zach admitted his for her. He had taken her on dates, offered to help her with her homework, and was a friend, even though she didn't realize how desperately she needed one. He was kind, liked to take care of her, and was genuinely concerned for her welfare. Just the sight of his tall frame and wide smile on his handsome face had her heart fluttering in her chest. If she left, what would become of their relationship? Setting those thoughts aside, she concentrated on finishing her paper for Senior English.

《《—》》

J.J., knowing the personalities of the animals under his care, approached Lady first. Talking soothingly, he reached out his hand. She stretched her nose forward to verify that he was the one who kept her safe in the barn and her feed bin full. Relaxing visibly, she didn't shy away as he took her reins. Continuing to speak softly and stroking her neck, he directed his next words to Zach as the young cowboy walked up to Lady.

"Samson will follow his favorite barn mate, and then you'll be able to pick up his reins," J.J. instructed.

Leading Lady out of the trees and back towards Ethan and Carli, he heard, and sensed, more than saw, Samson following and Zach stepping next to the big gelding and collecting the leather straps as they dragged the ground. J.J. slowed, careful of where he led the horses, guessing Carli would need some more time with Ethan, if only to get him to his feet.

Carli's concern was easy to read. The crease between her brows was back, and to keep the moment from becoming too intimate, he broke eye contact, and from his seat on the pine needles he looked to the right and observed Shaun and the poachers. It appeared the sheriff had things under control. To his left, J.J. and Zach had both horses and were making their way to where he and Carli remained on the ground.

"Much to Samson's displeasure, it appears the bears are out of hibernation," Ethan said.

Carli laughed, dispersing her worry. "So you remember our previous conversation and what landed you here."

Ethan smiled, more at the freeness of her laughter than the situation. "Are you alright?" he inquired.

"Of course. But I think your head needs to be looked at. I'm sure Shaun has called for an ambulance."

"Give me a hand?" he asked, and extended his.

194

She was about to argue, but the expression on Ethan's face warned her to not protest his health. Rising from her crouched position, her rifle still in one hand, she extended her other one, which was enveloped in Ethan's much larger, and stronger, palm. With smooth, graceful ease, he rose to his feet. Standing toe-to-toe with her, inches taller, it took him a moment to gain his balance. He blamed it on the bump at the back of his head. As he swayed slightly, he noticed the concern reenter her expression.

J.J. and Zach stopped a few feet away with the horses.

"Neither of them seems to have retained any ill effects from the ... what happened?" J.J. questioned, his glance moving from Carli to Ethan.

She gestured with her head in the direction of the elk still in the tree. "Carcass drew a bear."

J.J. shook his head. "Poor Samson. He's had a rough day. Confronted by one of his demons. Scared boy," he added sympathetically, then reached out a hand to pat the sorrel's neck.

"Stan is here," she announced as an ambulance pulled up behind Shaun's vehicle. "Let's have him check your skull," she spoke to Ethan. To Zach she said, "Cut down the elk. We can't leave it here, and there's no way in hell we're letting those bastards have possession."

Zach handed Samson's reins to J.J. and made his way to the carcass in the tree.

"I'll keep the horses from the commotion. Let me know if you want to take them back or catch a ride with Shaun or Stan. I can ride Samson and pony Lady," J.J. suggested.

"Thanks," she said as she began walking with Ethan toward the game thieves, Shaun, and the emergency vehicle beyond.

"Hi, Stan. This is Ethan. Samson spooked and Ethan took a tumble. Knocked his head pretty good on the ground." She kept the commentary running as she led Ethan to the rear of the ambulance, where the doors were open so he could sit on the bumper.

Stan busied himself with pulling on blue latex gloves, then parting Ethan's hair to view the wound. A wad of white gauze appeared and was pressed to the back of the patient's head. Before he could begin the requisite questions to determine the mental status of the client, Ethan told him what he needed to know.

"Name's Ethan Brooks. Today is March 30, 2013. I was riding Samson when we came across a poacher's camp. The scent of the game brought in the bear. I was unprepared for Samson's reaction and wound up on the ground. There is no blurred vision, no nausea. Some dizziness upon standing."

Stan nodded. "You've done this before. Did you lose consciousness?"

Ethan looked at Carli, who nodded her head.

"The emergency room in Laramie can check for fractures or brain swelling or bleeding, and confirm a concussion. I have to take you in."

Ethan wondered how it would look on his report that a hospital visit followed a fall from a horse, instead of the usual gunshot or knife wounds. He eyed Carli, then Stan, then shifted his attention to Shaun.

"Don't suppose you would let me go on my own recognizance?"

Stan shook his head. "With a head injury, if something happens to you, I lose my job. And I love my job."

"Give me a minute?" Ethan asked Stan.

Stan looked at Carli who nodded slightly. He took Ethan's hand and placed it on the gauze used to staunch the flow of blood from the wound.

Ethan made his way to Shaun, who stood at the back of the pickup truck. Carli followed.

"We heard that Bear Tanner was shot, but none of us are involved," one of the men on the ground explained.

"You alright?" Shaun asked as Ethan stepped up next to him.

Ethan's gaze traveled from the four men on the ground, to the gun on the tailgate, to Shaun.

"Need any help?" he countered.

"Vince will be here—" he stopped as his deputy parked next to his own vehicle. "*Is* here, so we'll bag the evidence and take these guys to the office. You want to stop in after your visit to Laramie, I wouldn't turn away another set of eyes and ears."

Shaun's gaze was steady, and Ethan recognized grudging respect and cooperation, so he nodded, then turned to Carli.

"Are you staying here?" he asked her.

Her eyes were on the gun that Dan set on the tailgate. "Shaun—" she started.

"I know. I'll send it to Cheyenne and they can test it, see if it's a match." He waited for her to argue, but when she remained mute, he added, "Go with Ethan. I'll let you know how things turn out. So far, they're cooperative."

She nodded. Turning in the direction of where J.J. continued to stand with the horses, she waved, then pointed to Stan's van. Taking a moment to watch as J.J. mounted Samson and led Lady in the direction of the lodge, she then shifted her attention to Ethan.

He took her hand in his free one, and led her back to the ambulance. Stan would insist he ride in the back, and he would convince the EMT to allow Carli to keep him company. He had more questions for her, and it would be some time before they were alone again.

Stan secured a bandage to Ethan's head, then closed them in the back and began the drive to Laramie. It would take an hour to arrive at the hospital, and at least that long before Shaun could return to his office with the poachers. He glanced at the rifle that Carli still held in her hand, then at the one that tightly gripped the rail of his gurney.

"Tell me what has you so troubled about the situation with the poachers."

CHAPTER 22

Carli looked at her watch, then calculated the possibility of catching Doc Miller at his home office.

"Can I use your phone?" she asked.

Ethan removed it from his waist and handed it to her. "Care to share?"

She began dialing. "If Doc Miller is available, it will save time in driving to Laramie and waiting in the ER."

She paused, then glanced out the side and back windows to gauge their location. They were almost at the highway that led to Centennial.

"Doc Miller? Carli Tanner." She smiled and held Ethan's gaze. "I'm fine, but I have a ... client who took a tumble from Samson. We're with Stan now, but if you could see him, it would save us a lot of time." She paused again, then smiled wider. "Thanks, Doc. We'll be there in about ten minutes."

She ended the call, then leaned over to reach through the window separating the back from the front of the ambulance and tapped Stan on the shoulder.

"Doc M is available and waiting for us."

"We're supposed to go to the ER—" he began.

"The Doc can diagnose a concussion, too. Even X-ray Ethan's head if he decides it's necessary. Please, Stan," she implored.

He sighed heavily. She took that as agreement and maneuvered herself back to sitting by Ethan.

"The gun on the tailgate is the same kind that's missing from the safe in the basement," she told him, answering his earlier question.

"Do you think they found it at the Ridge?" he asked, trying, without much success, to get the pieces to fit.

"I don't know. Maybe Shaun was able to get an answer from the clients."

"Could there have been a break-in at the lodge?"

"No," she shook her head. "That's the first thing Shaun would have told me when he picked me up at the airport."

The ambulance turned sharply to the left, then stopped. A moment later Stan opened the back door and found Ethan sitting at the end of the gurney. Deciding that they had already bent enough of the rules, he kept the clipboard in one hand and offered the other to Ethan as he stepped down to the parking lot outside Doc Miller's office. Before Carli could lead the patient a step further, Stan shoved the clipboard under Ethan's nose.

Ethan raised a brow, then took the board and pen, signed the bottom of the top form. Handing it back, he said, "Thanks for the ride, Stan."

"Anytime."

Carli, rifle in one hand, reached back into the ambulance and snagged Ethan's pack from the floor. Sliding it over her shoulder, she extended her hand to take his elbow, and led him toward the white-haired gentleman standing in the open doorway of his medical practice.

"Thanks, Stan!" she called over her shoulder as the rear doors of the ambulance slammed closed.

"Doc Miller," she began, her attention on the town's only doctor.

"Carli, glad to see you're healthy. And this is—" he left the question implied.

"Ethan Brooks. Ethan, Doc Miller," she introduced.

Doc Miller peered through his glasses at the bandages on the side and back of Ethan's head, concern marring his normally jovial features.

"Take Mr. Brooks to the first exam room. I'll be there in a moment."

He stepped aside and allowed them to enter his office as he took the clipboard from Stan. Scanning the notes the EMT made concerning Ethan, his eyebrows raised at the notation of the loss of consciousness and brief dizziness upon standing. He scrawled his signature on that page, and the next one, taking responsibility for the patient. Nodding to Stan, he entered his office to find Ethan seated on the padded exam table and Carli hovering, her rifle still in her hand.

"So," Doc Miller began, "how is it that you ended up involuntarily removed from Samson's back?"

"His extreme dislike of bears," Ethan answered.

Shifting his gaze to Carli, Doc Miller suggested, "You can set the rifle there, in the corner. Haven't been threatened by one since my marriage to Ellen."

She chuckled, then placed the gun in the corner. Turning to see Ethan's questioning gaze, she said, "Doc's second wife, Ellen, used some ... encouragement to get him to commit."

Ethan sat quietly while the physician checked his temperature through his ear and blood pressure with a cuff around his arm.

"Lost my first wife to cancer. Ellen had worked in the office here, and one thing led to another. We were together for almost three years before she became ... adamant about getting married. Best decision I ever made."

Ethan gave the doctor a half-smile at the visual of the man being led to the altar by a rifle. Wincing as the bandage was removed, he was then told to hold a clean piece of gauze against the wound that continued to seep.

"Scalp wounds are copious bleeders," Doc Miller said conversationally. "Nausea? More dizziness? Blurred vision?"

Ethan answered in the negative to each of Doc's questions.

"Might need a stitch or two to close the head," Doc Miller continued.

When he shined the penlight into Ethan's right eye, then his left, then his right again, he made a sound of confirmation.

Turning the light off and standing upright, he no longer had the friendly smile that had graced his face.

"I assume when you landed, it was on your back?" Doc asked.

"I'm not sure. One minute I was looking at the bear, then the sky." Ethan turned to Carli, realizing his confusion.

"When Samson reared, Ethan slid back and to the right. I didn't see him do anything to break his fall."

Doc Miller nodded, then moved to where he could palpate Ethan's back. Besides dust and a few pine needles that clung to his shirt, the patient showed no discomfort. If he felt any, the Doc judged Ethan wouldn't admit it.

"You walked in here fine, but I'm guessing that by tomorrow morning you'll be quite sore. Only take acetaminophen, as you have earned yourself a concussion, and other pain relievers tend to increase bleeding. Not as severe as I would have predicted given the scalp laceration, which will need stitches. Keep it dry for a few days. If you develop any of the symptoms I've asked about, head to Laramie."

He carried on his monologue as he gathered the instruments needed to stitch Ethan's wound. At the mention of additional signs that the concussion might worsen, he made eye contact with Carli over Ethan's head. It was imperative that she understand the possible severity of the injury.

"I'll make sure he takes it easy, Doc," she said.

Light conversation was made as Doc Miller numbed the area around the wound, shaved away a little of his patient's hair, and installed four stitches to close the gap in the scalp. He asked after Carli's siblings and expressed condolences for Bear's death. She shared that the funeral was set for Tuesday and that the details were in the write up in the Wyoming newspaper. He inquired after her most recent trip abroad, and if she had heard anything regarding the gallery in New York.

"Gallery?" Ethan asked, his first words since the doctor began to stitch up his head.

"You may not know, Mr. Brooks, but Carli is a very talented photographer. She's been working with a gallery to have some of her pictures at a showing."

"Really, it's the gallery manager who is trying to convince the owner that my pictures are of more than topless natives and zoo animals, which I believe is a direct quote," she clarified, then shifted her weight to cock the other hip as Ethan offered her a half-smile at her description.

"That would be exciting. I understand that it often takes just one show, and an artist can break into the business, become a household name overnight."

She shrugged. "Maybe. If I was interested in becoming a household name. Those in journalism already know who I am. Allows for movement in the industry."

"I thought you loved your job," Ethan said.

"I do. My notoriety ensures that Scott gets me whatever I want. Which, fortunately for him, isn't much," she paused and raised a brow. "Have you thought about publishing any of your sketches or talking to a gallery in Baltimore?"

Ethan snorted and shook his head. "That's part of my work. I highly doubt that others would be interested in," he hesitated, rolling his eyes up and to the side as if to glance at Doc Miller, who was out of his line of sight, "everyday people."

"I find the common citizen rather fascinating myself," Doc Miller interjected. "There are more people with innate ability in this world than those who become recognized for their talents. If you have one, show it off."

She smiled. "Ellen's been at work in the studio?"

"Woman creates faster than she can find a home for what comes out of the kiln or off the easel," he mumbled.

"Maybe she's ready for another showing in L.A.," she suggested, to which Doc Miller expressed an expletive under his breath.

"Sounds like you have to pick your battles," Ethan said with his gaze on Carli. "You either make room for what is created or you go through the hassle of pushing it away."

"We certainly have the room, and Ellen always convinces me it's worth the work of a show to share it with others," he answered, unaware of Ethan's coded communication.

Carli added a second meaning of her own embedded in her comment, "Ellen started out with drawings of how she wanted the remodeling of the house to look, and the first couple of throws on her wheel were more about creating utilitarian pieces than ones for sale. Now, after a few shows in California, she has quite a following."

Before Ethan could respond, Doc Miller announced that he was done. With strict instructions, and completed insurance forms, he sent them on their way.

Stepping down to the parking lot outside the building, Ethan looked to the right, then to Carli who stood on his left.

"Any ideas for getting back to the lodge?" he asked.

"Are you up for a short walk?" she countered.

"Sure."

She set off to the left, Ethan falling into step next to her, as she began a recitation of the history of Centennial. They made a right on the next street, then walked down a couple of blocks to the sheriff's office. Shaun's vehicle wasn't there, but a car with a sheriff's emblem on the side was parked in front. He followed her up the steps and into the office. Esther wasn't in, but a young deputy sat at the desk the receptionist had occupied when Ethan came to the office a few days ago.

"Hi, Denny," she greeted the deputy warmly. "How was your sister's wedding?"

"Hey, Carli. It was great. But, are you alright? I got the call that Shaun was bringing in poachers from the Preserve and that you had stumbled across their camp. What happened?"

Denny was twenty, just out of the Law Enforcement Academy in Douglas, with short enough hair to match his less-than-average height. Ethan watched the play between the young deputy and Carli with amused interest. Denny stood and rested his hand on his holster like an Old West gunslinger. Carli played her part as a beautiful woman plying her wiles to get what she desired, which in this case was a ride back to the lodge.

She tossed her hair over one shoulder, then raised the rifle she held in her hand. "Well, I had to use this, and Ethan, he's one of our clients, took a tumble from Samson when the bear got stubborn about leaving."

Ethan's gaze swiveled back to Denny, and as predicted, the deputy's eyes grew round at the prospect of facing off with a bear. He raised a brow at Carli's exaggerated excitement.

"I'll tell you the details if you give us a lift back to the lodge," she offered.

"I can't. Shaun wants me here to help book the poachers," Denny declined with a shake of his head.

"We were there. It'll take Vince and Shaun a few hours to do all their police work. Stan took us to Doc Miller's. We left the scene less than two hours ago. It'll only take fifteen minutes to run us up to the lodge. I promise, you'll be back here long before Shaun and Vince."

Just when it looked like Denny would hold his ground, she shifted her rifle to rest it on her left thigh, while she placed her right hand on her hip, drawing her elbow back behind her, effectively thrusting her breasts against her buttoned-down shirt, which was open far enough to show off her cleavage. It was obvious to Ethan what she was doing, and it was all he could do to not laugh out loud at the wide-eyed expression of Deputy Denny.

"Please, Denny?" she pleaded, leaning a little further forward.

Ethan thought that if the counter wasn't there holding Denny up, the young man would have fallen face first into Carli's shirt.

"Uh ... alright, Carli. We'll make it quick," Denny said, and followed Ethan and Carli out the office door, locking it behind him.

The older, more experienced FBI agent guessed driving wasn't the only thing Denny would be quick at. Carli, placing herself to take the front passenger seat, and the deputy driving the government-issued sedan, meant Ethan was relegated to the back seat, behind the Plexiglas separating the driver from the criminal that would normally occupy that space.

Before they had reached the end of the block, Carli made good on her promise. With details that he would have deemed irrelevant, and enough enthusiasm to inspire a small army, she retold the tale of their day. He did become interested in the events between his head connecting with the ground, and then opening his eyes to find Carli leaning over him. Missing the shot she fired into the air to scare the bear and the arrival of Shaun to take over watching the poachers, he was grateful that the trespassers were cooperative. Though he would like to think that Carli needed him for protection, he realized that she was quite capable of taking care of herself, at least when faced with a bear. She reached the anticlimactic conclusion of his stitches as they entered the parking lot in front of the lodge.

"I'm glad you're alright," Denny said, putting the car in PARK, but leaving the engine running.

"Thanks, Denny, and thanks for the ride," she said, placing her hand on his forearm.

Shaking his head, Ethan reminded Denny that he was there and would need the back door unlocked so he could get out. Walking around the front of the vehicle, he met Carli at the base of the steps by the front door. Glancing through the windshield, he recognized the expression of a love-struck youth.

"Effective, if a little cruel," he said to Carli.

"Cruel? He would have copped a feel if you weren't there."

"You're welcome."

"Well, I think we're even. He got an eyeful, and an earful, and we got a ride."

She began climbing the steps and Ethan's gaze was immediately drawn to the back pockets of her jeans. He couldn't blame Denny for the deputy's infatuation. Moving to block Denny's view of Carli's retreating back, he followed her inside the lodge. He watched a moment as Denny drove away, then shut the door.

"Carli, are you alright?" Ray asked as he came from behind the counter.

"I'm fine. Our client, however, has a slight injury. A few stitches in his head as a result from Samson rearing and dumping him."

Ray looked past Carli to Ethan. The man didn't seem to be too affected by his fall. Shifting his attention back to Carli, he gestured toward her rifle.

"You have to use that?"

"Fired a shot into the air to scare the bear. Shaun showed up before I had to use it on the poachers," she paused, her brows drew together in thought. "Do you know anything about them?"

Ray nodded his head. "We've seen evidence the past few years. They didn't stay in the same place. Bear knew some of his inventory was missing. They've been coming in the spring, but always gone by the time we had found their camp."

"Do you know what was taken?" Ethan asked, wondering why Bear hadn't mentioned this to his children, or at least to Shaun.

"Around a dozen elk, half-dozen deer, they got a cat one year, a young bear, not sure on the number of antelope, javelina, or the other species Bear stocks on the Preserve." Ray tipped his hat slightly back on his head.

"You'll have to know accurate numbers in order to press charges or ask for restitution," Ethan advised.

With hands out in supplication, Ray responded, "That's not my territory. And now that Bear is gone, it will be the responsibility of whoever inherits Tanner's Outdoor Adventures."

"And that would be me," said the voice of a platinum blonde in her mid-fifties, who looked years younger.

"Son of a bitch. Just when I thought today couldn't be any more difficult, I arrive home to find it infested with a sewer rat."

Carli's words were more animated for their tone than the false excitement she used to feed the story to Denny. Almost without thinking, she brought up the rifle and leveled the barrel at Darla.

Ethan stepped up behind her, and with a hand under the stock, continued the movement, the barrel finally pointing up at the ceiling. With a little more force, he removed the weapon from her grip. Ray hadn't moved, except to sigh in exasperation. The blonde woman pretended to be offended.

"Honestly, Carli, is that any way to greet your mother?"

Carli snorted at the woman's question. "Ethan, Darla Tanner, *ex*-wife of my father's."

In a mind that thrived on solving puzzles and deciphering human motives for behavior, the attractive woman standing across from him, paired with her name, had the electrical currents in his brain firing at the connection. By her own admission, Darla Tanner had just placed herself at the top of his list of suspects.

CHAPTER 23

Not everything needed to be bagged and tagged as evidence. Dan, Paul, Jerry, and Bob were forthcoming with answers and information. As Shaun questioned the men, Vince catalogued nearly everything in their camp, including their truck. Zach was given permission to use one of the tarps in the bed of the truck to wrap the elk. After pictures were taken, the ground that had absorbed the blood that drained from the animal was doused with what remained in the five-gallon water containers the poachers had brought with them in the hopes that the diluted smell would deter other scavengers. He called the lodge and requested that Zach and the elk be picked up, since both county vehicles would be crowded with those that were placed under arrest, and their firearms.

"I purchased it at a gun show in Denver. I have the permit and the sales receipt in the glove box," Dan informed Shaun.

"Where were you on Monday?" Shaun asked.

"Here," Dan answered.

"Were you scouting? Just camping? I fail to believe that you four have been here for a week and that's all you've gotten," he gestured over his shoulder where the elk had been hung in the tree.

Dan exchanged a look with his three friends. Before he could contrive a lie of omission, Paul spoke from his seat on the ground.

"We got a couple deer. Took them to a meat processor in Laramie."

Shaun thought a moment, then nodded. "I'll be paying Billy at Buckshot a visit."

"How do you know that's the place?" Jerry questioned.

"Because Billy is always out to make a fast buck, no pun intended. He's been warned about taking game without proof of a tag, or when it's not in season," he paused and looked at the four men who had been living in the Wyoming wilderness for a week. "This isn't the first year you've been here, and Billy has been a help from the start," he stated, then watched as none of the game thieves met his gaze.

Vince handed him the permits and necessary paperwork for each of the guns in the camp. They were all legal, even the one Dan carried.

"So, Monday? Your location?" Shaun asked again.

Jerry answered, "We were at the end of the canyon, on the east slope. We had set out early and were scouting for what was available. Just before we stopped for lunch, there was a shot from behind us," he gestured towards Miner's Paradise. "It was particularly windy that day, carrying the rifle report all the way up the canyon."

"I think we saw where Bear Tanner, the owner of this Preserve, was shot. We had heard the announcement on the radio when Dan checked the weather report two nights ago. Yesterday, up on Wolf's Ridge, we saw an unusual sight and guessed at what we had found." Paul was hoping for confirmation, but Shaun wasn't discussing the details of his father's death with these men, criminals, who stole and trespassed.

When the sheriff remained mute, Bob picked up the story. "Like Jerry said, we didn't see any game on Monday, unless you count the squirrels."

"Having each other as an alibi won't necessarily stand up in court." He handed the papers back to Vince, then withdrew his handcuffs. "I have three more pair if you think I'll need to use them," he said, holding each man's gaze as they shook their head.

"Vince, take these two," he gestured toward Dan and Paul, "and I'll take the other—" he was prevented from finishing by the arrival of one of the outfitter's business trucks.

Ray shook his head at the camp the poachers had established. It couldn't be seen from the highway or the road that entered through the south gate. They had picked a prime spot, and he guessed these were the same ones who had stolen from the Preserve in previous years. His quick assessment assured him that Shaun and Vince had the situation under control. To his left, Zach waved his arms indicating the location of the elk. He maneuvered in front of the sheriff's vehicles, then backed up to where Zach directed.

Once the four men were secured in the rear seats of the sedan that Vince drove, and Shaun's SUV, the weapons stored in the trunk of the sedan, Shaun approached Ray and Zach. The two of them struggled to place the elk in the bed of the work truck, so Shaun helped by lifting one side of the tarp that held the carcass. A few grunts and minutes later, and with the tailgate shut, Ray and Zach climbed into the cab and headed for the lodge.

The poachers' vehicle and their remaining gear would be left here. Denny and Vince would return to catalogue everything else, break camp, and impound the truck. Shaun started down the road toward the south gate, where Ray and Zach waited for the sheriff's vehicles to pass so they could secure the perimeter of the Preserve. On Highway 130 headed towards town, he began to review the scene of their camp, the answers they gave to his questions, and his gut feeling that the poachers were telling the truth about not firing their weapons while scouting on Monday. He realized he was no closer to solving the case.

The guns were a confusing puzzle piece. If it wasn't an accidental shooting, and these men were innocent of murder, who else would wish Bear Tanner harm? Glancing at the clock on the dash, he guessed Ethan and Carli were still in Laramie, and with him filing the paperwork on the game thieves, that left Sam alone with Darla at the lodge. Pulling up in front of the office, he sighed. A day that started off poorly with Ethan's inquiry regarding a missing weapon, ended with more questions and uncertainty.

«« —»»

"Six-thirty. Dinner's ready," Sam's voice called from the doorway of the lobby.

Carli heard, rather than saw, the clients abandon their chess game and books and conversation as they filed into the dining room. For the last fifteen minutes she and Darla had engaged in a heated discussion as to Darla's purpose for showing up at the lodge. Ray had left to retrieve Zach and the elk, and Ethan had encouraged them down the hall behind the stairs to reduce disturbing the clients. He placed Carli's rifle in the rack that hung on the wall opposite the stairs. The sun had set and twilight was quickly fading, leaving them in shadows.

Carli crossed her arms under her chest. "You and Dad divorced. There is nothing here for you. Abandoning your husband and three young children typically ensures you won't be mentioned in the will. There is no reason he would have left anything to you."

"Everything reverts back to the surviving spouse," Darla spoke, trying, and failing, to keep the smugness from her voice.

"But you're divorced. Have been for—"

"I never signed the papers. Bear had them drawn up, but without my agreement, well, we're still married according to Albany County and the State of Wyoming."

Carli opened and closed her mouth, unsure what to say in response to Darla's claim. She knew her father well, and couldn't believe that he would not pursue whatever means he had to in order to be free from this woman.

"Verifying the records can be done, but it may take a while to file the request and search the archives. Perhaps Sam would like some help with serving the clients?" Ethan spoke quietly into the lull, deciding this was the place to end their argument.

212

When she didn't move right away, he took her hand and led her down the hallway and across the lobby. He guessed she was still too stunned by Darla's proclamation to realize he held her hand. As they approached the dining room, full of clients and Sam delivering platters and bowls of food, Carli tugged on her hand, and he released it.

"Dad would have had a copy of every correspondence with Darla," she whispered, leaning close to him so Darla, who followed behind, couldn't overhear.

Giving her a half-smile, he said, "Then it's fortunate that you're familiar with your father's filing system."

Sam looked up as they entered, worry disappearing as the two who called Shaun to duty seemed to be unharmed. "Carli, Ethan. I didn't know you had returned. Are you alright?"

"Of course. Ethan has a bump on the head, Shaun arrested the poachers. The worst of it was arriving here to find this," Carli jerked her thumb over her shoulder at Darla, who stepped around her and took a seat at the table.

Sam pasted on a smile and glanced at the clients, then back at Carli with a meaningful stare. "Yes, well, it's a good thing we have an extra chair at the table. Carli, give me a hand in the kitchen?" Sam gestured with her head towards the other room.

Carli's gaze met Ethan's, then she followed her sister through the swinging door. Ethan took advantage of the other open seats at the table and placed himself across from Darla. His fingers itched to sketch her and the nuances of her expressions he had already observed and classified during her initial conversation with Carli. He would bet that each of Bear's children shared a similar opinion of Darla Tanner, and he understood their reasons. In nearly every society, if a parent were to leave, it was more common for the father, but when the mother abandons the family the scars were deep and often poorly healed. Smiling benignly at Darla, he took his turn as the plates and bowls were passed his way.

"You're sure you and Ethan are alright?" Sam worriedly wiped her hands on her apron.

"We're fine. Stan gave us a ride to Doc Miller's, then I persuaded Denny to bring us back here. When did she arrive? And I know you didn't invite her."

"I wouldn't even know how to reach her, and there is no reason for her to be here."

Carli snorted. "Apparently, she believes that her and Dad were never divorced. She thinks she'll get it all."

Sam's eyebrows met her bangs in the middle of her forehead. "Well, at least she isn't staying here. She has a room in Laramie."

"Ethan said we would be able to verify with Albany County what, if any, paperwork was filed. We also need to search the storage area and Dad's office. He'll have a copy of any papers regarding Darla, and I'm sure a copy of his will. Have you called Dad's attorney?"

Sam nodded.

"Then we get through the meal—I promise to behave," Carli held up her hand to stall any of Sam's protests, "and Ethan and I will see what we can find."

"It's going to be a busy night. Shaun at the office, J.J. on his way back with the horses, Zach, and Ray out at their camp … I hope we survive the next three days with Darla. You know she'll be around," Sam held Carli's gaze.

"Yes, she will and I'll be damned if she'll stay a moment longer than necessary or gets a single antler from Dad."

Sam smiled. They all would agree on that.

«« — »»

Ray drove slowly down the rutted road, made worse each year by the freezing winters and the runoff in spring. It was another half-mile to the highway that they would take to the main entrance of the Preserve. A full-service experience, Bear had installed a building behind the lodge, away from the barn, cabins, and parking lot, for the specific purpose of cleaning game. Large sinks, slabs of steel tables, drains in the floor, and a thermostat set usually at forty-five degrees, it was called 'the corner' since 'coroner' was too close to the human equivalent. Though Zach had remained quiet about what he had seen and heard from Shaun and the poachers, Ray wasn't surprised when the young guide began asking questions as soon as they made the asphalt.

"Did you know about the illegal hunters?" Zach asked, keeping his gaze out the windshield.

"Over the last few years, Bear and I had discussed it. He had noticed missing game that was unaccounted for. About three years ago we had stumbled upon the remains of their camp while making repairs to the far east fence."

"Why didn't you tell Shaun?"

Ray was quiet a moment, then glanced at Zach. The boy's mother had done a stellar job in raising a moral, socially-conscious child. Of course Zach would want the authorities notified. But Bear was from a different generation, and raised with a different set of rules.

"Bear didn't see any reason to bother the sheriff. Trespassers could be easily dealt with. He just never caught up to them."

It was Zach's turn to look at Ray's profile. He knew Ray and Bear had started the business. He had heard them argue recently, not the content, just the raised voices. Though the employees had speculated amongst themselves, none had asked Ray what would happen to the lodge with Bear gone.

"Will you press charges? Will you keep the lodge open?"

"If Shaun needs my input, but because he and Carli caught the thieves in the act, I hardly think I could be of much help," Ray paused as he turned into the drive. Weighing the questions Zach would ask, and knowing he couldn't, or wouldn't, respond to all of them, he gave the second answer. "The future of the lodge won't be up to me, Zach. Bear bought me out years ago. Part of the discussion for the sale was that he would leave it all to the kids." Ray drove past the lodge and parked beside the corner. He shut off the engine, then turned to the young guide. "Our relationship was complicated. Just let it be. What happens now is up to Shaun, Sam, and Carli."

When Zach closed his mouth, signaling he wouldn't ask or argue, Ray opened the door and climbed down.

The wheeled table was the same height as the lowered tailgate. A few pulls, and the elk on its tarp was transferred to the steel slab, then wheeled inside. Ray closed the door behind them and took two knives from the hooks on the wall, handing one to Zach.

"We're missing dinner," Ray said conversationally.

Zach smiled. "I like leftovers, especially chicken."

They both chuckled, then began to work on the elk. Two hours later, large hunks of meat were in the walk-in freezer, pieces of hide and unusable parts were discarded in thick garbage bags, and the two of them, having washed the blood from their hands and arms, left the corner for the lodge and whatever Sam had saved for them.

Once inside the kitchen, they watched as the barn lights turned off, and a minute later J.J. joined them. He reported that Samson and Lady were taken care of and apparently recovered from the ordeal with the bear. Zach rattled off the details of clearing out part of the poachers' camp and that Shaun would be entertained for the next few hours with paperwork. He and J.J. speculated about the future of the lodge and who would press charges against the game thieves. Ray remained quiet as they foraged through the refrigerator, and was the first of the three to announce he was turning in for the night. J.J. and Zach silently watched Bear's best friend and oldest employee, wearily leave the kitchen.

CHAPTER 24

They had agreed that Ethan would search the files on the computer while she dug through the stacks of papers that covered every flat surface in the office. Carli knew the password, so he wasn't forced to stretch his hacking skills. Fingers tapping lightly on the keys, he opened and read e-mails, files, and documents. Though his focus was on the screen in front of him, the rest of his senses were registering Carli's every move.

She smelled of horses and the wilderness, neither of which he found offensive. Her movements were methodical, her voice quiet except for the occasional grunt of understanding or mumbled curse at something confusing. Having started at one corner, she had worked her way around, compiling a stack of papers she deemed important. Receipts for a vague item or a scribbled note in her father's shorthand, phone numbers with no names, and an old, faded, file folder filled with what appeared to be legal documents, were all part of her own pile. In a casual, habitual movement, she tucked her hair behind her ear.

He paused in his search and raised his gaze to her profile. She wasn't classically beautiful, but attractive, and he wondered how much of that was influenced by her way of life. Her skin was tanned due to her time out of doors. She wore little, if any, make-up, and her hair was natural without the aid of dye, curlers, or gels. He guessed her career dictated that she travel light and surmised that her upbringing on the Preserve ensured she wasn't preoccupied with the usual womanly pursuits of fashion and

Hollywood drama. That might be one of the reasons he was drawn to her. He'd had his share of coiffed and powdered women, full of pretenses and games. Fake. Carli was … real. Assuming she was being honest in the assessment of her life, she had no reason to play the part of a Drama Queen. The more he considered, the more he realized the danger of being with such a woman. Even if she didn't say the words, he would be able to read her emotions. And what would he do if he recognized something more than enjoyment? Or sorrow when he left? That had him scowling, irritated that he had allowed his thoughts to take him so far away from his task. It was then that she turned to look at him, read his expression, and raised both brows.

"Did you find something disturbing?"

If you only knew, Ethan thought. Instead, he answered, "There appears to be a digital journal. Would Bear have kept his personal, daily accounts on his hard drive?"

She closed the folder she was holding and circled to the other side of the desk. Setting the file on her short stack of what she would attempt to make sense of later, she leaned next to Ethan to see the screen. Apparently he had tried a few passwords to get into the program, but the red 'x' and the message 'password is incorrect' indicated he hadn't been able to gain access. Glancing at the keyboard, and seeing that Ethan's hands rested in his lap, she used one finger and tapped in a code. Pressing 'enter', they both read 'welcome to your daily journal', to which she stood and laughed out loud.

"Anyone who would read this would know it to be a joke. Dad wouldn't title something with the mundane words of 'your daily journal'. But …" she said, and leaned over again, took the mouse, and clicked on the trash can icon in the lower right corner. The page they were viewing faded, and the real document appeared. Scrolling down, she shook her head. Her father, who loathed record keeping, had entered deliveries, client arrivals and departures, visits from the veterinarian, what was removed from inventory, and the date on which each event happened. He had even included talks with employees and a word or two about what was discussed.

Ethan leaned forward, attached the entire file to an e-mail, and sent it to himself where he could view it later on his laptop. It must have been several years' worth as it took a minute before the 'sent items' icon disappeared. He turned to look up at Carli.

"There has to be something in here that will tell us what he knew, and who shot him. What did you find?"

"Some unusual scraps of paper, and a folder that seems to have been around for a while."

"Anything interesting in it?"

"Unsigned divorce papers."

He turned the office chair to fully face Carli, but remained seated. "That doesn't mean Darla will inherit everything. We're still verifying with the county."

She nodded. "I know. But what if she's right?" Her voice dropped and there was a little fear, a little disbelief.

He rose to his feet and placed his hands on her shoulders. "I learned on my first case not to assume much about suspects, to look at the facts, and to keep searching until answers were uncovered. It's a waste of time and energy to speculate before there's enough information to begin to put the pieces together."

Her eyes were wide and trusting and he fought the urge to promise her that everything would be alright. What he didn't fight was Carli as she leaned a little closer and turned her lips to meet his. It wasn't the kiss of a stranger, but of a lover, and had his brains dropping to his jeans in a breath.

The hum of the computer was interrupted by the groan she elicited from him. Hands shifted from her shoulders to her cheeks where he caressed her skin with his thumbs. Her hands wrapped around his neck and pulled him closer, her breasts brushing against his chest. Carli's taste, the warmth of her smooth skin, the increase in the amount of her body coming in contact with his, heated his blood. Remembering where they were, the thought drifted through his mind, which was quickly turning to haze, that he should step away. And he would, after another moment. But that thought came too late.

She trailed her hands from his neck, around his shoulders, down his back, to the hip pockets of his jeans. There her hands rested, then pulled him closer. At the evidence that he was quite excited to be held by her, she returned the groan of pleasure. She didn't know where this would lead in the long term, but for now, her libido was voting for the use of several condoms. She hadn't been with anyone for a while, and Ethan was a fine example of the male species. Why not indulge while he was here? To that end, knowing that the door to the office was closed, she moved a step back, then lowered herself onto the table behind her. Vaguely, she registered the shifting of the mounds of papers and files around her, but was more interested in the feel of the man in her arms than any mess she might make of her father's filing system.

He followed her back and down, fascinated with where Carli wanted this thing between them to go. As she pulled him between her thighs, her heels wrapping around the back of his knees, her direction was blatantly clear. His knuckles grazed the tips of her breasts on their way down to the bottom of her shirt. Her sharp intake of breath added to his excitement. Inching his fingers beneath the hem, he felt the smoothness of her belly, and the snap to her jeans.

Encouraged by his attention to her flesh, which seemed to crave what he offered, she was relieved that he hadn't abandoned his skill at kissing her. Not wanting Ethan to be the only of the two to revel in the warmth of the other, to fuel the desire between them that seemed to burn hotter each time they touched, she maneuvered her hands over his holstered weapon, under his shirt tails, and onto his heated back.

"Carli?" Sam called through the door, her voice followed by a knock.

At the same time, Ethan's cell phone rang at his hip. Breaking the kiss and stepping back, he answered the call just as Sam opened the door and peered around the edge.

Glancing at the FBI agent's profile, then at Carli, who sat on the table by the computer, Sam entered the office. She started to ask if they had found anything, then stopped when Ethan began speaking.

"Yes, it's still open," he said, looking at Sam as she hesitated, mouth open. He turned to check on Carli, and noticed the slight flush to her face.

She moved to the desk and closed all the open files on the computer, then shut it down. As she waited for the screen to turn black, she busied herself with collecting the items she had found in the office.

Sam narrowed her eyes. "Are you alright? You look a little ..." then she glanced at Ethan who had moved a few feet to the opposite wall and stood with his back to them as he spoke into the phone. "Did I interrupt something?" she asked, a brow brushing her bangs as it rose.

Carli offered her sister a half-smile. She wasn't adept at lying, but even she didn't know what this was between her and Ethan. Finally, she shook her head, knowing that Sam wouldn't pursue with questions. For now. She straightened and began to move towards the door, papers in hand.

"My boss," Ethan explained, replacing his phone at his belt. Shifting his gaze from Carli to Sam, he asked, "What's up?"

"Just wanted to inform you that Darla has left for the evening. She will return tomorrow morning, when she has requested a tour of the grounds and all improvements since her last visit," Sam paused, batted her eyelashes, and with a fake smile added, "I will be indisposed in Laramie. Zach, Ray, and Donna are all scheduled to be with clients. It will be Sunday, so Alyssa will be here until noon. I vote we pay the girl fifty bucks to entertain Darla. Unless, of course, you would rather have the—"

Carli shook her head. "Hell, no. If you give Alyssa fifty, I'll chip in another fifty. Hazard pay," she explained. Walking past Sam and out the door, she paused in the hallway as her sister and Ethan followed.

"We found a few interesting items," Carli raised the papers in one hand as she closed and locked the door with the other. "I think Dad's legal forms are all here. Ethan found some journal entries on the computer. We're off to search the storage area."

Sam wrinkled her nose. "Careful. It's not used much, so who knows what surprises you'll find." She paused at the foot of the stairs. "I have ranch business to discuss with Matt. See you at breakfast," Sam included Ethan in her statement, then turned and started up the stairs. "Oh," she said, and called back over her shoulder, "Tim came in just as Darla was leaving. Said he spent the evening with a friend in Laramie and was going to his room to finish some work."

Carli watched as Sam disappeared at the top of the landing. She would have to check with Tim about his 'friend', as well as how much he had sent to Scott. Turning around, she found the lobby empty, the fire extinguished except for a few red embers, and only the glow from the dimmed track lighting above the reception desk to illuminate their way to the front door.

Ethan followed her through the lobby, where they paused to grab their coats from the hooks by the door. Once they descended from the veranda to the parking lot, he fell into step beside her. The chilled air had him tucking his hands in his pockets. That's what he told himself, but the alternative was to intertwine his fingers with hers. And if he did that, they would detour to his cabin for the remainder of the night, the storage area forgotten.

The call from Sloan forced him to rein in his desire for Carli. He hadn't updated Micah because he didn't have much in the way of facts or evidence, only more questions. Reporting that he had taken a fall from a horse and his growing attraction to a family member of the deceased would not fit with the cool, secluded, calculating agent that Micah Sloan knew, and he wouldn't do anything to lead his boss to believe much else.

The storage building was one of the first outbuildings constructed on the land, Carli informed him. "It's held everything from tools while Dad and Ray built the lodge, to holiday decorations. Hardly anyone goes in there now. Anything that's needed on a regular basis is stored in the room at the end of the veranda. Shaun's key," she said and held up the piece of metal before inserting it into the lock. "Everyone else has their own, or access to one, for the tack room in the barn, Dad's office, and the basement," she ended her explanation as they stood under the small overhang attached to the wall above the storage door.

She unlocked the padlock, turned the doorknob, and before she stepped inside, reached around the doorframe and turned on the lights.

"Dad trusted the people he hired, but since there wasn't much that was used in here, and with the confidential files, not everyone had, or needed, access. He kept things secure in case there was a client with sticky fingers."

Stepping into the crammed space, Ethan blinked at the fluorescent tubes suspended from the ceiling, then at the stacks of boxes that filled the fifteen-by-fifteen storage space. From floor to ceiling, leaving just enough room for the light fixtures, cardboard boxes lined the walls and formed two rows down the middle of the space. Barely enough room to walk between the stacks, he noticed that the boxes were all marked clearly with black, permanent marker. What wasn't easy to understand was Bear's shorthand. A set of three letters followed by two numbers, and on some there was a third number. Breathing in dust and stale, cold air, he glanced at the top row of boxes that was above his head, and felt the space grow smaller. The quiet click of the door as Carli closed it, had the hair on the back of his neck standing at attention. As his breath quickened, he closed his eyes and attempted to steady himself.

"Ethan?"

Carli's soft voice had his eyes snapping open. Turning his head to look at her, he tried to tamp down the panic. Fingernails bit into his palm as he curled his hands tightly into fists.

She reached back behind her and opened the door. Seeing Ethan's eyes dart to the space behind her, she stepped aside and used her foot to maneuver the brick that was utilized as a door stop, to the space in front of the solid plank of wood. The night breeze eased past her and brushed the dark strands that fell against Ethan's forehead. She sighed as he relaxed.

"A little claustrophobic?" Her question wasn't sarcastic or demeaning.

"A lot, actually," Ethan answered honestly. "Tried hypnosis once." He shifted his attention to the boxes and attempted to decipher the code. "Doesn't interfere with the job. In fact, it helps."

She moved to stand next to him, glancing from the writing on the boxes to Ethan's face. "How?"

"Allows me to empathize with the victim and predict what the perpetrator will do next."

Wanting to see his eyes, she touched his arm.

He paused in his study of the boxes and looked at her. Her gaze held concern, and questions. She didn't want to know how it helped him, she wanted to know how he had developed the fear. Did he trust her? Giving her the story would be crossing yet another line in this assignment. If she was involved in the murder of her father, there was nothing in his experience that she could use against him. His instincts told him she was innocent, and if that proved to be true, the tale would add another layer of intimacy between them.

"When I was six, a kidnapper took me from a grocery store parking lot. He stepped up to my mother and punched her hard enough in the face that she lost consciousness. After stuffing me into the trunk of his car, I was crammed onto the floor of a closet in the house he had rented. He demanded a million dollars from my father, who was one of the highest-level civilian aeronautical engineers working for the government. Roy Carter got his fifteen minutes of fame. He believed his demands were met. We stepped outside the house, which was surrounded by federal agents, in order to climb into the car that supposedly had the money in the trunk. It was agreed that we would be allowed to drive off, and he would leave me at a bus bench a few blocks away. I bit his hand hard enough that he lowered the gun held to my head, which, unbeknownst to my six-year-old mind, was the signal for the sniper," Ethan sighed and looked again at the stack of cardboard in front of him. "My parents insisted on therapy. That's when I started to draw. First it was my nightmares, then people," he shrugged. "And the panic attacks from being in cramped, dark places is the only thing that I've kept."

Once Carli's sister had been rescued from Rutgers, Sam hadn't wanted sympathy, only understanding and to be treated as if the incident hadn't changed her. She gave that to Ethan now in her expression and a reassuring touch of her hand.

"Then you know all about Sam, and everything she went through."

Carli's words and touch brought his attention back to her. "And other cases like us, yes." The empathy he felt for families who were victims of abduction was reflected in her eyes. "So, now that you know my darkest secret, do you also know this code that's on all these boxes?"

"Of course," she began, but hesitated at a scuffling noise. Brows drawing together, she backed up, then walked down the next aisle. "Ethan, say something."

"Actually, I think I've said more than enough already," he answered, but moved down his own aisle, his hand coming to his waist to withdraw his weapon from its holster.

They reached the end of their respective rows at the same time, and with Ethan's words, came more rustling. She lifted a bucket, which was used to catch water from a leak in the roof, off of the stack against the wall. Seeing that it was empty, she turned it over, placed it on the floor, and stepped up to peer into the corner on top of the row of boxes. Not knowing which of them was startled most, she let out a curse as she jerked back and lost her balance. There was nothing to grab onto but smooth cardboard. She toppled backward and would have fallen against the stack behind her, except Ethan was there.

Her back landed against his chest and he caught her under her arms. The sound of the bucket as it was knocked over echoed loudly in the quietness of the storage area, upsetting the resident who had claimed it as her own. Angry at the intrusion and the commotion, the mother opossum hissed and bared her teeth over the edge of the box. Ethan glanced up, then began laughing.

Placing her feet under her on the floor, Carli turned from the interloper to Ethan. She was warmed by the mirth in his eyes, the strength in his arms as he continued to hold her, his forearms under her shoulders. It took her only a moment before she joined in his laughter. The opossum, however, failing to find any humor in the situation, gathered her babies and scurried along the top of the boxes to where the vent was, and the grate should have been. They disappeared through the hole in the wall to outside the storage shed where it was free from humans.

Their laughter faded as Carli regained her balance and stepped away from Ethan.

"Thanks. You saved me from serious injury and making a mess from toppled boxes," she smiled.

"My pleasure," he responded as he replaced his weapon, and his chin gestured towards the creature that expressed discontent. "Thought they had the joint to themselves."

"They'll return once we leave and it's dark and quiet again," she said, then turned her attention to the boxes and Ethan's request at deciphering the code. "The first letters are an abbreviation, the numbers are the year."

"F. EM. 99?"

"Former employees, 1999," she answered.

He moved down the aisle, towards the door, and found two boxes marked as containing employee records for 2011 and 2012. In the containers on the opposite side of the aisle was something that interested Carli. While he dug through files, she pulled pictures from her childhood. Some were in albums, but most were in paper envelopes with the negatives. Her mind strongly voiced the opinion that they should be scanned and made into digital files, while her heart softened and tripped at the memories. She recounted a few stories aloud that were illustrated by whichever photograph she held in her hand.

Thirty minutes later, she placed the pictures back inside the box with a vow to do something with them. Ethan had selected a few files of possibly disgruntled employees that would be investigated. They left the storage building and walked across the grounds towards the lodge.

"What will you do about her?" he asked.

She shrugged. "I'm a live and let live kind of gal. I'll go about my business, and she'll do what she's always done."

He glanced at Carli. "Are you talking about the opossum or Darla?"

"Both. We can keep the missing grate between us. And as soon as the funeral is over, and Darla is left empty-handed, she'll crawl back to her own shelter on the coast."

He steered her toward the steps of the veranda. They were the only two outside, and as he looked up, one light in an upstairs bedroom turned off, while another continued to glow.

"Sam. Tim," Carli answered his unasked question, following his gaze. Stepping onto the first stair, she turned to him, now eye to eye, and, she couldn't help realizing, lip to lip.

"How's the head?" she asked.

"Fine."

"No symptoms?"

"None. Just to make sure, I'll be up a while, reading," he said, and raised the files.

"I'll be working early tomorrow. I'm actually surprised Scott hasn't contacted me about the pictures for the issue."

"Would Tim have sent them?"

"Only some of the digitals. I do all the developing."

"And the ones you took today?"

"Film. Those will be the first to get done."

He nodded. "I'll wait until you're safely inside."

"You still think someone here is trying to eliminate all of us?"

"My job is based on fact and safety."

She raised a brow, the shadow of which he could see from the faint light in the lobby. "And I'm your job?"

"Yes. And quickly moving past a distraction to ..." As his voice faded, he wondered why the silent, lone agent in him suddenly felt the need to spill every memory and thought in his head.

"To what?" Her voice was soft and he felt himself drawn to her.

"Something," he answered vaguely, as his lips pressed to hers.

It was meant as a test of his self-control. Could he kiss her, then leave her? Gripping the files in one hand, the other balled up in his coat pocket, he took just enough to remind him that Carli was unusual, and because of that, he needed to be cautious. Ending the kiss with a closed-mouth press of his lips, he straightened.

"Sleep well," he told her, his voice slightly gruff.

"You too," she said, then turned and entered the lodge without another word.

Maybe, after he found the pieces to solve the case, he could leave Wyoming with himself intact.

Closing and locking the door of Cabin 4 behind him, he turned up the heat and opened his laptop. He took his time reading through the employee files, but there was not enough written to warrant a murder. Setting the files aside, he propped himself against the headboard, his legs stretched across the quilt that covered the bed.

It was the way she spoke so freely about her memories, came the unbidden thought. Even with his eyes closed, her dynamic words, he knew, would match her expressions as she shared a little of her past. And he realized he would have to draw it. Carli, sitting on the floor of the storage area, the box flaps open, a photograph in her hand.

His computer beeped, and he knew the answers, or at least the path to the missing pieces, would be found in Bear Tanner's journal. He opened his e-mail, then the attachment. After reading the entry three days before Bear's death, he reached for his pack, which he dropped off in the cabin upon their return from Doc Miller's, and pulled out his pad and a pencil. Glancing at what he had sketched on their ride, he turned to a fresh page and began to record his impressions from Bear's words.

Two hours later, he set everything on the nightstand and closed his eyes. As he slept, the pictures on his pad and the words from the journal mingled and moved in his mind. He was convinced that the murderer was someone Tanner trusted, and that in itself was the greatest betrayal.

CHAPTER 25

Denny had stayed the night at the office to keep watch on those that occupied the cells. Vince was to relieve him at eight that morning. It had taken hours to file the paperwork on the four poachers. Fortunately, they were cooperative and didn't ask for legal representation, probably guessing that a lawyer wouldn't be able to do much besides suggest that they not answer questions, which would only delay the inevitable, since they were caught with their hand in the proverbial cookie jar. Shaun guessed it was due to their lack of funds that instigated their criminal activity in the first place. All of their permits and receipts for their hunting rifles checked out, and they remained staunch in their plea that they did not shoot, by accident or otherwise, Bear Tanner.

Shaun had arrived home just before midnight and was exhausted enough to slip into sleep without one of the aids he had to employ with increasing frequency. Waking up with the alarm on his cell phone coming from the floor and wherever his pants landed the night before, he glanced at the clock on the wall across from his bed and realized he had an hour before leaving for the lodge. Collecting a T-shirt and a pair of shorts from the floor of the closet, for which he had yet to make doors, he sat on the edge of the mattress and tied his running shoes. Raking his hands back through his hair, he sighed heavily, then made his way to the exercise room downstairs.

There was something about hard, sweaty, physical exercise that cleared his mind. A pot of coffee couldn't accomplish what an hour running, framing a house, or hand- sanding planks for the floor could do to put events into perspective. Sissy wasn't going to take him back unless he gave her a diamond ring. Darla would remain at least through Tuesday, and he would do what he could to be somewhere besides the lodge when she was there. He admitted that he would need Ethan's help, and the FBI's resources, if they were to determine what happened on Wolf's Ridge. And in two days' time, there would be an official service to say good-bye to his father.

A shower and a change into street clothes of jeans, boots, a long-sleeved, buttoned-down shirt and his coat, followed his run. He arrived at the lodge just in time to relieve Alyssa of the leftovers before she began the rest of her work in the cabins. Since it was Sunday, most of the clients were checking out, having arrived the previous week. Ray would make a couple of shuttle runs to the Cheyenne or Laramie Airports for those who hadn't rented their own transportation. Zach had the day off, but he knew the younger man would spend the afternoon with Alyssa since she would be done cleaning and doing laundry by three. Until then, Zach and J.J. were to help Denny clean up the camp of the game thieves. He would have to check the schedule himself to find out how many clients would be arriving in the next couple of days.

"Why don't you put it on a plate and have a seat at the table?" Alyssa asked, her hands in the dishwater, her long, blonde hair pulled back into a high ponytail.

"It would just make more work for you," he answered, scooping up the remaining eggs with a wooden spoon in one hand and a piece of bacon in the other.

"Well, it's not like one more dish is going to make a difference," she gestured toward the mountain of bowls and pans that didn't fit in the dishwasher.

A few more bites had him looking up from the now-empty skillet. He moved to her side to add it to the unwashed pile. Though he moved slowly, he must have caught her daydreaming. As he reached forward to set the pan on the counter next to her, she jumped, raising her right arm in a protective posture. He cursed under his breath.

"You startled me. That's what I get for thinking about this afternoon instead of paying attention," she explained to cover her reaction, then returned to her task.

He peered intently at her profile, searching for signs that Jim had lost his temper recently. "How are things going at school?"

"Fine. I finished my report for English. It's hard to believe that graduation is only two months away."

"And your birthday. And prom. Lys, you got a lot going on."

"I know, and it will all be over so quick."

"How's your dad? He find any work?" He knew the answer but wanted to get a good look at her face.

She turned toward him and shrugged. "Daddy hasn't found anything in town. Said when the weather warms up he'll take a day and go to Laramie, see if any sites need a new crew member."

No bruises. Alyssa had always covered for her father. 'Clumsy', 'not paying attention' were common excuses. She was too old to call social services and have them do anything, and she wouldn't press charges. Bear had given her a job when she was fifteen, and Shaun assumed the responsibility for looking out for his father's employees. Of course, Zach had a much closer relationship with Alyssa.

"What are your plans this afternoon? Must be something good," he said.

Her entire face lit up. He had seen the expression before on Sissy. What would it take for him to feel what they felt?

"Zach's taking me to town for a late lunch and a matinee. They're showing the new Sara Miller movie."

It wasn't long ago that Shaun had taken Sissy to a show. He didn't remember the movie, only the warm, feminine body pressed against his. Perhaps he should have a talk with Zach.

J.J. peered around the kitchen door. "Hey, Shaun, Alyssa," he paused as both of them turned to face him. "The last of the clients just checked out. They have their own vehicle, so looks like Ray

Michele Venné

will only have one trip to make to the airport today. Turk hasn't been out in a while. I'm going to ride him south, along the river. Should be back in an hour. Then I'll go with Zach to clean up the camp."

"You be careful," Shaun warned him.

"Always," J.J. said, then disappeared from the doorway.

"Anyone coming in today?" Shaun asked.

"I don't think so, but you know where the schedule is."

"Sam? Carli?" he continued with his questions.

"Laramie. Upstairs."

"Mortuary? Darkroom?"

She turned towards him, cocked a hip and rested her hand on it. "Now, if you know so much, why are you asking me?"

He smiled at her mock censure. "Because I like to talk to pretty girls."

She shook her head. "Well, this one is already spoken for," she said and returned to the sink full of suds.

"Thanks for breakfast," he said as he moved toward the door, coffee cup in hand.

"Thanks for saving me from keeping the leftovers," she called after him.

The schedule hung on the clipboard, the same as it always had. Zach was off, and Alyssa would be later that day. J.J. was out riding. Donna had the day to herself and he guessed she would spend it by taking her mom out to lunch in Laramie. There were no guests due to arrive until Wednesday, and that reservation had a question mark next to it. Sighing in relief that the lodge would be empty of clients for a few days, he glanced at the clock, did a little figuring, and decided he had about an hour and forty-five minutes before Ray returned from the airport. He pushed away the slight annoyance that Sam had gone, by herself, to Laramie. Perhaps she was far enough away from the lodge and Centennial that if someone was intent on causing the Tanners harm, she would be safer among the citizens of the city rather than on her own wandering the Preserve. Leaving the front desk, he unlocked his father's office with the idea to locate a few phone

234

numbers regarding the business, and perhaps he would get lucky and discover, in the stacks of files and papers, something that resembled a will. He wasn't concerned about what Bear Tanner would have left to everyone, he was just curious as to the future of the lodge and Tanner's Outdoor Adventures.

«‹‹—»››

There was excitement that fluttered in her veins. This would be where her human eye, through the lens of a mechanical device, attempted to capture what only the mind had previously interpreted. Being in the darkroom was only second to being outside, whether that was a rural, urban, or complete wilderness setting. She enjoyed her digital pixels. Even changing the color, the brightness, erasing a scar or smoothing a wrinkle could, and often did, alter what the original composition was and, Carli felt, made it less 'real' in its depiction.

Here in the darkroom, images could still be altered, though she chose to leave the scars and wrinkles that allowed her subjects to speak the words of their lives. One after another, film spools were opened, placed in a film reel, then dropped into a developing tank. Exact minutes of agitation were counted, then film was unwound and dried. Using the enlarger, the images were transferred onto photo paper. Processing trays filled with developer, then stop bath, fixer, and a final rinse, received the sheets as the chemicals allowed the images to become visible. She had done this for enough years, in various darkrooms, that she had devised a routine. Her economical movements were influenced by a second longer or shorter in one tray or another, a dial turned or a knob adjusted on the enlarger. This familiarity allowed her to entertain other thoughts.

Of Ethan, for example. She refused to waste energy on denying her physical attraction to the man. He was smart, talented, adventurous, and she enjoyed their verbal banter. Chuckling, she realized she had listed his qualities as if she was writing a personal ad looking for someone like him. His panic attack in the storage area last night would qualify as a tragic flaw, her mind glomming onto the words 'classic hero', though she believed him when he said it helped, not hindered, his work ability. Using tongs to move the paper from tray to tray, then to the line behind her to dry, she brought her thoughts back to what they knew.

Which wasn't much, she realized. There was the small lead with the poachers and their rifle. Ethan didn't believe he would find anything in old employee files, but, as he explained to her, he was eliminating suspects. She must be off the list with the way he had kissed her, unless he subscribed to the old adage of 'keep your friends close, your enemies closer'. If he still believed that she, or Shaun or Sam, could have killed Bear Tanner, then her astute judge of character had permanently fled.

Ethan's physical reaction to her in the office, and she guessed the other times they had found themselves wrapped in each other's arms, would be difficult to fake. Wouldn't it? He was a man, most certainly, and she knew she had curves in all the right places. Then there was his concern for her safety.

She transferred the last three pictures from the tub of stop bath to the final rinse, just as a knock sounded at the door. When she heard Ethan's voice, the corners of her mouth drew up into a smile. *Silly*, she thought, *to have such anticipation at seeing him.* But the chastising did little to dampen her naturally pleasant and upbeat personality. After attaching a corner of the picture with a pin on the line, she made her way around the table of equipment and bottles of chemicals to the door, where she turned the switch off, shutting down the red light outside. Unlocking the door, she opened it to see the man who had occupied her thoughts and touched off the unusual beating of her heart.

«««—»»»

It was the sound of his watch alarm that pulled him from a short night's rest. Lifting his head from the pillow, Ethan squinted at the bathroom light that spilled from behind the partially closed door. Flipping onto his back, he turned off the alarm and stared at the ceiling. Recovered from his panic attack, and the ensuing embarrassment, his next thought was of the woman who fell into his arms. He snorted at the double meaning and rolled out of bed.

Missing breakfast was part of the plan. It was a priority that he eliminate suspects, and the files he took from storage would help to shorten the list. Then there was the growing desire towards Carli. His tired mind last night had convinced him that being apart from her for several hours would douse the flames. Realizing that may not be the case, he turned the water valve in the shower to the cool side of warm. Ignoring the directive to keep the stitches dry, he put his head under the spray and removed the dried blood from his hair.

Dressing in clean clothes, the ones from yesterday dirty and bloody from his fall, he sat on the edge of the bed and began to review the employee files. After the third one, he stood to pace the length of the cabin. What he concluded last night was true. No words of revenge or a parting of ways due to theft or wrongful treatment of a client or fellow worker were documented. Each employee was given a bonus and a letter of recommendation upon termination with Tanner's Outdoor Adventures. There was nothing here that pointed to a suspect.

He set the last of the files on the table beside his computer. There was quite a story in the words Bear Tanner had left behind. He read the last three months of entries. Bear had brought in a lot of money, and spent quite a bit on importing animals, transfer fees, vet bills, and salaries. There were notes about conversations with Zach and Alyssa, and projects he had worked on with Shaun, presumably on the house Shaun was building. Notations filled the days regarding clients and what was hunted, where they had taken down each animal, even the number and weight of fish caught from Little Shy River or William's Lake. Carli's lesson on the code that marked the boxes in storage helped to decipher Bear's shorthand in his journal. All but one mark. An asterisk. There was no legend anywhere in the text to explain this symbol.

He would review it again, record the dates, and perhaps Zach, Alyssa, Ray, or Shaun would know what it meant.

Pulling on his coat and grabbing the stack of files, he left his cabin for the lodge. There was one business truck and Shaun's vehicle in front of the lodge. The parking lot was void of any rental cars, except his, so the remaining clients must have checked out, and someone had taken the van on an airport run. He walked through the empty lobby to the dining room. No one was there, and the table was clean. There was noise from the kitchen, so he pushed open the door to find Alyssa closing the dishwasher.

"Morning," Ethan said, then eased into the kitchen.

Alyssa jumped anyway. "Jeeze-Louise. That's the second time someone has startled me this morning."

"Sorry," he apologized, noticing all the food was gone, the counters clean.

"It's alright. You've missed breakfast. Not that there was much left, but Shaun beat you to it. I can fix you a sandwich, or there's leftovers from last night," she suggested, and left the options open.

He waved away her offerings. "I'm fine for now. Thanks. I was wondering if you could tell me where Carli is?"

"She's in the darkroom. Upstairs, at the end of the hall."

"Is Shaun with her?"

"I don't think so. She usually works by herself. If the red light is on, don't walk in. Tim may be with her, but I'm not sure. I haven't seen him yet this morning."

He smiled his thanks and left the kitchen. There were no new marks on Alyssa, so either she stayed out of the way, or whoever used her as a punching bag must have taken a break. Shedding his coat and tossing it across the back of one of the couches in the lobby, then balancing the stack of files on top of it, he made his way up the stairs.

From the landing he could see the red light. If she had been inside working through breakfast, he thought she would be close to being finished. There were rooms along both sides of the hall, and with the doors closed, the lights overhead were on all the time. With the amount of snow that fell every year, it wasn't beneficial to have skylights installed. Reaching the end of the hallway, he shifted from one foot to another like a nervous teenager. He wasn't excited to see her, wasn't wanting to smell her skin, taste her lips. She didn't move him beyond a casual affair. He was lying about the first and hoped the second was true. His hand, raised to knock on the door, was stilled by a voice from behind him.

"I wouldn't. Carli tends to get grouchy when she's interrupted."

He turned to look over his shoulder and offered Tim a half-smile. "How long have you worked with Carli?"

"Long enough to fall under the category of common-law marriage."

"You know each other well, then," he said, shifting to face Tim and walking a few steps back down the hallway.

Tim nodded, then stuffed his hands in his front pockets. "If you're expecting me to divulge secrets, you're asking the wrong guy."

Ethan shook his head. "Lucky for her you're protective."

"Fortunate for you, despite Carli's brains and beauty and talent, she doesn't flip my switch."

"You would marry her?" Ethan raised a brow.

"The moment I met her. If she was interested in being a homebody. Women like Carli are rare." Tim narrowed his gaze slightly at the FBI agent. Physically, Carli could do worse. The man certainly oozed masculine energy. He would have to observe them together and see if either showed anything beyond casual interest.

Ethan raised his arm and pushed his fingers through his hair. Tim glanced from the man's biceps, to his broad chest and flat belly, then the gun at his waist that peeked out from under the flannel shirt he used to cover the weapon. *Yes, Ethan was quite a man,* Tim thought.

"She has no desire to be married and stay home?" Ethan asked, deciding that Tim could offer an interesting perspective, and needed information.

Tim shrugged. "Why should she? She's making a very good living at something she loves. Why change? Besides, with her schedule, dating is a challenge. Doesn't matter if you meet her in New York or one of the villages she photographs. She doesn't stay in one place very long."

"You were with her when she was notified about Bear's death?"

Tim leaned a shoulder against the wall. "Yes. Damn near fainted. Scott, the editor at the *Views*, has yet another new assistant. Uncaring bastard sent three words, 'Bear is dead'. My guess is the assistant didn't bother to find out who Bear was. Just sent the telegram. Bear and his kids were real close," Tim paused, then raised his brow. "Are you thinking Carli had something to do with her dad's death?" He knew the answer in Ethan's silence. Shaking his head, he said, "None of them would do anything to harm another. They all genuinely like each other, which is unusual in families these days."

Spoken with such conviction, Ethan could easily discern Tim's feelings for Carli. Tim loved her, but not in the romantic sense. The thought arose that should they be in elementary school and he broke Carli's heart, Tim would punch him on the playground. He wondered at the devoted friend's reaction if it occurred now.

Tim watched Ethan's face and the emotions that showed themselves. One corner of his mouth tipped into a half-smile. "I care deeply for Carli. I see that you are interested in her ... company. Shaun won't be the only one to kick your ass if you make her cry. Carli never cries."

Ethan offered a smile at the picture of his 'ass-kicking' being done by Tim. "I'll keep that in mind."

Tim nodded, then pushed himself off the wall. Glancing at his watch he turned away from Ethan, saying, "She's probably close to done. If you knock now, she may not be too pissed at the interruption."

Ethan watched as Tim descended the stairs and disappeared from sight.

Smiling and shaking his head at the warning and the relationship description, and remembering Tim's recount of Carli's reaction to the telegram, he knocked on the door. The red light turned off, and the door opened. The expression on Carli's face when she saw him was far from upset at the intrusion.

"Hi," she smiled.

"Morning," he answered, his dimples deepening as he smiled back at her.

"Want to come in, see the pictures from yesterday?" Carli stepped aside and opened the door wider.

He entered the darkroom. Once his eyes adjusted to the dim lighting, he saw the lines of pictures on the other side of the table. She closed the door behind him, and it was then he noticed the quiet music. Drums and flute. He glanced over his shoulder and raised a brow in question.

"It helps put me in the mood," she paused, then decided to clarify as neither of them apparently needed anything for their libidos to rev into fifth gear. "Helps me remember the climate, the people, the environment. I buy locally when I can. Have even done some of my own recordings. Different regions, continents, require their own sound."

She slid between him and the island in the middle of the room where the trays were set, to point to the photographs. Beginning a monologue of the pictures from Africa, then the ones from South America, she kept her eyes on the prints, her hands gesturing as the stories were told. Anecdotes of an animal that returned to the same place to forage or hunt, a village woman and child, of relationships she had forged with the locals as well as those from charity organizations. Doctors Without Borders. Peace Corps. And the accusation that she had a friend in every harbor and airport.

He studied the photos, feeling them come alive with her descriptions and stories. Her passion for what she captured on film, how the exposure of the areas helped the local citizens, was obvious in her voice and body language. His interest shifted from the pictures to the woman. Carli embodied the excitement, compassion, the very lives of those captured by her camera. She had an international reputation and was an extremely talented artist. The more he studied Carli's expressions, felt her laugh tickle his skin, absorbed her enthusiasm, the more solid Tim's threat became. She was open and honest, beautiful and intelligent. There was no one to retaliate for him, should she break his heart. That thought had his feet frozen to the floor.

There had been no close relationships since Mac Waise died. If she hurt him, it would be his own damn fault for allowing it to happen. He had remained successfully unentangled for years. The soft curls of her blonde hair, the brightness of her hazel eyes, could tip the scales. And he wasn't willing to fall victim. Resolutely, he shifted his gaze back to the pictures. A lioness stalked her prey among tall, dried grass. Did the photo breathe with the predator? Or was it the life of the one who captured the moment that had infused that movement into the print?

She removed the pictures of the footprints and the stained dirt of Wolf's Ridge. Some of the passion related to her work flowed away, leaving her quiet, serious. She didn't know what she had hoped to discover by producing the pictures. They were just as grizzly in their replication as the real thing. A few more on the line were of the surrounding forest area. The last one she removed was one of Ethan. His dark hair had fallen across his forehead, he wore a half-smile, just enough to accent his dimples, and there was laughter and desire in his eyes. She handed it to him.

"You're quite photogenic."

"I turned down a cover shot for *Male on Parade* for my interview at Quantico," he returned.

"Really?" Her voice rose slightly with amazement.

"No. The press and my sometimes-undercover status don't mix," he said, shuffling the photo of himself to the bottom of the stack depicting their time on the ride yesterday.

He would give the prints to Shaun to add to the file on Bear Tanner. Glancing back at the line of pictures, he voiced his opinion.

"All those award panels that presented you with trophies and plaques and checks, knew how to judge. You're excellent in your craft, Carli," he complimented, taking his gaze back to her face.

"Thank you, Ethan. It means more coming from one with equal talent." Her voice was soft and she stepped towards him.

He shrugged. "A talent born of necessity."

"But birthed in its own right," she said with another step.

"The lioness," he gestured with a tip of his head toward the line of photos, "she breathes because of you. Your observation, your interpretation, are clearly imprinted on the paper," his voice ended roughly as Carli stopped just in front of him, heat in her eyes.

"So many compliments. One might be led to believe you have an ulterior motive, Mr. Brooks."

She leaned in slightly, turning her face up to his. He remained where he was as a test of his control. Her tongue moistened her lips, then she caught the bottom one between her teeth.

"I believe, Ms. Tanner, you are already aware of any intentions I may have, which I assure you I will attain. In good time."

"I've witnessed little of your actual ... passion, that you feel so absolutely certain you will be able to wield. The accomplishment of anything does begin with intention, Mr. Brooks, but if the road leads nowhere, well ..." she said as she shrugged, and placed her hands in the back pockets of her jeans.

The posture caused her breasts to thrust forward as the vee of her shirt tightened around her bust line, revealing the very tops of one of the places Ethan longed to see, feel, taste. Her expression was a mixture of innocence and barely chained desire. He set the pictures on the counter beside the trays. Without moving his gaze from her eyes, he realized his previous conviction to hold himself away from her had evaporated. He closed the distance between them.

The first taste spun his control to the nether regions of his mind. Both hands came to Carli's jaw as he took the kiss deeper. Her hands wrapped around behind him stoking small fires beneath his clothes, heating his body and the room. His hands made the trek from her cheek, down her neck, to the buttons that held the material covering what he sought. Releasing the first three, tiny fasteners through their holes with his nimble fingers, he slid his palm inside her shirt and across her breast. Stroking his thumb along the edge of where lace met skin, he felt her nipple harden against the center of his hand. That response quickened the blood in his veins and accelerated the urgency to have more of her.

With her hands under his shirt, she enjoyed the play of muscles across his back as he moved and shifted to continue undoing her buttons. Her body's reaction was swift and definite. It seemed that every part of her being was voting unanimously to have Ethan. Her mind bumped along with logistics, the how and when and where she could enjoy him for as long as he remained in Wyoming. The willingness of her physical responses, the reveling in sensations, barely left enough space for her heart, which softened, turned, opened to possibilities her mind had yet to contemplate. Nerves were electrified, senses revving.

The rest of the buttons fell from their holes, leaving the front of her torso open to his gaze and touch. A front clasp that held the cups together over her breasts was released just as easily. Both of his hands rose to cover her. As his thumbs caressed the hypersensitive tips, he nibbled his way across her jaw and down her neck. Gently, he pressed her back against the counter behind her, wedging himself between her thighs.

She leaned forward, nearly beyond reason with the electrifying sparks Ethan instigated with his steady touch. Her palms measured his back, ribs, and abdomen, then her fingers undid the fastening of his jeans, and pulled the zipper toward the floor. There was a primal moan of pleasure, and she was unsure as to which one of them emitted the sound. She was adventurous when it came to sex, but had never had the experience in a darkroom. The ones at college were too busy, at the *Views* in New York it was shared with other photographers, and would be considered in poor taste to use such a public area for something that she preferred to keep private. She equated it to having sex on a copy machine. But here, in her own darkroom, there was nothing to stop her and Ethan from following through on what they both obviously desired. Pushing her hands between Ethan's jeans and his skin, she was interrupted by a pounding on the darkroom door.

"Carli? Carli! The storage shed is on fire."

Alyssa's banging and frantic voice was followed by Carli and Ethan righting their clothing. Carli reached the door first. Flinging it open, she stared into a panicked face.

"Tim has a hose on it and I've called 911. We could use some help," Alyssa said, her gaze shifting to Ethan as he stepped up behind Carli.

Leaving the darkroom door open, the three of them trotted down the hall and the stairs, then out the front door of the lodge.

CHAPTER 26

It was quite simple, really. Acquiring a gas can and fuel from a station in Laramie, the person purchasing it was assumed to be just another anonymous farmer or rancher. Pulling off the highway and hiking down the drive and around the parking area to the storage was the most strenuous part. No one was around, including the sheriff, whose car was parked in front of the lodge. Splashing the gas against the side of the building, then leaving the plastic container at the back, offered a certain excitement that zinged through the body. Just like in the movies, the match lit on the first strike, and blue flame topped with bright yellow, licked at the line of gasoline around the perimeter, the accelerant urging the flames up the walls of the structure. Stepping back from the heat to watch, for just a moment, the design of fire on the wall. It wasn't certain that important documents were stored here, but why take the chance that Bear, in his convoluted filing system, didn't have several copies of his will. By destroying the storage building, it was one less place to search later.

The growing height of the flames and the great cloud of smoke that billowed into the air was the signal to sneak back across the land between the shed and the highway. The only thing left to do would be to change into different shoes, and dispose of these muddy ones at the first opportunity.

«« — »»

How the hell did Dad ever manage to find anything in here? Shaun questioned in the silence of the office. Not knowing if

Carli had already gone through the stacks, he shuffled files, but didn't find anything of interest. He had just sat in the office chair, when the 911 call came in on his cell phone as a text message.

Fire-outbuilding at the lodge.

He shot out of the chair and out of the office, neglecting to lock the door. He smelled it as soon as he opened the front door, and seeing the location of the smoke, knew it was the storage shed. As he rounded the corner, he saw that Tim had stretched out a hose from the corner of the lodge and attempted to keep the flames under control. Once the Centennial Fire Truck arrived, they would tap into the hydrant in the parking lot and the fire would be extinguished. But that wouldn't happen before there was serious damage, or complete loss, to the structure and its contents.

"Keep the ground soaked around the building. If the needles catch, we could lose more than this shed," Shaun yelled to Tim as he skidded to a stop a few feet from Carli's work partner.

Tim nodded and redirected the puny stream from the garden hose to the area around the sides of the structure. There was electricity going to the storage shed, but a short would only occur if the light switch was engaged. Shaun moved around the closest corner of the storage building and was now facing the side that was furthest from the front door of the lodge. In the shadow of the wall was the melted plastic remains of the gas container. Arson. But why the storage unit? Why not the lodge? Or the barn, if the purpose was to destroy property?

Through the flames that reached up and devoured the wooden walls and roof of the building, Shaun saw Ethan. Their eyes met, then Shaun pointed at the bubbling plastic. Ethan nodded, and they both returned to the front of the building where Carli was directing the fire truck to the hydrant.

In their methodical way, the town of Centennial's firefighters unwound hoses as one attached an end to the hydrant, while two others directed the flow. It all looked quite serious, as they were dressed in their flame-resistant pants and jackets, hardhats and visors, and gloves to keep the heat from their hands.

Carli moved to stand next to Tim, who decided he was only in the way with his hose, so had backed off and left the fire to those who dealt with the orange monster on a regular basis. Turning to locate Ethan, she found him at the rear of the fire truck where he stood conversing with Shaun. It appeared as if they took turns nodding and gesturing towards the structure that was quickly being consumed by flames.

"Are you alright?" she asked Tim.

He nodded. "Of course. You know, I live in New York City for excitement. Out here in the country, things are supposed to be calm and uneventful."

"Depends on your definition of calm. There's always activity at the lodge."

"But it seems to have raised to another level, beginning with Bear's death."

She pursed her lips. He was right. They had never had a fire, never had a client get hurt while out riding, except Ethan. In fact, she knew that over the years there were very few injuries incurred by clients or staff.

As the color of the smoke changed to reflect more steam than ash, Carli looked to where Ethan and Shaun continued to talk, then noticed the Cadillac that drove into the parking area. Darla. The company van used that morning to return clients to the airport pulled up next to Shaun's vehicle, with Ray in the driver's seat.

"No accident," Shaun said.

Ethan shook his head. "Who would be able to obtain—" he began, then answered his own question. "Never mind. Everyone had access."

"To the gas cans for the snowmobiles, chainsaws, things like that, sure. But Dad's cans were all metal."

Understanding bloomed on Ethan's face. It was arson, with the firebug bringing their own accelerant.

Shaun continued, "They expected the container to melt. If it was an employee, why make it obvious that it's arson?"

"The Marshall may be able to figured it out."

"Not before whoever did this has a chance to try something else. Maybe they want us to know the level of destruction they're capable of."

"If that was the case, why start off with murder, then digress to arson?"

Shaun thought a moment, then glanced at the flames being doused by the spray from the firemen. "Unless it isn't the same person."

"You think your family has more than one enemy?" Ethan's brows drew together at what this could mean.

Shrugging, Shaun turned back to the agent. "Or they're partners. One removes the head, the other makes the rest so uncomfortable that they leave."

"Bear Tanner was worth a chunk of change. Money is always a motive. Who stands to gain the most from Bear's death?" Ethan looked at the wilderness around him, the lodge, barn, and the growing group of spectators. Carli and Tim were joined by Alyssa, Ray, and Darla, all with appropriately distraught faces.

"None of us know. I was searching Dad's office hoping to find something—" Shaun started.

Ethan shook his head. "Carli and I were thorough in our search there last night. She found several official documents. Haven't had the chance to find out if she read them," he paused, then, watching Shaun's features, asked, "Did you know that your father kept a daily journal on his hard drive?"

Shock, disbelief, then laughter answered more than the sheriff's words. "I knew my father very well. If he has something like that, he had a damn good reason for doing it."

Looking again at the smoldering sides of the storage shed, Ethan shifted a few of the puzzle pieces, and decided that none of Bear's children were responsible. Nor were former employees or clients. That left current employees. And Darla. Zach and Alyssa were off the list. J.J. could not reasonably account for his whereabouts when Bear was shot, and he was absent this morning as well. The will could be contested, if Darla was indeed still married to Bear, by either the wife or the children, depending on how Tanner distributed his worldly goods.

The roof had caved in, but three of the four walls remained standing. Mostly. The cardboard boxes and their contents were mush from the water. Before Ethan could ask, Shaun revealed they were thinking the same thing.

"Whoever sparked the gas, had to have known, or guessed, that Dad kept files in the storage shed. They must have been attempting to destroy—" he paused, then looked at Ethan. "Legal papers. The will." He glanced at Darla, then added, "Or divorce papers."

Needing to tie up loose ends, as others began to unravel, Ethan asked, "What did you discover about the gun Bear had with him on Wolf's Ridge?"

Shaun sighed. "It wasn't the model Carli said was missing from the safe in the basement. The one Dan Rogers, one of the poachers, has is most likely clean. All of their weapons are registered, their permits in order."

"Then the game thieves are unrelated to Bear's death, but obviously not this," Ethan gestured towards the remains of the storage structure.

"I agree."

"Where is the gun that Bear had with him?"

"The client said he gave it to Ray once they arrived back at the lodge."

Both lawmen turned their gaze towards the older man that stood between Carli and Darla. Shaun guessed that Ray had cleaned the weapon and stored it someplace. The idea that Ray had any part in the recent happenings at the lodge never entered his mind.

Reserved, aloof, refusing to participate in the funeral plans. Ethan's one conversation with Ray hadn't produced much in the way of information. Looking at his expression now, Ethan would define it as relief. That the fire was out, or that he had yet to be implicated?

"I want you to take a look at the journal your father kept. I sent the file to my laptop. Do you have time today?"

Shaun tipped his wrist to look at his watch. Gauging how long it would be before the fire truck left, contacting the Fire Marshall, and returning to the office to sign off on the transfer of the poachers to Cheyenne, he shifted his gaze to Ethan.

"After dinner?"

Ethan nodded. "Keep me informed on the Marshall's report. And you may want to locate Bear's rifle."

"Already planned on it. Just to eliminate suspects, I'll gather the weapons stored at the lodge and send them to ballistics in Cheyenne."

"I'll call them in the morning, make sure they understand this is a federal investigation," Ethan offered.

Shaun smiled. "I knew you would be good for something."

The agent chuckled, then left Shaun to his duties as sheriff, and moved to join Carli and the crowd of spectators.

«««—»»»

There were several issues that Sam felt she needed to see to personally in Laramie, all regarding the services for her father. The nine o'clock meeting with the funeral director at the mortuary went well. Since Carli and Shaun had no opinion on the matter, she had chosen a simple urn to be on the dais in the church. She decided that they would ride to Wolf's Ridge, once things were settled, to spread Dad's ashes. Because it was on private property, they wouldn't need a permit to do it legally. There were papers to sign and details that she hadn't even thought of, all outlined in the brochures given to her by the mortuary.

The next stop was the bank. Though she was friends with the bank manager and was therefore able to open the accounts over the phone, she did have to sign the forms to make it official. She knew that her father had an extensive list of friends and acquaintances, as she contacted them all with the news of his death, but she didn't realize their generosity. Tens of thousands of dollars had already been collected. Deciding to leave the accounts open for three weeks, she signed more forms for the funds to be automatically transferred to the organizations at that time, and the accounts closed.

Her meeting with the pastor at the church wasn't until one-thirty, so she decided to have lunch at a café in Laramie. As she munched on a salad, she scrolled through her to-do list on her phone, feeling a sense of accomplishment that the list was dwindling. She hadn't heard any updates from Matt, and was on the verge of assuming all was well at Crystal Springs, when her phone chimed, alerting her to a text. Setting her fork on the table, she switched screens and read the message.

Fence repaired. Cattle moved. Sold Ace. Bonita is in foal.

She smiled. Bonita was one of her favorite mares. Though she was in foal last year, she had gotten sick and had reabsorbed the fetus. With fingers crossed, she hoped Bonita would stay healthy and carry the foal to term. She was a bit sad to read that Ace had found a new home, but Matt would only sell if the owners fit the profile of what the horse needed. There was always the clause in the Bill of Sale that the horse returns to Crystal Springs should the owner, for a variety of reasons, decide the horse no longer fit their needs. Her father didn't think that was a sound business practice. Only four horses had been returned, and she decided she would rather have them back than to not know their fate.

So the fence was fixed, but how long would it be before there was another breach? And would Cole be as understanding? She had just sent a message to Matt, when her phone chimed again as she received a text ... from Cole. Trying not to smile, attempting, half-heartedly, to deny the quickening of her pulse, she schooled her features as she read what he had written.

Thanks for the flowers. Sorry to hear about Bear. Alice.

It wasn't from Cole. Alice must have insisted that he notify Sam and so he sent a text message with the words stated exactly as his mother had spoken them. Not wanting to be rude, and setting aside the disappointment, she typed her response.

253

You're welcome. Heal quickly. Thanks for your thoughts. I'll see you next week.

Pressing SEND, she set her phone next to her plate, then dug into her purse for her wallet. Laying bills on the table and gathering her things, she guessed she would be back at the lodge by three. If luck was with her, Darla would be elsewhere. The last thing she wanted, or needed, was the woman imposing herself into affairs that did not concern her. As she turned to leave, her phone chimed again. She looked at the screen as she made her way to the door of the café. The waitress nearly ran into her as she stopped suddenly to stare at the message.

Look forward to your return. Be safe. Cole.

With apologies streaming from both women, Sam hastily exited the restaurant. Fumbling for her sunglasses, as she squinted into the afternoon sun, she wasn't sure how to feel, or if a response was warranted. Climbing into the cab of one of the trucks from the lodge, she decided to do nothing, and dropped her phone into her purse. Attempting to put the matter out of her mind as she navigated her way onto Interstate-80, then the highway towards Centennial, the questions wouldn't leave her alone. Why would Cole care if she was home or not? And why would he want to see her? To request payment for the fence? She hated this. When she was tired or overly stressed, her mind seemed to just wind in circles. There were no answers, and it was useless to speculate.

Everything was set at the church. There were volunteers to direct the florists where to put the wreaths, the placement of the urn, and to set up and take down extra chairs. The family would not be required to do anything. Crossing the last item off her list for the day, she dialed Carli's number as she drove through town towards the lodge.

There was no answer on Carli's phone, and Shaun's vehicle was not in front of the sheriff's office. Resting her arm on the door of the truck, the breeze from the open window ruffled her bangs. She was looking forward to a quiet evening at the lodge, maybe arriving at a consensus with Carli and Shaun as to the future plans of Tanner's Outdoor Adventures.

Just before she reached the driveway, she smelled it. Smoke. Sitting up in her seat, she turned cautiously into the drive. A wave of relief washed over her as the lodge came into view, apparently still intact. That was quickly followed by irritation as she recognized the Cadillac parked next to the sheriff's vehicle. Climbing down from the cab, she looked around. The gutted, blackened remains of the storage shed squatted among a puddle outlined on one side by the deep, dual-wheeled tracks of what must have been the fire truck. There were no new rental cars in the lot, and she hoped there weren't any recently made reservations for the next few days.

Feeling exhausted and her head spinning with questions, she trudged up the steps of the lodge and entered the lobby. Darla was seated in the center of one of the sofas facing the fireplace, which was void of the afternoon fire due to the warmer spring weather and the absence of clients to enjoy it. Because it was Sunday afternoon, she knew that Alyssa was not here, and therefore Zach would be gone as well. She assumed J.J. was in the barn, and Ray was probably starting the evening meal. Carli, with hands on hips, stared out the side window, her back to the front door. Shaun was nowhere that she could see, and Tim stood halfway between Darla and Carli, a weary expression on his face.

To stall for time, she slowly closed the door, removed her coat, and greeted, tentatively, those in the tension-filled room.

"Good afternoon. What happened to the storage area?"

Carli turned just enough to look over her shoulder at Sam. Tears were close to the surface, and Carli rarely cried.

"Arson. Someone poured gasoline along the perimeter."

Sam couldn't keep her eyes from darting to Darla. "Was anyone hurt?"

Darla raised a brow. "Don't look at me. I arrived after the fire trucks. Clearly, someone wants the Tanners gone. Really, I didn't think Bear had any enemies."

"Except the vermin—" Carli began to mumble under her breath.

Darla got to her feet. "I had nothing but respect for your father—" she responded.

"Please! Enough!" Tim cupped his hands to the sides of his head. "The two of you have done nothing but argue and trade insults for the last thirty minutes! I would prefer for you to stew in silence than continue to be privy to this nonsense." Placing his hands on his hips, his look of censure darted from Darla to Carli, before it changed to a plea for help as he turned toward Sam.

"Well, no one asked you to stay," Carli grumbled, arms crossed under her chest as she faced the center of the room.

"If I left, there would be nail scratching and hair pulling. It really doesn't place either of you in a very mature light to lower to such behavior."

Before anyone could respond, Ray emerged from the dining room to announce that he would serve dinner early if everyone could be civil.

"I've lost my appetite," Carli said, her long strides carrying her to the door where Sam continued to hover. Pulling her coat from the rack, she called to Tim, "I owe you a glass of whiskey. Coming?"

Tim glanced at Ray, then Darla, then stepped around the end of the sofa, grabbed his jacket, and squeezed out the door.

Carli turned her gaze to meet Sam's, the same question hung between them. With a sigh, Sam took her coat and followed Carli out the door. As was her habit at Crystal Springs, the truck keys hung from a belt loop. Sam removed them and informed her sister that she was too upset to drive when Carli held out her hand for the key ring.

"Fine," Carli muttered, climbing in the truck from the passenger side, then sliding to the middle of the bench seat.

Tim sat next to her, and Sam, behind the wheel, didn't ask or say anything until they were on the highway. She left the window down, deciding Carli needed the fresh air. About halfway to the

Rockin' R, Sam guessed her sister had settled enough to give answers.

"Any idea on who sparked the shed?"

"Shaun and the Marshall went over everything. Nothing definite."

"Where is Shaun?" Sam asked.

"With Ethan in Cabin 4. Did you know Dad kept a diary on his computer?" Carli turned to look at Sam.

"No. What did he write?"

Turning her gaze back to look out the windshield, Carli said, "Just the events that occurred each day. Since Shaun was around more than you or me, Ethan thought he might be able to decipher some of the codes Dad used."

Sam, having driven on rural roads since she was fifteen, was not bothered by the dips and curves. At Tim's rather loud swallow, Carli requested that they arrive at the 'R not covered in vomit from one who was sensitive to the twists and turns of vehicles. Sam decelerated, and continued with attempting to discover what had triggered the scene she had found at the lodge.

"Why do you allow Darla to get to you?"

Carli dragged her hand through the curls that bounced in front of her eyes and exhaled heavily. "I don't know. It's like I read the sign 'Danger, Crocodiles', but I wade into the water anyway. I guess I'm hoping one day I'll actually win."

Tim snorted. "Honey, you don't have a big enough bitch gene in you to contend with the likes of that California witch."

Carli tucked her hands inside the pockets of her coat, then glanced at Tim. "Thanks."

"She'll only be here until Wednesday, at the latest. Once we meet with Stevens, it should clear up all the speculation regarding the lodge." Sam slowed as the neon sign for the Rockin' R came into view.

Turning into the dirt parking lot, and rolling up the window, Sam asked, "What is worth enough to you to ignore, or even be civil, to Darla?"

"A hundred dollars," Tim answered.

Carli scowled at him. "That's not—"

"Take it or leave it. It's burning a hole in my pocket," he said, tapping his shirt, "ever since it found its way here when you were unable to send the photos on time."

"The fire was a bit of a distraction," Carli argued, following Tim out of the truck.

"An excuse, you mean, in an attempt to renege on our wager. A bet is a bet, Dear Carli, and if you want the cash, you'll not engage in the display I was forced to witness this afternoon."

Sam stared at the two of them. They stood toe to toe, with Tim several inches taller, yet not backing down from Carli's glare. She imagined they conversed this way occasionally. Since they had become work partners, the rest of the Tanners compared them to a married couple. She had often wondered if they might have been, had Tim been straight.

"Fine." Carli turned on her heel, and without waiting for Sam or Tim, stalked toward the door of the Rockin' R.

Sunday evenings were typically the slowest for the restaurant, and tonight was no exception. Sissy was behind the bar washing glasses, and only four tables and five bar stools were occupied. Jackie, who worked part-time here and part-time at Doc Miller's in town, smiled at Carli as she entered, followed by Sam and Tim.

"Eating out tonight, Hon?" Jackie asked.

"Maybe. Drink first," Carli answered, tipping her head to the bar on her left.

"Sure. I'll check back later. And Carli, Sam," Jackie paused until both pairs of hazel eyes held her brown gaze. "I'm sorry about Bear."

"Thanks," Sam and Carli voiced in unison, then offered a small smile to the waitress.

The three took stools at the bar, and Carli raised a finger to get Sissy's attention.

Wiping her hands on a towel, the beautiful brunette walked the length of the dark, wooden counter, stopping in front of Carli, who was flanked by Sam and Tim.

"Hey, Sissy. We'll need some Kentucky," Carli requested.

Ignoring the tray behind her where the well liquor was kept, Sissy hooked her foot around the corner of a crate under the counter, to pull it out. Stepping up, she reached onto a glass shelf and brought down with her a special bottle of whiskey. Toeing the crate back under the counter, she turned and grabbed three shot glasses. Setting them on the bar in front of each of them with one hand, then removing the stopper from the bottle, she filled each glass to just below the rim. More than a shot, but not so full it would spill. It was, after all, the finest whiskey.

"I'm sorry about Bear," she said, pouring the liquid to exactly the same level in each glass without wasting a drop.

"Thanks," Sam answered.

Sissy's gaze was on Carli, who nodded slightly. When she turned to replace the bottle, Carli laid her hand on the bartender's wrist.

"Leave it."

Sissy offered a nod of her own in understanding, and set the bottle on the scarred wood in front of Carli. She wandered down the bar, refilling glasses as needed.

Carli leaned back on her stool to include Tim and Sam in her toast. "To the best father, the smartest businessman, an upstanding citizen, a phenomenal outdoorsman, and friend to most of the population in Wyoming."

Gazing at the dark brown liquor in her glass, she felt the tears gather once again. Better to have the tears express the burn in her throat than her grief over losing her father. She brought the glass to her lips, closed her eyes, and drained the shot in one swallow. Sam followed, and then Tim. All three glasses were replaced on the bar. She lifted the bottle and refilled the tumblers. The next round went the same as the first. By the fourth refill, they began to sip.

"You were right," Tim stated, speech slightly slurred by the rich alcohol on an empty stomach. "This is the best Kentucky makes."

Carli offered him a half-smile and sipped again.

Tim watched her closely. She could always out drink him. He would be passed out with one glass of the local brew, and wake up hours later to find Carli with flowers in her hair, dancing with the villagers around the fire. She was all those things he had told Ethan about that morning. What he didn't include, was courageous. He knew she was holding herself together by sheer force of will. Carli rarely saw the need for tears, and had never had the experience like the one she was in the middle of now. He wanted to stay close to her, to be there when her strength gave out and the grief overwhelmed her. As he sipped, he wondered how Ethan would handle the normally pulled-together Carli in the throes of the realization that her father was gone. That, he decided, would be the test of the man's intentions, and feelings, toward his best friend and gifted work partner.

CHAPTER 27

There were pros and cons to being the boss. Hiring and firing people, deciding which projects held merit, or pulling the plug on ones that drained the budget, only fueled the God-like complex that people in his position wielded as deftly as a Samurai does a sword. Scott preferred to think that he had more compassion than some of his colleagues. A few of his employees, however, seemed to enjoy pointing out to him that he is just as big an asshole as his contemporaries. And those that he allowed that privilege meant more to him than just being an employee. Carli Tanner was not only the most talented photojournalist on his staff, and one of the best in the business, she didn't take any of his shit, for which she had earned his deepest respect. With respect, came 'like'. Scott 'liked' few people in his life. He tolerated most of the staff at the *Views* because without them, he would not be the top shark. Other editors at various publications were mere competition, players in the game.

He rocked back in his five-hundred-dollar executive chair, then spun far enough to gaze out at the view of Manhattan from his twelfth-floor office. Absently straightening his tie, he thought of the drawbacks of 'liking' an employee. His assistants were never around long enough for him to form any attachment to them. As long as the rest of the journalists and section editors did their job, he left them alone. But it was Carli who prompted him to contact his own father. Surprised by the call, Scott's father wondered if he had suffered a heart attack from his job, or had gotten fired by the Fortune 500 company that owned the magazine. No, he had assured his father, everything was fine. They hung up after an awkward twenty-minute conversation. A phone call that he would not have instigated had Bear Tanner not been shot and killed, and Carli not been one of his most 'likable' people.

Spinning his chair back towards his computer screen, he looked again at the digital prints Tim had cleaned up and sent. Tim was the first demand Carli had made when he offered her the job. Her reasons were valid, and though he allowed her to team with one of the staff already on the *Views'* payroll, he didn't think it would last. Apparently, her hard-ass routine with him during her interview was a one-time event. Carli Tanner produced articles that sold his magazine. If she needed a partner in order for him to continue with his seven-figure bank account, he would find a way to justify the extra travel expenses. Fortunately, the corporate board was thrilled with Carli's work and so they didn't question Tim's role.

These were the shots from Africa. They were phenomenal, as was all of Carli's work, and the hard-on he was developing was more for the sales and prestige of the *Views*, than for the beautiful and talented artist. Carli had made it clear that their relationship would be one of employer and employee only. She had guaranteed, at her interview, that *International Views* would increase their subscriptions and circulation, as well as win coveted awards, with her on the team. At first he thought it was false bravado, and believed a night spent in his bed would show Carli her place. He chuckled now at the swiftness with which she had gained the upper hand, and produced for him in ways even his inflated ego could not have predicted.

Glancing at the clock on the wall, and the enormous calendar under it that listed sections and articles to be completed and formatted by particular dates, he opened his e-mail and tapped a message. He needed the prints he was sure she had developed by now, as well as the preliminaries for South America. The expense report could be filed when she and Tim returned to New York, which he hoped was by the end of next week. One World Piece, a premier gallery in the City, had contacted him regarding a collection of Carli's prints for a showing. Since she was often unreachable through phone or e-mail, the gallery manager thought to connect with her through Scott. He added to his e-mail that if she would send a message to the gallery, it would get them off his ass, as they had become quite persistent in reaching her. Pressing 'RETURN' after typing his name, he added a post-script.

Accounting contacted me about a telegram request during you time in Africa. Your location was denied, but it was agreed that a message would be sent. No idea who requested it, only that the message was 'Come home'. Hope you can solve the mystery.

《《—》》

Collecting his pants from the floor of the hotel room, Worthington removed his wallet from the back pocket and took out three hundred dollars in cash. Glancing over his shoulder as he stood next to the bed, he tossed the money on the sheets beside the body of the prostitute he had spent the last two hours with, distracting himself from the stresses of his campaign. Taking his pants with him, he closed the bathroom door and turned on the shower. Misty, he knew, would be gone when he emerged.

Though he hadn't heard from Darla, and they agreed she would only contact him after the will was read and she took possession of the property, there was an unease that began to settle around him. He trusted Darla to follow through on the plan. Well, as much as he trusted anyone. Perhaps it was these forays into Monterey that were making him nervous. His campaign announcement was made and the press had begun to request interviews, follow him to his office, and even called the house and spoke with his wife. Rose would handle the inquisitions as if she was born with the ability. Her sights were set on the White House and anything she could do to assist her husband's campaign was done with precision.

As predicted, when he opened the bathroom door of the hotel, Misty was gone. He finished dressing, dropped the room key in the box in the lobby, and handed his parking ticket to the valet. Settling his sunglasses on his nose and snapping the seat belt of his Mercedes, he drove from under the portcullis of the hotel to the highway that would take him north to Carmel. Settled that he would stay away from Misty and Monterey, he relaxed into the leather seat as the soft sounds of jazz floated around him, and his thoughts drifted to timeshare cabins in Wyoming. His chosen career was politics, and to win at politics required copious amounts of cash. To his mind, the end always justified the means.

«««—»»»

Shaun sent the rifle with Denny and the poachers to Cheyenne. Ray had no issues with giving it to the sheriff, and apologized for not mentioning it sooner. Neither Ethan nor Shaun thought anything would come from the ballistics testing. Ethan had called the Cheyenne Police Department earlier and made them aware of the investigation and the FBI's involvement. There was nothing useful so far from the arson investigation, except that there was still a threat.

For the past three and a half hours, Shaun and Ethan had exhausted every lead they had in the shooting and the fire. They were left with few answers, especially to the one, gigantic question glaring right in front of them. Who killed Bear, and why? While Shaun read through his father's diary, Ethan was flipping pages in his yellow legal pad and sketching ideas and theories that were formed between the two of them, possibilities to track down, other incidents to investigate.

"I remember this date. Dad had called and said he couldn't come by to help with installing the cabinets in the kitchen," Shaun paused and looked up at Ethan who vacillated between sitting on the edge of the bed and pacing the length of the cabin. At Ethan's questioning expression, Shaun continued, "I'm building my own house. Dad would come by and help with all the major projects. I had built the cabinets and needed a hand to hold them in place while I mounted them on the wall."

Ethan nodded. "My father usually decided he needed my help on home improvements at a time that I would rather have been at the beach or in the water. We had a summer cabin in Martha's Vineyard," he tipped up the corner of his mouth. "Once the rich and famous started to frequent the coast, my parents sold it. Now they're in Arizona half the year, Baltimore the other half. Dad made sure my education included which end of the hammer to use."

Shaun chuckled, remembering his own father saying much the same thing. "So, I remember this date." His eyes were back on the computer. "Two weeks earlier, there's the same symbol. Different day of the week ..." Shaun's voice became quiet, his brows coming together as he scrolled down the screen, peering at the asterisk and the dates.

Ethan's phone chimed. "Brooks," he spoke into the device.

The screen showed the main number for the FBI Field Office in Baltimore. When Micah's voice was in his ear, Ethan walked out of the cabin, closing the door quietly behind him.

Shaun glanced out the window, and by the light outside the door, saw Ethan walk the length of the porch in front of the cabin. He went to the computer case to look for the power cord for the laptop. On his way to the dresser, where the case was, he picked up the pad of paper with which Ethan seemed to spend a lot of time. Flipping through the pages, he saw himself, Sam, Alyssa, Zach, J.J., Ray, and a great number of sketches of Carli. His first thought was that the FBI agent was a talented artist. The next, that Brooks was attracted to Carli. He didn't blame the man. His oldest sister was quite a woman. A few of the drawings appeared more ... personal, as if Carli showed a side to Ethan that few were privileged to see. The sketches seemed alive. Nuances were captured in pencil that Shaun had only witnessed with Carli's photographs. The protective brother role made him want to know Ethan's intentions, but the practical side reminded him that Carli was an adult and capable of telling the agent exactly what she thought of him, or what might occur between them.

Tossing the pad back on the bed, he reached into an outside pocket of the computer case to search for the cord, when he found a stack of file folders. Intending, at first, to pull them out so he could feel the bottom of the pocket, the title of the one on top caught his attention. He glanced out the window and saw Ethan facing away from the cabin, one hand holding the phone to his ear, the other hand pushing his hair back from his face. Shaun read the other labels, then opened the first folder. Murder. Interviews. Parent reports. Autopsy. Crime photos. Bloody, grisly details. The last line he read before Ethan opened the door was, *child, age 9, found dismembered, sexually assaulted. Taken from school. No witnesses. No suspects.*

Ethan paused on the threshold, one hand on the open door. "Reading those files is in violation of about ten federal laws."

Shaun looked up, the brief expression of deep hurt and confusion flashed on his face before the schooled features of the town sheriff reappeared. "What the hell are these?"

Closing the door, Ethan answered, "Unsolved cases. Federal cases." He left the question unasked.

"I was looking for the power cord. Seems there's a lot about you I don't know," Shaun said, his gaze shifting to the pad on the bed.

"All you need to know, whatever is pertinent to this case, I'll volunteer," Ethan offered, took the files from Shaun and replaced them in the case, then set the power cord on the bed.

Ignoring Ethan's warning, Shaun asked, "Are those the kind of cases you work? Are they all crimes against children?"

Sighing, Ethan set his hands on his hips. There were no rules forbidding case discussion in general. Not that rules had ever kept him from doing what needed to be done. They usually just forced him to be more creative in his solutions. Releasing his hands to his side, he nodded.

"How do you sleep at night?" Shaun gestured toward the case that held the files and pictures.

"Better than some. I just … find a compartment for it. Refuse to allow it to take over."

"So, it hasn't affected your personal life? You have a lot of friends, a girlfriend or wife?" Shaun knew he was prying, but also hoped that if Ethan found a way to deal with what was in the files, he would have the answer to eliminate Shaun's own ghosts.

Ethan snorted, then took the power cord and moved to the table and the beaming laptop. After attaching the cord and plugging it into the wall, he sat in the opposite chair Shaun had used. He held the younger man's gaze and briefly wondered at their differences. How many murders did a small town sheriff see in a year? What was the worst he had to deal with? A rollover of a tourist driving too fast on the mountain roads in winter? Shaun was old enough to no longer be considered a rookie in any force. Ethan had learned long ago that even if people weren't in law enforcement, they still experienced gruesome events.

"No, I don't have many friends. That's more a choice than lack of opportunity. The job, as you know, demands a lot. Few women tolerate being second in a relationship."

Placing his hands in his front pockets, Shaun realized how much he and Ethan were alike. "You probably think a small town, what does this sheriff know about tragedy? I've seen enough that I don't always sleep well at night. Hell, there are times I don't sleep." He chuckled, but it lacked humor. "Dad was my best friend. An incredible woman wants to marry me, but I can't seem to commit to her." Shaun relaxed his arms by his sides. "I've wanted this career since I was a kid. I just wish …" as he searched for the words, Ethan offered a multiple choice answer.

"You had time, energy, something left to give that isn't tied to the job, tainted by what you see and hear. You wish there was a way to banish the demons."

Neither blinked, nor breathed. They both knew Ethan spoke for every lawman. How does one protect and serve, and not be consumed by the injustices of humanity? The silence in the cabin was broken by the ring of Shaun's cell phone. He turned partially away as he answered, only to swivel back towards Ethan at the message.

"Shaun, it's Sissy. Carli, Sam, and their friend knocked off a bottle of John's best whiskey. There's no way any of them are fit to drive."

Despite the music and a few loud voices, he heard Sissy's concern clearly.

"Thanks. I'm on my way." Replacing the phone at his waist, he grabbed his coat from the back of the chair. "Seems my sisters and Tim have imbibed a little too much at the Rockin' R."

"I'll come with you," Ethan offered, snatching his coat from the end of the bed.

Shaun counted vehicles as they climbed into the his SUV. "They must have taken the truck. You'll have to drive it back."

Ethan said nothing as he buckled his seat belt and Shaun's tires left the gravel drive for the paved road. The time on the dash indicated he and Shaun had spent four hours in his cabin pouring over files and theories.

Without preamble, Shaun said, "How do you feel about Carli?"

Ethan, realizing his raised brow in the dark was lost on the driver, answered vaguely, "That she isn't a suspect. She's a talented photographer. Her skills at horseback riding are better than my own."

"Facts. Look, I know you've been here only a few days, and you'll be returning to Baltimore soon. I've seen the way you and Carli interact."

"Is this the protective brother speech?" Ethan queried.

"Yes. It is. I know the two of you are going to do ... well, I would rather not think about that, but it wouldn't be fair if I didn't warn you. Carli ... she's only fallen for a couple of guys. Each relationship seems to be a little deeper. And each time they end, she becomes a little more ... like me." His voice started off loud, but now was barely a whisper in the quiet of the vehicle. "If I had my way, I would dissuade you completely. But as much as I

268

care for her, I've never attempted to control her." He looked at Ethan, who nodded.

He looked away the same time the sheriff took his eyes back to the road. *That's a record*, Ethan thought. Warned off the same woman by two different men.

Shaun slowed as he pulled into the front of the Rockin' R. There were about a dozen cars in the dirt lot. The blue and red neon from the four-foot 'R' that flashed near the roof, reflected off the hood of the sheriff's vehicle. One hand on the keys, the other on the door handle, he looked again at Ethan.

"Carli hardly ever drinks, and so to have her too inebriated to drive ... well, Agent Brooks, you're in for a treat. A drunk Carli Tanner is an unusual sight. Unforgettable, and rare."

Both men exited the SUV and made their way to the front door of the Rockin' R.

CHAPTER 28

You have reached the office of Maxwell Stevens. We're sorry for the inconvenience, but our office will be closed until Tuesday afternoon due to a family emergency. Please leave your name, number, the reason for your call, and it will be returned promptly by Tuesday evening. Thank you.

Pressing 'END' and closing the phone, it seemed that no new information would be forthcoming until the will was read with everyone present. If Lady Luck was in the vicinity, then the fire would have destroyed any copies of the will or divorce papers. That was one less building for the construction crew to demolish. Now it was a matter of scooping up the charred ruins and hauling them away.

It was quiet here with everyone gone. The lodge was set far enough back from the highway that headlights and engine noise didn't reach the veranda. Bear liked the quiet. Well, now he would have an eternity of it. Sighing, all thoughts of the robust outdoorsman were set aside for visions of vacation rentals. Cabins, parks, a clubhouse, a recreation building, groomed trails, and an expanded stable were the highlights of the development that were planned. It was all about family fun and adventure for those who would place a large portion of their life savings with Wyoming Lifestyles for the privilege of using the facilities a few weeks a year. For the developers, the amenities would entice more buyers, who would line the pockets to overflowing of those who made the vacations possible. They were so close to beginning the construction. Within a week, if all continued according to plan. The excitement was making it difficult to sit and wait. Perhaps the horses needed to be checked. A stroll on a crisp, spring night would feel good.

《《—》》

With only a crescent moon, the stars shined brightly. Each pebble he tossed into William's Lake set off ripples that reflected the starlight, much like the eyes of the girl next to him. It wasn't unusual that they would drive down to the lake after being in town for dinner and a show. Alyssa picked the movie this time. A comedy. He laughed, of course, and sometimes just because she did. When it was his turn to pick the movie, it was always an action flick, something with explosions and guns and where the bad guys were either caught or killed at the end. The loud *bangs* would have Alyssa clutching his arm, her face turned into his shoulder. It gave him the opportunity to protect her.

Having tossed the last rock into the water, he turned to look at Alyssa. She was laying on her back, staring up at the night sky. As an elective during her senior year, she was taking Astronomy and Geology. He hadn't paid as much attention in school as he should have. It wasn't that it was too hard. He was just bored. Listening to her share stories from the Greeks and Romans regarding the cosmos was like taking a class for free, or getting the information from a book without having to read it. The added bonus was how Alyssa's voice wrapped around him. She would change the pitch and tone to depict different characters, would ask him questions, then pose some of her own. What amazed him most was how smart she was, especially since he knew her father.

He stretched out next to her on the quilt that was laid on the ground. Propping himself up on one elbow, he kept his other hand to himself. Just looking at her, with her pretty face and her body relaxed, made him feel good. He knew he was in love with her, and the ring he had purchased was proof that he was serious about making their relationship permanent. She would be eighteen on Friday, and that was when he would give it to her. It wasn't an engagement ring. He was afraid she would not consider attending college if they were to get married right away. There was a churning in his gut if he allowed doubt to enter his plans. She would go to college, perhaps meet someone else, and leave him. Or she wouldn't attend college and he would feel guilty for keeping her from any future besides being his wife.

With his head close to hers, it seemed natural that she reach up to take off his straw hat with one hand, draping the other behind his neck and encourage him to close the distance between them. He didn't resist.

Zach never allowed a chance to kiss her slip by, for which she was grateful. Not that she'd had a lot of boys to compare him to, but of the three she had kissed, Zach was skilled. He didn't slobber, and he showed her there was more to kissing than sticking his tongue down her throat. It took just one press of their lips, months ago, that first set off the zinging in her veins, the heat in her belly. The fluttering in her heart, the constant smile, the feeling of excitement that filled her when he was near, or when they were alone, like now, was addicting. She wondered, not for the first time, if she would always feel this way with Zach.

That thought never scared her. A couple of her friends told her she was too young to really be in love or think about getting married. But she knew. Zach was the one for her. His palm on her flat stomach was warm. His hands were a little rough from the work he did at the lodge, but they felt comfortable when they held hers, his long fingers lacing them together. Always sure and gentle when he touched her, he never rushed, but seemed to savor just holding her.

They had talked about sex when Zach officially asked her to be his girlfriend. She told him she was ready, but he refused to give her father any reason to keep them apart, and that included statutory rape. They had done some things, but even when she told him she wanted to go all the way, he refused, saying they should wait until she was eighteen, a legal adult. That would be on Friday.

Zach said he made plans for them, but kept them a secret. She was excited. That would be the night she would give herself to him. She was naïve. They each were just beginning to know the other's body, where to touch to bring sounds of pleasure. Tonight was no different, yet each time they were together, it wasn't the same. She rolled on top of Zach, then felt the vibration in his pocket.

With one arm still around Alyssa, he reached his other hand into his jeans and withdrew his phone. It was time. He set the alarm on his phone so he could return her before her curfew, and keep Jim Lockhart from finding a cause to pick a fight with her.

"What will you be working on tomorrow?" she asked as Zach stood and, keeping her hand in his, helped her to her feet.

"A few repairs. Hay is supposed to be delivered, so J.J. will need help setting up the pallets and probably re-stacking the remaining bales from the last delivery."

He relinquished her hand as she reached down to take the quilt from the ground and shake the pine needles from it. She folded the blanket and followed him to his truck, where he held the door open for her.

"Did you finish the essay for English?" he asked.

"Of course." She watched as Zach walked around the front of the truck, settled his hat back on his head, then opened the driver's side door.

"I'll miss seeing you tomorrow," she told him as he slid behind the wheel.

"Just enjoy your day off. Tuesday will be …" he wasn't sure how to describe a day filled with people, everyone swapping stories about Bear Tanner, and, he was sure, tears.

"Sad, but happy, too," she finished for him.

He glanced at her as he started the truck and headed back down the only road that led to the lake.

"Happy?"

"How many stories involving Bear will make people laugh?"

He smiled. "Alright. I see your point."

She turned up the radio, then sang along to a country song about life. Reaching across the seat, she took his hand as they drove to the house she shared with her father. He pulled into the dusty drive that circled in front of the dilapidated structure. The porch light was on and the glow of the TV could be seen in the living room. She sighed, then leaned toward Zach.

He met her in the middle and kissed her goodnight. "I'll see you later."

"Yes," she said with one more press of her lips to his.

Then her seatbelt was off and she was out of the truck. She turned to wave just before disappearing inside the house.

Zach slowly pulled through the circular drive. He didn't want to leave her with Jim Lockhart and wished for the day they would live in the same house. Until then, he would hold a certain amount of fear for Alyssa. She denied that her father had trouble controlling his anger for several months after they started dating. Then she admitted that she had done something that provoked her father. He had spent countless hours trying to reason with Alyssa that the way her father treated her was wrong. It was abusive. The last time Jim lost his cool, she called in sick to work and stayed home from school. When she showed up at the lodge, the swelling was gone from her lip and cheek, and she tried to tell him the cut on her lower lip was a cold sore. Alyssa wasn't good at lying, and when her eyes slid away from his face, he knew what had happened. Shaun had explained to him what he could and couldn't do when it came to protecting Alyssa and upholding the laws of Wyoming. That was one of the few times Zach had used words his mother had always frowned upon. As he drove to the lodge, he thought of the ring he would give to Alyssa on Friday. Whether she married him or left for college, she would be safe from Jim Lockhart in another two months.

«« —»»

Tim didn't know how she did it, or how he ended up with the side of his face pillowed on one hand, resting on top of the bar, drool collecting between his fingers, as she sang and shook her hips in front of the juke box. Sam had disappeared, he thought, into the ladies' room some time ago. But then, time ceased to have meaning after half a bottle of whiskey. He tried to lift his head, but the alcohol had paralyzed him, and it took all his concentration just to keep Carli swimming somewhere in his field of vision. Attempting to swallow, he realized his tongue felt thick and he knew from experience that he would feel every cell in his body tomorrow, as all ten billion of them screamed insults to his intelligence for allowing Carli, again, to bring him to Death's door.

Despite Carli's uncanny ability to never appear completely wasted, she would occasionally have alcohol, but rarely drank to the excess she had tonight. The only way he knew she was as drunk as she ever got, was he had watched her consume nearly half the bottle herself. Sam had given up trying to keep pace with her big sister. Tomorrow, they both would be nursing the mother of all hangovers. He briefly wondered if Sam was getting sick in the ladies' room, and if he should check on her. Carli was fine, though his code of chivalry required he ensure she was safe. A cold breeze brushed his face, and he rolled his eyes toward the door. *Oh, swell. The cavalry,* he thought, as Shaun and Ethan entered the Rockin' R.

The whiskey had burned, and if he could peel his face off the bar, he would do his best to make Carli pay for the pain he would have to endure tomorrow. She cared a great deal for him, didn't think she could have any other work partner, and sometimes she just wanted him to tell her no. No more boats. No more seafood. No more whiskey. But his feelings for her wouldn't allow him to sit by and have Carli drink to the memory of her father alone. Sam was her sister. That was different. He was her friend, and more.

Bear Tanner had excellent taste in alcohol. He stocked his cabinets with the highest quality liquor, and his children had inherited his good taste. Unlike Shaun and Samantha, she had inherited the anti-drunk gene from her father. As a teenager, she had tried a few times to experience the feeling of not being in control, but it eluded her. Like Bear, her body metabolized alcohol the same as it did a cheeseburger. The three of them had finished the bottle Sissy had taken from the shelf behind the bar, and she knew she had drunk half the bottle herself. The result? Her inhibitions were lowered, but nothing was distorted or blurred, she didn't feel sick, and she would be free from any ill effects tomorrow.

With one hand placed on either side of the jukebox, she peered through the glass. No live band on Sunday night, so she began dropping quarters into the machine and choosing her favorites. Some were rock, others were country. They all echoed the emptiness in her heart over the death of her father. Tonight she would said good-bye. The funeral on Tuesday and spreading his ashes on Wolf's Ridge were formalities. So she played songs to wish her father well and attempted to express the pain in her chest. And because the tunes were loved, she thought nothing of serenading the jukebox.

She glanced at the hallway that led to the restrooms and wondered if Sam was alright. The country song ended, and a rock ballad that included lyrics about 'flying to the angels' started. She closed her eyes and sang along with the lead singer. When the chorus began, she turned around and belted out the words. On the second line, she opened her eyes and saw Ethan and Shaun standing just inside the front door.

Sissy went to the end of the bar and leaned over the width of the wood to talk to Shaun. Without pointing, Sissy informed the sheriff that Tim was near comatose, Sam was in the restroom, likely vomiting the very fine whiskey into the toilet, and though Carli was still standing, she probably shouldn't drive home.

Carli recognized all this without skipping a word of the song or removing her gaze from Ethan. She watched as Shaun bent down to talk to Tim's face, which was still on the bar. His left hand formed the 'okay' sign, to which Shaun just shook his head. Tipping the empty bottle to read the label, he turned toward

Ethan, said something as he walked past the FBI agent, who nodded, then continued toward the hall and the restrooms.

Ethan hadn't taken his eyes from her, but she guessed he had gained all the information he needed about who was in the bar and possible exits. He started toward her, weaving his way around tables and chairs to the edge of the space reserved for dancing. The corner of his mouth raised to a half-smile as she danced and sang her way to meet him. Without losing her stride, she reached out and took his hand, then led him onto the wooden dance floor.

Both of her hands slid slowly up Ethan's chest to meet behind his neck. She would have been temporarily satisfied to tease him with her voice and sway of her body, but he placed his hands on her hips and drew her closer. Only a few inches from his face, she softened her voice, then let it fade as the song ended. He continued to move with her as the jukebox paused before beginning her next selection.

"Incredible with a camera *and* a voice that recording studios would love to hear. You're full of talents," he told her, fighting with himself to gauge her health and not allow the desire to begin its burn.

"Yes, well, those are the ones you know about so far," she said as the music swelled and another rock ballad blasted through the speakers.

He lowered his lips closer to her ear as he moved with her, enjoying the swing of her hips, the feel of her hands as they played with the hair that brushed his collar. "Are you drunk, Carli?"

She raised a brow. "Shaun didn't tell you?"

"No. He was rather elusive. Something about a sight to see, but that is how I already view you, Ms. Tanner."

She graced him with a full smile. "Agent Brooks, I don't get drunk. Rare metabolism. My inhibitions take a short vacation. That's the reason for the vocal performance."

"You have inhibitions?" he asked with all sincerity.

She threw her head back and laughed.

Her voice was pleasant enough, but the way she vocalized the songs on the jukebox, he wondered why she hadn't pursued a career in the music industry. And her laugh was ... throaty, carefree, and definitely inhibition-less. The thought flashed in his mind that this is how he wanted her. His hands held her hips close to his, their thighs brushed, her torso leaned away from him, the erotic column of her neck exposed to his hungry eyes, and his mouth, were they someplace alone.

She swayed forward and spoke close to Ethan's ear. "It is due to said inhibitions, Agent Brooks, that I have not tasted every inch of your skin, or allowed you the pleasure of experiencing some of my more personal ... talents."

He wrapped one arm around her low back and pulled her closer. His other traveled to her shoulder, where he encouraged her to rest against him, his face below her ear as he inhaled her scent. Ignoring the surge of heat between them, the press of Carli's breasts to his chest, he whispered a question to determine her emotional state.

"Why did you drink half a bottle of whiskey, Carli?"

Without hesitation, she whispered back, "My father is dead."

He shifted back far enough to look at her face. All laughter was gone. In its place was a woman a moment from shattering. Her world had been rocked from its comfortable orbit and she had yet to place things back where they belong. She was lost, confused, hurt, angry. He pulled her from the dance floor, leading her around tables, towards the bar.

Tim was sitting up, a glass of water in his hand. Sam stood next to him, one hand on Tim's shoulder, the other holding her phone. Shaun turned toward Ethan as he and Carli paused at the end of the bar.

"Who has the keys for the company truck?" Ethan asked, still holding Carli's hand.

"Here," Sam said, unclipping them from her belt loop and holding them out for Ethan.

He nodded, took the keys, then shifted his gaze to Shaun. "I'm taking Carli back to the lodge. You alright here?"

Shaun looked from Ethan to Carli. He knew his sister, and understood why she drank. Glancing at their hands, fingers interlaced, then back to Ethan's face, he understood the question. As sheriff, this wasn't the first time that he would have a few drunks to get home safely. As Carli's brother, he knew that only with the amount of whiskey she had consumed would she allow herself to grieve Dad's death. He wondered if Ethan knew what he was doing, then with a nod, he vowed to check on Carli when he brought Tim and Sam back to the lodge.

Not waiting for further conversation, Ethan grabbed Carli's coat from the bar stool and opened the door of the Rockin' R. She didn't protest or drag her feet, but followed as he led her out of the building and through the parking lot to the white truck with 'Tanner's Outdoor Adventures' painted on the side. He unlocked the passenger door and waited while Carli climbed inside. Placing her coat on her lap, he closed the door and got in on the other side, sliding behind the wheel. He glanced at her as he started the truck. Her expression hadn't changed. She had fastened her seatbelt, but kept her gaze out the windshield. He flicked the radio off as they left the parking lot, and he heard Carli curse.

"Shit."

"What?" he asked.

"I still had another three dollars' worth of songs in the jukebox."

He didn't know if laughing would break her, so he said, "You're right. Shit. I could have had another three dollars' worth of dances."

She started to chuckle, but it was too much effort. The flood of grief that she had worked so tirelessly to hold back, broke free. With a sob, the tears started running down her cheeks. *Why now*, she asked herself. Men didn't *do* emotional women. Whether anger or sorrow, any drama, and most men made themselves scarce. She wouldn't blame Ethan for dropping her off at the front door of the lodge as he made his way, quickly, to Cabin 4.

But she knew why. She drank tonight so she could say good-bye to her father and begin to heal the hole he had left in her life. It was unfortunate that Ethan would have to witness her meltdown, but any pretense to hide her emotions from him went the way of the rest of her inhibitions. Crossing her arms around her middle as if to hold her shuddering, breaking insides together, she held her breath as Ethan's hand rested warm and sure in the crook of her elbow. He tugged gently until she released her left arm. A great sigh escaped between her lips as he wrapped his fingers around her hand and held her firmly. As the next stuttering breath left her body, she had the feeling that her hand was not the only part of her he was holding.

CHAPTER 29

J.J. yawned. It had been a long day, and he had even missed the shed fire. Making his final pass down the barn aisle for the night, he peeked over each stall door, ensuring that the resident was content for the evening. At the front of the barn, he turned off the lights and slid the doors closed. Tucking his hands in his coat pockets, he took the path he knew well enough that he traversed it without a flashlight. Rounding the corner of the lodge, he noticed that one of the trucks was still gone. As he climbed the steps to the veranda, headlights splashed across the front door. He turned, expecting to see the company vehicle, and grinned as he recognized Zach's truck as it parked on the opposite side of the lot from the lodge. Waiting patiently, and hoping for the opportunity to tease Zach, he leaned against a post on the veranda.

"Have a nice night?" he called out as the young guide made his way across the empty parking area.

"I was with Alyssa, so of course I did," the voice answered, belonging to the body barely outlined in the light of the crescent moon and the dim floodlight that lit the graveled lot.

"You're not limping. Did you finally convince her on what she's been missing?"

Zach climbed the first step to the veranda. "You know, there's more to Alyssa than what's between her legs."

"Yeah, like her cooking. A man could get used to that. You seem to be indecisive about what you want from her, but I'm a cowboy who knows exactly what I want. And in the case of that blonde-haired, blue-eyed, young, *hot*, female, I got more on my mind than blueberry muffins."

He was quick, but not quite quick enough. Zach reached out and knocked his hat from his head. Catching it as he stepped back and turned toward the door, he had the advantage as Zach was still four steps below the veranda. He pushed open the front door and darted across the lobby toward the steps leading to their quarters upstairs. Zach was close behind, slamming the door, ignoring the reprimand Ray would give them at breakfast for making so much noise, and chased after him. The sound of two sets of running boots on the wood floor filled the lobby. On the fourth stair, Zach reached out and snagged his coat. It slowed him down, but he shrugged out of it and continued up the stairs, his laughter now hindering his progress.

"Never mind her muffins," Zach was saying as he scrambled up the stairs carrying J.J.'s coat.

"I do believe there is a famous song about 'Blueberry Hill' that talks about *muffins*," J.J. said, turning around and placing his hands on his chest as if he were cupping breasts.

Zach slowed to a walk as his room was the first on the left and J.J.'s was on the opposite side of the hall, at the far end by Carli's darkroom. He smiled at J.J.

"C cups would be just your size," he said and tossed the coat to the larger and slightly older cowboy.

Catching it, J.J. asked, "Does she know what your plans are?"

"I'll tell her when I take her out for her birthday."

He walked backward a few steps towards his door. "Assuming I don't sweep her off her feet by then."

Zach smiled. "I don't think you have it in you, Old Man."

He placed a hand on his chest as if he were wounded. They both laughed.

"Hay delivery is tomorrow," J.J. reminded him, swinging open his door.

"I'll be there," Zach said, letting himself into his own room.

Tossing his coat over the back of his desk chair, his hat on the desk, he toed off his boots, and pulled his belt from the loops. As he untucked his shirt and began to unbutton it, he paused and pulled out the drawer on his nightstand. Sitting on the edge of the bed, he withdrew the velvet box and opened it.

The deep blue sapphire rested in the middle of the silver setting and was flanked by two diamonds. Though it wasn't big, only three-eighths of a carat, it was Alyssa. It represented the blue of her eyes, her beautiful soul, and his commitment to her for as long as she would have him. Closing the box, he stretched out on the bed, one hand behind his head, the other holding the box as it rested on his chest. He closed his eyes and dozed with visions of Alyssa and the promise ring.

«« —»»

"Are you serious?" Shaun asked.

Tim's hand over his mouth was enough to convince him to pull over. Again. This was the third time Tim had gotten sick since they left the parking lot of the Rockin' R. It had taken a month to remove the odor of vomit from the last time someone had puked in his vehicle, which also happened to be a drunk that he had picked up at the Rockin' R for disorderly conduct. Tim's only defense was that Sissy was afraid he would be camped at the bar all night.

Shifting the vehicle into PARK as Tim barely opened the door before his stomach contracted again, Shaun didn't realize someone could vomit so much and still have anything left in their system. He watched as Tim unbuckled his seatbelt and, with more grace than he would have thought Tim possessed, Carli's red-haired work partner exited the vehicle and made his way to the first tree.

"Going to arrest him for indecent exposure?" Sam asked from the back seat.

He looked from the open passenger door to the rearview mirror. If she had gotten sick at the Rockin' R, she kept it to herself. When he let himself into the ladies restroom, she was at the sink splashing cold water on her face. She had yet to follow Tim's example, so he guessed she wasn't as drunk as Tim.

"I think he's suffering enough," he answered. "Are you alright?"

"I'll have a headache tomorrow, which will make me far better off than Tim." She was quiet a moment, then leaned forward, placing her elbows on her knees and spoke through the grid that protected Shaun from any violent criminals he may have to transport. "She'll be better for it, you know."

He nodded.

"She doesn't let herself cry. As close as she was to Dad, if she doesn't grieve, it will destroy her."

Sighing, he rubbed his forehead. "What do you think of Ethan?"

"I think he'll take care of her."

"What if she's more than he can handle?"

"Carli has us, and Tim. She'll be alright." She glanced out into the dark and noticed that Tim was on his way back to the vehicle. "But there's something about Agent Brooks. The way he looks at her. Did you notice their familiarity with each other when they were dancing?"

"Hard to ignore," he said, putting the SUV into gear as Tim closed the door.

Fastening his seat belt, Tim offered, "Ethan won't hurt Carli. Already told him I would kick his ass."

Shaun glanced in the rearview mirror and saw Sam smile. "Good to know. I think I'll check on her anyway," he said.

The remainder of the drive to the lodge was quiet. Tim seemed to finally have come to the end of his stomach contents. The police radio squawked, but Vince responded to the call of a disabled vehicle on the Interstate. He wasn't surprised to see the van, both trucks, and Zach's truck all in the parking lot. Ethan and Carli were here, and there was one light on upstairs that he could see from this side of the lodge. Zach's room.

"I'll just make sure everyone is accounted for," he explained, climbing down from his SUV.

286

The three of them mounted the steps to the veranda and pushed open the front door. The lobby was empty, only the track lighting over the front desk was on, casting enough of a glow to easily see their way to the staircase and up to the landing.

"Should I check on you in the morning?" Sam asked Tim as he opened the door across the hall from Carli's room.

"Depends on the time and what you bring."

"Eight. Coffee and whatever Ray makes for breakfast."

He made a face. "Make it nine and whatever Alyssa may have left behind and I'll consider answering the door."

"I'll see what I can do," she chuckled.

Tim entered his room and closed the door.

"He's a grown man who's traveled the world. I'm sure he knows what to do to recover from overindulging with Carli and fine liquor," Shaun spoke from next to her.

"I know. I just—"

"Want to take care of someone when they're feeling bad."

She gave Shaun a half-smile and a shrug. "Thanks for the ride home."

He wrapped her in his arms and held her for moments longer than necessary. She was safe, and he was glad she was here. Though he wouldn't admit it to either of his sisters, he missed them.

She stepped back and let herself into her room, softly clicking the door closed.

The one at the end of the hall opened, and J.J. stuck his head out. Seeing Shaun, he padded down the hallway in his socks.

"Everything alright?" he asked the sheriff.

"Just bringing a few home from the Rockin' R." He glanced at the dark space under Ray's door, guessing he was asleep, then turned to glance at Zach's room.

"Haven't seen Ray, but know that Zach arrived about twenty minutes ago," J.J. offered, following Shaun's gaze to the younger man's door. As they watched, the light was turned off.

"One more to check on," Shaun said, as J.J. nodded and retraced his steps.

He turned toward Carli's room. *Perhaps knocking first would be a good idea,* he thought, remembering the way Ethan had held Carli's hand. Sighing, he raised his knuckles to rap on the wooden door.

《《—》》

It was cold. Was the window open? The smell of gunpowder filled the nostrils. Behind closed lids, the picture wavered from the eyes and antlers of an elk to the flannel shirt and beard of Bear Tanner. Steel beneath the right index finger. Red and blue plaid in the crosshairs of the scope. A little to the right and up to account for the distance and wind through the canyon. The gun kicked. Blood blossomed. A pain in the hip had a shift occurring in hopes of finding comfort. Suddenly, all the images converged and the rifle report had the torso sitting up in bed. Beads of icy sweat collected and rolled down the creased forehead. Bear's face, splattered with blood, stared. Disbelief. Betrayal. Blinking rapidly, the image disappeared.

CHAPTER 30

Carli gripped his hand as if it were her only tether to reality. Her world had altered unchangeably and she was groping for sense in an act that was illogical, at least for everyone except the one that pulled the trigger.

This wasn't Ethan's first experience with a traumatized woman. His gut clenched painfully at the realization that as long as he held his position with the FBI, there was likely to be several more distraught families when the abduction occurred, which would turn to devastation if he wasn't smart enough to solve the puzzle before a dead child was the cost of his failure. He knew the words to say. Had taught the class at Quantico, written papers outlining how to handle the family and the media during and after the incident. But he had never been this close. When had Carli become more than a suspect? Someone different than an affected family member? Pulling up to the veranda, he extracted his hand from hers to park the truck.

She didn't wait for him to open her door. The numbness that had kept her safe since she had read the telegram was gone. The alcohol had done that. And now she would fall apart. Of all the times to be self-conscious, she was suddenly feeling embarrassed that Ethan would see her this way. The façade had shattered. Tears streamed down her face. She attempted to hold them back, but only had her breath stolen in great sobs. Gulping air, her eyes searched Ethan's as he held the lodge door open for her.

In the faint light from the lobby that fell between them, she saw what she hadn't found in anyone except her father and

Shaun. Strength. Courage. So, he wouldn't run, wouldn't drop her off at the front door and make excuses that gathering the pieces of a grief-stricken woman wasn't in his job description. He had recaptured her hand and its warmth softened her heart. Gesturing for her to enter first, he followed and quietly closed the door behind them.

As she climbed the stairs, each step seemed to require more effort. The wood was blurred with the tears that her eyes seemed to produce in excess. After a few steps, or several, she couldn't discern, the toe of her boot caught on the rise and she stumbled. Ethan caught her with his arm around her middle. Sagging against him, he understood that she had reached her capacity. He scooped her up and carried her the rest of the way.

Being tall and athletically built, he ignored her weight and cradled her against his chest. Knowing which door was hers, he bent slightly to turn the knob. Her room was sparsely furnished, containing a queen-sized bed and a desk and chair. He could make out several crates and assumed it was her equipment. Using his foot, he swung the door closed behind them and made his way to the bed than now sat in the near dark instead of the light from the hall.

Setting her on the bed, he began to move away, but Carli wouldn't release her hands from around his neck.

"Ethan ... please ... stay," came the stifled words between sobs.

"I'm not going anywhere," he spoke quietly. "Scoot over."

She released him long enough to move toward the middle of the bed, and then tears of relief joined the others as he settled next to her and gathered her in his arms. Carli clung to him and cried. Questions occasionally became clear enough in her muddled mind that they passed her lips. Ethan, with utmost patience, answered them all. When she would think about it later, she would realize that some of his answers were positive affirmations. He never promised anything, wouldn't downplay the grief that ran rampant through her. Instead, he confirmed that he had heard her, understood her reaction, and he didn't once attempt to take advantage of her emotional state.

Not knowing, or caring, how long he held her, stroking her back, her hair, allowing her to soak his shirt with tears and snot, Carli's eyes finally began to dry, her mind closing down in stages to sleep off the grief, and the whiskey.

"Let me get you some water," he offered, sliding off the bed and making his way in the dark to the bathroom.

He closed the door before turning on the light, not wanting to shock Carli. There was a glass on the counter by the sink. Rinsing it, his gaze drifted to the mirror and he gauged his reflection. His eyes were a little red from lack of sleep, the brackets around his mouth that set off his dimples when he smiled, had deepened. It was more than just another set of tears. They were Carli's, and she was more than just another woman.

Turning off the water, and then the light, he let himself out of the bathroom. Deciding that she was asleep, or soon would be, he pulled the desk chair after him.

"Carli?" he called softly.

"Hmm?"

"Drink this," he said, finding her hand and wrapping her fingers around the glass.

She sat up enough to drain the contents. "Thanks." She handed it back to him, amazed that her voice sounded so normal.

"Would you like some more?"

"Of you?" she teased, attempting to cover for her emotions.

"Of water," he clarified, but she could hear the smile in his voice.

"No. Ethan?"

"Yes?"

"Will you stay with me?" When he didn't answer right away, she added, "Just for tonight. It feels ... good to have someone here."

"Sure. Get some sleep."

She moved closer to where he sat in the desk chair. Unerringly, her hand found his. She sighed when he didn't pull away, but held her in the solidness of his palm. Perhaps it was the security of Ethan's presence, or the exhaustion of her grief and bout of tears, but sleep quickly claimed her.

As her fingers relaxed, he slowly withdrew his hand and settled more comfortably in the chair that would apparently be his bed for the evening. Dragging his hand though his dark hair, his attention was drawn to the window and the blanket of black spotted with stars. The air here was pure, fresh, clear. The skyline sculpted by trees and mountains. He couldn't see them, but knew what he would find in the morning. Shifting his gaze back to the body on the bed, he wondered what tomorrow would bring when they visited the Albany County Clerk's Office. How long would it take to find the killer? How soon would Carli fade from his memory? Shifting in the chair, he felt uncomfortable with the tightness in his chest at never seeing her after he left Wyoming. He suddenly wished for his sketchpad, a need that was interrupted by a knock on the door.

Before he could straighten from the chair, the door cracked open, spilling light from the hall across his face and onto Carli's sleeping form. The features were hidden in silhouette, but the build was that of a protective brother. He rose from his chair, blocking the light as he moved to stand in the doorway. Shaun backed up into the hall, and he followed, mostly closing the door behind him.

"How is she?" Shaun asked.

"Exhausted. Takes a lot of strength to deny grief."

"You're staying?" the sheriff inquired, gesturing with his head to the room behind Ethan.

"She asked me to. Look—"

"Tomorrow—"

They both spoke at once. Shaun closed his mouth and allowed Ethan to go first.

"The entries in Bear's diary mean something. We need to find out what, and soon."

"You and Carli going to the courthouse tomorrow?"

Ethan nodded. "I've already made a call. The file should be waiting for us. I've also requested property records."

"Why? I thought the FBI had all that information."

"It does. But any changes or inquiries are recorded with the county. It could point to someone who has a particular interest in Bear's holdings."

Shaun narrowed his gaze. "If Darla has anything to do with this, and I personally believe her to be a strong candidate—"

"Your belief is biased," Ethan interrupted.

"Then she wouldn't be dumb enough to use her real name," Shaun finished.

"But she would use her real estate company's."

Of course Ethan knew what Darla did for a living, Shaun thought, and nodded his agreement. "What do you want me to do?"

"Find the link between those symbols and whatever occurred on the days Bear felt was important enough to record. I'll call you before we leave Laramie."

He nodded and turned to leave, but paused and looked back at the closed door. "She's done, you know. Crying," his gaze moved to Ethan's. "Carli, being the oldest, has always been the strongest, bravest. Even when it comes to giving away her heart," he confessed, and without waiting for a comment from Ethan, his boots echoed on the wooden floor as he moved down the hall, the stairs, and out of the lodge.

He waited for the engine of the sheriff's vehicle to reach his ears before he reentered Carli's room. She hadn't moved. Taking his seat by the bed, he wondered if he would be courageous enough to walk away, and stay gone. Round trip flights to Wyoming were impractical, international flights would be impossible.

Leaning forward, one hand holding his head, the other dangling off his knee, he closed his eyes and sighed. Even entertaining a relationship with her was insane. They were each physically attracted to the other, and he knew from experience that getting laid would squelch that desire. Maybe that's all it was.

"Ethan?" her voice, hoarse now from her expenditure of emotion and brief sleep, pulled him from his thoughts that were only turning him around in a circle.

He dropped his hand from his forehead and peered into the dark. Unsure what to say, or how to respond, he realized nothing was required of him. Carli's hand unerringly found his. The breath halted in his lungs, just for a moment. If he hadn't been tired, his defenses down and thoughts jumbled, he would have missed the feeling, the warmth that spread through his chest. The touch of her fingers, the sigh of contentment that escaped her lips, the single stroke of her thumb across his knuckles, all set the alarm blaring in his mind. She settled back onto the pillow, her fingers still intertwined with his. In the faint light from the crescent moon now high in the night sky, he reached out and shifted her hair away from her face, gently tucking it behind her ear. Suddenly, international flights didn't seem so impossible.

«««—»»»

The front door of the Rockin' R banged open, drawing Sissy's attention. Justin and a friend walked to the end of the bar, laughing at some joke they shared. With a towel in her hand, she approached the pair. They were ranch hands that regularly spent their weekly check on booze, and came to the Rockin' R enough to cause trouble, but not severe enough to be banned from John's establishment. Jackie had gone to the back to get her purse and coat. Since there was no one in the restaurant, they were shutting down early.

"Justin," she nodded toward him. "It's late. We're closed."

"Hey, Beautiful! What do you mean it's late? I just got here. The party is just starting," he winked at her as he sat on a bar stool.

"No, it's not. You need to go home."

The smile dropped from his face. "This kind of attitude is really going to affect your tip."

"It's not attitude, and you won't be leaving a tip because I'll not be serving you. Come back tomorrow." She tried to relax, but there was something about Justin that made him more than just a mean drunk.

"Should I call Sheriff Tanner?" Jackie offered from the middle of the bar, the phone receiver in her hand.

"No. It's alright. Kevin and I can get a beer some other time," Justin offered, coming to his feet and backing toward the front door.

Sissy turned, her relieved expression finding Jackie. "Thanks," she sighed.

"I'll wait for you. No sense in giving him any reason to cause more trouble."

She smiled, tossed the towel on the bar, and went to retrieve her things. The parking lot was empty when they left through the side door. The realization that Justin and his friend were gone had her tired shoulders and aching feet longing for a hot shower. It didn't take much for the memory of the disgruntled customer to slip from her mind. Tomorrow was her day off, and she planned to start out by staying in bed past six. They all would be attending Bear's memorial on Tuesday, and then reporting to work, as the Rockin' R was sure to be full of funeral attendees. She slipped between flannel sheets, hoping Shaun was alright. He hadn't called her, hadn't said anything to her when he came to get his sisters and Tim. She would make sure he wasn't drowning in liquor when she saw him on Tuesday. The beautiful hazel eyes and pale blonde hair that had filled her thoughts for years, brought comfort, and a little concern, as she drifted to sleep.

CHAPTER 31

Cracking open one eye, she noticed the light that filtered through the partially closed, opaque curtains. She guessed it was about eight. Lifting her head off the pillow, she confirmed the time, then shifted her gaze to Ethan. He was slumped in the desk chair, legs askew, one arm dangled while the other rested across his belly, and the growth of beard that darkened his jaw added a particular edge to his handsome face. He had stayed. The corners of her mouth curled into a smile. She sat up and leaned closer to him.

Sensing her movements in his light doze, he opened his eyes. Sleep tousled curls, warm hazel eyes, and a smile that confirmed the storm had passed, filled his vision. There were no indications of the previous evening's meltdown. Straightening the kink in his neck, he sat up and leaned forward. Her hand on his knee as she adjusted her legs over the edge of the bed added a sense of familiarity. They hadn't engaged in any bed games, but he knew that their time together last night forged a deeper intimacy.

Stopping when his lips were inches from hers, he searched her eyes. There was relief, but nothing more. In realizing she hadn't mistaken his remaining with her as anything beyond human kindness, he returned her smile.

Deciding that her preference for dimples was something worth indulging in, she closed the distance between them. The kiss began as a warm, gentle press of the lips. He tilted his head to the side, and she took his bottom lip gently between her teeth, soothing the bite with her tongue. The smooth, wet stroke across his lip had him taking the tip of her tongue between his lips. A breath later, his hand cupped her jaw, and he showed her he was done teasing as he boldly entered her sweet mouth. With Carli's other hand fisted in the front of his shirt, he thought they would finally get what they were both starving for, what they seemed to be moving towards since their first meeting in the lobby days ago.

Yes, she cheered in her mind. Alone with Ethan, and they would be able to investigate what seemed to spark so easily between them. She tugged on the front of his shirt, so he shifted his weight and followed her down to the mattress. Their tongues danced and the heat in the room began to rise. She pushed his shirt up as her hands found his waist and ribs. Not wanting to waste time, the pressure inside of her building, she unsnapped his jeans and began to lower his zipper.

On one elbow to give himself room to unbutton her shirt and push aside the material, the tips of his fingers traced the lace edge of her bra. When a fist pounded on the door, he froze, then rolled onto his back and laughed. It seemed fate would once again keep Carli's tantalizing body from his hands and mouth.

Panting beside him on the mattress, she pulled her shirt together and mumbled, "Son of a bitch," as she went to answer the knock, which only caused Ethan to laugh harder.

Before she pulled the door open, she cast a glance over her shoulder, and seeing that he was standing and refastening his jeans, she scowled as she turned the knob.

"Oh, good. You're awake. Breakfast is ready and I was just going to …" Sam's voice trailed off as Ethan walked behind Carli and into the bathroom. With an expression that changed from relief to mortification, Sam stammered, "Carli, I'm sorry. I didn't know … I mean …"

Carli waved away her apology. "Ethan stayed with me last night. And nothing happened," she added, to which her scowl returned.

"Are you alright?"

"Of course. We'll be down in a minute," Carli said and began to close the door.

"I'll be working on the books. Zach and J.J. are in the barn, Shaun is in the office."

"And if I don't get to the bathroom ..." Carli said, and left the implication hanging.

Sam smiled and walked back down the hallway.

Sighing, Carli turned and pressed her back to the closed door. Ethan, arms crossed, leaned against the doorframe of the bathroom. Walking towards him, she raised a brow.

"Now we'll be the talk of the lodge."

"I don't know why. Nothing has happened."

"Despite our best efforts," she commented as she rounded Ethan's shoulder to move into the bathroom, and closed the door.

When she emerged minutes later, he was standing by the window. "Mountain tops and trees. I'm used to buildings and bridges that create the skyline."

"For as many places as I wake up in, this is my favorite view. The air almost shimmers. There's no haze or tinge to it from exhaust. The wind circulates the smell of everything that the forest is comprised of. Sometimes I can distinguish between snow or wildflowers or pine, and other times it's just ... Wyoming."

"Why do you have an apartment in New York City if this is where you want to be?" He turned to her then, and watched her familiar shoulder shrug.

"Convenience."

Shifting her gaze from the window to Ethan, she considered her answer. Easy for her job, the gallery that wanted her to do a showing, and an international airport. But her heart was here. She wondered how much longer she would be satisfied with the answer she had given him.

Two plates were set at the table, and when they finished and went to the kitchen to clean up, they discovered their dishes were all that was left. It was agreed that they would meet at the truck, for which Ethan still had the keys, in thirty minutes.

Ready for her trip to Laramie, Carli checked on Tim. Verifying that he was alive, but feeling as if he shouldn't be, she grabbed her digital camera and went to meet Ethan.

«<«—»>»

Bucking hay was part of the cowboy life, one which J.J. was very grateful to live. Attractive enough to get a woman for a night when he wanted, his free-spirit kept him from being interested in any kind of permanent relationship. Tanner's Outdoor Adventures wasn't the first employer that had hired him for his skills, and he figured it wouldn't be his last. Though he had liked and respected Bear, and the others who worked for the lodge, he was getting the feeling it was time to move on to another ranch, maybe a different state.

They had re-stacked the remaining twenty bales from the road-sider that had been delivered before the first snow, so he paused, set the hay hooks on one of the bales, and removed his gloves. Zach was younger than his own twenty-seven years, but in some ways seemed wiser. The younger ranch hand knew what he wanted to do with his life, including the woman he wanted by his side. He felt a twinge of … something. It wasn't jealousy.

"Did you get it?" he asked.

Zach looked at him quizzically, then comprehension dawned when J.J. pointed to one of his fingers.

"On Monday. I'll offer it to her on Friday. She'll be eighteen."

"Aren't you afraid you're making a mistake? Neither one of you is even old enough to drink."

Zach raised a brow and readjusted his hat as J.J. sat on a bale across from him.

"Age has nothing to do with it. She just …" his eyes looked beyond J.J.'s shoulder as he searched for a way to put his feelings into words. "She makes me happy. And I want to make her feel the same way. I think about her when we're not together. Shit, J.J., I've dreamed about kids that have her smile, her laugh," he shrugged. "I just know she's the one. And I don't want to lose her."

"You mean to me?" J.J. smiled.

"To anyone who has something I don't. More money. Their own spread."

"Better looks?"

Zach shook his head. "To a future without me."

J.J. sobered. "If she loves you, and she's never shown anything that would say different, you have nothing to worry about."

"That's why I'm giving her a promise ring. And I'm going to encourage her to attend college."

"Why?"

"Bear said I shouldn't rob Alyssa of her future—"

J.J. stood, cutting him off. "Well, Bear is dead. And if she goes off to school, she'll see what a big world it is out there and wonder if she wants to stay in a small town, or with a small town man." The words, laced with angst, surprised him, as did his suddenly blurred vision and moist eyelashes.

Zach stared after his friend as J.J. took his gloves and disappeared into the barn. The wrangler was generally genial, and he knew him well enough to know that J.J. was restless, unhappy with parts of his life. Maybe the ranch hand was jealous that Zach had found the woman that perfectly complimented him. He hadn't witnessed J.J. angry or upset about Bear's death, but then he hadn't been there when J.J. rescued Bear from Wolf's Ridge, or ridden with him to the lodge where Stan determined it was too late. Perhaps changing employers as often as the horseman did, meant J.J. just wasn't that attached to anyone. He rose from his perch and got to the next thing that had to be done. If J.J. planned to leave Tanner's, he would miss the friendship.

«««—»»»

He had skipped shaving that morning, deciding that the shaking in his hands would have nicked his chin. After his KP, he had taken one of the trucks to the north end of the Preserve to check the fence line. The sun had risen enough to shine over the eastern edge of the canyon, but had yet to warm the air. His gloved hands worked with the wire and pliers, but there wasn't enough to twist together. *Damn bull elks*, he thought with disgust, taking himself back to the truck and the supply of wire in the bed.

Lowering the tailgate, he reached in and pulled the wooden spool towards him. Something brushed his back, and he froze. A bird. It had to be. The frigid wind that blew up from the ground, moved off to the north, swirling and spinning and picking up pine needles and dust as it went. It wouldn't have caught his attention, had it not felt like a hand, and been icier than the cool, spring breeze.

Peering over his shoulder, he saw nothing but the dirt road that ran the fence line. Scowling, he shifted his gaze to the spool, cut a two-foot length, then returned to the breach. Though the sun now warmed his back, the chill remained. Once-nimble fingers pulled and twisted wire, cutting the excess and tucking the tail where it wouldn't likely gouge something if it pushed on the fence. That job completed, he looked again back down the road. Nothing. The breeze was now high in the trees, and he watched as the boughs swayed and heard the whistling of the wind between the pine needles. Deciding it was the lack of sleep and the encroaching family members, he climbed into the truck and continued down the edge of the Preserve.

«« — »»

The bell had rung, and Alyssa was shoving her things into her book bag when Ms. Hatch, her English teacher, approached.

"Have you given any thought to applying at University of Wyoming?" Ms. Hatch, tall and thin, and her smile always welcoming on Monday mornings, asked.

"I just don't see how I can," Alyssa answered with a shrug.

"There are scholarships, you know. I just hate to see talent wasted. And you have a lot of it. Your compassionate nature, your willingness to tutor other students, and your contributions to class discussions all would help you to be successful in college and in a career as a teacher, which you mentioned your interest for in your essay."

Alyssa gave her a small smile. It wasn't that she didn't want to go, but that she couldn't.

Unwilling to give up easily, Ms. Hatch continued, "Your father will survive on his own without you. He's an adult, as you will be at the end of the week." She had always made a big deal about her students' birthdays. Sitting on the edge of the desk next to Alyssa, she smiled as she addressed what else the girl might be considering.

"You relationship with Zach Murphy will still be as strong and wonderful when you graduate with your degree as it is now, if you want it to be. You can commute to Laramie, or live on campus and come home on the weekends to see him."

Alyssa averted her eyes to the strap of her book bag.

"I've always felt that there was a small window of time in which to complete a college degree. Not that students don't return later in life, but the longer you're away, the harder it is to begin a degree, or even return to school. It would be a tragedy for you to miss the opportunity, then wonder how your life would have been different had you continued with your education," pausing, Ms. Hatch could detect that Alyssa indeed had considered her pursuit of a higher education. "Well, I would be happy to help you fill out an application. Just consider your choices, Alyssa. All of them."

Alyssa glanced up and recognized the sincerity in Ms. Hatch's eyes. Before she could say anything, Mr. Sax, the Math teacher from down the hall, stepped into the room.

"Sorry to interrupt. Ms. Hatch, we have that parent meeting in the office in five minutes."

"Sure. Thanks," she said.

Alyssa stood, and, slinging the pack over her shoulder, offered Ms. Hatch a smile as she walked out of the room. She didn't know what she would have told Ms. Hatch had they not been interrupted. That she thought about going to UW, she wanted to be a teacher, was afraid to leave her father, and that she loved Zach? With only two months left before graduation, she would have to decide soon.

CHAPTER 32

Tired. That was the only remnant from her night of drinking and crying. Since Ethan still had the keys to the company truck, she rode shotgun, slumped low in the seat with her knees braced on the dash. With her eyes half-closed, she switched her gaze from the scene outside the passenger window, to Ethan. They had shared stories of previous evenings spent in a drunken haze.

"So, just like in the movies? The pool cue just snaps?" Carli asked.

"Assuming the object it hits is struck with enough force. Otherwise it leaves a hell of a welt."

"Is there a scar?"

He glanced at her, as her comment seemed a bit too enthusiastic. "I'm not sure. Only Big T and his cell mate know that answer."

She smiled and looked through the windshield, then straightened in the seat as they exited Highway 130. Taking her phone from the dash, she checked to see if Shaun had sent a text that she missed. Nothing.

In her early morning conversation with Tim, which was more him grunting answers and cursing her for being able to function, he had told her about the e-mail from Scott and their boss's question regarding the first telegram. She stopped at the office, where Shaun was reading through the diary entries, and suggested he search the date that the telegram was sent to see if there was a connection. He said he would get to it and let her know if he found anything.

She glanced at the packed parking lot. Mondays were apparently busy days at the Albany County Courthouse in Laramie. The clerk's office was on the first floor, closest to the basement, which held the files. She hoped that, with Ethan's influence, they would find the information they needed quickly. One corner of her mouth turned up at the prospect of kicking Darla out of the lodge.

"Whatever your expectations are, suspend them. We can't make any plans until we know, legally, what has been filed," Ethan cautioned her.

She was quiet as they entered the building, went through the metal detector, and only smiled up at him as he held the door to the clerk's office open for her.

"What makes you think I have 'plans'?"

"I know how you feel about your mother, and you have a particular … glint in your eye."

With brows raised and a sudden look of innocence, she whispered, "I do? Perhaps that has to do with the company I'm keeping today." Just to prove her point, she trailed her hand across his chest as she walked past him and into the office.

He growled and hoped to hide the immediate physical reaction to her touch. Had she trailed her hand across the front of his jeans instead of his shirt, he would have given himself away. Her nearness had its way with his blood pressure, and he was grateful that they had an audience which kept him from reaching for her.

After signing the form and producing his badge, the clerk was quick about handing over the files and leading them to a small room down the hall where they could view the contents in private. Ethan set the folder on the table and pulled out a chair for Carli. She ignored it and turned the file to face her. One by one, she set the papers aside.

Marriage certificate. William Tanner and Darla Lewis were married on April 4, 1979. Witnesses were Ray Foster and May Smith, John's wife. The paper was faded, but the seal of the State of Wyoming was in the center. She glanced at the lower left corner, and saw that they were married in Laramie County. Her eyes narrowed in thought. In 2004, the lines between Albany and Laramie Counties were redrawn due to the presidential election that year. The story ran in the Wyoming papers for weeks leading up to, and following, the special election held in May of that year. She remembered her father telling her of his attendance at Town Hall meetings in Centennial and Laramie. If there were no divorce papers here, they could check in Cheyenne, the seat of Laramie County.

Deed for the property, titled Medicine Bow Wildlife Preserve, was there. Road assessments. Taxes. Easements. No divorce papers.

She glanced at what Ethan was reading.

"There have been three inquiries into Bear's property. The most recent was an attorney. Before that, two separate real estate companies. It should be easy enough to find out information about them." He folded the printout and stuffed it in his back pocket. Disappointment showed on Carli's face and he guessed she hadn't found that which would sever Darla's tie to Bear Tanner's fortune.

"Can you call Laramie County? Ask them to check the archives for divorce papers that Dad might have filed?"

"Do you know when?" he asked, unclipping his phone from his belt.

She rubbed her forehead in thought. "Somewhere between '84 and '86. That's probably when he filed. I have no idea how long Darla sat on it before signing."

He was dialing by the time she had finished speaking. Another thought had occurred to him. There was a law on the books in Maryland that allowed a divorce to be final, even if both parties had not signed the agreement.

Once the clerk in Laramie County answered, he went through the required request and identification, then asked, "Does Wyoming have a law like the Beatrice Law in Maryland?" He held Carli's gaze as he waited for the answer. "The ruling was based on an absent spouse and a two-year period where they

couldn't be located. The judge allowed the divorce to be final."
There was another pause, to which Carli raised a brow. At
Ethan's smile, her other brow joined the first. "Thank you.
You've been most helpful. Yes. We'll be there before four."

"Well, Mr. Brooks, don't keep me in suspense. What have
you discovered?"

He scooped up the papers and the file folder, then opened the
door while Carli exited the room.

"We'll get to Cheyenne before four?"

"Of course."

"They're holding a record filed by Bear. In case you were
unaware, Ms. Tanner, Wyoming does indeed allow one spouse to
file, and dissolve a marriage, based on the absence, and failure to
locate, the other spouse."

She emitted a small squeal as she threw her arms around him.
Though he was caught by surprise, he wrapped her in an
embrace. In the brief moments before she stepped away, he
enjoyed the feel of her soft curves pressed against the front of his
body, her scent as it wafted around him.

"You, Mr. Brooks, are fantastic," she complimented, stepping
back, but allowing her hands to slowly unwind from his neck and
trail down his chest.

He took both her hands in his in an effort to control her
physical touch, and said, "And those are only my phone skills."

Returning the file to the clerk, signing out, and exiting the
building, he continued to hold her hand. Once they were in the
parking lot, she smiled up at him.

"So, what other skills do you possess, besides those devoted
to communication? Have any that would require a horizontal
orientation?"

He returned her smile as he held open the passenger door.
"Require? No. I sometimes like to be ... unconventional."

When he slid behind the wheel, she asked, "And these are
skills taught at Quantico?"

He chuckled and shook his head. "Skills are acquired because so much attention is paid to detail, information gained from the senses, and the right kind of encouragement."

She fanned her hand in front of her face as if to cool a blush.

Once they were on Interstate-80, and she was assured a good cell connection, she called Shaun. After informing him that they were on their way to Cheyenne to verify the file at the Laramie County Courthouse, she listened as he explained a few of the connections he was able to make between the asterisks in their father's diary and what he remembered had occurred on those days. The links were being made, and she felt like they were finally closing in on why the event occurred on Wolf's Ridge, and who was responsible.

«« — »»

Shaun rubbed his eyes. He had been staring at the screen for hours. There were connections, and he was feeling so close to making sense of everything, but he didn't have any more time today. Vince was off this afternoon, and he had to begin his patrol. He closed down the computer and locked the office door behind him. The lobby was empty, but Zach was behind the desk.

"Is Darla still here, or did she give up and return to her hotel in Laramie?"

"Last I knew, she was outside on the veranda talking with Ray." Zach yawned, then covered his mouth as he picked up the phone.

Shaun waved good-bye and went in search of Darla. He found her in one of the wooden rocking chairs on the west side of the lodge, alone.

"Where's Ray?"

"Said something about a repair to one of the cabins."

"I have news. Carli called from Laramie."

"She didn't find divorce papers, did she?" Darla attempted to keep the smugness from her voice, but didn't care that a little tinged her words.

"No, she didn't," he paused while Darla smiled wide. "She did tell me that they were on their way to Cheyenne. She reminded me that the lines between Albany and Laramie Counties were redrawn in 2004."

He watched as her smile began to fade. Then gave her the rest of the information that Ethan had uncovered. "Are you aware that Wyoming has a law, rarely used I would guess, that allows one spouse to end a marriage when the other is missing?"

Now her lips were turned down, then pursed together.

"Ah, I see this is news to you. Seems you have no claim on anything that belongs to Dad." When she failed to respond, he continued, "I don't expect to see you after tomorrow. Ever." Shaun turned and left a mute Darla.

As soon as he rounded the corner of the lodge and was out of sight, she shot out of her chair and began to pace. "Damn," she cursed.

Since she left Wyoming, she hadn't cared if the whole state imploded. Of all the things she could have contemplated to become an obstacle, a change in the county lines was not one of them. Even if Bear was able to dissolve their marriage without her signature, surely he left her something in his will. After all, she bore him his three beloved children. He owed her for that. Deciding she would need a plan to fight her grown children for what she was entitled to, she left the lodge and returned to her hotel in Laramie. She would feel more confident at the funeral tomorrow, once she devised a way to get the Preserve and follow through on the future she had with Councilman Worthington.

«« —»»

J.J. shuffled through the mail. Most were advertisements or cards sent to Bear Tanner or Tanner's Outdoor Adventures, either in thanks for an enjoyable vacation or in sympathy to the family for his passing. He paused when a return address caught his attention. Carmel, California. This would be his final check. He stuffed the envelope in his back pocket, then headed up the drive towards the lodge, where he found Zach behind the front counter.

"Any new reservations?"

Zach shook his head. "Just inquiries so far. I'm not sure what to tell prospective clients."

"Tell them you're not authorized to confirm reservations. Take their contact information, then hand it over to Sam."

Ray walked into the lobby. "How many do we have for dinner?"

J.J. raised a brow. "You're pulling KP twice in one day?"

"Just doing my part. At least we don't have clients."

"Because your cooking would chase them into town," he teased.

Zach laughed, knowing it wasn't far from the truth.

"Well, that will be one less meal I'll need to prepare," Ray mumbled.

Zach laughed again.

Ray turned back toward the dining room, and J.J. called after him, "Hey, Ray, I was only kidding!"

Ray waved away the apology.

J.J. turned toward Zach. "Is everyone expected here tonight?"

"As far as I know. Ethan and Carli should return anytime from Laramie. Sam is checking on things at the Rockin' R. Tim is upstairs. Shaun will probably come back by, and me."

J.J. tossed the mail on the counter. "Nothing for you. You'll probably want to have Sam open the cards."

"Where are you going?" Zach asked.

"Same place I spend most of my time," he answered, exiting the lobby and taking the back trail to the barn.

CHAPTER 33

Tuesday dawned colder than the previous day. There was a threat of a storm moving in from the Pacific, with Arctic air blasting down from Canada. Idaho was getting drenched. It was expected that rain, with possible snow flurries, would arrive in Wyoming by Wednesday afternoon. For today, the precipitation should hold off, allowing funeral attendees to safely travel to the church, then to the Rockin' R. John volunteered to close to the public and have food and drink only for those who were wanting to pay their respects to Bear Tanner.

The funeral began at noon. Everyone at the lodge was up early, breakfast was made, the horses were fed, and each had their assignment for the day. Sam and Carli had the duty of greeting guests. Alyssa, who took the day off from school, was in charge of the guest book. Ethan was head of security, with Shaun and Tim as back up. Vince and Denny planned on arriving late to the service as they ensured all attendees entered the church instead of lingering in the parking lot or the surrounding forest. J.J. and Zach would fill in where needed. Ray declined to be part of what he referred to as their 'stage production'. Donna, who would attend with her mother, offered to be another set of eyes in case something appeared suspicious. The church ladies would supply a light refreshment. Those that chose to take advantage of the meal and celebration at the Rockin' R, complete with a police escort, should arrive at the restaurant about two.

Ethan wore the only pair of slacks he brought with him. His weapon and shield were as much a part of getting dressed as pulling on his shoes. The news of what he and Carli had returned with was a cause for celebration at the dinner table last night. They had located the divorce papers in the Laramie County Courthouse, a granted severance of the marriage contract between Bear and Darla. As predicted, her signature was absent from the form. There were toasts raised that the 'evil witch' should vacate Wyoming, for good, after the funeral.

People began filing into the narthex an hour before the scheduled service. Some were already carrying wadded up tissues, others spoke in quiet tones. From Ethan's position opposite the front door, which was propped open despite the stiff breeze and cooler temperatures, he had a view of the parking lot and the front walkway. He could also keep Carli in his line of vision as she, with a smile pasted on her face, greeted friends, relatives, clients, and townspeople. Her warmth and sincere appreciation for each wish of condolence, he knew would be genuine. The uncharacteristic breakdown, according to her siblings, would allow Carli to be tear-free today. Glancing at Sam, who, despite her three-inch black heels was still a few inches shorter than Carli, wasn't as dry-eyed. Despite the dabbing she did at the corners of her eyes, her make-up held.

Some of the attendees had sent notes and pictures to Samantha regarding their memories of Bear Tanner. Those words and photos were combined into a video that ran continuously on a TV in the lobby. He scanned several cards and letters as they arrived in the mail, but found nothing beyond heartfelt thoughts. Moving behind the small group of people in front of the DVD, he eavesdropped to pick up comments. He continued to wind his way through the crowd waiting for the services to begin. Finally, the sanctuary doors opened and guests began taking seats along the side and back walls, and filling up the pews. Watching Carli and Sam, he relaxed slightly as they walked down the aisle to take their seats closest to the pulpit.

Shaun met him at the front doors, the receiving area now nearly free of those who came to pay their respects. The parking lot was full, and cars and trucks lined both sides of the road in each direction.

The sheriff rocked back on his heels, his hands stuffed in the front pockets of his slacks. "Dad would have laughed that so many people were making such a big deal out of his death," he paused, then shrugged. "He would have been touched by their kindness. Sam said thousands of dollars have been donated for charities in his honor."

"I've always thought the number of attendees at a funeral was a testament to how the life was lived. Bear Tanner lived well."

Understanding and respect shined in Shaun's eyes. He inclined his head forward in a gesture of thanks, then looked away as his vision blurred slightly, blinking to clear the tears.

"You can go in. I'll be here for any late arrivals," Ethan said.

Shaun offered a half-smile, then turned and entered the inner sanctuary. He forced himself to breathe and relax. As he sat between Samantha and Carli, he reached into the pocket of his dress shirt and removed the note card he had made. Staring at the words, he heard the music fade away and Pastor Leon shuffle papers on the podium. Glancing at Sam, he saw she had settled herself, her eyes dry. Shifting his gaze, he observed the profile of his traveling sister. She wasn't crying, and in fact, wore a slight smile. She, too, understood what Bear would have thought. Feeling his gaze on her, she reached out and took his hand. On his other side, Sam tucked her hand into the crook of his elbow. As different as each of them were, they were as close as siblings could be. They would need each other in the coming weeks and months as they adjusted to life without their father.

Ethan closed the front doors, as much to offer a bit more security as to shut out the increasing wind. No one was left in the narthex. He eased open the rear door of the sanctuary and stepped inside. The pastor was at the pulpit, and every seat was occupied. His eyes roamed over the crowd, watchful for anyone that might be suspicious. He identified all of the ranch hands, and Darla. She seemed to be overplaying the role of the widow. Since she was absent from the community breakfast that morning, Carli reassured him that Darla would be at the meeting with the lawyer that afternoon when the will would be read. The lawyer thought to answer their questions regarding the future of the lodge, and expedite the process by bringing the paperwork to the wake. If it wasn't for the 'selfish, money-hungry, sewer rat', a term he thought Carli edited for the sake of Alyssa and the fact that they were at the breakfast table, it would be a week before they met with Stevens regarding the future of the Preserve.

Shaun had found a few connections is Bear's diary. One of the days coordinated with a report of a breach in the perimeter fence. Not just any downed barrier caused by their elk or the neighbor's cattle, but a cut wire and uprooted posts. The others denoted times when they were short-handed. Despite the schedule, one or more of the employees was detained at another task, and was kept from being at a particular place and time. J.J., for example, was two hours late reporting to the barn when clients had scheduled a ride. His reason was construction on the highway when he was returning from a run to the airport. Another time Ray was four hours late, forcing Zach to take his shift in the kitchen to make dinner. Shaun remembered that Bear was particularly upset, but tight-lipped about the incident, as Ray offered no explanation. Ray and J.J. were both in the pews near the siblings. He would be interested to hear what Bear had left each of them. It may, or may not, add to their rankings on his suspect list. Money and greed were always popular motives.

Sam approached the podium and gave a short biography of her father's life, adding a couple of anecdotes of how he had molded her as a person. Shaun was next. He offered a humorous and fact-filled history of Tanner's Outdoor Adventures, giving examples of how Bear's values were expressed through the lodge to everyone who visited. Carli shared a few stories, having most of the attendees chuckling in their understanding, then sobered them with a 'Letter to my father, and best friend'. She had written it, Ethan realized, after her night at the Rockin' R. At the line of, "you held my hand, and didn't leave," she looked up and caught Ethan's gaze. Her honest eyes reflected that those words were for him. He felt an ease in his chest. A melting. Tipping up the corners of his mouth, he acknowledged Carli's reference, and gratitude. She finished her letter, and in the silence of an audience moved by the love of a daughter for her father, she folded her paper and looked out at the sea of faces, many of whom she knew.

"Dad will be missed, but that doesn't mean that he would expect, or accept, sadness at his wake," she paused and made a show of glancing at her wrist to check the time. "John at the Rockin' R has graciously reserved his entire establishment for those wishing to toast the departure of Bear Tanner. I do believe the beer is cold and the first round of whiskey is on the house. So, dry your eyes and send Dad off with the same revelry, kindness, and laughter that he lived with every day of his life. Thank you all for coming." She stepped down from the pulpit to join Shaun and Sam.

Carli took Shaun's offered arm, and with Sam on his other side, the three of them made their way up the aisle to the sanctuary doors. They formed a receiving line just outside the building. Some of the guests entered the Conference Room, opposite of the sanctuary, for the refreshments offered by the Church Committee. The employees and Tim followed the deputies and the other attendees to the Rockin' R. Ethan relaxed his vigilance when he realized that the crowd who remained at the church were the elderly and those with very young children. Carli, Sam, and Shaun enjoyed the laughter and stories that were shared by those who knew their father.

In watching the mannerisms of the siblings, he confirmed what had been his first impressions. They had similar facial features, hair of slightly different shades of blonde, and hazel eyes. All three were sincere and friendly, with Sam and Carli casually touching guests on the arm to emphasize or offer comfort. They smiled and laughed openly. Shrugging seemed to be a family trait. Though he had missed knowing Bear Tanner, the quality of his children was testament, a legacy, to the character of the man.

As guests began to leave, the Church Committee members cleared the tables and packed up the remaining food. Small groups had formed, attendees that had been reunited with other friends or past clients. This seemed to be the cue that those who stayed could fend for themselves. As if by some telepathic communication, Sam, Carli, and Shaun migrated toward Ethan and the doors that led to the narthex. Sam, having arranged everything, thanked the woman who was the head of the Committee. Moments later, the four of them were striding across the parking lot towards Shaun's SUV.

There was a brief conversation between the three siblings as to who they met and pertinent information they had learned about Bear and the lodge. A few miles from the Rockin' R, Shaun glanced into the rearview mirror and addressed Ethan.

"You're quiet. I didn't see anyone or anything that might have been a threat."

Ethan shook his head. "I didn't either. I suspect the Rockin' R will show much the same."

"Whoever shot Dad wouldn't come armed to the funeral. If they wanted to remain anonymous, and eliminate the rest of us, they would wait until we were alone," Carli said.

Sam blushed slightly as the memory of the brief, and terse, conversation with Shaun when he discovered she had left the lodge and gone to the Rockin' R yesterday by herself. She argued that she wasn't used to asking for permission to take care of the items on her list. But, he reminded her, none of them were accustomed to their lives being in danger.

Ethan stared at Carli. She was right, and he had known that the chance of something happening in the crowded church wasn't likely. Shifting his gaze to the rearview mirror, he noticed the tic in Shaun's jaw. He was sure their thoughts were the same.

"I think, Sam, it would be best if you left for Colorado soon," Shaun said.

"I was planning on leaving on Saturday—"

"Tomorrow. There's enough security at Crystal Springs to keep you safe. But I think whoever is causing trouble is either done, or they'll keep it focused on the lodge."

"Like the fire?" Sam asked. "I think whoever is behind Dad's death is finished."

"Or arson was someone else's idea," Shaun added, sharing one of the theories he and Ethan had discussed.

Ethan interjected, "The fire was a way to destroy something that they didn't want found."

"Like divorce papers?" Carli offered.

"Maybe. But Shaun's right. The focus seems to be the Preserve, and if Sam is in Colorado, that's one less Tanner to have as a target," Ethan said.

"Guess I'm outvoted," Sam mumbled. Turning to look at Carli in the backseat, she asked, "And whatever Dad's will says, you'll stay around long enough to see it through?"

Carli raised both brows. "My travel plans are on hiatus, but Scott isn't going to give me months. I have a career to return to and my apartment in New York."

Sam sighed and straightened in her seat to look out the windshield.

"But that's why we have phones and e-mails. Not to mention the sheriff that is so good at keeping in touch with his sisters," Carli said, leaning forward and patting Shaun's shoulder.

That made Sam chuckle. "Alright. But just because I'm at Crystal Springs doesn't mean I won't be able to come back at a day's notice," she paused, glancing at Shaun, "or that there isn't trouble at home."

He shot her a worried look. "What do you mean, 'trouble'?"

"Matt said that the fence was cut. Cattle on the JAR-C prompted a call from Cole."

"Still, you'll be better off at the ranch. And, if it happens again, you'll call Mitch," he said, making it a statement.

"What can the sheriff do—"

"Document. Look for patterns. Without the paperwork, nothing holds up in court."

Ethan knew all of that, but also witnessed where documents had held up the wheels of justice.

"So, you'll call and check on me?" Sam teased.

"Every day if I need to," Shaun promised.

Ethan knew that Sam was innocent of any involvement with the incidents at the lodge. With her at the ranch in Colorado, that left two Tanners to keep safe. He glanced at Carli and a clenching seized his gut at the thought that if he failed to protect Carli, something, or someone, could harm her. They were saved from further discussion as Shaun pulled into the front parking lot of the Rockin' R. It was full with what looked to be most of the guests that were at the funeral. Sam pointed out Steven's car.

It appeared that everyone had already consumed their first glass of whiskey on the house, as the raucous crowd was not indicative of a mourning. Tables were full, the bar was two-deep in places as people stood in groups, sharing stories of Bear, a drink in one hand, a plate of food in the other.

Sam glanced at her watch, then spoke loud enough to be heard over the voices filling the Rockin' R. "I'll find Stevens. John said we could use the back office. We need to let everyone else know—"

"I'll be sure to inform Darla," Carli interrupted, a peculiar smile on her face.

The four of them disbanded from their post at the door, the siblings ordering drinks and visiting with those who wished to express their condolences or ask after the lodge. Ethan began his surveillance of the crowd, wandering the periphery of the bar, always keeping Carli within view.

Occasionally, Shaun would scan the attendees, make eye contact with Ethan, then move on to another person who shook his hand, offered him a hug, or gave a compliment to his father. Alyssa, Zach, J.J., Donna, Ray, and Darla were all told of the impromptu reading of the will and converged in the narrow hallway at the far end of the bar that led to the kitchen and John's office.

Stevens had set his briefcase on the only bare spot on the wooden desk that John used to write checks and fill out deposit slips. The perimeter of the desk was covered with stacks of files and invoices. Of the two chairs in the small space, Stevens took one, Darla the other. She preened, while those invited arranged themselves in the tiny space, as Shaun and Ethan leaned against opposite sides of the open doorway. The hum of the restaurant and bar was in the background, yet loud enough that the attorney raised his voice to be heard over the noise.

Maxwell Stevens, an attractive man in his late forties, was dressed professionally in a coat and tie. The well-tailored suit showed off a body that had spent considerable time in a gym. His father, Maxwell Stevens, Sr., had retired from the father-son firm, and so Max Jr. had inherited Bear Tanner as a client. They had met on a few occasions, with Bear usually contacting him via e-mail whenever a legal question was raised regarding the business.

Max removed the file, which was over three-inches thick, from his briefcase, opened the cover, then paused. Fishing his reading glasses from the front pocket of his suit jacket, he wiped the lenses across his sleeve, then carefully perched them on the end of his nose. Looking over the top of the frame at his audience, he briefly made eye contact with each of them. Carli leaned against the wall, closest to the desk. Samantha stood on the opposite side. Shaun was in the doorway. They looked relaxed, as well they should. Having met each of them before, he knew they all had successful careers and full lives. He remembered they were close, and was sure they shared shock and confusion at Bear's sudden death. At his last visit to the lodge, Bear had introduced him to the employees. They were all like Mr. Tanner in their friendly greetings and quick, genuine smiles. When his gaze landed on the attractive, older woman who poised herself on the only other chair in the office, he raised a brow.

"I'm familiar with everyone here. But you, Ma'am, I haven't met."

Darla smiled sweetly and extended her hand. "Darla Tanner. Bear was my husband—"

"*Ex*-husband," Carli corrected.

"I never signed—"

"Didn't have to," Carli continued with a satisfied grin. "State of Wyoming allows a divorce to be finalized if one spouse is estranged from the family for a minimum of two years."

Max raised his other brow. "Brushing up on Wyoming law?"

"Out of necessity," Carli answered.

His gaze shifted back to Darla, who was shooting Carli an unpleasant look.

When Darla refocused on the attorney, she said, "I gave Bear three children. We had been in touch throughout their lives—"

Her monologue was interrupted by an expletive from the doorway, not so cleverly disguised as a cough.

Max pursed his lips to keep the corners from turning up. In all of his work with Bear and his visits to the lodge, Darla Tanner, current- or ex-wife, was never mentioned. Obviously, from the comments offered by Carli and Shaun, there was some animosity between the mother and her children. He sighed, knowing it was rare if there wasn't at least one shadow in the family portrait, and shifted his gaze to the back of the room and the man holding up the other side of the doorway. He didn't intend to referee a family feud, so he inquired about the man's relevancy.

Shaun answered, "Ethan Brooks is a ... friend of mine. I've asked him to attend this meeting."

Max nodded, then dropped his eyes to the open folder in front of him. He spent the past two days reviewing the extensive legal documents Bear had filed with the firm Maxwell Stevens, Sr. had founded. The holdings were extensive. There was a list of nearly every item that was on the property here in town, as well as that of Crystal Springs in Colorado. Without looking up, he began.

"As per my most recent conversation with Samantha Tanner, the middle child of Bear Tanner and the one in charge of legal matters, it was decided that specific details of the will be set aside for another date. The reading today will be strictly to reveal William Tanner's wishes for the business of Tanner's Outdoor Adventures, Crystal Springs Farms, and the employees of the lodge. Specific dollar amounts, labeling values of properties and items will be withheld at this time. Mr. Tanner has enclosed a sealed envelope for those of you in attendance today."

Max paused and set aside the top sheet of paper from the folder. Reaching into his briefcase, he extracted a stack of plain, white envelopes, all sealed, and placed them on the desk. Taking a moment to relish the power he held to make or break a life, a wish, and a family, he took a breath and continued with the 'short list', as Bear called it.

"Bear asked me to read this as he wrote it in his own words. If there are questions, the remaining legal documents are on file at the office." He turned over another page.

"The one thing on everyone's mind is the future of the lodge. Those of you in the room know that the Preserve gave me the privilege to offer unique experiences to the guests, as well as raise my children with a healthy respect for the outdoors. Anyone who has been in my employ has been part of the Tanner family. You will not be set aside and forgotten, simply because I am gone." Turning another page, Max was aware of the shift in climate in the room to one of loss and sadness.

"To my oldest daughter, I leave the entirety of Tanner's Outdoor Adventures." He continued through the gasps of surprise and disbelief. *"Carli, for all your worldly travels, I wish to give you a permanent home. You've always loved Wyoming. Though you won't admit it, you have a head for business. I entrust what I've built into your capable hands. Capture the sunsets and keep your art as the center of your life. Should there be a delay in you taking the reins, Max will have other papers for options that you are allowed. My wish is for your years to be filled with the happiness that I have experienced with the clients, employees, and my children at the Preserve. May you find comfort in raising your own children in the rich Wyoming wilderness."*

Max looked up as Sam took two steps to wrap Carli in her arms. There were no tears. The remaining attendees watched silently.

Sam stepped back, but tightly held Carli's hand. Ethan, observing from the doorway, noticed the collective sighs and smiles from the employees of the lodge, and the suddenly rigid back of Darla. When Sam shifted to face Max, Ethan watched as Carli, with her free hand, tucked her hair behind her ear, and glanced in his direction. Her eyes were dry and there was a smile on her pretty face. When her gaze turned to Shaun, Ethan also looked at the sheriff. There was relaxation in his shoulders and an answering grin. Max's voice continued from the far side of the office.

"To my middle child, Samantha, I leave you all that you have ever wanted. Crystal Springs is officially yours, lock, stock, and barrel. I know, Cowgirl, that you will prosper and always get back on the horse, regardless of the event. Remember to make room in your heart for love. There are provisions and papers in Max's office concerning profits from the lodge and the joining of properties. If you'll set aside your lists, and have a bit of a life, you'll know what I mean."

Carli moved toward Sam and rubbed her back. Ethan's gaze shifted to Shaun, whose knowing smile and shake of his head told him there was a story behind Bear's words of advice to find a life besides work. He briefly wondered if every parent had the same wish for their child, his mind momentarily taking him to the last visit with his folks, and his father inquiring if the FBI had rules against an agent settling down and having a family. Pulling himself from his revelry, he looked again to where Carli and Sam stood in front of the desk, and noticed the flush that bloomed on Sam's cheeks. Yes, there was definitely a story there.

Turning another page, Max continued. *"Shaun, my son, you have made me more proud than any father in Wyoming, hell, the whole United States. Your compassion and concern for others are admirable. My wish for you is that you save some of that for yourself. Find that which completes you, Son. You have your property, your house, and your career. You will receive a portion of the yearly profits from both the lodge and Crystal Springs. Being a public servant doesn't pay as well as it should. You will also have a one-third vote in the trust I've set up with Max which oversees the lodge, the farm, and all other enterprises. Max will fill you and your sisters in on those later. Shaun, find peace in your life, as I have found in mine."*

Ethan's gaze was on the profile of the sheriff. He wasn't smiling now, but instead the tic was back in his jaw as he clamped his teeth together. There was an extra brightness to the man's eye, and Ethan guessed it was tears that the sheriff would refuse to shed. Both Carli and Sam had turned to face Shaun, and if not for the people between them, would have taken their brother in their arms and held him. Shaun straightened away from the doorframe and stuffed his hands into the front pockets of his slacks. He dropped his gaze to the floor for a moment, and when he raised it again to his sisters and the employees who had turned to look at him, the moisture in his eyes was gone.

Max cleared his throat, effectively shifting everyone's attention back to him.

"The employees will continue to have a job, as Carli sees fit. The trust and its committee will be discussed in private at a later time. Two final thoughts. First, there are provisions that any grandchildren born will inherit an equal amount of land, no less than fifty acres, in prime, Southern Wyoming country. Finally, know that each of you have embellished my life. Best wishes for the rest of yours."

There was some rustling in the room that was silenced by Darla rising from her chair. "Mr. Stevens, surely that cannot be all that Bear left for you to read."

"Yes, Ms. Tanner. That is all he has on his 'short list'. I am quite familiar with all of Mr. Tanner's most recent requests. Your name was not mentioned," he paused, looked from Darla, whose face had gone from red to pale, to Carli and Sam, who grinned broadly. "However, he has left you an envelope. It was his desire that I distribute them after this portion of the reading."

Max took the stack of envelopes and shuffled through them until he found the one with Darla's name scrawled on the front in Bear's writing. He extended his hand across the desk, having come to his feet as those present began moving at the conclusion of the 'short list' reading.

Darla looked from Max's face to the envelope, and wasn't convinced it wouldn't be laced with poison. She took it from him, and shaking slightly, turned it over and stared at the sealed flap. What would Bear have to say to her? Her hope was that the lodge would default to the surviving spouse, but now she intended to fight Carli's find at the county clerk's office. Her alternate plan was that if Carli, Sam, and Shaun had inherited the property, that it would be put on the market, and she would still be able to gain control of the Preserve. Vaguely aware of Max calling out the names of the people in the room, she did register the attorney admitting that he had no knowledge of the contents of the envelopes, that Bear had only instructed that he distribute them. Sliding a manicured nail under the flap, she loosened the seal and withdrew the single piece of paper. She unfolded it, and holding it at diagonal corners, read the simple sentence.

Carli shifted closer, attempting to peer over Darla's shoulder. She felt reassured that her father had snubbed Darla even in death. Whatever he had written to the woman who gave him three children, she didn't know, as Darla refolded the paper, and without putting it back into the envelope, turned and left the office.

Having watched the expressions chase themselves across Darla's features, Ethan stepped back into the hallway as she squeezed past Shaun, who refused to move, and headed toward the bar and, he assumed, out the door of the Rockin' R.

CHAPTER 34

The envelope and the words it contained seemed to burn through the skin. Unable to set the paper aside, it was held between the hand and the steering wheel. The immediate panic that Carli alone had inherited the lodge and the land subsided as the scheming mind began plotting a way to keep that from happening. Unaware as to what 'other provisions' Bear had eluded to in his 'short list' should Carli not be able to take possession of the property and business, it was decided that it didn't matter. The unexpected obstacle Carli posed, needed to be removed.

Turning off the headlights as the lodge came into view, the vehicle coasted to a stop. Most of the funeral guests and family were still at the Rockin' R. Though the individual cabins were often locked, the lodge never was, mainly because someone was always in the lobby. It didn't take long to locate the master key ring behind the front counter, illuminated, as usual, with the track lighting overhead. Walking from the lobby to the storage room at the end of the veranda, knowing there was no one around, the door was left open as the search, and location, of the right items commenced. Within minutes, the storage area was again secured, the keys replaced, and the stairs to the second level of the lodge traversed.

At the end of the hall was the room that Bear had built, enticing Carli to visit her home and to remain for longer stays. This is where the oldest spent considerable time, so it seemed fitting that this is where her time would come to an end. The darkroom was unlocked. In turning on the light, it was noticed that the prints developed two days before continued to decorated the line strung across the opposite wall, not yet having been sent to New York by Carli or her colleague. Bottles stored in the cabinets were searched, then good fortune was realized when two partial containers were discovered on the counter behind the island that stood in the middle of the room. It was a simple matter to dump the contents down the drain, then refill them to their previous volume and replace the bottles where they would be within easy reach. The burn of the bleach and ammonia on the back of Carli's throat would be small retribution for the words that were issued forth from her mouth. Just to be assured that those bottles would be used, some of the liquid in the trays was drained as well.

Turning off the light and closing the door, steps were retraced to the transportation parked a short distance away from the lodge. The now-empty bottles stolen from the supply closet were placed in the vehicle. With a smile that the plan would be successful, the car started and crept slowly back down the drive.

«« — »»

For the next few hours, Carli, Sam, and Shaun mingled with those that remained, turning the wake into a true party. Carli's glass of wine was empty, and as she used it to gesture in her conversation with the person in front of her, Ethan appeared at her side. She blinked at him, slightly surprised, then smiled as he took her empty glass and handed her a full one. He grinned just enough to set off his dimples, and wandered away when the seemingly familiar heat sparked in her eyes.

As the crowd began to thin, he noticed that the employees were gone. J.J. had left early to feed the horses, Zach took Alyssa home, Donna returned to the house she shared with her ailing mother, and Ray had sought solace in having the lodge temporarily to himself, with the exception of Tim who mentioned there were work-related tasks that he needed to complete.

Carli hugged an elderly couple, then watched as they exited the Rockin' R. She set her wine glass on the bar and surveyed who was left. Shaun was seated at a table with some long-time clients. Sam was on her way to the restroom with two women Carli thought she recognized from the church. Then her eyes fell to Ethan who was making his way around tables to meet her at the bar. Whether wearing slacks and a dress shirt, as he was now, or jeans and a flannel shirt, his clothes outlined a masculine body that she really wished to get to know better. The breadth of his shoulders was contrasted by narrow hips that sat atop long legs. By the time her assessing gaze had reached his own, and her approving smile graced her lips, he was in front of her. In the depths of his eyes was the answer to the desire that, since having ignited between them, smoldered beneath the surface.

Without a word, he held out a hand to her. Not knowing what he planned, but sure it would be worth her while, she placed her hand in his. He led her to the dance floor where the empty stage was on one side, a playing jukebox on the other. Turning to face her, she willingly stepped into his arms. A sigh of contentment, of safety, of relief, escaped her lips as she closed her eyes and rested her head on his shoulder. She had shed her heels an hour ago, otherwise they would have been face to face.

He tightened his arms around her and felt his shoulders relax as the feminine curves of her body pressed to the hard planes of his own. They moved slowly around the dance floor, Carli softening with each exhale. The scent of her shampoo, or maybe it was just her, floated around them. For the next few moments, he shut out the visual world as he melted with her. Would it have been the same between them had they met at a different time, for another reason? How would it be when he finally got her alone and naked? That thought had his blood heating, his groin hardening. Pressing his hand firmly into her low back, he drew her closer. A groan emanated from low in her throat as she recognized his state. The slow thrum of her own circulation increased. He leaned slightly away from her as the song on the jukebox ended. The flare of his desire had a brow raising in silent question. Carli's half-smile was her answer. Stepping back, yet retaining her hand in his, he led her around the tables to where Shaun and Sam sat on two barstools.

There were only about ten people, themselves included, in the Rockin' R. John was behind the bar stacking glasses, and Jackie was putting up chairs. Sissy had gone home an hour earlier after confirming that Shaun wouldn't self-destruct. The few who remained took the hint, said their good-byes, and left.

"It's the least I could do," John said, waving off Sam's offer to drop off a check the next day for food and drink that was beyond what they had agreed upon. "Bear was a close friend," he shifted his eyes to Shaun. "Just find out what happened."

Shaun nodded, and with the keys in his hand, headed toward the door. Carli slipped her feet into her dress shoes as she and Ethan followed Shaun and Sam to the sheriff's vehicle. On their way to the lodge they shared who they had spoken with and stories that were told by clients and townsfolk. Pulling up to front steps, Shaun left the engine running. Sam climbed out of the front passenger seat, inquiring if Shaun would be by for breakfast.

"Tomorrow is Wednesday. That's my day to stop at the diner. Get caught up on the town gossip."

"For dinner?" Sam asked.

"Lunch. Then I'm taking you to the airport." He kept his gaze on hers and saw her resignation.

Without a word, she closed the door and met Ethan and Carli who were already out of the SUV and standing on the veranda. Headlights flashed over them as Shaun backed up and drove to his own house.

Sam glanced at Ethan and Carli. She realized that they wanted to be alone, so she claimed exhaustion, which was the truth, and took herself inside and up the stairs to her room. When they drove in, there weren't any lights on upstairs. Zach's truck was parked in its usual spot, which meant he, Ray, and J.J. had probably called it an early night. She hadn't seen Tim leave the Rockin' R, but guessed he had caught a ride with the employees. His door was closed, and it was quiet in the hall. Kicking off her shoes and laying on her bed, she blinked at the clock. It was just past ten, but had been the longest day. Tucking her hands beneath her cheek as she rolled onto her side, she decided she would do everything in the morning. Pack. Change her reservations. Call Matt. Her last thought before sleep claimed her was that by going home early, it meant she would have to deal with Cole sooner.

«« — »»

Carli turned away from the closed front door of the lodge and leaned into Ethan. The press of his lips cranked up the temperature that was already spreading heat from the closeness of their bodies on the dance floor. Her hands slid up his chest to lock around his neck, allowing her to snuggle against him. The warmth of his body was especially welcome since she didn't have a coat that could fashionably be paired with her dress. The wind that had been blowing all day didn't abate when the sun set. She shivered, her body confused between the chill of the air against her back and the fire growing between her and Ethan.

"Should we go inside?" he asked, breaking the kiss, but continuing to run his hands up and down her back, his lips pressing into her neck.

"Yes," she breathed, her response an answer to more than just a change in their location.

"Yours or mine?"

"Mine. It's closer."

"This won't be a onetime event."

"I would hope not," she said with a half-smile.

"I don't mean just tonight."

"After tonight, curiosity will be satisfied."

"That's highly unlikely."

"Well, we try it, and see how many opportunities arise before you leave."

He chuckled. "The opportunity has been ... arising since our first conversation in the lobby days ago."

Her hand trailed down the buttons of his dress shirt to the belt at his waist where two fingers hooked inside, and the palm of her hand rested against the evidence. "Then I think we should—"

She didn't finish her thought as the vibration of his cell interrupted the play of words that seemed to pass so easily between them. When he answered the phone, the expression in his eyes cooled considerably and she knew there would be no other kind of 'play' tonight.

Keeping the phone to his ear with one hand, the other continued to hold Carli to him. His gaze finally shifted from her lovely face to the space beyond her as Micah's voice filled his ear.

"Any news?" Micah asked.

"Nothing solid," Ethan said as Carli rested her head against him.

"I need you to split your time. We have an abduction. The local authorities have already issued an Amber Alert. All the information has been sent to you in an e-mail. I want you to take a look at it. Get back to me ASAP with your thoughts." Micah spoke in the usual hurried, East Coast manner.

"Can't it wait until morning? Sounds like all the basics are being done," Ethan tried to delay, holding onto a slight hope that he and Carli could be opportunistic tonight.

"You know the timeline. If we can get her back within forty-eight hours ... after that, the odds are—"

"I know. Alright. I'll send you my thoughts within an hour." He disconnected without waiting for a reply and sighed.

She stepped out of his embrace, and then quickly wrapped her arms around her middle at the instant loss of Ethan's warmth. "Work?"

He nodded. "Rain check?"

Carli smiled. "Still want to see Miner's Paradise?"

His gaze traveled the length of her body, imagining what it would feel like, taste like, when he finally had her to himself. "More than you know."

She glanced down at the front of his slacks as he stepped down to the graveled parking lot. With a mischievous grin, she told him, "I have a pretty good idea. Breakfast at seven. We'll hike out afterwards."

"Hike?"

"Easier than taking the horses. The terrain is rough, the vegetation thick. More of a chance to see a cat." She had made her way to the door of the lodge, her hand on the knob.

The dull glow of the parking area light allowed her to see Ethan quirk a brow and open his mouth to speak. Realizing in that moment how he would interrupt her 'cat' reference, she clarified, "Mountain lion. They like craggy areas, dense brush ..." her voice faded as she realized she wasn't helping her explanation any.

He chuckled. "We'll see you at breakfast. Go inside before you freeze."

Without another word, mainly because she was afraid she would give him something else to laugh about, she turned the knob and stepped into the lobby. Closing the door, she leaned against it and enjoyed the slight shiver that tickled her spine from Ethan's knowing chuckle. Pushing herself away from the wooden door, she took herself upstairs. There wasn't any light leaking out from under Tim or Sam's door, so she let herself into her own room.

She kicked out of her shoes and pulled her dress off over her head, letting it fall to the floor on her way to the bathroom. She needed a hot shower to warm up from the cold wind, then a cold shower to recover from Ethan's touch. Dressed in sweatpants and an oversized, long-sleeved T-shirt with a picture of the state of Wyoming on the front, she plopped on her bed completely wired from the day. Glancing around the room, hoping to find something to do that would dissipate the remaining energy left over from the funeral and the feel of Ethan's body, her eyes lighted upon her closed laptop.

Sitting in the chair at the desk where her computer was plugged in and powered on, she opened the screen and brought up her e-mail. Several were work related. Guessing they were condolences from some of her colleagues, she scrolled through them until she saw one that Tim had forwarded from Scott. Why hadn't Tim said something to her? Opening it, she scanned the contents, leaned forward in her chair, and read it again.

A telegram was sent to their location in Africa. She had never received it, which is how Tim had responded. Scott was wondering who had requested that she 'Come home', and how things were progressing so he would know when to expect Carli back at the office. If she had any time, he urged her to contact One World Piece Gallery about the show. Having received the digital files, his final request was for the remaining prints from Africa and South America.

She clicked through the rest of her e-mails, responding to some, deleting others. Closing the program, she leaned back in her chair and stared up at the ceiling. Who would have requested that she return home? If Shaun had contacted Scott, or rather Scott's assistant, Shaun would have told her when he picked her up at the airport. She would have to find out for sure if he sent one, or two, telegrams. If it wasn't Shaun, it had to have been her father. No one else would have had reason to call her home from a job that had taken her half a world away.

Sighing and pushing her hands through her hair, she recalled what her father had left for her. The lodge and the Preserve, "if she chose to take it". The clock read 10:30 PM. If she was to be any good for the hike to Miner's Paradise, the place Ethan believed where the shot was fired from that killed Bear Tanner, she at least should try to get some sleep.

She switched off the light and climbed between the sheets. Forcing her eyes to close, she was less successful in turning off her thoughts. The most difficult part of this trip was over. The funeral. She had never thought about what her father would do with the lodge, and now that he had entrusted it to her, a forgotten dream had new life breathed into it. She fished occasionally, but found it difficult to pull the trigger and kill one of the creatures that roamed the Preserve. If one attacked, or if she was starving, she might reconsider. Her dream, long ago set aside when she had embarked on her career, began to take form again in her mind. She had the land, established clients, and employees. The focus would be different, the intention of the Preserve would need to be shifted. *Great*, she scowled into her pillow, *now how am I going to get to sleep?*

Decisions had to be made, and ideas of the future filled her mind. It must have been the fatigue of the day, the frustration of sex with Ethan put off yet again, the myriad prints that needed to be finished and shipped to New York, the upcoming hike to the far side of the canyon, Sam leaving ... the realization that with a little time and some work, her future could drastically alter the course her life currently traveled ... that her thoughts gave up, and her mind turned over to sleep.

CHAPTER 35

His walk to Cabin 4 was the time he needed to settle the arguments in his head about not going to Carli after he looked at the information Micah had sent. He wondered at her thoughts of inheriting the Preserve and what was inside the envelope that she received. Hearing Bear Tanner's words for his children and employees, it was demonstrated how the man was in life and why Bear's death was taken hard by everyone. If he still harbored the possibility that Carli might have staged the shooting, her inheritance would be an incredible motive. He remembered her shocked expression and knew that no one in that room had suspected Bear's intentions. That led him to wonder if she would stay, or continue with her globetrotting career. Deciding he would ask her about it on their hike to Miner's Paradise, he recalled their earlier innuendo, and it brought a brief smile to his face.

Shutting the cabin door against the chilled wind, he turned the lock and powered on his laptop. As he read the information, his mind filed facts and his heart was steady, a complete contradiction to a short time earlier when he held Carli on the steps of the lodge. What he discerned from the report was that it was most likely the child's estranged father. Taken from a small town on the Jersey Shore, the vehicle was seen heading north on the Interstate. There was no family, on either the father or mother's side of the abductee, that lived north. A vacation spot? Someplace they had talked about going at one time? Abductors stuck to what they knew, an area or an industry where they had the opportunity for income and could reestablish themselves in a new community.

Micah had also sent pictures from the child's bedroom and a list of items that were missing. A backpack. Some clothes. A favorite toy. It all went together and told the story of who took the child, and where they were headed. Searching particular areas along the Interstate that might fit the profile, he had pulled up several websites. Just before his hour was up, he snatched his pad off the dresser, took a pencil from his computer bag, and began to pace. In between the strides that carried him from one side of the small cabin to the other, he drew. The Jersey Shore, cities like Newark to the north whose main industry were factories, and ones that had not turned into ghost towns because of the economy. He sketched the child from the picture the mother had provided to the local authorities. Then he drew the likely abductor, based on the picture of the child and the mother, and verified via the Motor Vehicle Department and a driver's license. The car, including the license plate, registered to the father, was drawn at the bottom. He paused, read his notes, studied his drawings, and felt the pieces slide into place. Taking the chair in front of his computer, he typed an e-mail to Micah telling him where to look for the child.

There was a rush of endorphins that flooded his veins. This situation would end well. The abductor meant no harm to the child, but his belly clenched a little anyway, knowing that too often that was not the case. A child could be taken for something to control, something to sell, or something that was used to fill a void in the perpetrator's life. The things he had seen on the job, how humans regarded each other, haunted his nights and seared his soul. Especially when he was not smart enough or fast enough in figuring out the clues in order to save a life. Some of his colleagues had turned jaded, cynical, permanently damaged from what they witnessed. He managed to hold it together, his heart torn each time another mother cried on his shoulder or a father threw accusations punctuated with expletives at him that he wasn't doing enough or that it was his fault if a body was recovered rather than a living child. Long ago, he promised himself that if he lost his edge, if he couldn't keep the horrific details of his job securely locked away in his mind, he would walk away from the Bureau, take his pension, and live out his days in a remote area far away from those he could no longer protect or save. But this was not one of those times. His gut told him he was right.

Micah-
The child and abductor are in ...

«« —»»

"I know what I said," she spoke harshly into the hotel room phone.

"And despite your constant reassurances, you have failed to come through in the end. I should have known better than to attach my funds to a—"

"Just because there is a glitch with the divorce papers—"

"And the will. How do you plan to fix that? Or will my campaign suffer because of your incompetence?"

She bristled at his tone and his words. "Of course I have a plan. I haven't invested this much time and effort to give up now. You know, I have a lot to lose with this project as well."

Councilman Worthington pinched the bridge of his nose. "I'll not debate this with you. I'll expect to be kept apprised of your *plans* and the outcome."

"My intention is simple. Remove that which blocks what I want."

"And how do you propose to do that?"

"There are some things, Councilman, that you may be better off not knowing," Darla paused. "You sound uptight, and about more than just the development." She left the question implied.

"Politics are not for the weak, Darla. It's been a difficult couple of days," he answered vaguely, not willing to tell her that he decided to cut ties to his favorite prostitute and that his wife was visiting her brother in Texas.

"Sounds like you could use a friend. Wish I was there," she softened her voice, turning it seductive, something she felt more comfortable with than being stern when defending her position and her plans.

Her insinuation was not lost on him. He sighed. "Yes, it would be convenient if you were here instead of there."

Convenient. Not that he missed her, or would have liked to see her. She pushed away the hurt by reminding herself what she had done to protect her interests, of which he had no knowledge.

"I can make you feel a little better," she purred into the phone. When he grunted his skepticism, she knew how easy it would be to prove it to him. "You know, I can still taste you at the back of my throat," she stretched her fingers out in front of her to examine her nails. "There's never been another man with such ... talent. You really do have incredible staying power, which really turns me on. I love how you ... twitch when you're really excited, the way your balls feel in my hand," she paused and made a fist, then smiled to herself as she imagined crushing the arrogant bastard's testicles between her manicured fingers. Keeping that to herself, she continued with her monologue. At the sound of his zipper lowering, she smiled wide and then began to talk in a way that the hookers in a back alley spoke to the johns, and sometimes to each other. In another two minutes, she had quietly lowered the phone to its cradle. The councilman was 'done', and she was through with this day.

«« —»»

Believing her father to be asleep, Alyssa crept through the living room and down the hall. She changed her clothes and got ready for bed, deciding that whatever dishes her father had used to make himself dinner could wait until morning. If she tried to clean up the kitchen now and woke him, it wouldn't be a pleasant scene. Climbing into bed and reaching over to turn off the light, she settled in, then let her thoughts wander.

The day had been difficult, but not as hard as it could have been. It hadn't surprised her that so many people showed up for Bear's funeral. The contact list in the computer at the lodge was extensive, and that didn't include all of the extended family or townspeople. In her opinion, what was said at the church was just perfect. It wasn't so sad that she cried, though tears gathered in her eyes. Maybe that was because her tears filled buckets when Bear's death was first announced. And there was Zach. He held her hand through the whole service. At the Rockin' R, he stayed close to her as others offered their condolences and appreciation for her work at the lodge.

On the way home, she and Zach had talked about the service and Bear's words when Maxwell Stevens read the will. They were both elated that Carli would inherit the lodge. If it had been Sam, they thought perhaps she would have sold it. It made sense that Bear wouldn't leave the business to Shaun. He loved being Sheriff of Centennial. They had speculated what Carli would do with the Preserve. She always enjoyed herself when she came home, and often led a trail ride or hike or mingled with the clients at meals. Selling it, they assumed from the attorney's words, was an option. However, they had agreed that they would want to stay on at the lodge, whether or not Carli continued to run Tanner's Outdoor Adventures.

Halfway to her father's house, she convinced Zach to pull over so they could read what Bear had written to them. She began to cry, then laugh, when she looked at the check he had enclosed. It was enough to pay for her first year at a community college, or a semester if she went to UW. Bear's words encouraged her to see more of the world besides 'this tiny corner of Wyoming', and to make something more of her life than Zach's wife. That amazed her. How did Bear know her secret dream? Everyone at the lodge knew she and Zach were dating, but she didn't think anyone knew they were in love.

Zach read his note to himself, then paraphrased the words when he shared them with her. He had been given a check as well, but when she asked about it, he just stuffed it into the envelope and pulled back onto the road. As she stared at his profile, willing him to tell her everything, she noticed his eyes glistening. Tears. She had never seen Zach cry. Not when Bear was shot, or any time since they had met. She didn't push. He would share it with her when he was ready, of that she knew for sure.

It was the image of Zach, strong and sensitive, quick to laugh and to encourage, that she held onto as she succumbed to sleep. And it was the harsh, angry shake and beer-scented breath that awakened her as Jim Lockhart held her by the arms and yelled at her to answer his question.

"What?" she asked, disoriented, finding it difficult to shift from Zach to her father. In the next heartbeat, she was fully awake and cringing away from his drunken face.

"I asked you a question, Goddamnit! And I want an answer!"

She held her upper arms close by her sides, her forearms crossed in front of her in an attempt at protection. "I'm sorry, Daddy, I didn't hear you. What did you ask?"

"Your job. Do you still have your job?" His eyes narrowed on her face.

Alyssa nodded. "Sam had Mr. Stevens read a preliminary will. Carli inherited the Preserve. Bear wrote that we would all have our jobs as long as the lodge was in the Tanner family." She didn't wince, refusing to show that his hands hurt. There would be bruises tomorrow and she would have to remember to wear long sleeves.

Jim was temporarily placated. So Lys would still have a job and the paychecks would continue to be collected. It would be just like Ray had said. Releasing her arms, he straightened from the edge of her bed and took a step back. A thought occurred then, about Bear's generosity. His brows drew together as he wondered if Lys might be holding out on him.

"He didn't give you anything?"

"Who?"

"Bear Tanner. He didn't leave anything to you in his will?"

"No," she blinked and dropped her gaze. Her eyes shot back to her father's face when he took a menacing step towards her.

"You're not lying to me, are you? Because you know how I hate liars."

She looked at his raised hand and knew that if she told him about the check, she would miss the next week of school. "No, Daddy. I'm not lying." Holding her breath, and his gaze as best she could, Jim Lockhart was convinced enough to lower his hand. It wasn't until he closed the door behind him that she let out the breath she was holding and flopped back onto her pillows.

There had to be a way to hide the check, or cash it where he wouldn't know. As she stared up at the dark ceiling, the dread of never being able to use the money, never going to college, never leaving this house brought useless tears to her eyes. Willing herself not to cry, for her heart to steady its rhythm, she rubbed her arms until a restless sleep took her.

«« — »»

The letter had been one of apology and slight confusion. Sometime before this past week, Bear knew there was something wrong. He didn't confront it, and probably believed that the issue would resolve itself if left alone. The resolution was his death. There was no money, or any mention of compensation. That would have been the epitome of irony, payment for murder by the murdered. Maybe Bear knew what was coming, though probably not on that day, at that time. Or perhaps he did have some inkling that his demise was at hand, but he chose to finish his days how he had lived them, which was full out, wide-open, spitting into the face of fear.

Well, no one would read the letter, so they couldn't accuse the holder of any foul play. Setting the lit match to the corner of the envelope, the flames were watched, the paper turned this way and that to feed that which consumed it, before it was tossed into the toilet and flushed.

The money that had been set aside through the years had accumulated nicely. To resign now would be logical. No one would place blame for the desire to leave the employment of the lodge. Losing someone such as Bear, the friendship and semi-permanency he offered to his employees, would be taken hard by everyone. Carli was sure to keep the lodge going, but she would just do it with one less person. The absence wouldn't be felt, and the remainder of this life could be filled with ease instead of the tough work that the Preserve sometimes required. The letter of resignation could be penned tomorrow and left for Carli.

CHAPTER 36

Stretching, then blinking open her eyes, she read the clock. 5:15 a.m. She could get an early start on the day by finishing the photos in the darkroom. Maybe Shaun could drop them off at the post office in Laramie when he took Sam to the airport. A frown touched Carli's lips. She missed her sister, and Shaun, when they weren't together. It was easier when she was out of the country, or at least working somewhere besides New York. Whether or not Shaun was correct that Samantha would be safer at Crystal Springs than at the lodge, she wasn't convinced. If someone was serious about causing them harm, they would find a way to follow through.

Taking a quick shower to help her wake up, she gathered some shipping envelopes that were preprinted with the New York address for the *Views* and headed for the door. Her gaze landed on her computer where the e-mail from Scott was stored. Who sent the first telegram? And why? And what was the connection between the dates and the symbols in her father's diary? On the table beside her computer was the petite purse she had taken with her yesterday. Poking out of the top was the unopened envelope from her father. Everyone had received one. Even Darla. She would have given her eyeteeth to read what he had written to his estranged *ex*-wife and the mother of his children. Withdrawing the envelope from her purse, she smiled slightly at his familiar handwriting. The letter, she decided, could wait. The pictures, according to Scott, could not.

The hallway was empty as she traversed its length to the darkroom at the end. Locking the door, as was her habit, and then turning the switch to illuminate the red light outside the door to show she was working, she set the envelopes aside and began to gather what she would need.

Removing the prints from the cord stretched across the back wall, she sorted them, placed them back-to-back with acid-free tissue paper in between, and began to load them into the packages.

Next were the rolls of film from South America. She carefully developed the film to create the negative, then shot the negative onto the photo paper. She noticed the low level of chemicals in the trays and added more from the half-empty bottles on the counter. Within moments, a strong smell filled the space of the darkroom. She blinked and turned toward the thermostat, as it was always on when she worked to circulate the air and keep the chemicals from becoming too overpowering. It was set in the usual position. Shaking her head slightly, she returned to the trays, tongs in her hand to transfer the prints from developer through rinse. Using the tips of her fingers at the edges of the paper, she began to hang them on the line. The images were fuzzy, as if they were overexposed and out of focus. With hands on her hips, she tipped her head to the side as she peered at the pictures, and then inspected the developed film. The negatives were fine. It didn't make sense.

Bringing her hand to her forehead to rub away the dull headache that turned quickly to a sharp stabbing, she felt the slight burn on her fingers. She sniffed them. Not developer. Turning to look back at the trays, the room spun. Reaching out to steady herself against the counter, her knees buckled and she leaned over the tray. Bleach. That was what burned her fingers. How did bleach get inside her darkroom? But bleach itself wouldn't cause her to react this way. The floor and ceiling tilted. Her head ached and her stomach churned. Out. She had to get out of the darkroom. Moving her hand, it bumped against the trays. Some of the bleach sloshing into the tray next to it. A white vapor rose from the counter. Unable to hold herself upright, she landed on the floor. The door. It was just there, on the other side of the island, perhaps six feet away. The stinging of her eyes caused her vision to blur as tears attempted to flush out the toxin. She dragged herself around to the end of the island, but that was as far as her Herculean effort took her. Her breathing became labored, and she squeezed her eyes shut.

Is this how her life would end? Instead of some remote location where she might contract a rare disease or parasite, her last day would be at home in Wyoming. A freak accident that allowed her to mix bleach and ammonia … how did they get here? Disappointment swamped her then, as she realized she would never know what it was like to share herself with Ethan.

«‹—›»

Excitement and relief flooded him when Micah called to confirm that his deduction was correct. The abductor and the child were located where he had predicted. That morning the child had been returned to the legal parent, the perpetrator arrested. He showered, gathered what he thought he would need for their hike, stuffed it all into his backpack, and headed for the lodge, believing that his demons were securely tethered.

The morning was cold, the skies overhead, cloudy. Setting his pack just inside the front door, he looked to the counter and saw Sam stifle a yawn.

"Morning," Ethan said.

"Morning. You're up early," she eyed him, wondering why he came in from outside when she thought he had been with Carli all night.

"I received some good news, work related, and I'm wanting to see Miner's Paradise," he told her, a smile on his face as his hands rested lightly at his hips.

"I would imagine good news in your line of work is good news for others, too," Sam worried her bottom lip, not even wanting to know the details of his career, and instead focused on his second comment. "It's quite different from Wolf's Ridge. You may get an opportunity to see some wildlife," Sam said, and glanced at her phone as it chimed and vibrated against the desk.

"Have you seen Carli this morning?"

Without looking up from her phone she answered, "Not yet. She's probably in the darkroom."

He briefly wondered at the message Sam received on her phone that would cause the scowl that creased her forehead. Taking the stairs two at a time, he saw that Sam was correct. The red light at the end of the hall alerted everyone that Carli was working inside. No one else was around, and he guessed that J.J., Zach, and Ray were out doing what needed to be done around the Preserve. He hadn't seen Tim since the early part of their time at the Rockin' R yesterday and wondered if the man was still abed, or out enjoying the early morning.

Reaching the door, he paused, remembering Tim's warning at Carli's grouchiness when she was disturbed in her darkroom. He decided he could persuade her to forgive him. Knocking on the wood, he glanced down at the space between the bottom of the door and the floor. Since it was void of a threshold, he could see a little of the light from the room. There was a shadow, something that disrupted the even dispersal of the dim light from inside. He sniffed, then became concerned.

"Carli?" His voice was loud in the empty hall.

When there was no answer, he banged on the door, then tried the knob. It wouldn't turn. He couldn't use his gun to shoot at the wood surrounding the doorknob in order to break in for fear a slug would hit Carli. Looking around for something heavy, he saw the fire extinguisher hanging on the wall to his left. Releasing the clamp, he removed the steel cylinder, and in one motion turned and slammed the base of it against the doorknob. By the time he raised it to take a second swing, Samantha had reached the top of the stairs and was demanding to know what was going on. The second blow dislodged the locking mechanism and he pushed the door open. The overpowering odor of hydrochloric acid burned his eyes and nose. Breathing into the

348

crook of his elbow, he searched the floor and found Carli's body a few feet from where he stood.

"Call an ambulance!" he yelled to Sam, who was halfway down the hall.

Taking Carli under the shoulders and behind her knees, he lifted her to his chest and darted around the door and partially down the hallway. Laying her carefully on the floor, he felt for a pulse. His eyes watered, he coughed, and he tried to ignore the tightening in his chest that he blamed on the chemicals rather than the unconscious woman in front of him. There was a thread of movement underneath his fingers. He stroked her hair away from her face and pleaded to her to open her eyes, to wake up.

Sam appeared on the other side of Carli, the phone to her ear. She answered the questions with single syllables, then looked at Ethan.

"Hydrochloric acid," he answered her unasked question.

Sam's eyes widened in disbelief and confusion. A couple more answers, then she hung up the phone.

"Stan is on his way. He said to get her in the shower. Cool water to dilute what she's absorbed through her skin."

He nodded and again scooped Carli from the floor. Sam opened the room Carli stayed in when she was home, and moved ahead of Ethan to the bathroom where she turned the shower on full. Not caring that he was fully dressed, or that the water was chilly, he stepped under the spray, Carli held in his arms. The wetness splashing on her face brought her around, coughing, trying to open her eyes, only to have the water wash into them.

"It's alright," Ethan reassured her as she struggled against him.

Setting her feet on the floor of the shower, he pushed her hair away from her face, and continued to steady her. The tightness in his chest eased as she began to ask what he was doing. Relief that she would be alright, punctuated by a few choice words she tossed at him for having her fully clothed in the shower, nearly had the corners of his lips turning up in a smile.

"The darkroom is filled with hydrochloric acid," he told her and waited to see if comprehension dawned.

Trying to take a deep breath, she fought against the cough and stood a little straighter. Blinking, she stared at Ethan, her hands fisted in his shirt as the icy spray pounded her back. Keeping her eyes locked on his, she recognized his concern, and something else that was more than the desire that had been flowing between them. The burning in her throat and eyes eased. She told him what she remembered.

"I wanted to finish some prints so Shaun could mail them when he took Sam to the airport. The fluid level in the trays were low. I took the bottles from the counter and filled them."

"You're sure you used the correct bottles?" he questioned.

Carli nodded. "I only keep photo developing chemicals in the darkroom. No one goes in there except me," she swallowed, and winced slightly at the rawness. Her brows drew together as she tried to recall when things didn't seem right. "I developed the film. Shot it onto paper. I took the first prints from the rinse to hang them on the line, and felt a burning in my fingertips. It was bleach. I got dizzy, then knocked into one of the trays, splashing the chemical over the edge. A white cloud rose up in the air, and that's when I knew I had to get out of the room."

At the sound of a man's voice from the lobby, Sam darted out of the bathroom to meet Stan.

"The cloud was chloramide vapor. Bleach and ammonia are a deadly combination," Ethan stated, then flexed his fingers into her shoulders to confirm that she was alive.

"I never have them in the darkroom."

"Who knew you would be in there this morning?"

Carli shrugged, then began to shiver. "Everyone knows. No one cleans the room or stocks it. I do. They all know that if I'm not in the barn or leading clients, I'm developing photographs. Especially early in the morning."

He reached behind her and turned off the shower. Assuring himself that she could stand on her own, despite her shivering from the temperature of the water, he stepped out of the tub, grabbed a bath sheet from the towel bar and wrapped her in it. Lifting her from the shower to the bathroom floor, he turned to find Stan and a partner filling the doorway.

"Glad to see you're conscious, Carli," Stan told her. "You need to remove your clothes," he shot a look at Ethan, "as they are still full of the chemical, though now diluted."

Carli nodded, then stared pointedly at Stan and his partner, someone she hadn't met. They backed out of the doorway, but when she shifted her gaze to Ethan, he simply reached out a hand and closed the door.

"I'm not convinced you're steady enough on your feet to do this alone."

"This is not the time or place to pick up where we left off last night," she began.

"And even though the thought of you naked, under me, on top of me, against the wall, is not far from my mind right now, my priority is your health."

Carli snapped her mouth closed. She didn't know if she should be shocked at all the ways he wanted her, or sexually excited. Either would have explained the flush she felt blooming on her cheeks, rising from the goose bumps on her flesh.

Unwrapping the towel and handing it to Ethan, she tried to undo the buttons on her shirt. The numbness in her fingers and the slight fuzziness in her brain kept her from completing the task. He simply brushed her hands aside, and in a utilitarian manner, removed her shirt. While she worked to pull her hands through her cuffs, he unzipped her jeans and pushed the heavy, soaked material over her hips and down her legs. Crouching next to her feet, he lifted them one at a time to remove her boots, then pull her pants over her feet as she steadied herself with a hand on his shoulder.

From his position on the floor, he looked up the length of her body and groaned inwardly. Carli's close-fitting clothes covered smooth skin over toned limbs. Despite his best intentions, his libido gave a jumpstart to the desire that seemed to be running at nearly full-speed whenever she was around. Taking the towel from the counter, he held it up in front of her.

"All of it. Off."

She sighed, and with her body hidden behind the cloth Ethan stretched between his hands, she shucked her bra and panties. Not wanting to face Stan and his partner completely naked, she took her flannel robe from the hook on the door, pushed her arms through the sleeves, then tied it around her waist. As Ethan tossed the towel over the shower rod, Shaun's voice could be heard through the bathroom door.

"Carli? What the hell happened?"

At her nod, Ethan opened the door and found four pairs of eyes with a mixture of concern, anger, curiosity, and wonder.

Stan took control. "If you think you can make it down the stairs alright on your own, Brad and I won't carry you to the bus on the stretcher."

Carli nodded, and the crowd moved away from the door.

"We need to check you out, put you on some oxygen, call the clinic," Stan continued.

She led the parade of concerned friends and family members down the hall, the stairs, and out the front door of the lodge. Stan and Brad walked with her, one on each side.

Sam followed, all but wringing her hands. This wasn't an accident, a case of inattention on Carli's part. Just like the fire that destroyed the storage shed, and the shot that killed their father, someone was sending a distinct message that the Tanners were unwanted. She wondered if the incidents at Crystal Springs were perpetrated by the same person, and if she would be any safer there, than here.

Shaun placed his hand on Ethan's arm in the hallway to halt his intention of going with Carli to the ambulance that waited in the parking lot. "What happened?"

Ethan gestured toward the darkroom, and they made their way to the partially open door, its knob hanging at an awkward angle. The odor had dissipated with the fresh air from the hallway. Glancing at the prints and film, then the open door, he wondered how much of her work was ruined.

"I came up here to find Carli. Sam informed me she often works in the darkroom early in the morning. As I started to knock on the door, I noticed a shadow on the floor blocking the light from inside. Then the smell. It wasn't strong, but was very different from the pine odor that normally permeates the lodge. I called out. No answer. I pounded on the door. Nothing." He paused and gestured to where the fire extinguisher sat on the floor. "I used that to break the doorknob. Found her passed out on the floor. Sam heard me, and I told her to call 911. While she was on the phone with Stan, he told her to get Carli into the shower. Dilute the hydrochloric acid."

"Looks like you need some dry clothes," Shaun dropped his gaze to Ethan's sodden shirt and jeans.

He glanced down at himself as if he just realized his state. Mumbling an expletive, he reached under his flannel shirt and removed his gun. It was far enough towards the back of his waistband that it hadn't been soaked, but he would need to clean it anyway.

Shaun, who had begun his own cursory look around the darkroom, glanced back at Ethan. "J.J. or Zach can get you a cleaning kit from the storage closet."

His brows drew together at that, since all the cleaning supplies were probably kept there. The assembly line of equipment and trays set up on the island counter were familiar to him. He looked at each of the trays, his scowl deepening as bits of paper, remnants of a photograph, floated in one of them. Leaning close, he took a cautious sniff, then backed away. Bleach.

Ethan took a pair of spare tongs and lifted two bottles from a large, plastic garbage can. Based on the other contents of the can, he assumed this was a recycle bin. Neither label alluded to a cleaning agent. Taking a sniff of each, his nose still recognized, despite the burn earlier, that one bottle had contained bleach, the other, ammonia. Carli hadn't mistaken the bottles. Someone had refilled them, then left the bottles for Carli to use. In the space of a few moments, his gut turned from red-hot fury that someone had wanted to cause Carli serious, if not permanent, harm, to ice that settled, and stayed, that told him they had nearly succeeded.

"I'll bag this stuff, get it to Cheyenne," Shaun said.

Ethan nodded mutely and left the darkroom.

Carli was sitting on the rear bumper of the ambulance, an oxygen mask over her nose and mouth. Her eyes appeared clearer, and she kept them on him as he approached.

"Feeling better?"

She nodded.

"Her vitals are a little off. Probably more from the ordeal than the chemicals," Stan told him. "The clinic is expecting us, but our patient here is reluctant."

Carli removed the mask and spoke to the EMT. "I don't need a ride in your bus, Stan. The burning in my eyes is gone, and I'm sure a cup of coffee at breakfast will get rid of the discomfort in my throat."

"You need—"

"No. I don't." Carli glared at Stan. She liked him well enough, had known him a long time, but he could be like a dog with a bone when it comes to delivering people to the hospital.

Stan huffed out a breath and looked to Ethan hoping to find an ally.

"What are the effects of exposure to hydrochloric acid?" Ethan asked.

"Burning in the nose, throat, and eyes. Coughing. It can burn the skin. A headache."

"With fresh air and rest, she'll be alright?"

Stan couldn't lie. He reluctantly nodded.

"I'll ensure she gets both," Ethan informed Stan, though his eyes were on Carli.

"She's a Tanner, Stan. It takes more than a little chemical mix-up to keep us down," Shaun added.

Exasperated, Stan got the clinic on the phone to inform them that the patient wouldn't be delivered. He listened and acknowledged that poison control would still be contacted and the incident reported. With the message conveyed to those at the back of the ambulance, he took the clipboard from Brad and began to make notes on the form.

"The darkroom is off limits until I get everything cleaned up and sent to town. I'm not sure how much of your work is ruined," Shaun left the statement unfinished, instead of saying, 'since Ethan had to break down the door and save your life from someone who purposely tried to end it'.

"It's alright. It wasn't the negatives, only the prints," Carli reassured her protective brother.

As Shaun walked away, he dialed the number of the Cheyenne Police Department to inform the forensics office he would be bringing in some evidence.

Stan shoved the clipboard at Carli, who initialed and signed at the places he pointed to on the forms. She stood, handed the mask back to Stan, then gingerly moved the two steps from the gravel of the parking lot to the bottom step of the veranda.

Ethan placed his hand on her low back, not so much to support her, as to fulfill the need to touch her and confirm for himself that she was alive.

As the ambulance pulled out, J.J. and Zach rounded the far corner of the lodge. Their jovial faces fell as they watched the red van drive away, both gazes swinging to where Carli, Ethan, and Sam stood on the steps of the veranda.

"Hey! What happened?" J.J. asked as the two of them trotted the distance to the group at the front of the lodge.

Ethan glanced at Carli, wondering if she would be honest with the employees about the incident.

"Someone switched the chemicals in my darkroom for bleach and ammonia," she explained.

Wanting to witness J.J.'s reaction, Ethan shifted his gaze to the head wrangler. Shock, then concern registered. Was he that adept at faking his expressions, or was he innocent of any involvement in the events that seemed to plague the Preserve and its occupants?

"Come on. We'll fill you in over breakfast," Sam offered as she stood holding open the door.

They all filed inside, Shaun waving off food and drink until he had gathered whatever evidence was in the room. He was halfway upstairs, the rest of them talking all at once in the lobby, when a voice from the door immediately hushed the crowd.

"I passed the ambulance on the driveway. Is everyone alright?"

All eyes turned and found Darla Tanner, dressed in a pale blue pantsuit with a floral blouse, and a slightly quizzical expression on her face.

CHAPTER 37

Ray flicked off the radio. A Wyoming news station just broadcasted a ten-minute segment on Bear Tanner. He supposed the man deserved that much airtime, being the icon he was for the state. Glancing out the window above the sink, he noticed the silence now in the kitchen, free from the radio and sizzling pans on the stove. With a plate of bacon in one hand and a platter of scrambled eggs in the other, he pushed through the kitchen door. Before he set the food on the table, he realized the dining room was full of people, none of whom wore a pleasant expression. He was just about to make a joke concerning worried faces so early in the morning, when Darla, the last of the party, paused in the doorway.

"What's going on?" he demanded, more than asked, as his gaze touched everyone, then landed on Carli's wet hair and bathrobe.

"Someone swapped my photography chemicals for bleach and ammonia. If Ethan hadn't broken down the door, I may not be here right now."

J.J. and Zach each inquired as to how it could have happened. Sam remained quiet and introspective, watching the play between Ethan and Carli. Everyone settled at the table, including Darla, who had words of shock and concern for her daughter. As Ray poured the coffee, he couldn't keep his eyes from straying to Darla. She found some place else to rest her gaze. Details and theories were tossed out over breakfast. Towards the end of the conversation Shaun took a seat at the table. The one always occupied by Bear remained empty.

"This confirms it," Shaun spoke to Sam. "You need to return to Crystal Springs."

"Already changed my reservations. Matt will be there to pick me up."

"Are you packed? The office in Cheyenne is waiting for the items I took from the darkroom."

"Yes. I threw everything together this morning before all of this happened," Sam gestured toward Carli, who raised a brow at being referred to as 'all of this'.

"Well, I think the biggest, unasked question is what Carli plans to do with the Preserve," Darla said, carefully setting her coffee cup on the table.

Shaun looked at Darla as if realizing for the first time that she was at breakfast. He knew that Carli and Sam shared his thought that whatever Carli's ideas were, they would not include Darla, and therefore, were none of Darla's concern.

Sam began to make their shared thought known, when Carli spoke directly to Darla.

"I know how much this place meant to Dad. He raised us here, and we all think of it as home. If he entrusted it to me, how can I turn it down? Yes, I have plans. The Preserve will continue. Dad believed in giving clients the adventure they sought. It brought him prosperity and lifelong friends. He was happy here and loved his life. That's something Shaun and Sam and I have in common. You, on the other hand, hate it here. Your life is in California, or wherever you've hidden out the past twenty years. Dad didn't need you. We're all grown up, and don't need you either." Carli placed her napkin on the table beside her plate, slid her chair back, and stood.

Ethan, who was sitting next to her and silently cheering her on as she expressed her thoughts in a sure, collected, controlled manner of speaking to a person who had done little in her life besides cause pain and disappointment, stood as well.

"Take a good look around, Darla. This will be the last time you'll be allowed on the property." With absolutely no trace of what she had endured that morning, Carli left the dining room.

Ethan exchanged a glance with Shaun, noticed that Darla's face had turned an unflattering shade of red, then followed Carli. Informing her that he would change his clothes and meet her in her room, he watched as she ascended the stairs and disappeared beyond the landing. On the short trek to Cabin 4, he checked the barrel and ejected the clip on his weapon. Everything was dry. It would fire if the need arose.

"Since you have your own car, that alleviates me from extending my manners and offering you a ride to the airport," Shaun said to Darla. Turning his gaze to Sam he added, "I'll be outside." A moment later, the front door of the lodge was closed with the sound of finality.

J.J. and Zach, feeling the family tension, yet relieved that not only was Carli recovered from the incident in her darkroom but would keep the Preserve operational, made excuses as to what had to be done around the property that day. They left the table, taking their dishes with them, and deposited the plates in the kitchen sink on their way out the back door. Ray, silent throughout the meal, began to gather the remaining plates. Sam helped and was the first to enter the kitchen.

Placing the dishes in the sink, she looked out the window that was set above the counter and ran the length of the entire wall. The pines and disappearing patches of snow, the squirrels and the birds that seemed to chase each other from branch to branch, reminded her of the Springs. She loved the lodge, but Colorado was where her heart resided.

Ray brought her out of her daze as he stood next to her, adding his stack of dishes to hers. With his gaze out the window, Sam studied his profile. She knew it as well as her father's.

"Ray? Do you plan on staying here? I know it will be tough, with Dad gone. I'm sure Carli could use your input on how to run the place."

He quietly considered how to answer her. Finally, with a ghost of a smile he shook his head. "No. I've stayed long enough. Too long, in fact. Unlike you kids, I don't love it here. Cold in the winter. Wind always blowing." He turned to look at Sam. "Your sister is a bright woman. She'll figure out on her own what to do. Not everything Bear did was right."

Sam placed her hand on Ray's arm. "Where will you go? What will you do?"

"Retire. Past time I did so," his voice shifted, along with his gaze, to the sink full of dishes, then the scene outside the window. "I would like to spend some time in the sunshine."

She didn't know Ray felt this way. He had been here as long as she had, a fixture in her life, like the lodge itself. There was an ache in her heart at the thought that she might never see him again. She wondered if the others knew how unhappy Ray had been.

"Why did you stay?" she asked before she realized she might be prying.

"Where else would I go? The pay was excellent, and Bear was my closest friend." He shrugged, and turned to face her.

There was sadness, perhaps some regret, and relief in his eyes. Sam wrapped him in a hug, something he haltingly returned.

"You'll keep in touch? Let us know where you are?" she asked hopefully.

Ray nodded, then brought his attention to the dishes. "You better get going or Shaun will come in here to collect you and the two of you will leave squabbling."

She stepped back and smiled up at Ray, who seemed to want to get on with the business of cleaning the kitchen. Leaving him, she passed through the dining room and dabbed at the corners of her eyes that seemed to always be moist these past several days. Pausing across the table from Darla, who had yet to leave, and in fact held her coffee cup with both hands an inch from her lips, she waited until the older woman met her gaze.

"What Carli said earlier, holds true for Shaun and me, too. The time has long since passed that we needed a mother. We have our lives, and you're simply not a part of them. It was your decision twenty years ago, and it is ours, now. You've never been to Crystal Springs, nor are you welcome." She felt as if she were going through the motions, her feelings either nonexistent or so confused that they were in hiding. "Have a nice life, Darla." It was said with as much sincerity as Sam could muster.

Without waiting for a reply, and not caring if she got one, she went upstairs to gather her things. Her suitcase was packed, minus the extra changes of clothes she had brought for the rest of her stay. Deciding that she would be visiting the lodge frequently in the coming weeks and months, she may as well have more clothes here. Her bed wasn't made since Alyssa would be changing sheets today when she came to work after school. She picked up her unopened envelope from the nightstand, smiled a little as her fingers touched the familiar writing, then placed it inside her purse. The complete opposite of Carli, who either carried nothing, or something just big enough to fit her driver's license and some cash, Sam carried a bag that contained everything she might possibly need in any situation. She knew it stemmed from her time in Carl Rutgers's company. If she only had a knife, a phone, some tissues …

Setting her suitcase in the hall outside her door, she walked slowly to the darkroom. There was fingerprint dust on the knob, the door, the counters, and the trays. A chill tickled her spine as she realized that Carli could have died that morning. The scent of hydrochloric acid and the chloramide cloud had dissipated, some into the hall, the rest through the ventilation. She should mention to Shaun that the filters should be changed, maybe even have the unit serviced.

Turning away from a room that had always brought joy to her sister, a place where her creativity came to life, she wondered if Carli would ever use it again. They had all been dealt a blow by the sudden death of their father. Harming Carli in a way that spoke 'sabotage', in a place that belonged only to her, could wound her sister, perhaps beyond repair.

She hesitated outside Carli's door. There was a strong need to ensure herself that her sister was alright. Her reluctance to leave Carli and the lodge and to return to the work waiting for her at the Springs, and whatever Cole had on his mind, was temporarily paralyzing. She squeezed her eyes shut, her knuckles poised to knock on the door. *Buck up, Sam. You're a Tanner after all, and Tanner's are made of tougher stuff,* she told herself. With a deep breath, and a stiffer spine, she rapped on the door that was immediately opened by Carli, who looked pretty peeved.

"Am I interrupting?" Sam raised a brow, her eyes going to Ethan who stood in the middle of the room, hands on his hips, half-obscured by the cases that traveled with her sister.

"Of course not," Carli answered, dressed in dry clothes. "We were just discussing the need to leave so that we could reach Miner's Paradise by noon."

Sam raised her other brow. "You're going hiking after what happened this morning?"

"Why not? Stan said fresh air would help me recover. There's plenty of it out there," she gestured to whatever place wasn't where she was standing.

"We can go tomorrow. You should take it easy today," Ethan suggested, a bit of anger creasing his brow.

Sam tried not to smile. Finally, her world-traveled, self-assured, brilliantly talented sister had met someone who would stand up to her, challenge her, care for her.

"You'll be going, too?" she asked Ethan.

His scowl deepened, but he nodded as he crossed his arms over his chest.

"And you know first aid? I assume they teach that at Quantico?"

He raised a brow, not entirely thrilled that Sam would take Carli's side.

She took the expression to be affirmative, and then finally smiled. "How much safer could Carli be than away from the lodge, out in the Wyoming spring air, with her own FBI agent?"

Carli wasn't sure if she should smile or frown. Sam was on her side in the discussion she was having with Ethan concerning the state of her health and what she could, or should, do. But then the words, 'her own FBI agent' sat a little funny with her. Because Ethan was employed by the FBI, it made sense that he took it upon himself to see to her safety. She wondered if he had feelings of guilt due to the incident that morning.

When neither answered her, Sam wrapped her arms around Carli. "Be safe. I'll see you soon."

Carli hugged Sam. She had hoped that they could visit longer, but understood Shaun's need to do what he could to protect his sisters and his belief that Sam's safety would be ensured at the ranch.

"We'll need to meet and go over the rest of the paperwork that Max Stevens has for us," Carli said to fill the space and keep the emotions of loss away.

"Yes, of course, but we should wait until all this ..." Sam waved vaguely, unsure how to address the shooting, the fire, and the darkroom chemicals. "Is, well, you know," and Carli nodded. "I have the guest book so I'll begin to send thank you notes. I may have to call or e-mail you and Shaun since I wasn't able to meet everyone ..." she sighed and realized that she was rambling to delay leaving.

Carli knew, as big sisters just seemed to know stuff, so she ushered Sam out the door. "If Shaun has to come get you, he'll be even more sour than he already is. Go. Have a safe flight. I'll be fine." Carli stepped back, a wide smile on her face.

Sam snagged her suitcase and pulled it behind her, then lifted it up as she descended the stairs. Shaun was waiting for her, leaning against the side of his SUV, the back passenger door open. After she tossed her bag inside, he opened the front passenger door for her, then closed it once she and her purse, which was more of a backpack with its myriad contents, were settled.

They were both quiet as they drove down the long, graveled driveway, the state highway through town, and didn't speak until the vehicle was speeding down 130 towards Laramie.

"She'll be alright," Sam finally spoke into the silence of the vehicle, punctuated occasionally by the police radio.

"Damn right she will. And so will you. I called Matt this morning." Shaun glanced at her. "I wanted to make sure he knew about what was going on here, and to increase the security at the Springs."

At her scowl, an obvious disapproval of him contacting the farm just in case she wasn't as forthcoming with the information about what had occurred on the Preserve as he believed she needed to be, he decided to refrain from sharing with her that he had also contacted the JAR-C Ranch. He figured the more eyes he had to keep Sam safe, the better. Years earlier, Sam and Cole were inseparable. He knew at one time that Cole was in love with Samantha, and had hoped, despite Sam's arguments to the contrary, that those feelings would, whether still present or not, have Cole offer his assistance. He hadn't been wrong.

"Don't make this harder on me than it is, Sam. I need you to be safe. Ethan will keep Carli out of harm's way, especially now that whoever is doing this is obviously out to … hurt her, and maybe you, too."

In an unexpected change of conversation, Sam asked, "Did you know that Ray is leaving?"

"No."

"I had a conversation with him in the kitchen this morning after breakfast."

She thought about the words that Ray used. There was something that seemed a little off, like she was missing part of his message. She shared with Shaun what their father's oldest friend had confessed amidst a pile of dirty dishes. Her brother didn't answer right away. Instead, he clenched his jaw so the muscle ticked in his cheek.

Finally he said, "I'm sure Carli will share her plans with us in detail and, assuming she's going to remain in Wyoming, she'll be looking for help in running the business anyway."

She made a noncommittal sound and stared out the windshield. Carli was smart, but didn't know the intricacies of being an entrepreneur. There was also something that Shaun knew that he wasn't sharing with her. The remaining drive was peppered with short comments volleyed back and forth of mostly inconsequential matters.

Dropping her off at the curb outside the terminal, he removed her case and set it on the walkway next to her. "Whoever is doing this, means business. Don't take unnecessary risks. Call me." He held her gaze until she acknowledged the gravity of his concern. He gave her a quick hug, then stepped back.

"Just because you have a gun, a badge, and a penis, doesn't mean you're immune to the insanity of this person. Don't take any unnecessary risks. Call me," she repeated his words back to him.

The word referring to what set him apart from his sisters, coming from Samantha, her bangs just over her brows, her dirty-blonde hair in its customary braid, her small stature and unlined face, would have made another man laugh aloud. Not Shaun. He took her seriously, and though he preferred to think of his sisters as virginal, he knew they both could sling the words of sailors to cut off someone at the knees, raise them beyond the clouds, or express their thoughts in the most succinct way possible.

"Right."

Sam turned and entered the terminal, pulling her suitcase behind her. Shaun waited until the doors slid shut before he replaced his sunglasses and climbed back into the SUV. Winding his way from the airport to I-80 that would take him to Cheyenne and the forensics office at the rear of the police building, he mulled over the words Ray spoke to Sam. 'Should have left long ago.' 'Past time to leave.' 'I don't love the lodge like you kids.' He didn't think Darla had it in her to pull the trigger and kill Bear Tanner. The property damage caused by the fire was minimal.

But the incident with Carli was personal. Everyone knew she was the only one who used the darkroom. She never would have stored bleach or ammonia amongst her developing chemicals. When cleaning needed to be done, she used soap and warm water. Carli was not a careless person, nor was she suicidal.

Shaun rubbed his forehead as he braked at a red light. He should have thought to inquire as to Darla's whereabouts from the time she left the Rockin' R last night until she showed up this morning. Pulling into the Cheyenne Police Station parking lot, he thought of the reading of the will. Bear had left Carli the Preserve. If someone else wanted it, they could take it if Carli was ... gone. Putting the SUV in PARK, Shaun grabbed his phone and dialed Ethan.

"Brooks."

"Is Darla still at the lodge?"

"No. I saw her pull out as we started towards the trailhead."

"Shit," was his first comment, "What?" was his second.

Ethan decided to respond to the second comment first. "Fresh air and her personal FBI agent. We're on our way to Miner's Paradise. I need to see—" he didn't finish his thought. Carli had paused on the trail ahead of him, hands on hips, and stared at him.

"Yeah, I get it," Shaun said. "Carli?"

"Fine. Why the question regarding Darla?"

"Dad didn't leave her anything. If she thinks she deserves something, she may believe that Carli stands in her way."

The ice was back in Ethan's gut, but he kept it from showing on his face. Instead, he said, "Understood."

As lawmen, they knew the stakes had been raised. They had a possible suspect and a real powerful motive. He glanced around at the trees, the rocks, the incline on this side of the canyon, and felt a slight comfort that Darla, if she did wish to eliminate Carli to get her hands on the Preserve, couldn't, wouldn't, follow them here. Her obvious dislike of the outdoors, coiffed hair, expensive shoes and clothing, were not conducive to a perpetrator that would hike into the wilderness to take another crack at removing that which might be considered the embodiment of her anger and unjust treatment. Believing that for the immediate future they were relatively safe, he silently shared the expletive Shaun voiced earlier at the sheriff's next words.

"On the way to the airport, Sam told me about the conversation she had with Ray. A few of his comments seemed … strange. I have a couple things I want to check out. I'll see you at the lodge for dinner," Shaun said.

"Sure," Ethan confirmed, then added, "You can have her picked up. Taken in and questioned. You know what she's driving. If she's serious, she won't leave until she has what she wants."

"Right," Shaun agreed and hung up.

He made the necessary calls, then hauled the evidence boxes into the lab.

《《—》》

Ethan replaced his phone at his belt and knew Carli would want a report. To keep her safe, he needed to be honest. She had a long history with Darla and might know how far the woman would go to acquire what she felt she deserved. Shaun also seemed to have concerns regarding Ray Foster. The wind picked up, reminding him that they had a destination. The sky began to cloud over, and if he could judge the weather in the wilderness of Wyoming, he might say there was a late spring storm approaching.

"Let's hike and talk. I'll fill you in on what Shaun is up to."

She relaxed her arms by her sides and continued up the trail.

"Were you aware that Ray planned to leave the lodge?" he asked.

She stumbled, then turned part-way around and shared her shocked expression with Ethan. "No."

"Can you run the Preserve without him?" he inquired, then asked something he should have last night after the reading of the will. "What do you plan to do with the Preserve?"

With her eyes on the trail ahead of her, she took a breath and voiced her dream aloud. "In Kenya, the government has worked with animal activists to alter the focus of their richly inhabited land. What used to be a game preserve is now available for safari only. Visitors shoot animals with cameras, not guns. Except poachers," she added, remembering the men they had surprised a few days ago.

"And you plan to execute the same conversion?"

"It will take some planning. The purchase of cameras, increasing the number of trails. I would like to expand what Tanner's has to offer during the winter months. Of course, new clientele will need to be contacted, and we'll lose some of the long-standing clients Dad had acquired."

She was quiet as they climbed the steeper switchback. Allowing the excitement to flood her imagination with ideas, she put aside many of the 'hows'. Did she *need* Ray? He was a master tracker and knew a lot about the animals that the Preserve stocked. She had studied enough at her father's side to know his business philosophy. For the jobs Bear had outsourced, she saw no reason to not continue those business relationships. The accountant, lawyer, insurance company, veterinarian, the Rangers who worked the forests and BLM land from where the animals were transported, would continue to benefit from their contracts with Tanner's Outdoor Adventures.

"No. I don't *need* Ray Foster. It's surprising that he would choose to not be a part of the Preserve, as he has been for so long. But I'm a believer that people should do what makes them happy. If he isn't happy here, then he needs to move on. I'll miss him. He's lived at the lodge since it was built. I'm sure everyone will be sorry he's leaving."

"How well did he and Bear get along?"

No matter the topic of conversation, or where else he tried to rest his gaze, it strayed back to Carli's heart-shaped ass. Her jeans were a perfect fit, from her narrow waist, hidden from view by her lined flannel shirt, down her long legs that seemed to never tire, to the well-worn hiking boots that appeared to know and traverse the trail as if on their own. The comment he had made to her that morning about the positions he wanted her in when they came together were pictured in his mind with his palms spread over the roundness of her bottom. With half his mind on the conversation and the other half below his belt, he had to strain to hear her answer.

"They were best friends. About the time I turned fifteen or sixteen, their relationship ... altered, I guess is the way to describe what I observed. When I asked Dad about it, he said that relationships are never stagnant. They change. It was as if he started to treat Ray more like an employee rather than a business partner."

If the two had a falling out, and Ray was forced to stay on at the Preserve, that could create resentment, and resentment could be reason enough to kill. Depending on how trapped Ray felt, maybe the only perceived escape would be if Tanner's was no longer run by Bear. Ray, having been such a long-standing feature of the Preserve, had the knowledge of where Bear was going with the hunting party that morning, the terrain of the canyon, and was even a seasoned hunter and therefore knew how to adjust his gun in order to make the shot. If Ray had a strong motive, and opportunity, then why the other incidents? And if he was planning to leave the business, what would there be to gain by getting rid of Carli? Unless it wasn't Ray who torched the storage area and swapped the chemicals in the darkroom.

"What is it? Ethan, are you alright?"

Carli's concerned voice reached his ears, and he realized he had finally drawn his attention away from sex with her to something completely involving his job. Her equally worried countenance swam before his refocused gaze.

"Who would have the most to gain if you were not able to inherit the Preserve?"

She blinked at his question. "Not Sam or Shaun, if that's what you're thinking." Hands on hips, the concern rolled into defensive anger.

"I know. Who else?" His fingers wanted his pad and pencil, *needed* them to make the connections visually.

"None of the employees. Max alluded to the sale of the Preserve if I failed to take possession. That would, most likely, leave them without a job."

She paced to where the bend in the switchback allowed her a view into the canyon. Crossing her arms under her chest, she tipped her head to the side and thought. Faces and names flashed through her mind. From behind her, Ethan voiced his conclusions, but left out the name of who he suspected of the shooting. His words flowed with her thoughts. Glancing up at the clouds, the first flake caught her by surprise.

"We're almost there. Let's keep moving. Hopefully this is all the clouds brought with them," she said.

One more switchback and they were near the top edge of the canyon. The trail leveled out, but the terrain remained uneven and dense with brush. Despite being under cover of the trees, the snow had increased enough that the flakes swirled on the wind as the temperature dropped. She pulled her flannel shirt snuggly against her.

"Darla," she finally answered. "She was so adamant that Dad hadn't divorced her, that he would have left her … something."

"Perhaps there was a check in her envelope."

She shook her head. "No. I was watching. She was the only one who opened the envelope in John's office. Perhaps she believed there would have been something in the letter to prove us wrong."

"I got a good look at her as she left. Her face was red. I think it was anger rather than embarrassment."

Stopping on the trail, her hair blew across her face as she gestured with her head. "Here. There's a clear shot between the trees to the top of Wolf's Ridge."

Squinting up at the clouds, obscured by the branches, the realization hit her that this wasn't a quickly passing storm cloud, but a front that brought with it substantial precipitation. Watching as the flakes began to collect on the ground, she considered returning to the lodge now or finding shelter on the rim of the canyon.

Moving off the trail, closer to the edge of where the ground dropped away, there was a clear view of the opposite side of the canyon. He had been at the bottom and on Wolf's Ridge. Both had seemed to set Miner's Paradise further away than it was. Perspective. Instructors had talked about it in the couple of art classes he had taken. In Baltimore, it would have been easier to gauge the height of the buildings and distance between landmarks. Scowling at the flakes that appeared to increase, he noticed the view across the canyon was less than optimal. He wasn't a sniper, but knew that someone with skill could fire a killing shot. Peering through the swirling snow, first being blown one way and then another, he raised his hands as if holding a rifle. Standing, the shooter could have been seen from Wolf's Ridge through binoculars, so he squatted, but the steepness of the edge of the canyon made it tricky to keep his balance, which meant the killer had been sitting. Looking around, he found the spot where pine needles had been cleared away. He sat on the ground. The nearest tree, just to the left of the cleared area, had a piece of bark that was chipped away. He touched it. If there was gunshot residue, he couldn't tell for sure without acetone, the most commonly used chemical to detect if a gun had been fired. It was possible that the shooter used the tree to steady the rifle.

"Ethan?"

Climbing to his feet, dusting off dirt, leaves, and snow, he turned to face Carli. "Would there happen to be an old hunting lodge around that we could hide out in until this storm blows over?" he asked.

"No. But there's a mine about a hundred feet up the trail." At the paling of his face, she added, "We would go inside as kids. It has a narrow entrance, but then opens into a room you can stand up in. And it's not that far underground—" she stopped as his jaw tightened. "Either that, or we head back to the lodge. But in this weather, with the snow and wind, we'll be soaked and may end up with hypothermia."

371

He looked up the trail behind her, then into the canyon and the direction of appropriate shelter. "Right. Mine shaft it is."

She turned and led the way back to the trail, then to the mine entrance. It was cut into the side of the canyon. A bush growing near the opening effectively hid the mine from the view of anyone who wasn't looking for it. She paused at the mouth of the shaft and examined the ground in the front and to the sides. Satisfied, she straightened and turned to face him.

"Looks like we're the only ones here." At his puzzled expression she said, "No cats … mountain lions. No prints … none have marked this as their own …"

When it looked as if she would explain further, he held up his hand. "I get it. No paw prints, no 'spray'."

She nodded. "If you like, you can close your eyes and I'll lead you in," she offered.

"How will you see where you're going?"

Giving him a half-smile, she shifted her pack over one shoulder, unzipped a compartment, and extracted a flashlight. A strong gust whistled through the trees, sending the snow sideways.

He had admitted that he was a little claustrophobic and why. But he wasn't castrated, and his pride refused to allow him to be led into a cramped, dark place by the woman he was protecting.

Holding out his hand for the light, he said, "What kind of FBI agent would I be if you went first?"

A handsome, brave one who wasn't afraid to admit he was a little scared, she thought, then handed over the flashlight. He held out his other hand and, as she had done several times, placed her hand in his. The warmth that he seemed to always possess immediately thawed her fingers, then the heat continued traveling directly to her low belly. If she listened to the whisper in her mind, she knew for certain that it was more than her hand she placed in his care.

With the wind at their backs, they crouched and wiggled through the narrow opening. The light shined forward through the dark space, thick with dust, and illuminated the rocks and dirt that constituted the top, bottom, and sides of the mini-tunnel. In an effort to keep his rising panic under control, he concentrated on where he placed his feet and moved in such a way as to reduce the number of times his broad shoulders bumped against the sides. To Carli's credit, she attempted to distract him by telling a story of her childhood when she and her siblings played 'Miner and Sheriff'. She chuckled and asked if he could guess who always wanted to be the sheriff.

The short distance seemed infinite as his phobia reached out of his head and snaked towards his heart. Life-sustaining breath came and went in short bursts, hesitating in mid-inhale as if there wasn't enough air and suffocation was moments away. The claws of the irrational fear tightened in his chest. At her words, he realized his fingers were doing the same to her hand.

"Ethan, it's alright. Another couple of feet and you can stand."

Shining the light further in front of him, the darkness widened just ahead. Reaching it, he cautiously rose from his crouch. She was right. The 'room' was tall enough for him to stand up in, but barely. The ceiling was supported by a series of timbers spaced about two feet apart, the dirt held together by the roots of the foliage that grew topside. Near the tunnel that they had just crawled through, there was a crevice in the ceiling. Moving closer to it, he felt a cold breeze from outside as a few stray flakes found their way through the crack to the floor of the room, where they instantly melted.

Significantly warmer out of the cold, snow-driven wind, Carli planted herself on a wide, smooth rock, setting her pack at her feet. Rummaging around in one of her zippered pockets, she pulled out a container of water and a tiny case with a screw top that contained wooden matches. She was very aware of Ethan and his movements around the shaft. Though his panic seemed to have subsided, there remained a pent-up energy. Sitting quietly and sipping from the water bottle, the image of a caged mountain lion came to mind. When it appeared he had satisfied himself with the width and length of the room, he came to stand in front of her.

"Here," she said simply, holding the water out to him. "There's another bottle, so take the rest."

He did, then handed the empty container back to her.

"We could use some of the discarded timber to build a small fire to dry out our clothes and keep the chill away," she suggested, gesturing to the pile of wood against one side of the underground chamber.

He cleared a space beneath the crevice in the ceiling, pushing leaves and loose dirt aside. Setting some splintered pieces of wood in such a way as to allow air to flow under them to feed the flames, he unzipped his pack and withdrew the pad he used for sketches. As a general rule, he didn't throw away his sketches, thus the boxes stacked in the rented storage space in Baltimore. Flipping to the back, he ripped out a few blank sheets, wadded them slightly, and stuffed them under the carefully stacked wood.

"Here," she offered, holding out her container of matches.

A moment later, orange flames devoured the paper and ignited the pieces of timber. Old and rotten, it would turn to ash quickly. The familiar scent of burning wood filled the confined space, then wafted up and out of the room through the opening overhead.

Sighing, he settled on a rock opposite of where Carli had perched herself, each of them occupying one side of their makeshift campfire. Stretching his legs out towards the flames, his thoughts were divided between being temporarily stranded here with Carli, and the two suspects that needed to be questioned. He refused to acknowledge the shadows at the edges of his vision that wanted only to pull him into the memories of the trunk of the car, the floor of the closet ... After a few minutes of silence, with only the quiet breathing of the woman who sat across from him and the wind outside that could be heard through the crevice, it was Carli that voiced his conclusions, or at least those that he had arrived at so far.

"There are no maternal feelings that Darla harbors for me, or any of us, for that matter. Someone cold-hearted enough to walk away from her three children, probably wouldn't hold any compunction for getting rid of the one that stood in the way of her receiving what she has probably envisioned as hers for twenty years. But what I don't get, is why? She hates Wyoming. Hates the lodge. Would she try to kill me for spite?"

"It's a lot to risk just to get even. What else could she do with the property?" he asked aloud.

She tipped her head to the side. "Money. Everyone wants it. People have killed for less, as they say. If I can't take possession of the property and business, it's sold—" she stopped, then laughed, though there was no humor. "Why didn't I remember? Darla Tanner obtained a real estate license soon after she arrived in California. She used to brag about the million-dollar homes along the coast that she sold to famous people in the movie and music industries."

He remembered Shaun's comments about Darla's career and their speculation that she could have used her business as a front for any sales offers on the property.

"There were inquiries made by a real estate company regarding the value and availability of the Preserve. It could have been her."

"That explains the darkroom, but what about the storage fire?"

He shrugged, then realized it was a habit of Carli's. "Get rid of any paperwork or documents related to the divorce or the will. The longer that it's believed the divorce wasn't final, or any delay in discovering what instructions Bear had left for his holdings, was more time that whatever plan was set in motion could be concluded with, as Darla claimed, 'all possessions are gifted to the surviving spouse'."

After a moment of thought, she shot to her feet. "That bitch! What other species kill off their own for personal gain?"

Pacing the few strides that measured the width of the cavern, she pushed her hands through her hair, loosening the damp strands from each other, setting the curls to fall about her shoulders. Darla was capable of several cruel, misdirected deeds, but attempted murder? Was it that she needed the money that badly, or that her mother despised her that much? Did she feel a twinge of regret, of second-guessing as she refilled the chemical bottles? There was a slight contraction in Carli's gut as she contemplated being hated to such a degree. Maybe Darla owed money to someone. A real estate deal gone bad? What were her plans for the Preserve? Questions she had no answers for continued to be churned out by a mind that couldn't quite grasp any motive for murder.

Guessing her question was rhetorical, he remained silent. While her attention was on the possible deception of the woman who gave birth to her, he decided the rest might as well be shared.

"The shooter—" he started, then stopped as Carli whirled around to face him.

"Would not have been Darla. She never liked guns. For years, well, the time she was at the lodge, Dad tried to teach her how to hold a gun. 'If only for protection', he would tell her. 'What if someone broke in while I was out with clients, or there was a bear or a snake?'," she shook her head, her gaze on the memories of the past. "They fought about it. He never did get her to handle a gun, much less shoot one. She always claimed she couldn't kill another living thing ..." Carli's voice trailed off. Couldn't kill an animal to protect herself or her children, yet she broke that rule when she swapped the darkroom chemicals.

"I know," were Ethan's quiet words from where he remained on the rock by the fire, his eyes on the flames as he laid another piece of timber across the wood rapidly turning to coals.

When she didn't question him, he looked up and found her expression quizzical. The fire had warmed the earthen room. The hills and valleys of her body highlighted by the flames battled for his cognitive attention. He was here alone, finally, with Carli. The chance of an intrusion was almost nil. Though he hadn't checked his cell reception, there probably wasn't any in their underground bunker, and no one was around to interrupt anything that he had in mind concerning Carli and the soft curves of her figure.

"Whoever fired the shot that killed Bear Tanner knew his way around a rifle, and the Preserve," he stated, the case temporarily winning the fight.

"'His'?"

"Ray Foster."

Her look of disbelief transformed to one of humor, almost. "You're kidding! Ray and Dad were the best of friends. He's been at the Preserve as long as I have. What reason would he have for killing Dad? Not that he did."

"He wanted out."

"Out of what? Wyoming?"

"Yes, and any business arrangement the two of them had."

"They didn't. When Dad first purchased the property, he and Ray were partners. Some years after that, Dad bought him out. I remember an argument where Ray stated that he could quit if he wanted to since he no longer owned part of the Preserve. Dad said ..." she grew quiet as the words came to her as easily as if they were spoken recently. "'So, you plan to quit, like all the other times? It takes a man to stay here and carve out a life,'" she swallowed, realized the torment Ray must have felt, and wondered how many other conversations, or disagreements, she hadn't witnessed that had ended the same way, with her father questioning the manhood or values of who she had always believed to be his long-time friend. Why didn't Ray just leave? If he was bothered by the words, why not end the friendship?

"If discussions such as that one occurred often over the course of their time on the Preserve, I can understand being angry enough to kill. But at Ray's age, he must have believed he couldn't just retire." Ethan thought, then shifted his gaze from Carli to the fire. "Unless he was coerced into shooting Bear. For money. Or because he was blackmailed."

"I can find out how much Ray has been paid over the years. I wouldn't think there would be many expenses, so he must have saved most of it."

"Was he ever married? Had kids that he paid child support for?"

"No. No wife. No kids. That I know of."

"Could it be possible," he asked her, watching for her reaction, "that Darla and Ray are in this together?"

Carli's face was blank, then thoughtful. "If Ray kept his discontent hidden for so many years, then Darla approached him with this plan ... I could see how that would happen. Ray has always been friendly with Darla. I wonder if any of the marks Dad made in his diary would coincide with her visits."

"Do you think they were having an affair?"

She shrugged and took her seat again by the fire. "I suppose it's possible."

"That kind of relationship would give each of them more leverage on the other."

With her eyes tracing the contours of his face, she agreed. "Yes, intimacy tends to open doors, offer opportunities."

"But one must decide if the excitement, the desire to know, to have, is worth the risk."

In the moments that stretched out after Ethan's words, the wind howled outside their shelter. The only light came from their small fire.

"It appears the storm won't blow over quickly, so we'll be here for a while," he commented, watching the flakes of snow that descended from the crevice, then disintegrated in the heat above the flames.

"Shaun will figure out where we are. He knows about this mine."

"Probably won't come until after the storm."

"Probably," she agreed.

"So we're here for the duration."

"Seems so."

"I can think of worse places, and less friendly company," he said, and grinned enough to deepen his dimples.

She smiled invitingly. Between the warmth of the fire and the heat in Ethan's gaze, she became uncomfortable and slipped off her flannel jacket, laying it on top of her pack. Pushing her fingers through her hair, the curls were swept back from her face, drawing Ethan's eyes, which seemed to never miss a movement, or an expression.

He shifted from his rock to the ground next to hers. Without asking, he leaned forward, stretched out one hand to caress the side of her cheek, and continued towards her until there was nothing between them. As seemed to be his habit, at least where Carli was concerned, the first moment their lips touched, he inhaled, as if breathing for the first time in his life. The softening in his chest occurred simultaneously with the hardening below his belt. He ignored the first and fed the second by immersing himself in the taste and scent of the willing woman with whom he seemed so fascinated. Following Carli's example, he shrugged out of his coat and placed it on the ground somewhere behind him. He shifted her jacket to join his and, in a slightly clumsy move, leaned back and braced himself with one hand, while the other, shifting from her cheek to behind her neck, urged her to follow him.

Giggling, they landed noisily on the coat-covered ground, Ethan on the bottom and Carli sprawled across his torso, her legs already entangled with his. The moment of humor passed, and he bracketed her face, which hovered above his, with his wide palms. The atmosphere became charged with desire and excitement. This time it was Carli that initiated the kiss.

Lips and tongues tasted and felt, nibbled and experienced. Sometimes drawing sighs, or moans. She would not to be denied this opportunity to see and feel Ethan, and to take her time enjoying every bit of him. To that end, while she balanced herself on one arm, the other hand worked his shirt from his jeans, and with a little help from the wearer, whisked it over his head. Her hand roamed his chest and ribcage, all toned and hardened muscle from time in a gym, as being fit was probably a helpful, if not a required, part of his job.

Leaving trails of fire on his skin with her fingers, he was jolted back to reality when her hand bumped into his gun, still in the holster at his hip. Breaking the kiss, his breath coming fast, he removed the gun and set it aside, but still within easy reach.

"I don't have any protection with me," he confessed, not wanting to employ the unreliable method of birth control of pulling out.

"Are you clean?" she countered.

A moment of confusion showed, then he turned up one corner of his mouth, and nodded.

"I'm on the pill."

"Is there someone I should know about?" he asked, his smile fading, his brow raising.

She shook her head. "A 'sometimes' friend. The last time I was in New York he was rather creative in his excuses to not see me. Guess I'm just in the habit of popping them through the foil."

Momentarily doubting that Carli did much of anything out of habit, he was grateful that she had this one.

Lowering her mouth once again to taste his lips, she didn't stay there. The skin of his chest and abdomen, dusted with dark hair, was begging for her attention. Nibbling and kissing her way down his neck, across his chest, and pausing to swirl her tongue around each nipple, she took his ragged breathing to mean that he was enjoying her attentions. By the time she placed an open-mouthed kiss on his navel, she had his belt, button, and zipper undone.

Knowing there was much more that he wanted to do with her, he sat up and pulled her up with him.

"Save that for later," he told her, his voice rough with wanting.

Not waiting for her acquiescence, he rolled her under him, vaguely aware that she was mostly on their clothes that littered the ground. Her shirt was removed with their combined determination. Taking a moment to enjoy the lace bra that barely obscured her dark nipple, which seemed to pucker at his stare, he traced the edge with the tip of his tongue, then pulled her into his mouth. Arching up, she offered more of herself, and gave him access to the back closure, which was quickly undone. The straps briefly decorated her shoulders before he removed the garment. Lavishing attention first on one breast and then the other, a portion of his concentration was on relieving Carli of her jeans. In their increased frenzy to get each other naked, boots were kicked off and denim was removed. He found himself on his knees facing Carli, who was also on her knees. The erratic flames of the fire, affected by the wind that funneled through the fissure in the ceiling, highlighted the curves and planes of her body. There was never a more erotic sight than what he was experiencing. He had been with his share of women, all of them beautiful in their way, but none of them were Carli. The logical portion of his brain, the one that was concerned with protecting her from an unwanted pregnancy, told him that she would never go away. From his memory? He realized that wouldn't be so bad.

She reached for him, unable to keep still, to refrain from what she wanted more in that moment than her next breath. Ethan was warm, and he wanted her, as evidenced by that part of him that strained toward her. As she leaned closer, he enveloped her in his arms, his mouth tasting and touching her from neck to shoulder.

By some unspoken agreement, she straddled his waist as he eased back onto his seat, his legs crossed in front of him. It didn't escape his notice that her delectable, heart-shaped ass, fit nicely on his thighs. After that thought, there wasn't much he cataloged beyond the cloud of sensations that were Carli. The layers of information his awareness categorized were many and varied. Her skin, her words, mostly sounds of pleasure punctuated with his name on her exhale, the scent of their eventual union, infused his mind. Hands traced the creases of her thighs to the hot center of her physical being, and he smiled at her readiness. That smile was met with a caress of her tongue as she kissed him, taking his groan as she shifted her hips and slid over him.

In this position, there was no pushing or easing, but rather a settling. He barely had the time to catch his breath before Carli began to move. He allowed her, for now, to set the pace. Guiding her along his length, he was touched by her sweetness, his desire for her rising to a new level at her take-charge attitude. She knew what she wanted, what she liked, and he was humbled and grateful that it was him.

The fire that Ethan started inside of her days ago had grown to a raging inferno. His length and width were not a disappointment, nor was his single-pointed focus on her and her pleasure. She recognized his willingness to have her take the lead, and she reveled in it, knowing, and anticipating, the time when he would set his control aside. Enjoying the ache, she felt his caresses, his steadiness, his safety. Stoking the fire, she quickened the pace. The lightning flashed inside her veins as each nerve crackled with its own life.

One hand on the middle of her back, the other moved to where their bodies were joined. He was too full of her, of her desire, her beauty, her abandonment of pretenses and facades ... did she ever possess them? His thumb touched her core. Carli flew apart, leaning back into the strength of his arm, her mind, body, and soul reduced to ash. Unaware that she had called his name, she heard him mumble hers, then gather her close.

Rough breaths, sweat-slicked bodies, incoherent thoughts. The logs crackled, wind swirled through the crevice, and hearts were irrevocably tied. Eyes still closed, she tentatively wet her lips with the tip of her tongue, a simple movement that had him hardening inside of her. He shifted slightly, and a ghost of a smile graced her lips.

A bold, glaring thought intruded. Can you live without hearing her call your name at the precise moment she melts? *Yes,* he answered, though less fiercely than he intended. He would burn her out of his system, return to Baltimore, and continue with his life. With that thought echoing in his mind, kissed her.

She tasted the desperation and wondered at it. He maneuvered her to her back and renewed his attention on her body with a sense of urgency she allowed him. Eyes blinking up at the dirt ceiling overhead, she gathered the pieces of her heart and soul, her body and mind, and pushed them back together. They wouldn't fit. She would never be the same. Acceptance flooded her. The touch of sorrow at the loss of ... what, she didn't know, was all shoved aside as she gave herself over to the sensations Ethan created.

CHAPTER 38

"What do you mean he's not available? I need to speak with Wilson, now!" Worthington raised his voice, then rubbed his forehead with the fingers of the hand that weren't white-knuckling the phone.

"I'm sorry, Sir. Mr. Wilson is unable to be reached at this time. However, I will give him your message the moment he is available."

The too-pleasant voice of Wilson Construction's secretary grated on his nerves. If he couldn't postpone the groundbreaking on property he didn't yet own, it would be a scandal. At this point in his campaign, when the press was already digging around, it could ruin his chances for a seat in the Senate. He should have been more watchful since he couldn't trust the scheming bitch. The next time he saw Darla Tanner, his hands would be around her throat.

"Do that," he spoke harshly into the phone, then hung up.

Sitting heavily in his office chair, he looked again at the computer screen. Regardless of how successful the development would be in Wyoming, assuming they were able to take control of the Preserve, there was also Colorado. Though he had never personally met Bear Tanner, the man had impeccable taste in real estate. It was unfortunate that the land he sought was owned by Tanner rather than someone who needed to unload the acreage due to the struggling economy. He would just have to find a way to encourage whoever inherited the property, now that Bear was dead, to put it on the market. Accustomed to getting what he wanted, when he wanted it, the land in Wyoming and Colorado couldn't be an exception. His campaign funds depended on vacation sales.

«« — »»

He didn't know why he couldn't sleep. Maybe it was the safety of the lodge and his bed. Tim snorted. Used to sleeping, if one could call it that, on the ground, a cot, a straw mat, or, on the increasingly rare occurrence, in his own apartment in The Village, even the busy streets, the seemingly constant barrage of noise from clubs and taxis was more soothing than the silence of the wilderness. Maybe the precious hours of rest he was able to steal on other nights was enough, and now that he had the opportunity to get seven or eight straight hours, his body didn't know what to do. Carli had tried to convince him that there was sound here. The wind through the trees, the chirping of birds, chattering squirrels, an elk's call during mating season could all be heard, she said. Well, perhaps that was true, if one was actually interested in all the peaceful, nature sounds. For as long as he had worked with Carli and all the places they had been, he blamed it on his upbringing in the city. Sure, he knew animals, respected their territory and gave a wide berth to those which could cause him harm, like the cobra that curled up beside him during their first trip to India, but if he had his way, he would stay in metropolitan areas.

He paused on his early morning hike and took a drink from his canteen. No one was awake when he quietly left the lodge. He was restless, and after his one-sided argument on the sounds of the wilderness, he recognized the real reason for his wandering mind. Carli.

Squinting up at the branches of a nearby tree, he looked for the bird that called into the brisk morning air. From further up the trail, the song was answered. The sun, which had already risen above the horizon, was now showing itself over the eastern edge of Pine Canyon. Beautiful, he knew is what Carli would say if she were here with him. Her camera would be out and she would try to trick nature by taking black and white pictures of the Kodachrome surroundings. When two people were together twenty-four/seven they got to know each other's habits more intimately than just friends, and often in more detail than lovers.

He knew she loved her life. Traveling, witnessing the world and all its wonders, the connections she made with others, and the way in which she used her gift to bring it all back and share it with the subscribers of the *Views,* had been her dream. But that had changed. She admitted she had plans, and it wouldn't completely surprise him if she decided to stay here. And that was what interrupted his sleep. Without Carli and their life on the road, where would he be? The increase in the wind had him glancing up at the sky.

Clouds. Dark, grey clouds. Deciding it matched his mood, he changed direction on the trail and headed back toward the lodge. He would have to talk with Carli. If she planned on resigning, he would need to speak with Scott about a reassignment. Traveling as much as he did with the person who knew him the best, understood when he needed space, could always tease him out of a mood, had him believing he couldn't have that with any other colleague. The worst part would be the months and trips of trial and error to confirm what was already clear in his mind. He couldn't continue to journey internationally, doing the same kind of assignments with another photojournalist. Scott wouldn't be happy, but then he rarely ever was, unless Carli earned him an award.

He would need to have a plan, some suggestion to give Scott, to ease the news that the *Views* would be losing two of its international journalists. *Funny,* Tim thought, as he recognized that the idea didn't bother him as much as he believed it would.

As the roof of the two-story lodge could be seen between the branches of the trees, which began to sway greatly with the increase in the wind, the other reason for his lack of rest, albeit of lesser importance than his career, settled in his consciousness. Though he'd had a few relationships, there was something about

Charlie. It went beyond his communication skills, his sense of humor and adventure. The flight attendant's dark, attractive features were the extra piece that made the whole package something that not only caught Tim's hard-to-please attention, but offered the promise of something more.

The flakes, in increasing amounts, followed him the last half-mile to the lodge. With the decision made to contact Charlie again, and an idea he hoped Scott would go for, he entered an empty lobby. Snow had been stomped from his boots on the veranda, and his now-wet coat had been removed. Just inside the door of the lodge, he hung up the jacket, then looked over his shoulder. A smile formed on his lips as he moved to where a fire blazed in the hearth.

Stretching his hands out to warm them, he heard Zach answering a question. He turned around to heat his back and nodded a greeting at Zach, who raised his hand in acknowledgement. After a few more minutes on the phone, with what sounded like a prospective client, Zach replaced the receiver.

"Have you seen the snow outside? Do you often get storms like this in April?"

Zach looked up from making notes in the computer log. "When a cold front comes down from Canada and wet air pushes east from Oregon, we can get late spring snows. The weather guys are predicting only a few inches, if you care to believe them."

"Glad I came back when I did." Tim remembered the company vehicles in the parking area, but looked around and saw that only the two of them were there. "Where is everyone?"

"How far up the trail did you go, and when did you leave?"

"A couple miles. About 5 o'clock."

"You missed it all this morning. Someone switched the chemicals in Carli's darkroom and we had to call Stan. Ethan busted down the door to get her out. Shaun took the evidence to Cheyenne Forensics and Sam to Laramie. She's flying back to Colorado."

"Wait. What?" Tim moved away from the fire, his confusion and concern showing clearly on his face. "Where's Carli? Is she alright?"

"She's fine. Her and Ethan hiked up to Miner's Paradise. With this storm, they'll either be back soon, or much later, if they can find shelter."

Tim closed his eyes briefly and knew that if Carli was seriously injured, Zach would be more worried. Exhaling, he opened his eyes. "Tell me what I missed, and don't leave anything out."

Zach glanced at the clock and judged Shaun would return within a couple of hours. If the snow didn't let up, he would make his concerns known to the sheriff. He knew there were mines, hence the name of the ridge, but he didn't know if any of them could offer shelter, or if Carli and Ethan were exposed to the elements. Either way, he supposed they would be alright. Carli grew up here, and Ethan surely would follow her lead.

Leaning back in the office chair and looking up at Tim, he recounted the events of the morning. About halfway through, Ray appeared, dressed for the weather.

"I'm going out to check on the south gate and the highway. Sudden storms like this can panic tourists," he informed Zach and Tim, then left the lodge.

Zach again glanced at the clock, then continued with his story.

«« — »»

Darla waited for everyone to leave, then pushed open the door to the kitchen. Ray had just finished clearing the counters from breakfast. She noticed the slight shaking to her hands and tugged on the hem of her blouse, straightened the buttons, then the collar. Ray turned, but didn't seem surprised to find her there.

Tossing the dishtowel on the island in front of him, he kept his gaze on Darla. "Was it you?" he asked, his voice a mere whisper.

Darla's nervous hand came to her earring, then to fix her already perfectly styled hair. "We haven't come this far only to lose everything because Bear refused to give me what is mine."

"How many more?"

"As many as it takes. There's more than just your retirement that depends on this."

"I don't give a damn about the councilman's career."

"But you'll care on which side of the prison bars your remaining years are spent."

Ray's eyes widened slightly at her threat. "I agreed to the first, not the second."

"You agreed, and that's all that matters. I tried to fix what Bear wrote in his will, but my plan was interrupted. That means you need to finish this."

"How? Everyone is suspicious of everyone else. And I'm not even sure—" he paused, looked around as if someone might be listening, then lowered his voice, "where to find them."

"You know this Preserve as well as she does. Track her. End it." Darla's tone was intense, challenging.

"And if I don't?"

"You won't have to be concerned with making your flight to Florida." Not wanting to continue to threaten a man who should just do what he agreed to do, she left the kitchen, then the lodge.

It wouldn't be in her favor to contact Worthington just yet. She would wait until the body was discovered. Any more of his belittling, arrogant comments, and she would find a way to finish *him*. The bank would give her the cash that Worthington had promised. She didn't need him as much as he needed her. A man of his appetites wanted, desired, someone of her particular talents. She was able to do for him what few others could, in and out of the bedroom. So she would wait until Ray confirmed he found the ungrateful bitch who inherited what belonged to her. Then it would be her turn to gloat, to give the go-ahead to move forward with the project.

With that settled, the Cadillac drove smoothly through the falling snow and light accumulation on Highway 130 to Laramie.

Perhaps lunch at the steakhouse and a manicure at the spa would be the best way to wait out the storm.

«« — »»

By the time he left the police station, the snow was falling in earnest. If there was already an inch coating his vehicle, how much had descended upon the Preserve? And more importantly, had Carli and Ethan returned to the lodge? He waited until he was inside the SUV and on the Interstate back to Laramie before he pulled out his cell phone. Zach answered on the second ring.

"How much snow do you have there?"

Zach glanced out the window. "About two inches, and it's still coming down. The wind has slowed a little."

"Where are Carli and Ethan?"

"Still in the canyon, I guess. I haven't seen them." At Shaun's expression of distress, Zach wondered if he should have been more concerned. "Carli knows all the places to find shelter, if there are any. She grew up here, like you. I hadn't thought to be worried about her. I mean, it's not like it's a December blizzard."

"No, but if conditions are right, people can still die."

Zach considered the absurdity of whoever tried to harm Carli with the chemical switch actually orchestrating a snowstorm to do her in.

"Is there someplace on the ridge that she would know about to get out of the storm?" Zach asked.

Shaun thought, then nodded, even though Zach couldn't see the gesture. "Yes. I'm on my way. I'll stop at the lodge, see if they've returned. If not, the road that parallels the east fence line leads to a seldom-used trailhead. The climb is steep, but it's the fastest way to Miner's Paradise."

"You're not the only one who's concerned. Tim came back from his own hike. He had missed all the excitement this morning, so I told him what happened. Said he was going to do some work in his room, but he's come downstairs twice to see if Carli has made it back."

391

"Who else is there? Ray?"

"No. Ray left about an hour and a half ago. He said that sudden storms cause tourists to drive poorly, so he went to check the south gate and the highway."

"Did Darla come back?"

"No."

"I'll be there in about an hour." Shaun closed his phone and set it on the seat next to him.

So, Darla was not at the lodge, and neither was Ray. Could he trust Ray to be at the south gate or the highway that bordered the Preserve? An uncomfortable feeling settled in his belly. Was it because there was a possibility that Ray had killed Bear, or that he was feeling guilty because of the misplaced mistrust? First he had to ensure that Carli and Ethan returned safely to the lodge, then he would have a serious talk with Ray. Maybe Ethan should be there. His own history with Ray may cloud his questions and the interpretations of Ray's answers.

He placed one more phone call to the Cheyenne police officer that he knew was on duty and would do the checking for him. Had he thought about it before leaving town, he would have done it himself. It was another example of his slipping skills as a law enforcement officer. He couldn't seem to think clearly since his father was brought down from Wolf's Ridge, ashen-faced from blood loss, a hole in his chest.

"Hey, Ben. Shaun. I was wondering if you could do a check for me."

A few minutes later, he closed his phone. The landmarks out his window told him he had about twenty minutes before reaching Centennial. He would use the time to get his questions in order for Ray, and Darla, and wait for Ben to call him back with information. With determination, he set aside any delving into his grief, or his abilities to do his job, until he had some answers.

If Carli and Ethan were on the crest of the canyon, she would find the mine they visited more times than their father knew about, and wait out the storm. He could find them before anyone else. That 'anyone' being whoever attempted to kill Carli that morning. The two words, 'kill Carli', had the gripping in his gut intensifying. Who? Why? When? Someone who had a lot to gain. The only time the lodge was empty, was during the funeral. Everyone had left the Rockin' R at different times and in different vehicles. But it was only one that he needed to find.

Slowing down as he drove through Centennial, his eyes scoured the roadside for a company truck. There was no one on the highway east of town. Vince's vehicle was parked in front of the office, which meant Denny was out on patrol. He sped up once the 2nd Street shops gave way to trees, and again searched for Ray. Taking a few deep breaths to push the panic away, he hoped to find both the company truck and Carli at the lodge. Driving faster than was safe, he pulled into the driveway.

"Shit," he mumbled, shifting his SUV into PARK. No truck.

Almost colliding with Zach as he came through the front door, his expectant face was met with a shake of Zach's head.

"She's not here. Ray is still gone."

"J.J.?"

"Out at the barn."

"You and J.J. saddle up. Take the short cut up to the canyon's edge at Miner's Paradise. I'm taking the fence line. And Zach," Shaun paused, waiting for the younger man to pull on his coat and gloves, "bring your rifles and a first aid kit."

"You expecting trouble?"

"Seems trouble has been here for a while, and showed its face for this fight last Monday."

Zach nodded. Shaun exited the front door and climbed back into his SUV. Zach went through the kitchen to the back door and picked up to a jog towards the barn.

CHAPTER 39

The cool air of the mine brought Carli back from where she had spent the last ... two hours? She glanced at her watch. The wind had died down outside, but the snow continued to fall. Ethan had added more timber to the fire several times and now lay stretched out on their discarded clothes. Propped up on one elbow, he seemed fascinated with her torso and occupied his ever-busy fingers by tracing the length and width of each rib. When he increased the pressure on a spot close to her armpit, she giggled and squirmed in an attempt to move away. He responded by wrapping his arm around her and pulling her back against his body. She sighed and relaxed, interlacing her fingers through his.

"I finally found a weakness in the tough Tanner exterior."

"Being ticklish is not a weakness. It's a sensitivity."

He placed a kiss on her shoulder. "Seems there are quite a few 'sensitivities' that you have."

"Perhaps you're just particularly talented in finding them."

"It makes me wonder if there are others that I've missed."

She lifted his hand and kissed his palm. "I don't think so. We've been ... exploring for two hours."

"Ah, but it's our first trek into this territory. I don't intend for it to be our last," he told her, gently urging her to her back, and to where her mouth, so close to his, received his attentions.

And just that quickly, she once again wrapped him in her arms, her body responding to his as if they'd had years instead of hours discovering each other's preferences and pleasures. Her eyes remained open and focused on the crack above the flames that danced on the rotted timbers. Briefly, the snow that fell through the fissure was interrupted, the light that filtered in from outside darkened, as if a cloud passed over the sun. Trying to sort out the significance of that observation while Ethan used his mouth and hands to escalate her excitement, became difficult. In less than a minute, there was a rumbling that seemed to originate at the opening. Musty air and dust began to fill the space around them.

Without Carli saying a word, he rolled to his side, weapon in hand, pointed in the direction of the sound. When nothing charged from the darkness, he pulled on his jeans, grabbed the flashlight, and made his way toward the entrance.

She scrambled to find her own clothing. Nothing would be more embarrassing than someone finding the mine with her naked inside. Taking the time to put on her underwear and boots, when Ethan reappeared a few minutes later she was fully dressed and finger combing her hair.

"What is it?" she asked, seeing his concerned face.

"A cave-in."

"What? Even though this mine has been here for years, these braces are still good." To prove her point, she stepped to the nearest one and pounded on it. It didn't sound as solid as she thought it was. "Are you sure you looked in the right place?"

"Closed-in spaces are not my favorite, so I pay particular attention to them."

"Let me see. Maybe it wasn't a cave-in." She moved toward him, and he handed her the flashlight.

They crouched down as they entered the tunnel that led from the underground chamber to the narrow entrance. She shined the flashlight through the dust that continued to hang in the air. Beyond it was a solid wall of dirt and rock. Changing the angle of the flash, she inspected the beams of the tunnel. They were intact. Tentatively, she stepped closer to what should have been a portal to the outside and pushed on a rock. It didn't move. Using a little more force only earned her a little shower of dirt and pebbles as the sediment above the rock trickled down on her.

He grabbed her hand and pulled her back into the room where the fire had subsided to a few flames on the spent wood. While he grabbed the rest of his clothes, including his boots, Carli stood and looked through the crevice overhead. She was quiet, introspective. That, along with everything else about her, it seemed, caught his attention and he inquired as to her thoughts.

"Just before ... that," she gestured toward the entrance and what she had yet to be convinced was a cave-in, "I saw a shadow pass over the crack in the ceiling. The air stilled and the snow didn't fall."

He moved closer to her and followed her gaze. A few minutes passed as they both watched, waiting for the phenomenon to repeat itself. With the fire burning now only as embers, and the entrance closed off, the air began to settle, cool. He pushed away the fact that he was, temporarily, trapped inside the earth, and instead began voicing other alternatives to their predicament.

"Are you superstitious?" he asked her.

"Not particularly."

"Then what you saw was not the proverbial 'Shadow of Death' coming to claim two more victims."

"Then what was it?"

"'Who', would be a more appropriate question."

Her gaze met his. "Darla would never come out here. She wouldn't know the trail, and it's snowing."

"Who else is familiar with Miner's Paradise?"

"Everyone who works at the lodge."

"And who would come out in a snowstorm to take care of a 'problem'?"

"All of them. We've all gone—"

"That's not what I mean. You, Carli, are the 'problem'. Who knew we were coming here?"

"Everyone," she said again, exasperation and frustration at his comments and questions coloring her tone of voice.

"And who knows the location of this mine?" he continued to press.

She paced away the three steps that the space allowed, then turned to face him. Between them, a whiff of smoke climbed through the dimly lit space and out the crevice.

"No one besides Shaun, Sam, and Dad. Sam is on her way to Colorado, Dad is gone, and if Shaun came out here, it would be to get us back to the lodge."

"That leaves Ray, J.J., and Zach. I assume they can all track?"

"Of course."

"And if they got close enough, they would smell, and see, the smoke."

The naïve part of her brain wanted to ask why they hadn't come to bring them back to the lodge, but her rational mind, the one she relied on to keep her safe, to get her where she needed to go, had her asking the question at which Ethan hedged.

"But it isn't 'they'. You've already eliminated Zach and J.J. from your suspect list. Based on our earlier conversation, that leaves Ray. Has he followed us in order to do what Darla failed at? Make the cave-in look natural?"

When he was quiet, then gave a slight nod, her expletive matched the one voiced only in his mind.

"That son of a bitch! After all these years, he thinks to get rid of me so easily? There has to be a really, really good reason that he's allowed Darla to dictate what he does."

She was angry, and that was good. It would keep her from second-guessing their chances of surviving the storm and the cave-in. And it didn't hurt that he enjoyed seeing that spark in her eye when he knew her mind churned, fitting and discarding puzzle pieces.

"Shaun knows where we're headed. If we're not back when he gets to the lodge, he'll come looking," he said.

"How do you know?" she asked.

"Because he's a good lawman."

The note of respect was not lost on her. The two of them had battled boundaries, but then seemed to work it out. She wondered if Shaun would have the same feelings towards Ethan, who seemed to have all but a confession from those he suspected.

"We might be able to help him a little. You up for some digging?" she asked.

The thought of being in the cramped space of the tunnel was not his first choice. But being buried alive, should Shaun be detained, was even less appealing. He answered her by taking the flashlight, and a steadying breath, then leading the way through the tunnel to the pile of debris that locked them inside the mine.

«« —»»

He wiped his brow. Why was he sweating in the snow? Because of Darla and the damn climb to Miner's Paradise. He should have told her no, that her threats were no good, but she knew he would be lying, even if he escaped to Florida, or another state where there was sunshine instead of this unbelievable snow and near-constant wind. If it was just the greedy ex-Mrs. Tanner, he would have a chance at a clean break. But he would also have to contend with the California Councilman. With money came resources, and the ones that could find him no matter where he tried to hide.

So he came out in this late spring storm, tracked Carli and the guest, Ethan Brooks, who looked like more than their usual client, and did what Darla failed to do. A cave-in would be characteristic of an abandoned mine. There were no fingerprints to leave behind as he pried the rocks loose with his boot, sending dirt and stones to effectively cover the entrance. There wouldn't be enough wood to keep their fire burning. He would stall Shaun's rescue efforts as long as he could, giving the air a chance to clear the smoke. It's not that he disliked Carli, she was just an obstacle to be removed.

He glanced at his tracks, relieved that they were quickly being covered by the still-falling snow. Turning, he retraced his steps and made his way back down the trail. Muffled by the snow, where sounds travel yet their origin can be difficult to determine, came the high-pitched whine of an engine in low gear that caused him to pause.

Changing direction, he left the seldom-used trail, an offshoot of the one he had hiked to follow Carli, and continued towards the top of the ridge. The wind swirled up here, where the trees were thinner and the flakes caught the air currents from both inside and outside the canyon. Crouching beside a tree, he looked past the puffs of his exhales to the road that ran the length of the fence line.

A gust cleared the snow in the air at the same time the headlights of the black sheriff's vehicle rounded a switchback. Swallowing, the realization that his attempt to complete the job had taken longer than it should, would now force him to use other means to delay any rescue attempt. Shaun, who knew Miner's Paradise as well as Carli, would know of the mine she would seek as protection from the elements. He couldn't return to the lodge, or Darla, knowing that Carli would be rescued. Everyone was already hyper-vigilant with the shooting of Bear and the fire. With Darla's stunt in the darkroom, they would never again get Carli alone.

He looked around for a place to get a clear shot. To shoot Shaun directly was not what he wanted. It, too, needed to be an accident. If Shaun didn't survive, he might have a better chance to leave Wyoming undetected. A mistake was not sticking close to Shaun, keeping abreast of the connections he made. If all were eliminated from Shaun's suspect list, except him, then the sheriff would know who was responsible for Bear's death. After the next turn, the four-wheel drive road flattened, with a sheer drop off into the valley where the lodge resided on the far end.

Bringing the rifle to his shoulder, he peered through the scope and listened to the vehicle's motor. Another twenty feet and the driver's side front tire lifted up over a rock. A squeeze of his index finger. The report echoed, but not as loudly as if it hadn't been snowing. The black vehicle jerked to the left. A conveniently placed log tipped the SUV to the right. Just when it looked as if it would land wheels down, he fired another shot. The second window on the driver's side shattered and had the desired effect. The wheel was pulled to the right as Shaun ducked, sending the vehicle rolling over the side.

He scrambled down off the ridge and made his way back to the alternate trailhead and the company truck.

«« — »»

Shaun should have expected it. Should have known that the unhappy employee would make his way to Miner's Paradise, tracking Carli. He thought to arrive in time and save his sister and Ethan. Now, he himself would have to be rescued. Both employees riding to the ridge knew the trail he would use to arrive at the rendezvous point, and would make the call to Vince should he not meet them. Assuming he survived the roll ... that thought jarred out of his head as the SUV came to rest on its side, braced against two trees.

The first thing he noticed was the odd angle of the trees through the fractured windshield. Then there was the intense pain in his left shoulder. Had he been shot? Looking for blood, the only thing that seemed to be leaking was his left temple. He must have hit the doorframe, or perhaps it was from the broken glass. When he tried to move his arm, he cursed and left it alone.

The snow was falling from left to right, some of it drifting through the open space that used to contain glass. That meant the vehicle was on its right side. The airbag had deployed and now hung limply from the center of the steering wheel. It took some effort, with the use of only one arm, to unhook the seatbelt and pull himself through the missing driver's side window. He was slightly more graceful in his slide past the flat front tire to the uphill side of the slope that led to the valley below. Searching the top of the ridge and not finding any movement, he hoped the bastard was gone. Injured, out in the open, it would take only one shot to eliminate another Tanner. Needing to make the climb back to the road, he decided to take his chances that the shooter would assume he either died or had been incapacitated in the tumble down into the valley. Once on the ridge, if he could get a cell signal, he would call the office. Then he would find Carli and Ethan.

«« — »»

Zach had given J.J. as much information as he knew, which wasn't more than 'bring the horses, a rifle, and a first aid kit'. They were out of the barn, each of them riding one horse and leading another, trotting to the trailhead and a quarter-mile up the easy slope. Slowing as they reached the first switchback, J.J. cursed and pulled Buck to a stop. The echo of the shot bounced off the canyon walls. Turning to look over his shoulder through the swirling snow, he could see Zach's face mirrored his own. At the sound of the second shot, the horses were urged up the trail. J.J. took Lady's lead in his left hand, his right drawing the rifle from the scabbard that was attached to his saddle. Behind him, Zach did the same.

They each carried a cell phone, which wouldn't get a signal until they were at the top, and maybe not even then, as weather sometimes interfered with the bounce to the towers. Maybe they would get information from Shaun informing them that Carli and Ethan were safe, or perhaps what they found would instigate a call to Stan.

"Any idea where Carli and Ethan are?" J.J. called over his shoulder, the horses' steps muffled by the snow that collected on the ground.

"No. There's no cabins up here. Unless Carli knows about a place that gave Miner's Paradise its name."

"I wouldn't think any mines would be stable. They haven't dug anything out of this area in years."

"Desperate times," Zach commented, leaving the second half of the saying unsaid.

They continued up the side of the canyon, J.J. veering off the trail. "Short cut," he called out.

Zach had never taken this route, but he followed anyway. The horses scrambled up the steep slope, forcing the riders to lean forward over the necks of their mounts. He couldn't make out any trail that they may be following. About to voice his opinion of the guide's 'shortcut', J.J. pointed to a painted horseshoe nailed into a tree marking the hiking and riding trail of Miner's Paradise.

"Where do we search?" Zach asked as the horses were given the chance to catch their wind.

J.J. looked around. There was no sign of anyone with a gun, and the steadily falling snow had covered whatever trail Carli and Ethan may have left. He did the next thing on the list taught by search and rescue teams.

"Carli!" he yelled into the trees.

«« —»»

At the sound of the first gunshot, Ethan paused in his work at moving the rocks to the side and back of the tunnel. There was no way to tell from which direction the shot originated, nor if it was a rifle or handgun. He wondered if he misheard, if perhaps the sound was some phenomenon in the Wyoming wilderness with which he was unfamiliar. Then he heard the second shot. They were safe where they were, for the time being. He began to guess what they would face when, not if, they dug themselves out of the mine.

"There's no hunting parties out today—" Carli began, then realized her mistake. "If he tried to seal us in, then who is he shooting at? A bullet wound isn't exactly the way to mask a murder as an accident."

"It could be anything. Maybe a cat or a bear crossed his path." He didn't know, but talking offered a distraction from the cold darkness that surrounded him.

"Both, unless injured or sick, would leave a person alone. You don't think he would shoot at whoever thought to come rescue us, do you?" Her digging stalled, and she looked at Ethan over her shoulder.

"It could be the only thing he knows to do to protect himself. If he's desperate, that's good and bad."

"What do you mean?"

"Bad that he'll be reckless and perhaps unpredictable, but good because impetuous behavior often leads to mistakes, and arrests."

She shifted her gaze back to the blocked entrance as if the maze of soil, gravel, and rocks would offer her the answers.

He gestured to the rock in front of her, which was large enough that both of them would have to work at moving it. Shifting to crouch next to her, he placed his hands around the small boulder. She did the same, and they both pulled. It moved slightly, causing dirt to trickle down the sides.

"If we dislodge this, it may cause the rest of it to come tumbling down," she suggested. Looking at the precarious pile of rubble that obstructed the opening, she pointed to the top and side of the rock they tried to move. "If we get rid of—" she began, then pushed on the area she indicated.

"No!" He started to reach in the same direction, but only to pull her hands away.

He wasn't quick enough. When Carli pushed, the earth above them and between the timbers, came crashing down. Dirt, rocks of all sizes, and decayed wood, buried years earlier, filled the already constricted tunnel. When the avalanche stopped, he sat up. Having thrown himself between Carli and the falling debris, he took the brunt of the weight that had collapsed on top of them.

"Are you alright?" Ethan asked.

"I think so," she answered, and tried to remove herself from under the pile. When she winced, his face shifted from concern to a scowl. "My ankle. I think something really big hit it."

He clawed through the dirt and rolled the boulder off of her lower leg. His hands shook, and he tried to convince himself it was over concern for Carli rather than being underground in a tight space. When he lifted her pant leg, blood oozed from a cut across her shin bone, just above her boot, and when he gently touched the surrounding area, her curse and intake of breath let him know it was more than a scrape. Digging her free, they found she was otherwise uninjured.

"Sorry. That," she gestured to the pile as she gently moved her leg, "was not my intention."

He peered through the dust, swirled by the Wyoming wind. One corner of Ethan's mouth tipped up. "No, but it helped."

The collapse had formed a hole, two-feet in diameter, from the mine shaft to the outside. As they began to once again scoop stones and dirt away from the new exit, they heard something more promising than gunshots.

"Carli!" Her name, laced with worry, floated through the fissure that she had created.

She smiled at Ethan, then yelled back, "Down here!"

J.J. dismounted, handed the reins of both horses to Zach, then followed the voices. Kneeling a short distance away, afraid to cause more of a cave-in, he peered into the hole. He returned a wide smile as both Carli and Ethan gazed back at him.

CHAPTER 40

Storm clouds snuffed out any remaining light from the setting sun, casting premature nightfall over the Preserve. A fitting end to a dismal day. J.J. and Zach saddled horses and rode for Miner's Paradise. Shaun took the four-wheel drive trail along the east fence line. He expressed concern as to Ray's whereabouts in the storm before he left to find Carli and Ethan. Remaining at the lodge to receive phone calls and await everyone's return was Tim's offer to do something constructive. He was reassured by Zach that Carli knew the Preserve better than just about anyone, and that she would be safe from the storm. Crossing his arms, he scowled at the desk phone that hadn't rung since everyone left. No one needed to tell him Carli would be alright. Between her survival skills and the protection of the FBI, he knew she would walk through the front door, whole and healthy. And when she did, he would give her his two cents about going hiking in a snowstorm after someone tried to hurt her.

The darkness that descended outside soon seeped into the lobby of the lodge. He built up the fire, turned on all the lights, including those on the veranda, and stood by the window as he waited for Shaun's SUV or the horses or Carli herself. The snow had stopped, and the wind kicked up only what had collected on the ground. He realized he would be able to detect movement in the area surrounding the lodge, depending from which window he was looking.

Glancing around the empty lobby, he fought off waves of loneliness. Is this how it would be without Carli? He had a plan for his career, and hopefully Scott would agree on the new perspective. Even the thought of returning home to New York didn't ease his discomfort. The vibration in his pocket from his cell phone pulled him from his mood, and when he saw the number, he brightened.

"Charlie. Are you back in town already?"

"Heavens, no. I don't serve on the Leer. I guess I just was feeling a little ..."

"Lonely?"

Charlie sighed. "We were diverted south to Las Vegas. A colliding of weather fronts shut down Denver and Billings. I've got an hour before we can regain our place in line and head for San Francisco."

"Vegas is surely warmer than here. The weather has graced Wyoming with another few inches of snow."

For the next forty-five minutes, with a few interruptions on Charlie's end, the two swapped stories of the worst storms they had been in, and what they did to divert themselves from feeling alone in the world. Charlie ended the call with a promise to reconnect between flights. He volunteered the information that he would be back in Laramie over the weekend, and smiled warmly that Tim accepted the unvoiced invitation to meet again at the hotel. The two-hour flight went smoothly for Charlie, but the next two hours were not as calm for Tim.

When he wasn't fretting about Carli's whereabouts and why no one had returned, he was wondering what he would say to Charlie when they met. He had to return to New York, and Charlie lived on the West Coast. If he wanted to keep his job, he would need to let go of any possibility that he and Charlie could have a relationship. He had tried a long-distance arrangement before, and it ended poorly after months of being miserable. It was fast approaching the time in his life where non-committed relationships were no longer fulfilling. Just as he was about to move away from the window that faced the parking lot, headlights shined through the night as a vehicle approached the lodge.

《《—》》

Carli was sitting at the base of a tree, leaning against the trunk, her left foot propped on a rock and an emergency ice pack from the first aid kit rested on her ankle. Zach was checking the tack on the horses, and J.J. peered at branches and the snow around the mine. Ethan, the most vigilant of the group, had his sketch pad in one hand, and had just crouched next to Carli to give her a bottle of water, when his gaze and his weapon zeroed in on Shaun.

"Looks like I missed the party."

Ethan replaced his weapon and stood. "I think you're right on time."

Stepping around Carli, he met Shaun near the entrance of the mine, or where it used to be. Eyeing the gentle cradle of Shaun's left arm, Ethan asked, "You hurt?"

"Collarbone, I think."

"Did you receive or give the two shots?"

A dry chuckle that lacked humor escaped from Shaun's mouth. "Received. One shot took out my front driver's side tire. Second shot came through the side window. Must have rolled three or four times—"

"My God, Shaun, are you alright?" Carli interrupted, having left her seat to hobble to where the two men talked.

"I'm in better shape than my vehicle."

"Who shot—" she started, then clamped her mouth closed. "If that son of a—"

"Wait. No sense in throwing accusations." Shaun's gaze shifted to Ethan. "You told her?"

Ethan nodded, but remained quiet, as Zach and J.J. joined them.

"Are they still suspects?" Shaun asked. "Because we'll need everyone if we're to keep him from killing again." When Ethan shook his head, he shared with the guides, "This is Agent Brooks, from the FBI. He was sent here by one of Dad's clients, some director from the East Coast. We've been working together to discover who shot Bear, and why." His gaze turned towards the agent.

"Carli and I have a theory," Ethan said.

Disbelief. Confusion. A little fear. The reactions of Zach and J.J. were common. Shaun and Ethan, who had witnessed what humans do to each other, had moved on to heightened protection and locating those that were responsible.

"An affair. Blackmail. Money. All legitimate, if unoriginal, reasons for Ray and Darla to be scheming," Shaun agreed when Ethan and Carli had filled him in on their thoughts.

"The snow covered most of the tracks, but there's a partial under a branch, that also happens to have a few leaves missing," J.J. added, then led Shaun and Ethan to what he had found.

"I told you it wasn't a cave-in," Carli said from the tree that she leaned against.

Ethan looked over his shoulder and offered her a half-smile. "I agree. *Neither* collapse was natural. Both had a little help."

She shrugged and drank from the water bottle.

"No telling where he is now," Shaun said. "But we need to get back to the lodge." He looked at J.J. "I want you to wait for Frank. I called the office and Denny contacted him. The SUV is just over the ridge, maybe a quarter-mile down the trail, and another fifty feet below the four-wheel drive road along the fence line."

J.J. nodded, and with his rifle still in his hand, headed in that direction.

"We'll take the horses back. Denny has alerted Doc Miller, who has agreed to see me. Guess Carli will need to visit, too."

"You aren't in any condition to drive. I'll take you both," Ethan offered.

With that settled, Zach helped Shaun mount Buck, then sat astride Diego. Carli bent her left knee, and Ethan boosted her up onto Lady's back. That left Samson for Ethan.

Stroking Samson's forehead, he spoke quietly, "I don't blame you for spooking at the bear. I was a little scared myself." He smiled as Samson pricked his ears forward and white puffs came from the big horse's nostrils.

Zach led the way, then Shaun, Carli, and Ethan rode drag. There wasn't much conversation, and the going was slow in order to reduce the bumps and strains on ankle and collarbone. He was vigilant for cats and bears as he strained to see past the beam that the flashlight offered. Riding at the front, he was likely to spot eyes, belonging to two- or four-legged creatures, before the rest of them. Reins and flashlight held in one hand, the other kept his rifle aimed at the space down the trail.

Ethan knew Shaun and Carli struggled with the reasons why Ray would do what he did. He also knew that Shaun, like himself, stretched his hearing and his sight into the darkness around them, wondering if Ray would pick them off as they rode past. Samson paused and raised his head, causing Ethan to immediately draw his weapon. The silent wings of an owl floated overhead. Samson relaxed, his rider lowered his gun, and they continued on the path, into the valley.

Leaning forward to stroke the horse's neck he whispered, "Thanks, Big Boy. Keep up the alarm system."

What should have taken less time with the horses, took a little longer. A different trail than the short cut ended with them at the barn, which was dark, but the lodge, which could be seen through the trees, was lit up like a runway.

"I'll take care of the horses. You guys head to the clinic," Zach offered.

Shaun managed to dismount on his own, then watched with interest as Ethan helped Carli to the ground. The care the agent took, the way his hands lingered, the closeness with which he stood told him what the man would probably deny. Ethan cared deeply for Carli, and with the look on her face as she gazed back at him, the feeling was mutual. He refused to allow his mind to travel along thoughts of what might have happened between the two of them in the mine.

With Carli leaning heavily on Ethan, the three of them made their way to the lodge. Denny and Tim were in the lobby, apparently in some kind of deep discussion, when Shaun opened the door.

Tim's eyes searched behind Shaun, and relief had him coming to the door and Carli's side. "Are you alright?"

"My ankle met with a rock. Other than that, I'm fine."

"But we're going to see Doc Miller, just to be sure," Ethan added.

"Did you fall?" Tim pressed, not believing that the normally agile Carli could be so careless.

"No. There was a … cave-in," she answered with a look in Ethan's direction. "We were trapped in a mine and I moved the wrong boulder."

Tim looked from Carli to Ethan.

"Zach and J.J. found us soon after," Ethan finished.

"Frank called, said he picked up your vehicle and J.J. They're taking it to the yard," Denny informed Shaun.

"I'll be over there first thing tomorrow. Probably need to have it towed to Cheyenne Forensics. They'll be able to recover the slugs."

"Did you get shot?" Denny asked.

"Bastard missed me. I'm sure he believed he accomplished his goal."

"Which was …" Denny said, his gaze shifting between Shaun and Carli.

"To keep me from finding Carli, and if he killed me in the process, all the better."

"And the 'bastard' would be?" Denny raised his brows.

"Put a bulletin out for Ray Foster. We need to bring him in for questioning."

Denny nodded, confusion and excitement showing on his face. "Do you need a ride to Doc Miller's?"

"Got one," Shaun answered with a tip of his head toward Ethan.

The deputy left to inform Vince of the events and to speculate about where Ray would be, and how the older man would react if Denny was the one to approach him.

Shaun retrieved the keys for one of the company vehicles, then tossed them to Ethan. When Carli began to protest, that she was fine and didn't need to see Doc Miller, Ethan simply took her by the elbow and led her out the door. Shaun was quiet, and wore a half-smile as her protests fell on deaf ears. Ethan opened the passenger door and handed her up and into the van. Shaun climbed in the back, and when she turned to look at him, to attempt to have him appeal to Ethan on her behalf, she found an amused expression.

"What is so funny?" she demanded.

He watched Ethan walk in front of the van to the driver's side. "Quit complaining. You have a good man in Ethan. Let him, since you never let anyone, take care of you."

With her jaw dropped, she was quiet for the first time in minutes. Ethan slid behind the wheel and started the van. Glancing at her, with a raised brow, he wondered at her silence. Looking at Shaun in the rearview mirror, he guessed he must have missed some sibling communication. Carli stewed and stared out the side window, and Shaun was slightly amused. With arms crossed in front of her, she remained mute for the drive to Doc Miller's, so it was Shaun from the backseat that gave directions. It was past normal business hours when they arrived, but Doc Miller standing outside his office door, just like he had days earlier.

"How's the head?" Doc asked Ethan as he climbed down.

"Fine. But there's an ankle and collarbone that require your attention."

Both Carli and Shaun received x-rays. Carli, to confirm nothing was broken, and Shaun to verify the location of the break. Ethan's stitches were also checked, since he was 'in the office'. With a filled prescription and a sling, an elastic bandage and instructions of 'elevation and ice', the three of them left Doc Miller and headed back to the lodge.

Having a difficult time keeping her eyes open, Carli rested her head against the seat. The past week had been filled with more twists and turns than a scary movie. She was exhausted from her grief, the traveling, the intrusion of so many people, the unexpected visit from Darla, and two attempts on her life. Turning her head so she could see Ethan, she studied his profile outlined by the dashboard lights.

Protection was a given, as he was a lawman, but the balm he offered to her tattered soul was appreciated, and if she wasn't careful, coveted. Having sex with him was inevitable, and addictive. Something else she hadn't expected. *How will you handle the withdrawal when he leaves?* she asked herself. Shifting in her seat, she bumped her ankle, winced, and drew the concerned attention of the FBI agent that was turning into so much more.

"Once you have Ray and Darla in custody, it's over, right?" she asked to alleviate his worry.

"Questioning first. If there's enough to arrest him, he'll go to Laramie for arraignment. Hopefully the judge will keep him in custody until the trial," Shaun answered from the backseat. He gave up trying to get comfortable and said, "With Darla, we'll need a lot more evidence to arrest her."

"Like a confession?" she asked.

Shaun snorted. "And I would only believe it if she took a polygraph."

"In the meantime, both of you need to stay at the lodge. If you're wandering around, you just make an easier target. That includes you, Sheriff Tanner," Ethan added with his gaze on Shaun through the rearview mirror.

"I've slept on the lobby couch before," Shaun murmured.

"Shaun," Carli said, nearly twisting around in her seat, "Ethan and I were wondering if there was any correlation between the marks in Dad's diary and his arguments with Ray that you witnessed."

Refraining from shrugging, barely, he answered, "I'm not sure. I would have to look at the dates."

"Can you verify if Dad sent a telegram to me in Africa? Scott wants to know who requested my whereabouts. He can't ask his assistant, as that was probably three employees ago."

"What did the telegram say?" Ethan asked.

"'Come home.'"

After a minute to think through the fuzziness of pain and the medication, Shaun offered, "If Dad knew Ray was causing trouble, or was likely to, it's possible he would want you here."

"Why?" Ethan wondered, thinking that if Bear suspected Ray of possible foul play, he would want Carli to be far away. Often people equated distance with safety.

"We were all close to Dad, but with Carli, probably because she's the oldest and knew the most about Darla and the Preserve, his desire would be to sign the lodge over to her in person. He would have voiced his concerns, and probably restrained Carli from confronting Ray."

"No 'probably' about it," she mumbled.

"Then Bear might have suspected Ray. What about Darla?" Ethan questioned.

"If Dad thought she was planning something, he would have told us," Shaun said.

"So there's still the theory that they are working together to get the land and exact a personal vendetta." Ethan loosened his grip on the steering wheel as he pulled into the drive. The clock on the dash read 8:45 p.m.

Zach and J.J., having been delivered back to the lodge by Frank, met them on the veranda. The fire was built up to keep away the chill from the clear sky and the new snow that remained frozen on the ground. Tim had made an impromptu meal of sandwiches. Once Shaun settled onto the couch and Carli in her own bed, Zach and J.J. shut themselves in their rooms. Ethan sat heavily on the chair closest to the fire, facing the front door with the dining room to his right, and a cup of strong, hot coffee in his hands. Ray only kept a cell phone on him when he was on the Preserve. With his absence and not knowing if Darla remained in Laramie because of the storm, one of them would stay awake as a security measure. Everyone was on edge and Ethan volunteered to pull the first shift.

With his pad on the coffee table in front of him, he flipped quietly through the pages. Pausing at the ones of Carli, the lodge and the valley that spread out behind it, he felt an odd sense of comfort. The crackling from the wood brought his attention momentarily to the scent of pine. Even when they were inside the mine, there was a circulation of air, though it carried with it the odor of ozone from the snow, the smoke from the rotted timbers, the rich smell of the earth above and around them. Remembering the softness of Carli's skin, and her sighs, he leaned back in the chair and shifted his gaze to the fire. There was something about the air here. It made him want improbable things and edged out his fear of cramped, dark places.

Wiping his hand across his face, he began to think frantically. It was supposed to be simple. Get rid of Bear, and the Preserve reverts to Darla. He would get his share and retire quietly on the coast. But now, he not only killed one person, but probably three more. If Shaun was still alive, he would have called into the office. Did they know? Had they connected the dots and decided he was the one? He couldn't return to the lodge, especially with the rifle. And he had to get his alibi together, had to be seen by someone, somewhere.

Wednesday night. Poker at Ed's in town. The last time he was there he reassured Jim Lockhart that Alyssa would continue to receive her paychecks. He wondered if the man would be there tonight and decided it would be fortuitous if he was.

The front parking lot was nearly empty, but around back there were a dozen vehicles, including Lockhart's truck. He dug his wallet from his hip pocket and counted the bills. Enough to get him in the game. If Lady Luck visited, then he would have the opportunity to lighten his load.

He parked facing the street, then banged loudly on the metal door. A minute later it was opened, and the young ranch hand that he had seen there the last time, smiled at him.

"Ray. Come to lose your wages?" Justin asked, pushing the door wider so the newcomer could enter.

"No one plays poker to lose, Justin."

He nodded a greeting to a few other participants and took the empty chair at the table where Lockhart was shuffling cards. This was straight-up poker. Nothing wild, nothing better. Five-card draw. The ante was two bucks.

Jim dealt. "How are things at the lodge?"

"Empty. Slow. Alyssa told you Carli will be taking over?"

Jim nodded and dealt a few cards to a couple of the players. "She needs the job. After graduation, she can work forty-hour weeks. Summer is coming, which means the cabins will be full."

Ray took one card. Two players folded and Jim showed his hand. Two pair, Jacks over eights. Ray tossed his cards in the pile. Play continued. Everyone, at least those at the table with him and Lockhart, took turns winning the pot. He had been around long enough to know Jim was holding back.

As the hours collected, the room filled with cigarette and cigar smoke. When Justin tried to light a joint, he was harassed until he went outside. Cheap canned beer and liquor sat on the tables and filled bellies. Jim was working his way beyond his usual functioning drunkenness. The next hand lent itself well to Ray's plan.

"No IOU's, Ray. Either you raise, or you fold," Jim nervously thumbed the corner of his top card.

"Something better than a note. A rifle."

"You that sure you can beat me this hand?"

The pot between them had nearly a thousand dollars in it. Everyone had bet big, then folded. It was down to him and Jim.

"Rifle is worth six hundred. Sure enough for you?" He kept his gaze on Lockhart. A straight, ten high, was hidden in front of him. There were a few hands that Jim could have that might beat it.

"Alright. A rifle. I call."

He turned over his cards and a few expletives escaped from the players who were no longer in the game.

Jim sighed. "God must be on my side tonight." A straight, Queen high, showed in front of him.

Ray leaned back in his chair to cheers and boos and comments of disbelief. Jim held his gaze as his hands stretched out to scoop up his winnings. With the bills folded and stuffed in the winner's front pocket, Jim followed him outside.

It was past nine o'clock, and they met the pizza delivery guy at the back door. There would be a break to eat and clear the tables of empty cans and bottles, then play would resume until they decided to go home.

Jim, with rifle in hand, peered through the scope and pretended to track a deer across the parking lot. He looked it over, checked the action of the bolt, then smiled at Ray.

"Pleasure having you at the table tonight. Coming back for more?"

He was saved by Justin, who talked loudly to Kevin about needing help at Willow Ranch. A mountain lion had been spotted earlier in the day, spooked the cattle, but managed to get a calf before scattering the herd to the state land that bordered the ranch. He thought of the opportunity, then shook his head at Jim. Lockhart was smart enough to stash the rifle in his truck before entering the building and returning to the poker table.

Raising his voice to be heard across the distance that separated them, Ray asked, "Need another hand to gather the cattle?"

Justin paused, then shrugged his shoulders. "Might as well come along. They've got quads and lights, but the state land can be too rough for wheels."

He nodded and followed Justin to the Willow Ranch. They were short-handed, but organized. By midnight, only half a dozen cattle were still missing. He was thanked and sent on his way. Unable to return to the lodge until he knew the status of Shaun and Carli, he needed a place to spend the next few hours. The morning news would report accidents due to the storm. Being only fifteen minutes from Laramie, he decided he would visit Darla. It would be one more piece in his alibi.

The hotel lobby was deserted, but the young woman working the desk directed him to a phone. Zach slept with his cell, and J.J. often complained of friends in different time zones texting or calling at all hours of the night. No one would be at the counter, so he would leave a message regarding his whereabouts. That would buy him time.

He recognized Darla's rented Cadillac in the parking lot, so he knew she was here. Too exhausted to play twenty questions and speculate on the outcome of his earlier actions, he got his own room. After taking a hot shower and laying his head on the pillow, he believed that he was finally exhausted enough to sleep, and for the nightmares to stay away.

Ethan had locked the front door of the lodge, something he guessed had never been done. When he returned from the kitchen with another cup of coffee, there was a beep. Following the sound to the other side of the guest counter, he saw the message machine had recorded two voicemails. Pressing 'Play', he heard Ray's voice informing them that he was fine, and after helping Willow Ranch, decided to get a room in town. Which town, and a room in which hotel? He scowled, unsure as to whether he should wake Shaun to have the sheriff verify the location and existence of Willow Ranch, when the second message played. The foreman from Willow Ranch was calling to thank Ray for his assistance with the cattle. Unless the man paid someone to make a phony call, which he doubted as everyone at the lodge would know the truth, he was left with the knowledge that perhaps Ray had gotten a room and wasn't on his way out of Wyoming.

With cup in hand, he rounded the couch and found Shaun's eyes open and staring at the ceiling.

"He won't run. Not yet. He'll wait to see if the morning broadcast alerts the public to the disappearance of Carli and Shaun Tanner, and a guest from the lodge. Or, better yet, the recovery of their bodies."

419

"You know him pretty well."

"All my life. I also know criminals and how the media works in Wyoming."

Ethan sat in the chair and sipped from his cup. "Would you prefer to go after him, or have him come to us?"

A few moments of silence passed before Shaun answered. "When you first showed up, I thought you would take over. Big lawman from the East Coast. The Fed who knew nothing of how a small town sheriff dealt with the citizens under his protection."

He shifted so he was sitting up. When he looked, there was a hint of humor in Ethan's expression, not offense. He knew the FBI agent's deceptively relaxed body would be able to draw his weapon in a breath and protect anyone at the lodge. The sketchpad that sat on the table in front of Ethan reminded him of the man's talent, art that he shared with Carli, and his intelligent, unique thought process.

"But you proved to do what you said. You let me lead the investigation. Even now, close to apprehending Ray, you still defer to the local authority."

"I respect you as a person and a sheriff. You know Ray, and you know this Preserve. An arrogant fool I would indeed be to impose upon Centennial's law enforcement." He set his cup down, then looked again at Shaun. "He killed your father. Tried to kill Carli and then you. Tell me how you want to catch him."

Shaun nodded. "I have a contact at a Laramie TV station. I'm sure she would be glad to help, and that includes sharing the story with others in the business."

Ethan smiled and decided he liked Sheriff Tanner.

CHAPTER 41

Zach stared at the phone. Alyssa had a project due at school and wouldn't be able to come to work that day or the next. When he reminded her that Friday was her birthday and they had plans, she was unsure if she would be done by then. Saying she had to get to class, she promised to call him later, and disconnected.

"Alyssa won't be in for the next couple of days," he informed everyone at the breakfast table, unsure if he should discount the feeling he had in his gut as a result of the events at the lodge, or if Alyssa was in trouble.

He and J.J. had already been out to feed horses. The sun was up and the temperature was rising. Some of the new snow from the previous day's storm had melted, and the rest would be gone in another couple of days.

Carli had showered and dressed in her typical Wyoming attire of jeans and a long sleeved, buttoned-down shirt. Her face showed she was pleasantly rested, and with a few ibuprofen, her ankle felt better. She and Tim had taken on breakfast, the plates of eggs, sausage, and French toast, along with the coffee carafe and a bowl of fruit, decorated the center of the table.

Fortified with his own pain medication, and a little rest, Shaun scooped up eggs and began to fill everyone in on the plan he and Ethan had devised earlier that morning.

"So, you don't know the reason Ray mutinied," J.J. said, still in a state of disbelief.

"That's one of the questions he'll have to answer when we bring him in," Shaun said.

"And that's the reason for the false declaration that you, Carli, and Ethan are missing and presumed dead?" Zach had lost interest in breakfast since he was really in the mood for blueberry muffins.

Before Shaun could give any further confirmation, his cell chimed. Answering it, he rose from the table and moved towards the lobby as he listened to the fellow police officer.

"Shaun, it's Ben. Got some information for you. Darla Tanner is staying at The Blue Sky Chateau. Did you need a tail on her?"

"No. I have the feeling she'll be coming around. If you hear some shocking news later this morning, don't believe it."

"A little cloak and dagger?"

"Enough to catch a killer."

Ben was quiet a moment, guessing the sheriff had a suspect on the shooting of his father. "Anything I can do to help?"

"Not right now. Thanks."

When Shaun turned back toward the table, he saw Ethan standing in front of the window at the end of the dining room, his phone to his ear. Turning around, their gazes connected. Ethan nodded, then replaced his cell on his belt.

"The real estate companies that had logged the inquiries at the clerk's office, have someone in common. Darla Tanner."

"So she was after the property the whole time. She must have coerced Ray into shooting Dad," Carli said and set her fork down, her appetite suddenly diminished by the conspiracy of murder.

"Ray may not have taken too much urging. If he built up enough resentment over the years, maybe all it took is the promise of some retirement cash," Shaun added as he took his seat and sipped his coffee.

"So we just wait?" Zach asked.

Ethan nodded.

"It's not like there isn't anything to do," J.J. mentioned. "The list of repairs is on the clipboard behind the counter. And this being the first Thursday of the month, Dr. Richmond will be making his rounds."

With a raised brow, Ethan looked at Carli.

"The vet that has a contract with the Preserve. He mends anything that might be wounded, vaccinates the horses, and checks the arrivals of whatever Dad has ordered." Her gaze shifted to J.J. "You've been here, and I've been ... away. Do you know if a shipment is due to arrive?"

"Everything is in the book in the office."

"Would you mind helping me get caught up?"

J.J. smiled easily. It was his sincere friendliness and charm that awarded him jobs and dates. "Anything I can do to help the new boss."

"So you're planning on staying?" She looked at him with a hint of desperation. Yes, she knew the workings of the Preserve, but there were things she hadn't dealt with because she hadn't been around.

J.J.'s smile decreased a little in its brightness. "For a while."

"What would make you stay ... longer?"

Before he could piece together a story to convince her it was time for him to move on, Zach interjected.

"Carli, what do you plan to do with the Preserve?"

All eyes swung to her. She took a sip of coffee, as much to gather her thoughts as to collect her courage to voice, and make real, what she had only shared with Ethan. The fact that she did open up to him was cause for her to examine her motives. That, she would do later.

Setting her cup down, she answered, "Tanner's Outdoor Adventures will continue, but as a safari, not as a hunting mecca." In the silence that met her declaration, she hurried to reassure them that the lodge would continue to grow in prosperity. "We'll offer all we do now, with hiking, horseback riding, and fishing, but instead of hunting parties, we'll take people on photo shoots. I would also like to expand the trails in winter for cross-country skiing, snowshoeing, and snowmobiling. I think Buck and Samson wouldn't mind pulling a sled for holiday clients. There would be classes in photography and film development. We could add a business center, purchase a couple more canoes for the lake. Maybe have a geologist test the mines. Some of the tailings may still contain—"

"Stop," Shaun said.

Carli closed her mouth and stared at him.

"You've been thinking about this for some time. How come you never shared your ideas with Dad?"

She shrugged. "Would he have listened?"

"He might have."

"His dream was the Preserve catering to hunting enthusiasts. I'm envisioning a new clientele. More families. People who are interested in conservation instead of stuffed trophies."

After a moment of consideration, Shaun smiled. "I think it's a fantastic idea. Probably save a bunch on insurance, too."

J.J. and Zach laughed.

"Now I know what to tell people when they call. Which, by the way, should I be taking reservations?"

Carli smiled at Zach. "Yes. Please take reservations."

Tim had been silent, watching the players in the game, listening to the information. When Carli began speaking of her plans for the Preserve, he knew he was right in making his own. With her confirmation that Zach, and anyone else who answered the phone, should make a reservation, there was a relaxing of his shoulders. He brought his hands together in applause.

"Brilliantly rehearsed and performed. I knew you would have great plans for this place."

"You knew I would stay here?" She tipped her head to the side, touched by his support.

"Wyoming has always been your home. And really, how many more awards can you win for Scott anyway?"

She chuckled. Of course Tim would understand. A bit of sadness entered her voice when she inquired what he would do.

"Return to New York, use up my remaining vacation days getting over my separation anxiety from you, then meet with Scott about a new feature."

It was Carli's turn to applaud. "And whatever you offer Scott, he'll take the deal. He won't want to lose a top-notch journalist."

Tim inclined his head in recognition of her compliment.

"Zach and I will start with KP, then I'll meet you in the office, show you what I know," J.J. offered.

"Zach, J.J., since the two of you will be out on the Preserve, you'll need to be extra cautious. We hope that Ray and Darla return to validate what they'll hear on the radio and TV. They may not use the front door. Keep you cells with you, and anything suspicious call me or Shaun," Ethan instructed.

The two younger men left the table, hands full of dishes.

"I would like to spend some time with your laptop confirming the dates in Dad's diary," Shaun said to Ethan. "Then I need to get to the office and bring Denny and Vince in on our plans. I'm also waiting on the results of the evidence from the darkroom incident." He rubbed his forehead as he recognized the tension headache gathering there. "Frank will probably have a report on the condition of my vehicle." Shaun looked up at Ethan. "And you?"

"Also waiting for information from the office. I'll be patrolling the lodge and manning the phones."

"But I can do that," Carli interjected, beginning to get excited about her new project.

"After you spend some time reacquainting yourself with your darkroom."

Her expression changed to one of guarded protest.

"The longer you stay away, the harder it will be to go back," Ethan told her, his voice quiet, but full of encouragement.

Shaun and Tim watched the interaction between Ethan and Carli, each forming a similar opinion. They agreed with Ethan. Carli needed to 'get back on the horse', otherwise she would develop one excuse after another to stay away. The artist in her would dry up from being denied access to her creativity.

"There will be time for that after Ray and Darla are behind bars," Carli told the three men at the table whom she knew cared about her.

Ethan rounded the table to stand beside her. "There's time now, while we wait for the suspects to take the bait and show up to confirm the news." He held his hand out to her and waited.

When she realized she would get no support in her procrastination from Tim or Shaun, she pushed her chair back, and to show she was willing and not afraid, put her hand in his. Shoulders back, standing tall, she allowed him to walk next to her out of the dining room and across the lobby to the foot of the stairs. She paused.

"Is your ankle bothering you?" Ethan asked.

She shook her head.

"The phone hasn't rung, and I have the headset, so there's no reason to stay at the counter."

She nodded.

"Would you like me to help you up the stairs?" There was a teasing smile on his face, and he held her hand as she strongly gripped his.

She shook her head, but remained rooted to the floor.

He tugged gently on her hand and began climbing the steps, a reluctant Carli behind him.

"Any sane person would have second thoughts about returning to the scene where an attempt was made on their life," he told her. "Those who allow fear to control their lives end up quitting their jobs and selling their houses so they don't have to deal. Only the brave conquer those demons."

They had reached the top of the stairs and it occurred to her that Ethan was right. She was more afraid than she realized. And fear was not a Tanner trait. *Spit in the face of fear*, her father had said. *Don't let it keep you from living your life.* She could hear his voice, his words, and was reminded of all the times she had been afraid. Falling out of the tree, confronting the mountain lion, returning to school when her first boyfriend broke-up with her but spread it around that they'd had sex when they didn't. When she had read the telegram that Bear was dead.

Ethan walked down the hallway with her, his quiet strength lending itself to her since she couldn't seem to come up with

426

much on her own. At the doorway to the darkroom, she released his hand and took a steadying breath. Wiggling the knob that hung loosely now in the wooden door, she pushed it open and saw the fingerprint dust on the counters and realized that a couple of her trays were gone. *That's alright*, she decided. She didn't want them back. Stepping inside the room, she noticed the odor of bleach and ammonia were gone. Her prints that hung on the line, when she first realized that something was wrong, were still there. She instinctively moved to where the negatives sat on the back counter. They had been developed just fine. It was only the pictures that had been ruined.

Leaning against the doorjamb, his arms crossed in front of his chest, he watched her. Tentative at first, probably afraid of the ghost that she had almost become, she looked around, then began to touch things. Her negatives, her equipment. She removed the prints that, even to his untrained eye, weren't right, and tossed them in the trash. Running water in the sink, Carli retrieved her bucket, soap, and sponge and began cleaning the counters, wiping them free of any fingerprint dust or essence left behind by Darla. The strong, brave, intelligent woman that had come to mean more than she should, was reclaiming her space. He didn't leave, didn't comment. Watching her move with sure, graceful actions, he felt a sense of pride. How could he think she would do anything else?

Replacing the missing trays with extras from the cabinet, she removed the gallon jugs and double-checked the labels. Opening the first one, she placed her nose carefully above it and sniffed lightly. Developer. With a small smile, she poured it into the tray. Filling and rearranging her equipment to her satisfaction, she looked around and sighed. Ethan was right. If she waited, it would have been harder. Glancing in the direction of the door, she saw him there, as she knew he was the entire time she cleaned and rearranged her equipment.

Wondering if he knew what his smile did to her, she rounded the island and stepped up to Ethan. Without a word, she wrapped her hands around his neck and kissed him. The touch of lips, a gesture of thanks, wasn't all that she wanted to say. He enveloped her in his embrace and pulled her closer, so she asked for more and he willingly gave it. The kiss deepened, his heady taste fuzzing her brain.

There was gratitude, heat, and more in her kiss. He gave the same back, his thoughts flying from taking her here to completely erase what had happened, to how he was going to get on a plane and leave. That caused a stutter in his breath, and he ended their moment of intimacy.

Bright, expressive, hazel eyes traced the features of his face, lingered on his lips, then floated up to meet his gaze.

"Thank you," she said, her voice filling the space between them. "Now, I have work to do," she added and stepped away.

He backed out of the room as she closed the door, then smiled as the bulb on the wall turned bright.

«« —»»

Alyssa set the phone next to her on the bed. Carefully, she replaced the bag of frozen peas on her split, swollen lip. Squeezing her eyes shut to stop the tears, she winced and gingerly touched the swelling beneath her eye. She had been so careful. He had been happy, or what passed for happy when it came to him, for weeks. The house was clean, all her chores had been done so he wouldn't even notice if something was out of place or needed doing. But it was her fault. She knew what would happen if he found it.

This whole incident could have been avoided if she had just given it to Zach. But she was afraid of what he might say or do. They had talked the night of the funeral about remaining in Centennial and continuing to work at the lodge. Did he wonder if she would take off after graduation? Why didn't she just tell him? Sighing, she knew why. If she told Zach that she wanted to go to college and use the check that Bear had given her, he might have panicked and broken up with her. Maybe he would have threatened her, bullied her into staying in town and at the lodge. But didn't she want to stay with Zach?

With a groan, she lay back on her bed, her thoughts spinning. One part of her pointed out that Zach had never intimidated or terrorized her. He had only been kind and funny and supportive. But he would turn on her if his happiness was threatened. Men were unpredictable, so she had to be careful. Shifting the frozen peas from her lip to her eye reminded her that she hadn't been careful enough earlier that morning.

She reread what Bear had written to her. Tucking the letter, the check, and the brochure for Wyoming University into the small compartment of her backpack, she left it on her bed as her phone chimed. The text was from Emma, one of her friends and her partner in Physics.

Patrick just walked by and he smiled at me! Do you think he'll ask me to prom?

She laughed. Emma had a thing for cowboys, and Patrick played the part well. He was on their high school rodeo team and split his time between his horse and his personal cheering section, many of whom were underclassmen girls who thought it would be cool to go out with a senior.

Don't know. Did you smile back?

OMG! I forgot!

She shook her head, scooped up her backpack, and sent a quick response as she walked down the hall to the living room. Her father was in the kitchen pouring more coffee, but her eyes were on the rifle that lay across the couch. He didn't own a gun like that. A .22 rifle, to shoot at beer cans in the backyard or to scare away salesmen, is what he kept behind the front door. She knew from working at the lodge that this was a more expensive gun, similar to one used by clients that came to the Preserve to hunt game.

Thinking that her father might forget that it was there and sit on it, she reached forward to lift it from the cushions and set it next to the end table, leaning up against the wall. The gruff voice from behind startled her, the task forgotten, as her backpack shifted. Without the small compartment zippered closed, the movement had the envelope falling, from the place where she thought to keep it hidden, to the carpet. Turning quickly at the presence of her father, having learned it was best to keep him in front of her, the jostling of the pack only gave the paper more momentum as it fluttered to the floor.

It laid there, between them. Her father took a step into the room, and she took a step backward, in the direction of the front door. Scared, blue eyes widened as they stared at the treasure Bear had given her. Her breath stilled as the letter, check, and brochure had partially fallen from envelope.

"What's that?" Jim Lockhart asked, stepping forward to pick the papers up from the floor.

Terror held her by the throat. There was no sound, lie, truth, or excuse that squeezed past vocal cords, frozen like the icicles that hung from the roof in January. Run! *Her mind screamed at her, but her feet refused to move.*

Jim straightened and looked through what he had in his hand. Wyoming University. A letter. A check. The last is what caught his attention. He stared at the amount and the signature, then back at the brochure. Unfolding the letter, he recognized the signature at the bottom as the same as the one on the check. He heard noise coming from the person in front of him, but the words made no sense. The familiar roaring began to fill his ears.

"What is this?" he demanded again, though he knew the answer. It confirmed what he feared. Alyssa planned to leave him. She had money and had lied to him about it. "You bitch!" he yelled, tossing the papers in the direction of the couch.

His fist shot out faster than she could move.

"I was going to tell you! I'm sorry! I'm sorry!" The words left her aching jaw like a litany.

"You're not sorry! You're a lying, sneaky bitch that needs to be reminded that your place is here!"

His knuckles again caught her in the face. Her backpack fell from her shoulder, the force of the blow driving her to her knees. Big hands wrapped around her arms and hauled her to her feet. Her blonde hair was across her face and kept her from seeing the backhanded hit that came from the other side. Stars were sent spinning in her head. Legs too weak to hold her up crumpled, arms that were finally freed raised to cover her head. Curling up in a ball to protect her stomach should the kicks come, she continued to apologize between sobs.

The hand in her hair forced her to look at him. But he was a shadow, black and evil and so familiar, behind what he pointed at her. The new rifle was an inch from her face. Its barrel seemed as big as a cannon. Her breath stopped in her lungs and somehow his words penetrated the ringing in her ears.

"You try to leave, thinking you can have a different life than this, and I will pull the trigger. I'll find you, no matter where you run or hide." Not waiting for acknowledgement that his words had gotten through, he scooped up the check and envelope from the floor by the couch, then stepped over her and out the door, rifle in hand.

Alyssa lowered herself to the floor where the tears that flowed now were in relief. He had left and couldn't smell the urine that soaked her jeans.

CHAPTER 42

When Ethan descended the stairs, Shaun was waiting for him.

"She's working," he answered the unasked question.

"She's alright?"

He nodded. "The laptop is in Cabin 4 if you have time to look at the dates."

Glancing at the clock that hung on the wall behind the front counter, Shaun nodded and moved toward the door.

"Here's the key. I have a few things I want to check out."

Shaun took it and made his way to Ethan's cabin. The day was degrees warmer than the previous one, and it seemed odd to have the parking lot so empty. He glared at the space where the truck that Ray had taken was normally parked. Heat burned in his gut at the betrayal. The remainder of his strides had his mind filing the pieces of evidence, the facts they knew, and their suspicions. Climbing the steps and letting himself inside the cabin, he realized how much was guesswork.

They didn't have a gun or fingerprints, only opportunity and a few coded phrases that perhaps they had bent to fit their means. The same could be said for Darla's attempt to take Carli's life in the darkroom. He didn't think forensics would come back with anything definitive regarding the evidence he had delivered.

Easing into the chair and powering on the laptop, he wondered if they had enough to arrest either of the suspects. If Ray and Darla heard the announcement on the news and came snooping around the lodge, he at least had enough to bring them in for questioning. Would Ray protect Darla if he thought she would give him up to save herself? He was beginning to think that if he didn't get a full confession, the courts wouldn't have enough to convict. Allowing them to walk away from the crime of killing his father was not an option. None of the Tanners would be safe until the two of them were behind bars.

He opened the diary file and focused his memory to place dates and events together. It took about half an hour before a pattern emerged. Fence breach, dead animal, important client cancellation, major repairs. They all coincided with Bear admitting to a tough day or a foul mood due to an argument with Ray. If Ray wanted out desperately enough, would he sabotage the Preserve? Shaun believed the man killed his employer, and presumably best friend, so these other incidents were petty in comparison. Was Ray trying to force Bear to close his doors?

His phone chimed. The number on the display told him he wouldn't have to return to the office to await this information.

"Totaled," Frank informed him. "Damn lucky you're alive. Air bag probably kept you from going out the window. Your slow speed on the trail helped the trees to stop the roll. Want me to write it up?"

Shaun rubbed his forehead. "Please. I'll contact the county and get the paperwork started for insurance and a replacement vehicle. Thanks, Frank."

"You okay? I mean, you walked away with just scratches?"

"Broken collarbone, some cuts from the glass. But, yes, I walked away."

He remembered from yesterday the urgency he felt to find Carli, wondering what condition she might be in, as he took the trail up the backside of Miner's Paradise. Could he have done something to prevent rolling his vehicle? Perhaps if he had placed the pieces together quicker or thought to predict Ray's desperation.

"Damn lucky," Frank repeated.

Closing out the program and shutting down the computer, he was interrupted by another call. His suspicions were accurate. No useable fingerprints. Chlorine bleach and ammonia were confirmed to be in the bottles. Minimal proof, and probably not what a prosecutor would use unless this was all they had. Confusing the jury with evidence that didn't convict might pass in court, but it depended on which judge drew the case. It wasn't enough for a guilty verdict, and anything else was unacceptable.

Both Ray and Darla had opportunity and motive. He had an easier time wrestling Darla into the role of 'killer for money'. What would she do if she purchased the Preserve? Stevens alluded to the sale of the land if Carli failed to take possession. Unless Darla had won the California Lottery, where was she getting her financial backing? In all the years that she had been gone from Wyoming, he never cared where she was or what she did. Maybe now was the time to set aside his dislike for the woman who birthed him and find out what she had been doing, and with whom.

Locking the cabin door behind him, he returned to the lodge. He walked through the front door, and was met with Ethan's weapon drawn and trained at his heart. Neither moved or breathed. The air itself paused in its flow from the open door into the room. Ethan clicked on the safety and set his gun on the table in front of him. Shaun noticed that the fire was reduced to embers, and the agent had been bent over his pad of drawings a moment before the door opened.

"I'm going to the office. I need to take care of a few things." Shaun looked at the clock then added, "The announcement will be made at the top of the hour. It will take them an hour to get here from Laramie."

"Anything on the dates?"

"Every one of the asterisks matches with an incident, which coincides with some disagreement Dad had with Ray. I think Dad was leaving a trail. Maybe that's why he asked Carli to come home. He knew something was going to happen." Shaun exhaled loudly. The whisper in the back of his mind was not as startling as the words spoken aloud.

"Carli is still in the darkroom. Tim is upstairs doing something for the *Views*. Zach and J.J. have wandered through and reported that there is nothing amiss among any of the buildings around the lodge." Ethan gripped his sketchpad, as he was on the verge of making a connection, and hoped Shaun would be satisfied with the report and do what he needed to do at his office.

"I'm fifteen minutes away. You see or hear anything—"

"I'll call for backup."

Shaun took a set of keys from behind the counter, then closed the front door of the lodge. A moment later Ethan heard the engine of the van, then listened as it faded away down the drive.

9:55 AM. He shook his head. There were too many variables and too many unknowns. A firefight was not what he expected, but he learned long ago that expectations and assumptions meant little in his line of work. Replacing his gun at his waist, he got up to pace. Behind the counter was a radio. He turned it on and waited through a few commercials. The grave voice that announced the disappearance of a guest from Tanner's Outdoor Adventures, as well as Carli and Shaun Tanner, reminded the audience of the family's recent loss. *Well done*, Ethan thought. Would the suspects hear it and return to claim the Preserve?

Flipping through the pages with his rendition of Ray, Darla, the money amounts and notes of what they knew for sure, he strode from the window to the dining room and back. Ray was reserved, not saddened, by the news of his lifelong friend's death. Refusal to participate in the funeral and his announcement to retire. Blocks of time unaccounted for. Very little affection shown to the three kids that he knew and had lived with for almost thirty years. Arguments can lead to resentments, which can, especially with the addition of the promise of cash, equate to motivation.

Darla was more difficult to read. If she presumed she would inherit the Preserve and had a real estate deal on the line, desperation could lead to attempted murder. But most real estate agents don't have the means by which to purchase something the size of the Preserve. Who, then, was she in business with? He glanced at the figures. Acreage, cost, resale, zoning. A doctor?

Too far away for a major medical center. A lawyer? Only if the land was to be converted to something else where the investment would be a quick payoff. A politician? He scowled. Ready money, knowledge of laws, and a continued source of income. Depending on the future use of the land, it could bring in more cash.

Moving to the desk computer, he pulled up the Internet browser and started searching. Forty-five minutes later, with more connections made, he looked up to see Tim descending the stairs.

"Just you?" he asked glancing around the empty lobby. Noticing that Ethan was working on the computer he continued, "Find anything useful?"

"Some loose strings. When pulled, there will be some unraveling."

"Enough to put them away? Carli, Shaun, and Samantha don't deserve this," Tim stood on the other side of the counter and spoke quietly. "Not that anyone does, but to be deceived by Ray ... and have your mother turn on you? Losing Bear was hard enough. Being worried that someone wants you dead ... in all of her traveling, with everything we've seen and done, she's never been like this. On edge. All that nervous energy ... afraid. That's not Carli Tanner."

Ethan understood Tim's concern. He had seen it in the victim's families of every case he worked. "It could be what protects her. Once we have Ray and Darla in custody, the fear will drop away."

"I hope you're right." He noticed, not for the first time, the look on the agent's face when speaking of Carli. A fierce protection that is born of deep feelings. This recognition made him wonder if Ethan realized he was in love with Carli. He hoped that love would keep Ethan from leaving, or maybe it would get him to return.

"Needed a break from the computer screen," Tim said, walking down the hallway towards the supply room. "Thought clean towels and a shower might refresh me."

Ethan watched him leave, then shook his head. He should be glad Tim was gay, otherwise he would never get the opportunity to be close to Carli. *Close, hell*, Ethan chided. He *needed* to touch her, kiss her, breathe her in. She did something to him. Soothed his fear. Made him feel what he had shut down and locked up when he lost his partner. Instead of pushing it away, he wanted to embrace it. From the first moment he kissed her, she made that forgotten part of himself come alive. What would he do with it, how could he tame it if he stayed in Baltimore? But what would he be if he left the Bureau?

Looking at the clock, there was still time. He took his pad and went to the kitchen. The coffee pot was empty, so he went through the motions of preparing another. Through the gurgling of the coffee machine, he heard his phone ring.

"Brooks," he answered.

Micah, it seemed, wasn't just sitting behind his desk the past couple of days. He had done some poking and flushed out a few interesting facts.

«««—»»»

Carli stretched her back. Maybe everything was catching up with her. The ordeal in here yesterday, the hike, the cave-in, the horse ride back, even the sex. She was in shape, but all the strenuous exercise was making her sore in places that weren't accustomed to such movement. With only one roll developed, and those prints hanging on the line, she left the darkroom and decided it was time to contact Scott.

Sitting felt good. So did seeing that she had received an e-mail from One World Piece.

Ms. Tanner-

We are in the process of finalizing the details for your show next month. Unfortunately, one of the local artists who was to share the show with you in the gallery has opted to send her pieces to North Carolina for an art contest. We know you are busy, and with the recent tragedy in your family, would certainly understand if you were not available to assist us. We're looking for another artist to fill the wall space in the gallery. We thought that with your connections, you may know of someone who has photos or paintings or drawings that would be interested in the showcase we are designing around you and your work. If you know of such an artist, please contact us immediately. Any questions or concerns regarding the show can be directed to Barbara West, the gallery manager.

We wish you well. See you next month.

Cecil Marks,

One World Piece, NY

She smiled and sent her reply. Ethan wasn't completely opposed to showing his art, though he called it 'work', and meant it literally. She should be able to convince him. With that done, and feeling restless waiting for Ray and Darla to show, she thought to seek out Ethan and speak to him about the gallery in New York.

Closing the door behind her and making her way to the top of the stairs, she remembered his sketches of everyone at the lodge, especially the ones he had done of her. Talent, absolutely, the man had it in spades. And not just for art, she smiled to herself remembering their time in the mine, as she hoped for more of his attentions before he left for Baltimore. That thought had the smile slipping from her face. Would he miss her? There was something in the way he looked at her, touched her, that told her there was a lot beneath the surface. With her commitment to the lodge, would she be able to handle it when he left? How often could she fly to the East Coast? Shaking her head, the confusion dispelled with the voices emanating from the lobby.

«« — »»

Shaun sent Denny home and Vince out to the highway beyond the entrance of the Preserve. He wanted his deputy close should things fall apart and they needed backup.

Having spent the last half-hour, unbeknownst to him, in the same way as Agent Brooks, he discovered the Internet was loaded with pictures and articles. Obviously Darla had envisioned herself moving up the food chain. First with a local with a lot of pull in a small town, then leaving Bear Tanner and attaching herself to various elected and promoted officials. A police chief, a judge, the mayor of a California town, population three thousand-five hundred. Her most recent acquisition was Councilman Ted Worthington from Carmel. And Worthington had just announced his candidacy for the State Senate. Here was the financial backing. What the newspapers didn't tell him was what they planned on doing with the land once they had possession.

The blinds were partially closed, and to anyone who drove by, the sheriff's office would appear to be empty. He had parked the van in the back, leaving the front lot void of all vehicles. Deciding it was time to head back to the lodge and be part of the welcoming committee, he moved toward the counter where Esther usually sat. She had taken the day off to spend it with her granddaughter. Stretching his good arm out to retrieve his hat from the hat rack, he looked out the window and swore. Darla's Cadillac cruised by with two people in the front seat.

Settling the hat on his head, he retrieved his keys and phone from his belt, then left through the back door, locking it behind him. He dialed Ethan's number. Though the seconds ticked off on his phone, there was no connection.

"Dammit," he muttered, climbing clumsily into the van.

Exiting the rear parking area, he hit the brakes as a garbage truck made its way down the side street, and stopped in front of him, blocking the lot's driveway as the arm reached out for the can. He hit redial. Still no connection. No lights or siren to hurry the truck along, he was forced to wait the thirty seconds it took for the trash collector to dump and lower the container, then move down the street. There was no sign of the Cadillac at the four-way stop at the end of the block, nor could he see it anywhere in front of him.

«« —»»

Deciding to saddle Buck and Samson and check the fence line on the north side between the Preserve and Medicine Bow National Forest, Zach and J.J. led the horses from the barn to the far corner of the lodge. They would tell Ethan what they planned, and assure him that they would call if they found anything.

Zach was laughing at a joke J.J. had told, when the scene unfolding outside the front door of the lodge halted their steps. J.J. cursed under his breath and Zach was too stunned to agree. Thinking to help the situation, J.J. reached back to remove his rifle from the scabbard.

«« —»»

The blackout curtains kept the morning sun from entering the room. Having no idea how long he had slept, Ray rolled over and squinted at the bedside clock. 8:30 AM. Perhaps a change in location kept the ghosts away. Deciding that it was time to get out of bed to see what the day would bring, he turned on the radio and shuffled his way to the bathroom.

Opening the door to allow the steam to escape from his shower, he tuned in to the tinny voice on the bedside radio. It was the top of the hour and there was breaking news. Moving to the side of the bed in order to pull on his boots, he stilled his hands as the DJ announced the disappearance of Carli and Shaun Tanner. There was speculation that perhaps the siblings had taken the family fortune and run off to a more exotic place than Southeastern Wyoming. Possible foul play was mentioned since a registered guest at the lodge was also missing. Deputies in Centennial were organizing search parties to comb the Preserve and the surrounding areas. Anyone with information was urged to contact the authorities.

He squeezed his eyes shut. They would expect him to show up this morning, concerned and demanding that he lead one of the rescue groups. He could track and had lived for more than twenty years on the Preserve. Could he look Zach, J.J., Vince, and Denny in the eye and tell them he had been playing poker, rounding up cattle, and sleeping, alone, in a hotel room and that he didn't know where Carli and Shaun had gone? Lying to Bear for years should have given him enough practice. It would be odd if he didn't return to the lodge.

Replacing what few items he carried back into his pockets, he used the room phone to call the front desk and ask to be connected to Darla Tanner's room.

"Of course I heard the news. Where are you?" was her response.

"Room 114."

"I'll meet you downstairs in five minutes. If we don't appear, and express appropriate worry, it will look suspicious." She hung up.

Typical, he thought. Always wanting to do whatever it took to uphold appearances. If it was discovered what they had done, their cellmates wouldn't care a whit about appearances.

Twirling the keys around his fingers, he waited by the front door of the hotel lobby. When the elevator doors opened, a look of concern matched the pale pink pantsuit that Darla had draped herself in that day.

"Why are you here?" she asked as if she only just thought of it.

"A long story," Ray answered, purposely short to keep from engaging the woman in conversation. The more he was forced to see her, the less he could stand the sight of her. They exited the hotel and headed to their respective vehicles.

Rounding the back of the truck, he glanced at the tire just past the driver's door. He paused while unlocking the truck and looked again. Flat. He must have picked up a nail in the lot behind the bar the previous night. It would take time to get it plugged, and he needed to return to the lodge.

Hurrying across the dozen parking spaces between the truck and Darla's Cadillac, he caught her as she was backing out of the space. The knock on the window startled her and she slammed on the brakes.

"You about gave me a heart attack Ray Foster. What's wrong?" she threw at him when she rolled down the passenger window.

"Truck has a flat. I need to ride back with you."

She nodded and waited while Ray climbed in next to her. Her scheming mind remained quiet until they reached Highway 130.

"We have to appear concerned," she began.

"I have no problem with that. I don't know if Carli is alive or if she and Ethan are still buried. Shaun may not have survived the vehicle rolling down the cliff. And if either of them tells someone that they suspect me of killing Bear ... well, I'm already concerned."

"What makes you think they'll put anything together and point their finger at you?"

"Just a feeling. They were ... distant at the funeral."

"It was you who wanted to pout at the ceremony, and even at the Rockin' R."

He looked at her now, with her hair perfectly curled, just the right amount of make-up, and earrings that matched her outfit. Difficult to believe that the woman had a killer's heart.

"What did Bear give you in the envelope?"

The only agitation she showed was a tightening of her grip on the steering wheel. "Nothing of any consequence. He was just as heartless and selfish in his words from the grave as he had been when he was alive," she paused to steady her breathing and chanced a look his way. Ray's profile reflected his age in the crow's feet at the corner of his eye, the gray whiskers that had begun to cover his cheeks, the deepening wrinkles under his jaw. "And Bear's final words to you?"

"I burned the letter, then flushed the ashes. He wrote that if anything 'accidental' befell him, that he would know it was me. Told me he had left clues for anyone who might look into his murder."

"It's difficult to cover your hate. I know." She made a rude noise. "At least I attempted. More than I can say for the three demons that I birthed."

443

He had the urge to mention she was the Devil herself, but he refrained. It would make all he had been through worthwhile if Carli and Shaun remained missing. Eventually, the sheriff's vehicle would be discovered, but hopefully it would contain only a corpse.

"Don't you think the authorities would look to you first if there is a hint of wrongdoing in their disappearance?" he threw at her.

"Kill my own children?" she said in mock horrification.

"If you were successful, I wouldn't have to clean up after you."

"And if you had killed Bear earlier, he may not have changed the will."

"Changed the will? You were out of it when you left."

She fumed silently, then said, "Why did you not mention that Wyoming redrew the boundaries for Albany and Laramie Counties? Or alert me to the new divorce law?"

He turned to look at her, his face a mixture of disbelief and self-preservation. "I didn't know you planned to kill your husband so you could inherit his land and sell it off to the politician you've been sleeping with!" The volume of his words steadily increased until he was yelling.

"Keep your voice down!" she snapped back as they slowed to drive down 2nd Street in the middle of Centennial. "You wanted out as badly as I wanted the bastard dead. Don't you dare blame me for all of this."

He crossed his arms over his chest and wordlessly seethed the remaining distance to the lodge. True, he agreed to the plan and carried out his part. But he would be damned if he would allow her to place blame. Bear got what he deserved. The controlling, arrogant ass would no longer belittle or order him around. As soon as Carli and Shaun were found, alive or dead, or when the end of the week arrived, he would take his things and leave Wyoming for good. If Darla neglected to send him his share, he would remind her what he knew of her scheming and her hand in recent events.

There were no cars outside the sheriff's office. It was reasonable that they would be at the lodge. But as they came to the end of the drive at Tanner's Outdoor Adventures, instead of finding a parking lot full of search and rescue volunteers, it was nearly empty. Would they have congregated elsewhere? Had they discovered the bodies and just hadn't reported the findings to the media?

She stopped in front of the steps to the veranda. They climbed out of opposite sides of the car and looked around. Ray was the first one up the steps, and left the door open for Darla. The lobby was empty. No one was behind the front counter.

"Maybe we missed the search teams," Darla began.

"Doesn't make sense. Everyone should be here," Ray said more to himself than to the woman who continued to chatter behind him.

"You don't think—"

"No. I don't believe he did. Or maybe he thought the wrong thing. What was it, Ray, that Dad did that pushed you over the edge?"

Darla and Ray turned simultaneously to stare at Carli, alive and whole, three steps from the bottom of the stairs.

\

CHAPTER 43

A motor home pulling a boat, and driven by one of the first tourists of the season, crawled along the highway ten miles below the speed limit. Shaun imagined the passenger, most likely the wife, pointing out the snow-capped peaks in the distance and the bright green of the pines that lined the road. The double yellow that marked the center of the asphalt that twisted and rolled through the countryside, along with steady on-coming traffic, kept him from passing the large vehicle in front of him. Reaching Vince on the radio, he explained his ETA at the lodge, then sent his deputy there ahead of him. Attempting again to contact Ethan, Shaun sighed with relief when the call went through, but then swore when Ethan's voicemail sounded in his ear.

《《——》》》

Setting his phone and coffee cup on the dining room table, Ethan drew his weapon from its holster and held the gun down next to his thigh. He heard two voices, but at the addition of the third, his adrenalin kicked in, flooding his bloodstream. As he came fully into the lobby, he recognized the backs of both suspects, as well as Carli advancing on them from across the lobby floor.

"Thank God you're alright," Darla began to gush and moved to meet Carli in the middle of the room.

"Don't touch me," Carli said, her voice a quiet blade of steel.

Darla stopped where she was.

"You failed to kill me in the darkroom. Obviously I was rescued from the mine that Ray tried to use as my tomb. No

447

doubt an attempt to do what you could not," her cold gaze shifted from the woman in front of her to the old man who stood a few feet from the fireplace. "Tell me Ray, why did you do it? How could you kill Dad?"

"I think that's a question that should be asked at the police station," Ethan said, announcing his presence.

Darla turned to look at him, and guessing she might have an ally in Shaun's friend, asked, "Where is the sheriff? We heard it announced on the radio that both Carli and Shaun were missing. Ray and I expected the parking lot to be full of search and rescue teams."

"On his way, I imagine. You two drove through town, and he was at the office."

"But there wasn't a sheriff's car out front," Darla continued.

"Because Ray shot out the tire and sent it rolling down the cliff yesterday," Carli, hands on her hips, continued to stare at Ray.

"Ray, why would you do—" Darla turned on him.

"Shut up! You conniving motor mouth. Everyone can see your concern is as fake as your eyelashes," Ray snarled at Darla.

"Don't you dare speak to me that way!"

"It's true," Ray continued. His heart beat fast. Understanding how a caged animal felt, survival instincts began to take over. "If you want to know what happened to Bear, ask Darla. She had it planned from the beginning. Knew how much the property was worth—"

"I was not the one who pulled the trigger." She stared at him, disbelieving that he would confess, here, now, when there was very little reason, besides speculation from Carli, that they would suspect her or Ray of any wrongdoing.

Before she recognized his intension, Ray grabbed a poker from the stand that held the fireplace tools and came at her, the piece of metal lifted overhead.

Carli, uncaring if the two of them killed each other, and rather shocked that Ray moved as quickly as he did, remained rooted to floor. Why would each blame the other? It didn't matter who schemed and who used the gun. Her father had been betrayed and was dead.

Ethan raised his weapon and took a few steps towards the two suspects rolling around on the floor. He noticed Tim standing behind Carli, towels in hand, but did not expect him to join the fray in trying to separate Darla and Ray. Linens fell, forgotten, to the wooden planks as Tim crossed the distance to the rug in front of the fireplace in an attempt to end the childish display. The three of them struggled briefly on the floor before Ethan reached in to help Tim, whose arms were around Darla. With Ray freed from the bottom of the pile, he scrambled to his feet.

Ethan crouched to retrieve the fireplace poker, when Darla elbowed Tim. He stepped back, lost his balance when his heel caught on the edge of the rug, and fell, head first, into the coffee table. Shifting his gaze from Darla to Ray, Ethan's breath hitched in his chest. The man had wrapped his arm around Carli's throat and held her up against him. She was taller than Ray by a couple of inches, so she was forced over backwards as her hands pulled at Ray's forearm. Ethan aimed his gun and stood at the same moment that Ray reached behind him and retrieved a rifle from the rack by the door.

"You don't want to do this," Ethan said, dropping the poker on the floor behind him.

"But I will. I'll scatter her brains all over the lobby."

Ethan's gaze shifted the three inches from Ray's eyes to Carli's.

Recognizing the unasked question, she confirmed, "There's a round in the chamber. Dad didn't believe in keeping unloaded weapons. 'Worthless', he called them."

Ethan removed a set of the sheriff's handcuffs from his belt and tossed them in the direction of Tim, who had recovered from his kiss with the table and gained his feet. "Put those on her," he directed.

Realizing Darla's rented Cadillac was his only means of escape, Ray demanded, "Give me the keys, or instead of planning it, you'll have to witness your daughter's death."

Continuing to play the part of the concerned parent, Darla pulled the keys from her pocket and threw them at Ray. He released his hold around Carli's neck to catch them, then grasped one of her arms and twisted it up behind her back, all the while keeping the rifle cocked and aimed at Bear's oldest child.

"You're coming with me," he growled in her ear, forcing her to walk backward with him out the door and down the steps of the veranda.

"Hundred bucks you won't get far," Tim said to Ray, but meant the words as encouragement for Carli.

Ethan followed, matching step for step the retreat of a desperate killer who held a hostage as a shield of protection. Carli was nearly as wide as Ray, so Bear's long-time friend was conveniently safeguarded behind the woman who had, in a short time, taken up residence in his heart. To his left, he saw that J.J. and Zach had stopped to watch the scene of a fellow employee hold a gun to the new owner's head. Putting out his hand to stall the movement of J.J. lifting his rifle, he watched as Ray shoved Carli into the Cadillac, then followed her onto the front seat. Through a spray of gravel, they backed up, then accelerated down the drive. Aiming for a back tire, he squeezed off a couple of rounds, but missed as the Cadillac only gained speed and became blurred in the rising dust.

Launching himself down the steps, he approached Zach and J.J., who were steadying the horses from the unexpected shots and flying rocks. Holstering his weapon, he took the reins from Zach and swung up onto Samson's back.

"Call Shaun," he yelled over his shoulder as he kicked Samson into a gallop and followed the Cadillac, leaving Zack behind with his phone to his ear.

J.J. mounted Buck, and with the rifle in one hand and reins in the other, followed Ethan. He heard a shot, and through the cloud of dust ahead, saw the Cadillac's rear window shatter. Watching as Ethan leaned slightly forward in the saddle, his gun arm raised, another couple of rounds sounded in the air. He thought of the old westerns with the sheriff chasing the bank robbers, only this was 2013, Ethan was an FBI agent, and they were pursuing the murderer of Bear Tanner. Buck was gaining on the long-legged strides of Samson, when another shot preceded the Cadillac swerving off the road and smashing into a tree. The sirens were heard moments before the red and blue lights could be seen through the settling dust and pine branches. Behind Vince's car was Shaun in the company van. He pulled Buck to a stop and dismounted, holding his rifle at the ready in case the three lawmen needed a fourth gun.

《《——》》

Her arm stung and her head spun with the improbable, but very real event that was transpiring around her. With the muzzle of the rifle jammed against her shoulder, she slid across the seat as Ray climbed in next to her.

"What the hell are you doing? Killing Dad wasn't enough? You're making things worse—" she yelled as she was flung forward and then into the middle of the seat as Ray backed up, then sped forward.

The rifle was braced between his knee and the door, out of her reach. He swerved in an attempt to dodge the shots coming from behind them, and she decided that if she was going to survive this, which she had every intention of doing, she better use her seatbelt. Considering grabbing the steering wheel, she ducked instinctively when the back window was fragmented by a bullet. She had just sat up to look in the side mirror and saw Ethan following them. There was a jolt to the right, then her vision was filled with white.

A cacophony of noise and sensations assaulted Carli. Pain, a tightness in her chest, gravel and pine needles floated in front of her, and sirens that seemed to be growing louder, filled ears that were already on overload. She closed her eyes and rested her head back against the seat. A moment later, her door was wrenched open and Ethan was there.

"Are you alright?" His words penetrated the haze of her brain.

Her eyes blinked open to see Ethan's concerned face, then followed the path of his flannel sleeve to the gun he aimed at an unconscious Ray. Running like he had, and taking her with him, confirmed Ray's guilt in the act towards Bear. If she had any doubt as to his intentions when he left her and Ethan in the mine shaft, it was erased when picture of the rifle held to her head as they left the lodge flashed in her mind.

"I think so," she mumbled.

Shaun's face appeared in the driver's side window, and Vince through the windshield, which closely resembled a spider's web. The door was opened as Shaun reached in to check for a pulse. Straightening and lowering his weapon, since Vince kept his gun on Ray, he called Stan. He moved to the other side of the Cadillac, which would need to be towed, as Carli carefully climbed out with Ethan's help.

"Maybe you should wait until Stan arrives," Shaun began to protest at her movement.

"I'm fine," she countered, stood, then leaned back against the side of the car.

"Where's Darla?" Shaun asked.

"In handcuffs at the lodge," Ethan said, not allowing his hands to leave Carli.

His mind told him she was alright, but his heart had yet to regain its natural rhythm. Once she caught her breath, she leaned forward and wrapped him in a hug. He held her gently, yet fiercely, forcing himself to release the fear that Ray would kill her. She was here, in his arms, and the threat to her life would soon be arrested.

Stan and his partner arrived and checked Ray. They placed a collar around his neck and carefully moved him to the stretcher. Once inside the back of the ambulance, an IV was inserted and the hospital in Laramie was notified of the stats and condition of the patient.

"You're actually allowing me to take this one?" Stan asked Shaun.

"By the book, Stan. Vince will follow you and help with the paperwork." Shaun turned away to call Frank for another pick-up.

Glancing at Carli and Ethan, he recognized the expression of relief on the man's face. As Carli shifted, he looked into his sister's eyes. It appeared there were two choices for Agent Brooks. Either he remained in Baltimore and there would be two more miserable people in the world, or they would have an FBI agent in Centennial.

The rest of the day was filled with dealing with the consequences of apprehending two criminals, charging them with murder, attempted murder, assault with a deadly weapon, and kidnapping. The more charges he could pile on, the better the chances were that a jury would convict. And the Tanner family would accept nothing less.

Darla would be held overnight at the accommodations provided by the Centennial Sheriff. There were questions, and when answers were convoluted and vague, Shaun applied more pressure. The real estate license, news articles of Darla and Councilman Worthington, and the demand to know when she had gained access to Carli's darkroom, were eventually met with a request for legal representation.

Denny was given the night shift. With clenched jaw, partly due to the frustration, and the rest because of the pain in his shoulder, Shaun drove the company van home. Parking in front of the house that was slowly being completed, he tried to remember how long it had been since he had been there. The structure was dark, so apparently he hadn't left a light on the last time he walked through the door.

Pausing in the space between the kitchen and living room, he sighed. Denny had brought dinner when he started his shift, and Shaun had taken more pain meds hoping they would work faster with food. He was tired, relieved, sore. For the first time in weeks, he thought he might be able to sleep without the aid of a bottle or miles on the treadmill.

It was a new experience to shower and dry himself with one hand and very limited use of the other. With a towel tucked around his waist, he looked in the mirror. The bruise on his shoulder covered more area than he thought it should. The cuts from the broken glass were mostly tiny, red flecks. The gash at his temple would take some time to heal. He wondered how long it would be before the dark circles beneath his eyes disappeared.

Flicking off the light, he made his way to his bed by the glow of the partial moon through windows that he didn't bother to cover. Getting as comfortable as he could, lying on his back, right arm under his head, his eyes traced the shadows on the ceiling and refused to rest.

Where was the elation? The relief that it was finally over, his father's murderer under guard at the hospital and soon to be behind bars in the Cheyenne Police Station? Maybe it was the fact that Bear Tanner was still gone, the betrayal of the man's lifelong friend and ex-wife that caused the empty ache to continue in his heart. His sisters would be safe. That thought had his eyelids drifting closed. A corner of his mouth tipped up slightly at remembering Carli's speech that morning regarding her plans for the Preserve. His smile faded when he recalled the embrace between her and Ethan outside the Cadillac. He wouldn't mind having the agent around, and based on Carli's response, she would prefer if he stayed. What would she do if he didn't?

Pushing the thought away, he told himself that Carli's love life was her own. She would have enough to keep her occupied with the Preserve and moving out of New York. Shifting slightly, he was glad that J.J. agreed to stay on a while longer. Then he wondered if Alyssa was going to return to work on Saturday. It had been a few months since she called in sick or with some project due at school. And wasn't tomorrow her birthday?

«««—»»»

"I don't think I can Zach. Why don't we celebrate next week? We're going out for prom, right?"

Alyssa spoke softly into the phone so she wouldn't wake her father. He had come home an hour earlier, just before Zach called. She had been in the kitchen making dinner. The scar on her left eyebrow was a constant reminder to what might happen should she be home and not have dinner ready whenever her father returned from the bar.

Jim Lockhart had paused long enough to survey the bruises he inflicted that morning. With no apology, no word that he had eaten in town, he made his way down the hall to his bedroom, where he closed the door. That was the signal that she would be on her own for the evening. Once he closed his door, he rarely emerged until the next day for breakfast.

She sighed, ate her dinner, careful of her split lip, then placed the leftovers in the refrigerator. No longer did she believe it was necessary to hide the injuries from her father, as she knew he was never sorry for what he had done. However, she needed to keep this from Zach. Saturday was when he would next expect her to show up at the lodge, and she wondered if she would be able to hide the bruise with makeup, or have her lip heal enough to kiss him hello.

"But then it wouldn't be your birthday. And you have to eat, right? We can make it short, then you'll have time to work on your project." Zach looked at the ring in its box. He knew Alyssa would like it, but it wouldn't have the same significance if he didn't give it to her on her eighteenth birthday.

"How about if I call and let you know?" she proposed, hoping he would agree, then she could continue to call in to work if she wasn't healed enough.

Sensing the desperation in her voice, he acquiesced, as long as she promised to call him the next morning with an update. After telling her he loved her, he hung up and set the phone next to the ring on the nightstand.

Alyssa had been looking forward to her birthday. She hadn't mentioned any project that was due for school before yesterday.

If she wanted to put him off indefinitely, it meant that Jim Lockhart had used his daughter, again, as a means to express his disappointment over his own pathetic life. He hoped he was wrong. Deciding that he would take her out even if she called and tried to delay meeting him, he flipped open the file.

Carli had given him several jobs, and one of them was to review receipts from the past month and legitimize each one. She also wanted a report from him regarding the upkeep and condition of the cabins, outbuildings, and fence line. He liked Carli and was excited to be involved with her ideas about changing the focus of the Preserve. The job fit him perfectly. He loved Wyoming, being outdoors, talking with the clients, and fixing things. Shuffling through the papers, he made notes as Carli had requested. She hadn't mentioned a raise, but if he could convince Alyssa to marry him, he would need to be able to afford a house.

Stretching out on the bed, his back propped against the headboard, his mind drifted off to what his life would be like once Alyssa was his wife. Between these pleasant visions and the events of the past week, Zach Murphy, for the first time since he came to work at the Preserve, and for years prior to that, fell asleep with the light on before 9:00 p.m.

CHAPTER 44

Carli removed the bandage from her ankle before she stepped into the shower. That had been after a simple dinner of sandwiches and whatever was left over in the fridge to top off a day that she could never have predicted or anticipated. With Ray and Darla in custody, quiet serenity, what she realized she loved about the Preserve, returned.

Once Shaun continued his duty as sheriff and secured the two people responsible for recent events, including the shooting of their father, she had directed J.J. and Zach to do whatever needed to be done to return the Preserve to a state acceptable for clients. They were both amenable to following her directives, for which she was grateful. With Ray gone, she would need their help. She had given Zach files and requested that he bring her up to date on the condition of the Preserve. Similar instructions were given to J.J., who reported, when Ethan was out of the room, that Samson had received extra treats. She had replied that they were well deserved.

Zach and J.J. had retired early to their rooms with the assignments she had given them. Shaun called her throughout the afternoon and evening to keep her updated on Ray's condition and Darla's request for a lawyer. There had been the phone call to Samantha to reassure her sister that she was fine and to share the change in direction of the Preserve. A new phone message had been recorded regarding the shift in the activities and amenities soon to be offered at Tanner's Outdoor Adventures. She decided that the next day would be soon enough to contact

Stevens and take possession of the Preserve, and begin to procure reservations.

Ethan had left the lodge after dinner, mentioning the need to complete paperwork. In the statement were the presumptions of flight reservations and that he would be awake for some time. She remembered the feel of him when he held her in his arms outside the Cadillac. It was more than relief, more than confirming for himself that she was alright.

It was 9:15 p.m. when she stepped into the hallway and closed her bedroom door behind her. With the topic of conversation to be the show in New York, she made her way to Cabin 4. The curtains were drawn, but the light shined from inside, so she knocked on the door. She waited, arms wrapped around her middle since she neglected to put on her coat before heading outside.

When the door opened, there was a moment where her breath caught and held. She knew her emotions showed in her eyes, but there was nothing she could do to hide them. This was the man that had saved her, supported and understood her, pushed her to return to the darkroom, and had made incredible love to her. *Love.* It was that and not just sex. But it was sex that oozed from Ethan with his dark hair falling over his forehead, shirt unbuttoned, jeans, and bare feet. The day's growth of beard and the dark-lashed eyes that warmly held her gaze were enhanced by his genuine smile of pleasure at finding her outside his door.

"It's cold. Come in," he said.

She smiled and walked into the cabin. Under the smell of pine from the materials that were used in the cabin's construction, was the scent of the man. At the first whiff, warmth began to spread from the center of her chest, and she had to focus on why she had come.

"Your flight is for tomorrow morning," she left the statement open, hoping he would offer her ... something.

"Changed it to Sunday. Sloan, my boss, will want to see me Monday morning."

"A couple of extra days of recreation?"

"You could say that. I find I enjoy the ... air, here in Wyoming."

He stayed where he was and watched as Carli moved to the other side of the cabin, her eyes taking in the lighted bathroom, the files he had stacked on the dresser, the curtains that hung in front of the window. Despite the obvious evidence of her still-wet hair that she had showered, he could smell the scent that seemed to be hers alone.

"Have you ever been to New York?" she asked.

He raised a brow at her change in conversation. "A few times."

"Are you available next month?"

He shrugged his shoulders, then wondered if she was asking him to meet her at her apartment in Manhattan. His heart beat a little faster. Could Carli be proposing a long distance relationship?

"One World Piece, the gallery in New York who is hosting a show of some of my photographs, has space for another artist. Apparently, the local that they had booked, withdrew and tossed their lot in with another gallery in one of the Carolinas."

Ethan shook his head. "My sketches are work related. I can't have the faces of suspects and victims hanging in an art gallery."

"Not all of your drawings depict the unfortunate. You rescued me this afternoon. Saved me from being a murder victim." She smiled mischievously. "Can't say I didn't fill the role of suspect at one time."

"But you were part of an investigation. It would be a breach of confidentiality to post anything related to the crime," he told her, sliding his hands inside his front pockets to reduce the need to reach for her.

She picked up the pad that lay next to his laptop and flipped through the pages, then stopped at the ones he had drawn during their time at Wolf's Ridge. There was one of her riding Lady in front of him on the trail, eating lunch, pointing out some landmark, and one with her and the rifle, which must have been before she shot into the air to scare the bear since Ethan had been unconscious afterward. *The poachers. Was that only last week?* she shook her head at her silent question.

"These ones, of our ride. You could submit these," she suggested.

"Not without permission—" he began.

"I give it." Her gaze held his, the pad of sketches between them.

The teasing faded from her eyes and was replaced with something else. Something more serious. He knew that she was giving him more than her permission to display his sketches of her. She had given him her body, and he knew that without asking, just a touch, a look, and she would give herself again. Admittedly, that was the reason for the change in his flight reservations. He wanted to be with Carli as often as possible in the hours that remained, and prepare his mind, and heart, to leave her.

The thought of displaying his sketches had never occurred to him. Without any formal art training, and since his 'art' was used as a tool for him to make connections between elements in a case, there wasn't anything worth giving to the gallery. But the sketches he had done of Carli on that day were innocent enough. There was nothing that related directly to the murder of Bear Tanner, which was the reason he was sent to Wyoming. It wouldn't be as if he were trying to sell his sketches, to make a name for himself as an artist. He was an FBI agent.

"Alright," he agreed.

She smiled. "I'll get you the information on where to send them."

"Later," he said, plucking the pad from her fingers and setting it back on the small, crowded table. Taking her hand, he asked, "Is that why you came here?" He tugged gently and kept his gaze on hers as she stepped closer to him.

"Sure. Why else would I have come out here at 9:15 at night?" Her eyes traced the features of his face, then her hands slid up his chest to encircle his neck.

"Maybe for the artist?" He kissed her cheek, then her jaw, allowing his lips to find the scented soft spot below her ear.

"The art is a reflection of the one who created it. It is difficult to love one without the other."

He let the words, *her* words, slide over and through him. She respected his ability, had suggested he do something with his talent before this offer of a gallery showing. Did she 'love' him in that meaningful sense, or was she using the word as having a preference for his art, and for him? His lips found hers and he sank a little deeper. What would he do if her love was real? The sharp talon of fear that slid close to his heart with the thought that he could lose her, allow her to somehow be hurt or threatened because of his job, was dulled by her touch and the emotions she allowed to guide the kiss.

He eased her T-shirt over her head and let it drop to the floor. His blood raced through his veins when her hands slipped beneath his open flannel shirt, removing it from his shoulders. He reluctantly released her to shrug his arms free, then placed his hands on either side of her face and deepened the kiss. Stepping forward, forcing Carli back a stride, he followed her down onto the bed. Reaching up to turn off the bedside lamp, he was reminded of how the glow of the fire in the mine cast tiny shadows on Carli's body. The only light now was the one from the bathroom.

In a choreography of cooperation, Carli's boots and their remaining clothes were pushed off and away. The more that skin was exposed, the higher the excitement ran. She seemed content to allow him to set the pace, but he knew, from previous experience and her personality, that her complacency would be short-lived.

As he trailed kisses down her neck and past her collarbone, she tunneled her fingers through his hair, steering clear of his stitches, to keep his mouth where she wanted it, which was bathing her nipple with his hot tongue. Creative people rarely relegated their talents to just their art. Ethan proved her theory by his inventiveness in his lovemaking. Mouth and fingers were never still, but instead changed in pressure and direction, thus eliciting varying responses. She understood his intent as he moved down her body, tracing her ribcage, being interested in her navel and the width of her hips, but the intensity with which he lavished attention on the part of her that ached for him, took her to another level. With the swelling of sensations inside of her, she wasn't in control, and didn't care. Her climax crashed over her, no thoughts in her mind as her brain was hijacked by swirling stars and the multitude of explosions along every nerve in her body.

A certain amount of pride rose up in Ethan that he could take her to such pleasurable heights. Her trust and responsiveness to his care of her, humbled him. Intoxicated from the saturation of his senses by everything that she was, he drunkenly worked his way up her body, then watched with avid interest as she came back to him.

"You are incredible," he told her, his voice gruff with wanting.

She blinked up at him. There was no more lying to herself. She was in love with Agent Ethan Brooks. A small part of her that had been influenced by what typically played out in relationships, or whatever this was between them, whispered in a pleading voice to keep the revelation to herself. She had tonight and another day and a half with this man, and she didn't want to spook him with what he could interpret as unreasonable and improbable. So her love for him would remain a secret. She would hold the realization carefully in her heart. Perhaps it would keep her company after Ethan left.

With a grin, she urged him onto his back and gave him a few more reasons to support his claim of her incredibleness. Their exploration was slow, pausing when a sigh of pleasure or a tightening of fingertips communicated that which the mind was incapable of forming into words. The rise and fall of the excited rush of adrenalin, the build and satisfaction of the ache within was enjoyed more than once.

When Carli climbed off the bed, then closed the door to the bathroom behind her, Ethan rolled onto his back and tucked one hand under his head. In the darkness of the room, he relaxed as his gaze traced the beams of the ceiling. There was nothing about this woman that was ordinary. The more time he spent in her presence, the more his heart softened. It was uncomfortable. He had vowed not to care deeply for anyone after his partner was killed. But then there was Carli. He would have more murder and kidnapping cases to keep him away from his residence in Baltimore. Carli would have the clean mountain air, her family, the Preserve, and her art. He frowned at the pictures of scenes from Wyoming that would fill his mind whenever he closed his eyes. And his sketches would remain a tool to solve crimes.

His scowl was unseen by Carli, who turned off the light before rejoining him in bed. Rearranging herself next to him, she sighed contentedly as he wrapped his arm around her to secure her to his side. Her fingers lightly traced the edges of his muscles across his chest and over his ribs. There was no pattern, but it seemed to soothe her. He was vaguely aware of the light touches he returned along her arm and hip. Eventually, they would have to discuss ... this. He was not looking forward to returning to Baltimore, alone. But that was a short time into the future, so he pushed the thought away. With a gentle kiss on the top of her head, he decided to be present and enjoy Carli now instead of attempting to predict how things would go when he returned to the East Coast. His pinched expression relaxed as he realized that the near-complete darkness of the room didn't bother him. It must be the woman beside him that gave him courage. How much would he need in order to risk a chance at having everything?

«««—»»»

It was the excitement of New York that had Tim up early. Though he hadn't even called to make reservations, the prospect of returning home and meeting with Scott was beginning to make him feel antsy. He had done all he could with the digital prints that Carli had taken, as well as edited the article she had written. In order to give Scott an example of what his plan would be, he had taken some shots yesterday morning and had written a rough draft of the piece. Carli's permission would be needed before he worked any more on the article. He guessed she would want to include information about her father, but that would be her decision.

The hallway was empty, all the doors closed. He knew it didn't mean much, since Zach and J.J. were early risers as there was always something to do, even if there were no clients around. He knocked on Carli's door and waited. The darkroom door at the end of the hall was half-open, the knob continued to hang limply. When he didn't hear any rustling inside, he cautiously opened the door.

Cases were stacked on one side of the room, her made-up bed on the other. He smiled, guessing Carli had occupied Cabin 4 the previous night. The absence of the smell of bacon coming from downstairs told him that if he wanted breakfast, it would be up to him. He closed her door and made his way to the kitchen.

Like himself, Carli had a fair number of friends in New York. There was one that she would see occasionally, but when he asked about their relationship, she laughed that anything besides a sometimes-availability would ever exist between them. More than once her 'special friend' had stood her up and she had called him at the last minute to join her for dinner or a concert. Those were the times when he was reminded of how easily Carli wore expensive cocktail dresses and nibbled crackers with caviar. She could be ultra-feminine and the envy of every woman at a club, banquet, or private party. Ethan had yet to see that side of Carli and Tim wondered if he ever would.

He ignored the ringing of the phone on the guest counter as he passed by, but smiled when Carli's voice spoke from the machine about Tanner's Outdoor Adventures. The only thing that greeted him in the kitchen was a half-pot of coffee. As he poured a cup, he noticed the clock read 6:18 a.m.

Cooking was one of his loves. He spent enough time in this kitchen over the years that he knew where things were. It was many times larger than his in New York, and it contained a few of the gadgets that he lusted after, but could never justify purchasing. Donning an apron from the drawer, he went about setting out ingredients. With the events of the last week, it appeared that no one had signed for the grocery delivery that he knew occurred with regularity, nor had anyone gone to the store to gather provisions.

The vibration of his phone in his pocket halted progress on breakfast. A text from Charlie. He smiled as he read the message, then sent one back. His day was looking brighter. Charlie had taken a charter to Laramie, where he would arrive later this afternoon. The rancher wouldn't be leaving until Sunday at noon, so perhaps Tim could join him for dinner at the hotel. This would be his opportunity to see if they could work something out with each of them on opposite coasts. He wouldn't approach the subject with high expectations. Though he had many friends, gay and straight, with Charlie there was just a little something uncommon.

«« —»»»

Carli was in the type of daze that sits lightly over the mind when one wakes, yet hasn't moved or opened the eyes. Feeling the warm skin of the man next to her, the delicious heaviness of his arm and leg that pinned her comfortably to the mattress, gave her tangible proof that their time last night was not part of her very active imagination. She smiled, keeping her eyes closed as Ethan kissed the top of her head. Snuggling closer to his chest, she breathed deeply. Exhaling, enjoying the feel of his warm kisses on her forehead and cheek, then inhaling as his wet tongue coaxed her lips apart. Shifting onto her back, she moaned as he moved between her thighs. In the next breath, he slid into her, easy, filling her to her heart. They rocked together gently in an age-old dance, cresting simultaneously, exchanging a sigh.

With all of her limbs heavy and relaxed, he eased out of bed and into the bathroom. The door was partly closed, the sound of running water filled the space of the cabin. He stepped under the spray of hot water and wasn't surprised at what had transpired between them. Even his thoughts of how he could change his life to wake up next to her every morning didn't shock him. And knowing her more intimately as he was beginning to, it wasn't a surprise when she stepped into the shower and wrapped her arms around his waist. It was a pleasure.

He had a mind for details and remembered that each of the cabins had their own forty-gallon hot-water tank. Whenever he and Carli came together, time seemed suspended. However long they were in the shower, the hotel-sized bar of soap had nearly disappeared and the water had begun to cool. She was quick about drying off and dressing.

With a towel around his waist, he crossed his arms and leaned against the doorframe.

"What?" she asked, pushing her arms through the sleeves of her shirt and pulling it over her head.

"Just noticing how different it is from you putting your clothes on and me taking them off."

She slowed in her task and raised her gaze to his. Despite how they spent the night, and the early morning, the heat of desire in his eyes caused her cheeks to bloom with a light pink. "Well, regardless of how much fun a bar of soap can be, I need to get to the lodge."

He smiled, setting off his dimples, which he knew were shadowed by his growth of beard. "Imagine if we had a full bar," he began, then enjoyed the deepening of her blush. "And there's no need to hurry. It's nearly seven and they'll all know where you are."

She stepped into her shoes, but left them unlaced since she would be changing clothes before making her appearance in the kitchen at the lodge. "Really? How?"

"They're men. They've seen us together. When you aren't the one brewing coffee at 5:30, they'll decipher your whereabouts."

She backed toward the door. Would J.J. and Zach say something to her? And if they did, how would she reply?

"I'll pour you a cup of coffee. If no one has started breakfast, you'll find me in the kitchen," her hand reached out behind her and opened the door.

He closed the distance in a few strides. Placing his hands along her jaw, he slowly lowered his lips to hers, kissing her sweetly. "Easy, Carli. No one will judge you. After all, you're the boss."

She blinked up at him, then smiled. Her panic had been that they would know she and Ethan had sex and that they might treat her differently. But the real reason she dressed quickly and wanted out of the cabin was her unsubstantiated fear that Ethan would put distance between them. Instead, he had shown that he wasn't going anywhere, wasn't shutting her out in the light of day. It was her own insecurities that placed the thought where she would latch onto it.

"Thanks," she said.

"For what?"

"For being you. For pulling me back from irrationality."

"You're welcome."

She left him standing there as she squeezed through the door, then closed it, leaving her out on the veranda. Looking both ways as she descended the steps of Cabin 4, nothing moved besides the breeze in the branches and the birds. The sun was up and would soon be over the ridge. She squinted at the sky, then turned toward the lodge. The parking lot was empty except for Ethan's rental, Zach's truck, and the remaining company vehicle.

Easing open the front door, she peered around it and found the lobby empty, and no fire in the fireplace. The aroma of coffee relaxed her. She may have been concerned about what the guys would say or do, but at least they had made coffee, which meant the horses were fed and it was business as usual.

After sneaking upstairs to change her clothes, she pushed open the kitchen door and was relieved to find Tim, dressed in an apron, preparing breakfast. What she wasn't ready for was his candor and challenge.

With ingredients chopped and waiting to be added to the egg batter, pans and tins set out for the stovetop and the oven, Tim checked to see that he had everything ready and wiped his hands on a kitchen towel. Carli entered through the swinging door, and with a smile on her face, wished him good morning as she poured herself a cup of coffee.

He leaned against the counter and commented on what he saw, and what he knew in his heart. "It must be, after a night like you and Ethan shared. Oh, don't try to deny it," he told her when she raised a brow at his words, though her slight blush gave her away. "Your bed wasn't slept in, and only hours of physical pleasure with a man who loves you could give you such a glow," he paused while Carli choked on her swallow of coffee. "The question is, do you love him enough to let him return to his life in Baltimore, or fight for something that happens only once in a lifetime?"

He remained quiet, knowing she would respond with denying words, but wondered if she would be brave enough to admit her feelings to herself, to Ethan, and grab hold of what they had with both hands.

《《—》》

Councilman Worthington pinched the bridge of his nose. Darla had one phone call, and she called him. Not only did she not get the property, by any means available to her, but now she was the resident of the Centennial Sheriff's Office. Conspiracy to commit murder. Attempted murder. Real estate fraud. There was even mention of blackmail, her against Ray, who had recovered from the auto accident and currently occupied a cell in the Cheyenne Police Station. She wanted him to provide legal counsel.

"My association with you at this point is over. Take the lawyer the State will offer."

"If you don't do something to get me out of here, I'll share with them who was financing the project," she threatened, refusing to take the blame for events that transpired on the Preserve.

"You're hardly in a position to intimidate me."

"I'm in the perfect position for you to give me whatever I want. If your name appears in the press and is linked to the death of Bear Tanner, your hopes for the Senate—"

"Alright. I'll see what I can do."

"Start with a lawyer. Then bail money." She would get what she needed from him, or gladly hand him over to the police.

"Just ... keep your mouth shut. I'll make a few calls." He hung up, then roughly loosened his tie. The calls would be made, and this ... problem would be dealt with.

"It's me," he spoke into the phone, not identifying himself by name or using an introduction. "The prisoner is Ray Foster. He'll be arraigned in Cheyenne, Wyoming. It would be in everyone's best interest if he failed to appear before a judge."

"Ten G's, same as last time, Boss?" the gruff voice asked around a toothpick.

"I'll wire five now, in good faith that you'll complete the job," Worthington said, tapping the keys on his laptop, knowing the laborer would check his account before any steps were taken to eliminate the threat.

"Sure thing, Boss. Anything else?" One of the four televisions was tuned to a Cheyenne station, while the computer was opened to a list of contacts in the Cheyenne Police Department.

The councilman paused in deciding what to do with Darla. Both suspects eliminated the same way may cause more suspicion than just one. "That's all for now."

Hanging up the phone, he began to pull the scattered pieces together. Ray would be dealt with, which left Darla and Wilson Construction. Mr. Wilson had expended a great deal of energy making himself unavailable for a conversation. He was tired of waiting. Checking his e-mail while the call went through, he was once again listening to the kind receptionist.

"Listen," he interrupted her. "You have done a remarkable job in stalling me from speaking with Wilson. Some ... events have occurred that alters our contract. Either you get him on the phone now, or I sue for libel. My business partner was just arrest for murder. The media gets hold of that, they'll find Wilson, and Wilson Construction, in bankruptcy court."

"Just a moment," was the receptionist's reply.

"I don't know what game you're playing, but—" Wilson began a moment later.

"Shut your damn mouth, Wilson. I'm in the middle of cleaning up this mess and refuse to add your company to the list."

"What the hell are you talking about? I was told I would be taking orders from Tanner, that you were a front and didn't have the cash."

Worthington squeezed his eyes shut as his teeth ground together. What else had Darla done without his knowledge? He would have to deal with her sooner instead of later.

"Tanner has been arrested. She never had the cash. It's been me all along."

"The trucks are on their way." Wilson pushed his hand through his hair.

"Call them back. The property was deeded to the eldest daughter who has no intention of selling."

"Sure, I'll do that. Then you'll owe me for just the mileage and the hours."

"I owe you nothing. If you had taken my calls—"

"If you had the Tanner woman under control—" Wilson interrupted.

"You would know there was trouble," Worthington continued. "Consider this a courtesy call to save your ass."

After a moment of silence, Wilson hung up.

Worthington called his lawyer. The contract would be voided. No money would change hands. A friend would be notified, one that specialized in criminal law. They would see about a deal, review the evidence, and look into previous litigations tried before the judge assigned to Darla's case. "There's nothing to worry about," the voice said. He hung up the phone, then popped a few pills that were prescribed should he be 'worried'. Glancing at his watch, he guessed Rose, his wife, would still be at home working in her office. Since his regulars were either in jail or in the next town, Rose would have to do.

CHAPTER 45

Frank had a busy day with the Sheriff of Centennial. He met Shaun at the impound lot at seven in the morning, hours earlier than he usually arrived. Though the dogs knew Shaun, if the gates were closed, they were on duty. It alleviated Shaun from being threatened by the two brothers and one sister, all Rottweilers, when he pushed open the gates instead of the sheriff letting himself into the yard.

While Shaun cleaned out the glove compartment, removed the rifle from the cargo hold, and took the box of ammo stored in the side pocket of his totaled SUV, he filled the sheriff in on the Cadillac.

"Rental company was quite nice about it. Said they would be appreciative if I could save them a trip and bring the wreck back to their lot in Laramie. You don't need anything out of it, do you?" he asked, then placed the sucker he held in his hand, back in his mouth.

Based on Frank's girth size, Shaun guessed the man ate more than candy for breakfast. He had the only tow truck in town and was often the first to respond when the Highway Patrol put out a call, but generally stayed out of Cheyenne and Laramie, giving the other companies their share of the business. Frank was known for picking up and putting wheels down on vehicles others were afraid to touch. He had been with Frank on recoveries and had witnessed people's surprise when the tow truck driver, dressed in overalls and heavy work gloves, explained the length of chain needed here or there, talked about the center of gravity for the vehicle, and which point was the fulcrum. The man was a closet physics nut.

"No. I have a warrant for her hotel room." Shaun thought a moment, then said, "You know what? Probably wouldn't hurt to look."

He handed the items from the SUV to Denny, who returned to his deputy's vehicle and placed them in the trunk. As Frank led him to where the Cadillac was secured on the flatbed, he placed a call to the judge. After a brief lecture about calling early on a Friday morning to secure another warrant, the judge granted him permission to search the rental. Hoisting himself up with one hand, he moved to the side of the Cadillac and looked through the window. Nothing on the backseat. The front was empty as well, except for broken glass and remnants of the air bag.

"The keys?" he asked over his shoulder to Frank who stood on the ground, watching.

"In the ignition."

Retrieving them, he shuffled his feet on the edge of the bed toward the trunk. The first glance told him the space was empty. With a closer look, he saw the partial outline of a container indented in the carpet and thought he caught a whiff of fumes.

"Any chance the crash put a leak in the gas tank?"

Frank shook his head. "All front end damage. Only fluids that drained out on the site were from the radiator. Makes things more exciting though if I were leaving a trail of gasoline down the highway."

Touching his fingers to the indentation on the carpet then bringing them to his nose, Shaun smelled the fuel. With the cool weather and the sealed trunk, it would take more than a few days for the stain to dry and fade.

"Denny, bring the kit," he yelled to the deputy who was on his way from his vehicle to the tow truck. "Frank, I think you'll have to call the car rental company and let them know that their Cadillac is now evidence in an arson case."

Frank removed the sucker from his mouth and the cap from his head to run his hand over the buzz cut that had grown out. "Well shit, Sheriff. That won't make the rental guys too happy."

"Probably not, but it will make the DA's day."

He took a few pictures with a digital camera, then a swab of the stain. Handing both back to Denny, he climbed off the flatbed. Readjusting his hat, he began walking towards the deputy's car.

"I'll make the call. You can drop the Caddy off at the Cheyenne Police Station, then head over to The Blue Sky Chateau and pick up the company truck. Ray claims it's in the parking lot with a flat front tire," he paused to retrieve his keys from his front pocket. With the use of the fingers on his left hand that were extended from the sling, he removed the truck key and handed it to Frank. "I'll make sure you get paid both ways."

Frank took the key and peered at Shaun. "It was a tragedy, what happened to your Daddy. You think your troubles are over?"

The sheriff stopped and turned to glance at Frank. "I think we know most of it. Assuming it goes to trial, the rest will come out." He shifted his gaze to Denny, standing next to the deputy's vehicle with the driver's door open, then the piles of cars and rusted metal and stacks of old wood and tires, then finally back at Frank. "Yes, I think our troubles are over," he answered with more conviction than he felt. Once Darla and Ray were arraigned, and hopefully held without bail, he might be more relaxed.

Frank nodded and headed towards the cab of his truck.

Shaun joined Denny and got in on the passenger side. "Drop me at the office. You and Vince are back on your regular shifts."

Denny left the impound yard and drove towards town. "Is Carli alright? I mean, if she was held at gunpoint and forced into the Caddy, which then crashed into a tree, I imagine she's pretty shook up."

Shaun glanced at his deputy. *Damn, the man still is in lust with my sister*, he thought. But it wasn't his place to reveal the feelings he knew she had for Ethan. That was between the two of them.

"Carli's tough," he said instead. "She'll be fine."

The drive to the sheriff's office was short. Denny kept the engine running as Shaun climbed out. As his deputy drove away, Shaun sighed. It would be easier to complete the paperwork with just him and Esther in the office. The clock on the wall when he walked in read 8:20 a.m.

"Morning, Sheriff," Esther said in her regular, pleasant tone.

"Esther. How's our prisoner?"

His receptionist, who also served as dispatcher, Gal Friday, and grandmother on occasion, raised her brow. "Don't you mean 'visitor'? And your *mother* is just fine."

He ignored her correction. "The Cheyenne van will be here in half an hour to take her into town. I'll be at my desk completing the paperwork for the transfer."

Leaving his office door open, he tossed his hat on the chair inside the door, shrugged out of his jacket, in which only his right arm was through the sleeve, and hung it on the rack, then sat heavily in his chair and turned on his computer. He set the prescription bottle he had taken from the pocket of his coat on his desk, then realized he would have to go back into Esther's domain to get a cup of coffee. Looking up, he nodded his thanks as his Gal Friday set a cup of the hot, dark brew in front of him.

Her gaze moved from the bottle of pills to Shaun's face. With a more studying glance, she could see the pain etched in the brackets around his mouth and the redness of his eyes. She knew not all of it was due to his broken collarbone.

"No one would give you any grief if you took some time off, Sheriff. It's been well over a week that you haven't looked like something the dog ate and then threw up. You've had a rough go of things, and it may not let up for a while, with the trial and all. It would do you some good to stay home for a day, work on that house of yours, maybe spend an afternoon fishing."

He wrapped his hand around his mug and sipped. "I'll take it under advisement," were his words, though his expression of gratitude said more.

She returned to her position at the front counter, and he focused his attention on paperwork and phone calls.

«« — »»

The first part of the day was spent in a casual meeting with J.J. and Zach. Donna couldn't make it in, so they had her on speakerphone, and since Alyssa was presumed to be in class, they texted her for clarification on certain items and her opinion on others. Carli felt more relaxed as the sharing of information and informal reports by Zach and J.J. assured her she wasn't that far removed from the business since she understand nearly everything that they told her. Excitement warred with overwhelm. She had ideas that the rest of them believed were doable and thought it would be the right thing for the Preserve. They agreed it would take a lot of work, and some time, to build up a new clientele. The meeting ended, and the three of them headed to the kitchen for a late lunch. Zach and J.J. remained there while she went to find Tim and Ethan.

"What do you think?" Zach asked, taking his time setting the last plate in the dishwasher.

"About what?" J.J. leaned back against the counter, content to allow the younger man clean-up duty.

"Carli's plans. Think they'll work?"

"Of course. Don't you?"

Zach shrugged.

"You were just as excited as the rest of us in there, swapping ideas and making decisions. What's really bothering you?"

He tossed the sponge into the sink. "Alyssa. She's been avoiding me, being vague about her availability for her birthday today. We've had plans for weeks."

"Maybe something has changed. She's officially eighteen now, perhaps she's found someone better," J.J. waggled his brows and smiled.

"I think that 'something' has to do with Jim Lockhart."

J.J. sobered. "Why don't you drive over there, check it out for yourself?"

Glancing at the clock, he knew Alyssa would be on her way home. He pressed her name on his cell. She answered on the second ring.

"Hi, Zach."

"Hey. How was class? Get your project turned in?" He held J.J.'s gaze, his friend obviously very interested in the outcome of the call.

"Fine. The project isn't due until Monday. I thought I could use the weekend to finish it, especially since there won't be any visitors at the lodge."

"Will you be ready in a couple hours for your birthday dinner?"

"Um. Well. I don't think—"

"We won't go out. How about a picnic at William's Lake? Just the two of us." If she agreed, then he knew there would be bruises.

"I suppose. If you pick me up after six-thirty, and bring me back early." She wondered if it was a mistake, looking at the mark on her cheek and the red of her split lip.

His stomach dropped to the floor. He nodded at J.J., who straightened and frowned. How badly had her father hurt her this time? They didn't need to contact Child Protective Services. They could just call Shaun. Now that she was eighteen, a legal adult, Zach would do whatever it took to convince Alyssa to press assault charges.

"Sure. I'll be there at six-thirty. Is everything alright?"

"Fine. See you then."

He replaced his phone on his belt and looked at J.J. "He can't keep doing this to her."

"As long as she stays in that house with him, he will."

"I'm giving her the ring tonight," he reminded J.J., shifting from foot to foot.

"You expect her to marry you, and what? Live upstairs?"

Zach had thought of a plan, added and discarded ideas as to how he and Alyssa would live. He had kept them to himself, but maybe J.J. would tell him if he was crazy. And he would have to talk to Carli. He shook his head and answered his friend.

"Cabin 9 is hardly used. It's set back in the trees, away from the other buildings. It's also the biggest cabin, and most costly to rent. With a little remodeling, it would be a place Alyssa and I could live."

"You would pay rent? What about Alyssa going to college?"

"I'll work something out with Carli. Lys hasn't said that she wants to go to UW. Since I'm giving her the ring tonight, I'll need an answer about her own plans."

J.J. stuffed his hands in his front pockets. The kid knew what he wanted and went after it. Couldn't fault him for that. Zach had a job and a future with a woman he loved. J.J. ignored the pang of envy.

"Cabin 9 would be a place to start. I don't think Carli would object. Just be careful Alyssa doesn't choose you over a degree. A regret is no way to start a marriage."

Glad that J.J. offered serious advice instead of his usual teasing, he opened the fridge to see what was available for a picnic. Not much.

"We missed the delivery on Tuesday. Guess it doesn't make sense to order the usual when no one is here."

J.J. peered over Zach's shoulder. "I don't have much to do today. I'll make a run to Laramie, get what we need. If you see Carli about Cabin 9, ask her about the grocery delivery."

Both of them straightened, and Zach closed the door.

J.J. clapped him on the shoulder. "Good luck tonight. If you need anything, call," he said with a smile on his face, though his voice held the seriousness of a possibly dangerous situation.

Taking the keys from the front desk, where he put them when Frank, after fixing the tire, returned with the truck Ray had driven, and a couple hundred dollars from the petty cash shelf in the safe in the basement, J.J. was off to pick up supplies.

Just as Zach was about to leave the kitchen in search of Carli, she, Tim, and Ethan walked through the swinging door.

"Did we miss lunch?" Tim asked as he peered around Zach and noticed the empty counter.

"There's enough for a couple sandwiches. J.J. made a run to Laramie for groceries. It's my job to remind you," he said to Carli, "that Tuesday is the regular delivery day. If you want to change the order, you have to call by tomorrow. We may not need the normal amount, since none of the cabins are filled. Well, except number 4."

Ethan gave Zach a half-smile then continued to share ingredients with Tim until another two lunches were compiled.

"If you have a minute, can I speak to you? Alone?" Zach added with a glance over Carli's shoulder at Tim and Ethan.

"We'll leave," Tim offered, taking his plate and a bag of chips with him as he pushed through the door.

"Any reason why we shouldn't take out a couple of the horses?" Ethan asked Zach, poised to follow Tim into the dining room.

He shook his head. "We feed at six. They get a little anxious if they aren't back in the barn by then."

Ethan smiled around his bite of sandwich and left the two of them in the kitchen.

Carli crossed her arms and leaned a hip against the counter. She remained quiet while Zach seemed to have a mini-conversation with himself.

"Today is Alyssa's eighteenth birthday. I had planned to take her to Laramie for dinner, and give her this," he explained, and pulled the ring box from his pocket.

Reaching out to take it, she raised her brows when she saw the setting. "You plan to propose? That's great, Zach. She'll love this." She returned the box and waited. There was more he wanted to tell her.

"If she says yes, I want to have her live with me. I know it isn't traditional," he held up his hand to stall Carli's opinion, if she had one, "but she needs to get out of that house."

"I have no issue with you and Alyssa living together. I only question whether or not the lodge is the place."

"I was thinking of Cabin 9. A few renovations, and it would suit the both of us fine." He held his breath as Carli seemed to think about it, then added, "We would both be here full-time. And it wouldn't be permanent. We would be saving up to get our own place. That could be done quicker if I got a raise." He watched as Carli uncrossed her arms, settled her hands on her waist, and raised a single brow. Pressing on, he offered, "I could use the money Bear left me to do the remodeling, and it would be the safest place—"

"Dad left you money?" she interrupted.

"I assumed he gave everyone a check with the letters he wrote."

"If he did, no one has said anything. It doesn't make sense that you use your own money to upgrade the cabin. Use what he gave you as a down payment on something that would suit the two of you." After a moment of thought, she added, "I think it would be great to have both of you here full-time," she paused. "A raise? Until I can hire someone else, you'll be responsible for more with Ray ... gone. I'll look at the books and see what I can do."

He grinned, but at her next words, became serious.

"Have you asked Alyssa to remain here instead of going to school? You know how Dad felt about a college degree, and I think she should be given the choice."

He nodded, realizing all his planning could be for nothing if Lys chose to attend UW.

"She's never admitted to anything that goes on in the Lockhart house," she dropped her hands and her voice. "You be careful. If Jim feels threatened, there's no way to know for sure how he'll react. You want to convince her to marry you, persuade her to press charges against that bastard." Carli's tone seethed with anger. "Alyssa is welcome to live here whenever she wants."

She waited for understanding to show in Zach's eyes. Leaving him alone in the kitchen, her gut told her not all was as it appeared to be.

Ethan and Tim talked quietly on the veranda.

Placing her fingers in the front pockets of her jeans, she looked across the empty parking lot. "Judging by the length of the shadows, I would say we have enough time to ride to the waterfall and back before dinner."

'You'll be one mouth less tonight. I'm meeting a friend in Laramie." Tim tipped his head back and waited to see what look Carli would give him.

Her eyes twinkled with knowing, and she turned up a corner of her mouth. "You and Charlie have a fabulous time. I won't wait up."

He chuckled. "Bet you a hundred bucks I'm back before midnight."

She nodded at him, then turned to Ethan. "Ready?"

"Always." He rose to join her and they descended the steps. Taking the path between the lodge and the barn, he draped his arm around her shoulders.

Perhaps she's gained a new best friend, Tim thought.

CHAPTER 46

It was 5:30 p.m. when J.J. called Zach.

"Are you at the lodge?" he asked, pulling into the drive, the bed of the truck and the front seat loaded with boxes of groceries.

"I'm the only one here," Zach answered, placing the dust cloth and polish back inside the tote.

"Then meet me around back."

Zach replaced the cleaning tote inside the supply closet, then went through the lobby to the kitchen, where he opened the door. J.J. was just backing the truck up to the steps of the veranda. While groceries were stored, he shared the outcome of his earlier conversation with Carli.

"If that's the way Carli feels, perhaps she'll give me a raise, too."

J.J. tossed the empty boxes into the bed of the truck. Tanner's Outdoor Adventures had stressed recycling as a way to conserve resources and preserve habitats long before it was the popular thing to do, and had a bin that was collected and transported to a recycling plant in Cheyenne. It was on his way to the front parking lot, where he would leave the truck in its usual spot.

"How many do we have for dinner?" he asked, pausing by the open driver's side door.

"*You*, have three. I'll be with Lys. Tim is meeting a friend in Laramie. That leaves you, Carli, and Ethan."

J.J. smiled. "Good thing I only picked up three filet mignons," he teased, knowing they were one of Zach's favorites.

Not to be outdone, Zach returned, "But I'll be dining lakeside, unchaperoned, with a beautiful woman." The smile remained on his face as J.J. shook his head and drove the truck around to the front of the lodge.

If he was to pick Lys up at six-thirty, he was almost late in getting ready. He had packed an ice chest earlier with what he could find in the fridge, but added a bottle of sparkling water and a few cookies from the bakery box J.J. had purchased. Apparently, the ranch hand missed Alyssa's baking. Setting the cooler by the door, he took the stairs two at a time to shower and change.

Ignoring any negative thoughts that tried to intrude and place doubts as to Alyssa's answer to wear his ring and live at the lodge, he instead practiced what he would say. They would discuss what her plans were after graduation, then he would share with her his thoughts for their future. With the ring in his pocket and his hat in his hand, he descended the stairs. He smiled and shook his head at the smell of charcoal coming from the barbecue on the back veranda. The cooler was loaded into his truck, and he was off to ensure himself a future with the woman of his heart.

《《—》》

"With everything that has happened, you haven't been to see the other reason people come to the Preserve," Carli said, pulling the saddle from Lady's back and walking into the tack room.

"The rest of Little Shy River and William's Lake?" Ethan asked, following her with Samson's saddle.

"You've heard of it?" She paused in adjusting the saddle and pad on the rack to look at him.

"It was—" he stopped himself from mentioning the FBI file and substituted, "on the map in the lodge."

He seemed to handle the tack fine, and it didn't take but a couple of times in the saddle for him to regain his seat on a horse. Though he had shaved that morning, the beginning of a 5 o'clock shadow gave him a rugged look that appealed to her.

"Tomorrow. We'll pack some lunch and I'll show you the tire swing we used to jump off of at William's Lake." It hadn't escaped her notice that as she talked, he moved closer to her, and now stood only a couple inches away.

"Do you mean," he began, and leaned forward, "that I'll be able to view you in a bikini?" he finished, his lips hovering above hers.

"Perhaps, if it warms up another thirty degrees. Or if you're lucky, less." Her eyes searched his and recognized the familiar desire.

"I've been known to be a gambling man," he confessed, then, without touching any other part of her, pressed his lips to hers.

It wasn't enough, she decided. Tipping her head to the side, she traced Ethan's bottom lip with the tip of her tongue. He captured it, sucked it into his mouth, and she gave in first to the need to touch him, placing her hands on his chest to steady her suddenly tilting world. The ring of her cell phone was preempted by the sneezing of one of the horses tied outside the tack room. She reluctantly stepped back, her fingers lingering on his shirt as she opened her eyes and placed the phone to her ear.

"Yes, we're back." She kept her gaze on the man in front of her and smiled slightly. "If you're grilling, the least I could do is feed," she paused, listening to J.J. "Of course I remember who gets what. We'll see you in about thirty minutes."

"Trading the feeding of many for the dinner of a few seems fair," Ethan said, then watched the seat of her jeans as she left the tack room.

"If you'll brush these two, I'll start with the feed cart," she called over her shoulder as she made her way down the aisle to the stack of hay just outside the opposite end of the barn and the feed room.

He stayed where he was, enjoying the silhouette of the woman whose body had him always thinking of sex, but her mind and talent encouraging him to consider other things.

Making quick work of brushing the dried sweat stains and checking feet for stones, he put Samson and Lady in their respective stalls. Hanging the halters in the tack room, he spied a tub labeled 'treats', and, prying off the lid, found apple-scented horse cookies. Taking a few, he returned to their stall doors. Holding them out to Samson and then Lady, he was fascinated by the many ways their upper lips maneuvered to take the treat.

"Dessert before dinner can spoil their appetite," she commented with humor as she lifted a flake of hay over the barn door to land in the feeder, then dumped a bucket of pellets into the feed bin mounted on the wall.

He raised a brow, watching Samson devour his pellets. "I don't believe they are aware of your philosophy."

She chuckled and continued down the shed row for the horses that were kept in the larger, outside pens during the warmer months. He helped her throw hay and empty buckets, checked the water tubs, and ensured that everyone was eating and feeling alright. The last stall inside the barn, across from the feed room, was stacked with straw and bagged shavings.

"These are left over from the winter. We bed the stalls to help keep the horses warm. About once a week everything is cleaned out and fresh straw or shavings is laid down," she explained from behind him.

"I thought maybe you used the straw for hay rides," he said almost innocently enough that she wondered if she imagined his hidden meaning.

"No wagon, but that's an idea. Perhaps a ride to William's Lake for a cookout or a swim to cool off might be something that would interest the guests."

He turned toward her, circled his arms around her waist, then moved her so she was inside the room, backing up toward the straw bales. "I think one would have to get hot first, before they cool down."

Her arms looped around his neck and her lips were too inviting for him to ignore. The fire that sparked between them was immediate and consuming. Straw that had fallen on the floor was raked to the side and seemed to beg to be taken advantage of, so he angled Carli in that direction. A step later, his shirt was pulled from his jeans, her tender fingers bringing fuel to the fire as it spread across his belly and up his torso. He broke the kiss long enough to help her remove his shirt, but before he could recapture her mouth, her lips were pressed to the center of his chest. The unexpected stuttering of his heart caught his breath, and when she looked at him with her brilliant hazel eyes, he inhaled deeply with a soul-felt knowing.

The touch of her hands on the button of his jeans brought him back to the urgency of needing Carli. Returning the gesture, her jeans were undone, his hand slipping skillfully inside. One moment is all he wanted to languish with the feeling that he was in love with this woman. It refused to dissipate with the texture of her skin, the taste of her mouth as their tongues tangled. Sliding her jeans down to give him access to what he wanted, caused her knees to weaken. Laying her in the straw, he chuckled as she hurriedly pushed his jeans away from what she sought. The laughter morphed to a groan as her fingers wrapped around him.

Any thoughts she had of a slow exploration and what she knew would be completion, was whisked away when Ethan rolled her under him. Her boots, in the way of her jeans, were toed off to land somewhere in the pile of bedding. Through the slipperiness of the straw stalks, the restrictions of half-removed clothing, and somewhere in the back of her mind the thought that J.J. might come looking for them if they failed to appear for dinner, she found what she wasn't aware she had been searching for. Ethan's touch ignited her physically. His artistic talent, caring, belief in justice, and daring sense of adventure connected with her heart. Striving to bring her pleasure, she opened her soul to his presence and reveled in the genuine concern for her safety. Instead of closing her eyes and riding the wave of sensations that swamped her, she kept them open and held his gaze. Would he see what she offered him? Would he be brave enough to take it?

Following her lead, he anted up. The love he saw in her eyes was reflected in his own. Their fingers were interlaced and he held them somewhere in the straw above her head. His face was a few inches from hers and it was enough to dissolve the rest of the world. Encased by her wet warmth, he tipped over the edge. Her name on his breath mingled with hers as an escaped sigh.

The truth was there between them, sparkling with something from the ether. He wouldn't ask her to leave this place where she spent her childhood and planned her future. Without forming the thought, or the multitude of arguments his mind might devise, he knew that if he wanted to live, to thrive in this life, then he would have to make a choice. Funny how the change, the decision, didn't raise great anxiety in his brain as it began again to function in the present.

She didn't want to speak first and break the spell that seemed to still be in place around them. So she smiled. He smiled back then rolled away from her. Above the scent of straw and horses, she smelled the barbecue. They began to straighten their clothes, pulling on boots, and finding their way to their feet.

He extended a hand to help her up. "Is it just me, or does lunch seem like it was days ago?" he asked, plucking straw from Carli's hair as she tucked her shirt into her jeans.

"It's all the physical activity," she offered, then laughed with him. "And the air. It seems that only when I am home do I have an appetite that rivals these guys," she gestured as they walked down the barn aisle to the horses munching on their hay.

J.J. eyed them both as they approached the back steps of the veranda. "Everyone alright?" he asked.

Ethan and Carli exchanged a look, but it was Carli who answered. "We were just discussing appetites."

"And observing the fulfillment of them," Ethan added.

J.J. raised a brow as Carli glanced at Ethan and tried to suppress a smile.

"Hungry?" he asked, lifting the lid of the barbecue to remove the steaks.

"Insatiable lately," Ethan answered, earning a chuckle disguised as a cough from Carli.

J.J. led them through the door to the kitchen, missing the piece of straw that Ethan removed from her hair and tossed on the veranda.

«《——》»

The only vehicle in the driveway was Alyssa's Honda. The house was dark except for a light at the back. *She must be in the kitchen,* Zach thought, and his stomach rumbled with hunger. The excitement he felt at the prospect of seeing her was something he wondered if he would ever get used to, or if it would fade over time.

The sun had set and it was on the far side of twilight. He mounted the three steps and knocked on the doorframe. There were a few moments of silence, then the screen door opened. Instead of giving him a hug and a kiss, as was her traditional greeting, she said a quick hello, then turned to close and lock the door. As if anyone would burglarize the Lockhart home. It was obvious from the state of the structure that there wasn't anything, besides what stood in front of him, of value in the house.

"Hey," he said softly, catching her around the waist as she tried to walk past him. When she looked up at him questioningly, he kissed her gently. "Happy Birthday, Alyssa."

"Thanks."

Even through the lip-gloss he could feel the wound on her lower lip. Deciding he would wait until they had set up their picnic to ask her about it, he walked her to the truck and held open the passenger door for her. Well acquainted with how she moved, he noticed there was stiffness. Defensiveness. His brows drew together in the beginning of a scowl.

She seemed to relax a little on the drive to William's Lake. Her ramblings regarding events at school and the conference via texting that morning with Carli just seemed to fill the space of the cab with white noise. He was careful to keep anger from his voice and make the appropriate sounds to reassure her that he was indeed listening.

He turned off the paved road and drove the short distance to the water's edge. Handing Alyssa the blanket, he grabbed the ice chest and they set up in their usual place. It was his turn to carry the conversation as he unpacked the cooler and poured the fizzy water into plastic cups.

"Cheers," he toasted and touched his cup to hers. He sipped, then figured that delaying the conversation would only make things more uncomfortable between them.

"Lys," he waited for her to look at him. "I have some things I need to talk to you about, and I don't know how ..."

"Is everything alright?"

"You tell me. And I want the truth. How badly did Jim hurt you?"

She swallowed the bite she had taken without chewing. How could he know? She had used make-up, and it was dark. "What do—"

"Stop lying. I bought it the first dozen times you told me, 'I'm not graceful'. I've seen you carry plates stacked high, ride a horse, clamber over boulders on a hike without skinning a knee. 'I tripped on the steps', 'I banged my head on the door knob picking up something I dropped'. Enough. Tell me the truth. You don't have to protect him." His voice rose with each statement, and now she was half-turned to the side, away from him.

He reached out with both hands, took her shoulders, and wouldn't allow her to get by with the flinch. "Damn it, Lys. I've never hit you. I never will. I may raise my voice, get angry, but I love you. I would never hurt you that way."

"I don't mean for it to happen. It just does. I can't help it," she said, her words full of apology.

"Can't help what?" he softly asked.

"I always do things wrong."

"No, you don't. I've seen you work all around the lodge. You do things right. There are a lot of times you do stuff the rest of us don't. You see what needs to be done, and you do it. When Jim hits you," he paused, put his fingers under her chin and turned her head to face him, "he's the one who's wrong. It's not normal to take out *his* anger at himself, *his* frustrations over his shortcomings, on you, Lys. He's been beating you to make himself feel worthy. Superior. In control of something in his life where he feels so very out of control."

She blinked at him. How could he know? She hadn't ever thought to look at it that way. "Where did you get those ideas from?"

"My sister. She studied Psychology before switching her major to Political Science. I used to read and edit her papers," he shrugged. "What matters is that you don't have to stay there. You're eighteen today. A legal adult. You can walk away, Lys."

His hand slid from her shoulder to her fingers, where he picked them up from her lap and held them, interlaced through his own.

She opened her mouth to speak, but he told her, "Wait. It makes sense that if I suggest you leave, that I offer you some place to go. But before I do that, I need to know what your plans are. After graduation."

Her head was spinning with all that Zach was saying. "I'll keep working at the lodge," she began. The tears gathered in her eyes and her voice started to hitch as she thought of the check her father had taken yesterday morning. "I mean, it's not like I have money to go to college. And ... even if I did ... how would I ... he would never ..."

His thumbs wiped away the tears that tracked down her cheeks. "Do you want to go to school?" he asked, thinking of the check that Bear had left him. He may not need a down payment if Alyssa was elsewhere.

She hesitated. What did it matter if she wanted to go to college? Any chance of that occurring was snatched from her. "Yes. I had been carrying around a brochure about UW for weeks. They have an education program. I thought that being a teacher would be a schedule Daddy could ... live with," she finished, then began to cry in earnest. The vision of the rifle in her face and the verbal threat made her shiver and feel hopeless to control the stream of tears.

"Hey, Lys. You're alright," Zach murmured, shifting closer to wrap his arms around her shaking body. This was not going the way he had envisioned it. "Tell me what has you so upset. If it's not having money to go to school, Bear left me some. It was in the envelope with the letter everyone received at the reading after the funeral."

"Bear gave me a check, too. But … Daddy found it …" her sobs kept her from finishing.

"Oh, shit. He found the money, and that's what pissed him off enough to … to do this to you?"

He held her face in his hands. Her tears had begun to flush away the makeup she had applied. When his thumb touched the bruise under her eye, she flinched. He ground his teeth.

"What else did he do? He hit you at least twice. Did he kick you?"

She shook her head.

"Threaten you?"

She nodded hesitantly.

"With what?" he asked, struggling to keep his voice level to not scare her.

Closing her eyes so she wouldn't have to see the anger in Zach's, she told him everything. "I was leaving for school. My backpack wasn't zipped all the way. Somehow, he had gotten a new rifle. It was on the couch. I was afraid he would sit on it and it would go off. I reached out to move it, and he came up behind me. Told me to not touch it. I jumped. The envelope and information from the college fell out. He read it and … and … Zach, I've never seen him so angry. He hit me. When I was on the floor and started to get up, he took the rifle and …" her breath stopped in her chest. Zach was silent. He hadn't moved. Hadn't said anything. Would it matter if she told him the rest of it?

"Finish it. Tell me everything. Don't keep it inside where it'll fester into some nasty wound. He's given you enough of those. Don't allow him anymore."

Her eyes were open now and searched his. There was understanding, a tense anger, and the love she knew he felt for her. She swallowed, and said, "He put the rifle in my face and told me that if I left, he would come after me."

She waited for Zach to explode. Expected him to swear or to look for something to break, or hit. Instead, he wrapped his arms around her and held her. He whispered things like, 'it will be alright', and, 'he won't hurt you ever again', and, 'I love you, Alyssa'. It was the last that she clung to, the only thing she believed. The first was a wish, the second not even a promise worth making. But she let him hold her. It was here that she found some measure of safety, a chance to catch her breath before fortifying inner walls and deciding how to stay out of her father's way.

His mind spun with the fear she must have felt. The physical body would heal, but a rifle used to threaten a life would leave a deeper scar. Setting aside his own rage, he began to reorder his plan.

"You have to tell Shaun," he urged her, moving away so he could see her face in the moonlight. "No. Don't shake your head. If Jim is in jail, he can't hurt you. I'll give you the money to attend UW in the fall. You would make a wonderful teacher," he smiled at her, tucking a strand of hair behind her ear.

"If I tell Shaun, there will be a trial. Then I'll have to tell everyone. And even if he goes to prison, he'll get out one day. And he'll make good on his threat."

"One step at a time. We'll tell Shaun. Maybe you can make a statement to the lawyers or the judge. But that's later. Right now, you can't go home. If you go back there, Lys, he could kill you. I refuse to give him the opportunity."

"I don't have—"

"Yes, you do. Come to the lodge. Stay with me. At least until the fall semester begins, then you can live on campus. You'll meet a lot of new people ..." he swallowed. Hard. She could meet someone else. Someone who was smarter, would make more money, give her things he couldn't.

She tipped her head to the side. There was more that Zach wasn't saying. Shifting, she laid her hand on his thigh and felt something in his pocket. It wasn't his keys. This was square and hard.

"What's this?"

"Nothing."

"Zach—"

"The most important thing—"

"Is for you to be honest. You push me to tell you about … stuff, and now you're holding back? How hypocritical."

He scowled. "Now, wait a minute. Your daddy using you as a punching bag is very different from me asking you to—" he stopped.

Alyssa's hand cupped the box in his pocket. With a corner of her mouth tipped up, she asked, "Zach Murphy, were you going to ask me to marry you?"

Possible answers chased themselves through his mind. The consequences, some pleasant, others not, caused him to stall a little too long.

"If you were, and now you're not, is that because you're embarrassed by what happened to me?"

"God, no, Alyssa. I would never be ashamed of you."

"Then you're afraid if I go to school, I won't come back." At his moment of silence, she continued, "Some of the classes I can take online, others I can drive to the campus, but then come home." She watched the tic in his jaw. Shaking her head, she told him, "I have no interest in being with anyone else. I love you, Zach. I have since you came to the lodge."

"I don't want to hold you back."

"You're not," she said softly. "I can go to school and find a teaching job close to the Preserve. Maybe even in Centennial."

"So you'll tell Shaun. And you'll let me pay for … I don't know how much it costs to go to college, but I'll give you what I have."

"And …" she encouraged him when he stopped before telling her what she wanted to know.

"And Carli won't mind if you stay at the lodge."

"With you."

"With me?"

"Yes. Married people usually live together."

"Lys—"

She put her finger to his lips. There would never be anyone else for her. It didn't matter that she was only eighteen. She knew herself and she knew Zach, better than what she believed. He loved her, and that was real. As angry as he was at her father, he controlled it. No, she was wrong. Not all men hit when things didn't go their way. Zach was a much different caliber of man than her father. Even knowing what she had been through, he wanted her to be his wife, would consent to send her away to college because it was what she wanted. Her heart overflowed with the realization of what Zach was willing to sacrifice for her.

"Tell me what you planned to say, how you wanted tonight to be," she said.

Her tears had dried. With the admission of what she had endured, there was an inner strength that emerged. She wasn't upset. Alyssa was the smart, levelheaded, beautiful woman he had fallen in love with two years ago. He had never kept anything from her. If she was to make a choice, then she should have the facts.

"I wanted to take you out to one of the best restaurants in Laramie. A candlelit dinner, your favorite dessert, and then ask you about UW. Bear left me money, and instructions, that I might use it for the down payment on a house. It's not much, but it would be a start. What you found," he fished the jewelry box from his pocket, "is the promise ring I was going to give you. After college, if you planned to attend, I would have given you a real engagement ring. Well, assuming you wanted to marry me." He sighed. "When you called in sick, then put off having dinner with me, I was concerned. Seems I had a right to be," he kept his gaze on her face, seeing the bruise, the split lip. "I asked Carli if we could move into Cabin 9. It would take some remodeling, but Carli said the Preserve would pay for it."

She wasn't surprised. Zach was good at planning. It wasn't unusual for him to offer suggestions to clients when they inquired about amenities or what activities were available, depending on the season. He had thought out every contingency, even the one where he guessed what occurred yesterday.

"So, ask," she said.

He looked at her, puzzled.

"You said you had everything planned. We talked about school—"

"You're going?"

"I'll speak with Ms. Hatch on Monday about loans and scholarships. Save the money Bear gave you. So, ask."

"You'll talk to Shaun? Tell him everything? You'll press charges?"

She nodded, reluctantly.

"Then, Alyssa Lockhart, I promise to wait for you. I love you, and some day, when you're ready, you can be my wife. This," he said and opened the box, "is your agreement to remember I'm here. Will you wear it?"

She disentangled herself from him enough to take the box and peer at the ring.

"It's a sapphire, to match your eyes, and two diamonds on the side. The ring is silver. It's the best I could do with what money I had saved—"

She again stopped his words with a finger to his lips. He was nervous and rambling, and she knew he must feel the same thousand butterflies in his stomach that she had in hers.

"No," she told him.

Zach's eyes grew wide, his jaw slack. "No?" he whispered, dazed with disbelief.

"No, Zach Murphy. I won't 'wait until I'm ready'. If I accept this ring, this is a promise of marriage. We're engaged. There won't be anyone else. I don't have to think about it."

She didn't know if she recognized fear, but had a tremble of her own. What if Zach was buying time for himself? What if *he* wasn't ready to marry *her*? Setting the ring box on the blanket, she began to climb to her feet.

"Wait. Not so fast," he snagged her waist and gently tugged her back down in front of him. "You mean you want this to be your engagement ring?"

She nodded.

"You would marry me ..."

"Tomorrow."

He took the ring from the box and held her left hand. "Alyssa, will you give me everything I want in this world by becoming my wife?"

With a smile that rivaled the brightness of the moon, she answered, "Yes."

He slipped the ring on her finger, then kissed her knuckles. Her other hand cupped his jaw, redirecting his lips to her own. The first kiss was full of sweetness, of promise. When he released her ringed hand, she removed his cowboy hat, and the kiss changed to one of desire.

She laid her hand on his thigh, sliding it slowly up to the waist of his jeans. Tugging at his shirt until it was untucked, she slid her hands around his waist and up his back. The chill of the night seemed nonexistent. His tongue and lips created the excitement she had become addicted to, while his hands moved up her arms to her shoulders.

"Not unless you want to," he spoke against her lips.

She nodded her head. "I want to have all of you."

His agreement was in the kiss as he laid her gently back on the blanket. With one hand, he pushed the cooler out of the way and in that direction of the box lunches. He stretched out one leg and heard the bottle of water hit the dirt. Wondering if he remembered to put the cap on was a flash in his mind as Alyssa kissed his neck and then captured his lip between her teeth. Then nothing mattered except the two of them.

Through a less-than-graceful coordination, he managed to relieve her of her coat and top, while she unbuttoned his shirt. Sitting up to pull his arms free he struggled with his boots, and by the time he returned his attention to her, she was wearing her bra, underwear, and a grin.

497

Zach's answering smile was full of appreciation. Her perfect breasts, which complimented the rest of her curves, looked more inviting than ever encased in lace. Unsure of the color, and realizing it didn't matter, he enjoyed the contrast between her skin and the material. When she reached her hand out toward him, he could do no other than go to her. The goose bumps on her flesh had him pulling the edge of the blanket around them. He kissed her then, and knew that when his thumb stroked over her pebbled nipples, it was him and not the temperature that elicited her reaction.

The familiarity they had with each other's bodies was about to change greatly. Zach had been with only one other girlfriend, and knew that he would be Alyssa's first. The material that she hadn't removed, he did, placing his hands and lips on the newly exposed flesh. She helped him remove his jeans, and there, in the space of three breaths, he knew he had never been more in love with her, or more scared, in his life. Taking the condom from the pocket of his jeans, he covered himself.

There was so much of him that she wanted to feel and experience. She took his hand and guided it where she wanted it. Instead of fear or uncertainty, she was filled with trust and love. Finally, after so much time, countless nights where they stopped, though neither wanted to, they would finally know what it was like to be with each other completely.

The caresses and kisses continued to heat the skin and excite the blood. He wanted to do it right, but soon became lost in the feel of Alyssa and was driven by his care for her and the base need to lay claim to her. She wore his ring, not as a promise that sometime in the future she may want to be his wife, but an acknowledgement of her love for him and her desire to spend the rest of her life committed to their marriage. Wanting to treat her gently, he was moving slow.

"Zach, I'm not fragile. I won't break," she told him, his face above her, held between her hands.

Pushing into her with one thrust, he pressed his lips to her shoulder. There was no one around to hear her, no reason for either of them to still the sounds of pleasure.

"Are you alright?" he asked against the tender skin on the side of her neck.

"Yes. For the first time in a long time, I'm really better than alright."

Her body, new to the intrusion, but welcoming the sensations he continued to generate, began to move in an innate dance. There was something that she was reaching for, had experienced it before with Zach and his clever fingers, and wondered if it would be the same this time. So consumed in the feeling of finally having all of Zach, she didn't care what went where, only that the intimacy they shared never end.

Caught between his libido pushing him to find the release that he had dreamed of, and his mind wanting to draw out the experience, was the thrill that he was finally where he wanted to be. All those thoughts and pumping blood and rushing hormones tossed him ruthlessly over the edge. Resting his forehead on hers, his breath came in deep rushes. He had brought Alyssa to completion enough times that he knew he had left her behind. With his lips on hers, and one hand where they were joined, it was only a few moments before she trembled around him.

She sighed and relaxed, but immediately missed him when he moved away and out from under the folded blanket. Watching as he pulled on his jeans, then walk to his truck, she realized the feeling she was immersed in was happiness. There were no second thoughts about accepting his ring or giving herself to him. Putting her hand out in front of her, she gazed at the gift.

He wandered back towards her and couldn't keep the smile from his face. They were closer to making their future solid, permanent. He crouched down next to her, taking her hand and kissing it as he had done when he first slid the ring on her finger.

"We didn't get a chance to finish your birthday dinner," he told her, realizing his appetite had been more than filled.

"Amazing how certain ... activities can make me famished."

"It's getting colder. You should get dressed."

She searched for her clothes and tried to put them on under the blanket. "Well, this is silly," she muttered, and tossed the cover aside, standing without a stitch on to conceal her body.

He stood and backed up a step. His initial reaction was that someone would see her. What he viewed had an immediate effect on the fit of his jeans. He watched, fascinated with her movements and the order in which she clothed herself. Not ever having observed a woman get dressed, he vowed he would make an excuse to see her do it every day. Curling up the corner of his mouth, he admitted it would serve as a visual to what he would do at the end of each day.

The meal of leftovers and bubbly water were consumed among conversation about the future, and touches. It seemed that neither could exist more than a few moments without feeding the other a kiss or a caress.

"You're coming to the lodge with me, right?" he asked.

"Yes. I can get some of my things from the house tomorrow. There's only two months left of school. It would be easier to be at the Preserve. I could help out before and after school. And I'll get to see you every day." An intimate, knowing smile was shared between them.

They packed up the truck and drove to the lodge. He set the cooler inside the front door. All the lights were off, except the usual ones over the guest counter. Hands held between them, he led her upstairs to his room. He knew they would have to deal with Jim Lockhart tomorrow, and Alyssa's father wouldn't be so eager to let her go.

CHAPTER 47

Dim lights reflected off the glasses, half-filled with wine, and the silver utensils that rested next to the plates. They had ordered and were enjoying their salads before the arrival of the entrees. The youth of the waitress seemed misplaced in the quaint hotel restaurant with its attempts at luxury and the soft jazz emanating from the speakers. If Tasha, their waitress, was uncomfortable serving two gay men, she didn't show it.

Charlie had been uncharacteristically quiet, but since Tim didn't know him intimately, as this was only their third meeting, he wondered if perhaps his new friend was tired from the flight, or just in a mood.

He sipped his wine. "You seem … preoccupied, Charlie. Is everything alright?"

Chocolate brown eyes tinged with hurt settled on Tim's features. "I'm at an age, and have been living comfortably long enough with my sexuality, that this shouldn't bother me. It just seems that about the time I notice more acceptance in society, I meet up with someone of Mr. Randall Buford's bigotry, and it just ruins my day."

"This was the man on the charter flight?"

Charlie pushed his fork around in his lettuce, then finally set it against the plate. "Yes. A cattle and oil man from Texas who was in San Francisco inquiring after a yacht of some sort, then flew to Laramie to watch his youngest son compete in a high school rodeo competition."

"A man like that, despite his money, keeps himself isolated. I imagine a flight attendant of your *kind* put a crick in his hat."

Charlie shook his head and sipped his wine. "Probably the reason I usually stick with commercial flights to major cities. Mr. Buford, and a handful of assistants and secretaries, were relegated to retrieving their own refreshments. He was quite embarrassing. Told me to stay away from him and those that accompanied him. Threatened to force the plane to land on the nearest dirt airstrip and walk me off the aircraft at gunpoint ..." Charlie's eyes refocused on Tim's for a moment, then he looked down as his fingers twirled his wine glass. "He surely wasn't accustomed to being around gay men. That I can understand. Dealt with his kind before. But the comment that ... I should have been drowned at birth," his gaze again met Tim's, "was a new one. It seems that no matter how I try to protect myself, or how much education is available regarding homosexuality, it occasionally shocks me that there are still people that harbor such hatred." Charlie's voice grew quiet.

Tim placed his hand on Charlie's and gave a reassuring squeeze. "It may seem that there are more people who don't accept or don't allow anything that is different from what they are. The misunderstanding and misinformation that homosexuality is a choice or a disease is fading away. Usually it's the older generations, those from particular parts of the county, or from certain religious backgrounds that continue with intolerance."

A ghost of a smile curled the corners of Charlie's lips. "I've always believed that every human is one of God's children. If He wanted us different, He would have made us differently."

Tim gave one more squeeze to Charlie's hand before releasing it.

"I have been remiss in pursuing any religious sect. The church that my family attends groups homosexuals and people of varied ethnic backgrounds together. Neither are accepted within their ranks. Maybe that is one reason why intolerance continues to be pervasive in those circles," Charlie said.

Tim swallowed his bite of salad and shook his head. "I don't think lumping all religions, or even all spiritual leaders, into the pile of propagating prejudice is fair. Then you would be in the same category as your Mr. Buford."

The waitress arrived with their meals, and the flow of conversation changed from subject to subject. Charlie was excited and supportive to hear of Tim's plan for his new position at *International Views.*

"Have you been to New York?"

"A few times," Charlie answered.

"I hear they have openings for flight attendants at the major airlines." He left the invitation implied.

Charlie raised a brow. "I've been on the West Coast for ten years. I have friends, my apartment."

Tim shrugged. "I can introduce you to my friends on the East Coast," his tone became more serious. "I've enjoyed your company, Charlie. I think we can have something, if we want. It's alright if you're not interested."

"And I like you, Tim. Believe me, I comprehend how difficult it can be to find the right partner. I just don't know if I can uproot my life again."

"Understandable. But the offer is there. Even if you would just like to meet for dinner when you have a long lay over."

Talk shifted to one of recent events regarding world news. Tim enjoyed the lively conversation, while Charlie kept Tim's offer in the front of his thoughts. Insisting he pay the bill, Charlie left a heavy tip for the waitress since they occupied the table for a few hours and she continued to pay attention to them as customers.

Charlie walked Tim to the company van in the parking lot. "Cold," he said, realizing he didn't bring a coat with him from his hotel room.

"This is the last of the freezing temperatures. Should be reaching into the seventies by next month," Tim replied. "I had a good time. Thank you."

"I did as well."

They stood beside the van, Tim a little taller than Charlie. He nervously tossed his ponytail over his shoulder, then lowered his lips an inch at a time. The tentative brush of firm lips sent a thrill through him. Charlie angled his head to the side and returned an open-mouthed kiss. The intimate touch sparked the fire. Tim cupped Charlie's jaw and enjoyed the feel of the man's warm palm on his chest. Lips and tongue tasted wine and coffee and the sugared dessert, as well as the desire. Tim stepped back and ended the kiss, temporarily feeling the burn of Charlie's whiskers against his own cheeks.

"We could be really good together. Think about New York."

Charlie nodded, then watched as Tim climbed into the van.

The window rolled down, and Tim stuck his head out. "Have a safe flight."

Charlie smiled, then waved. He watched until the van disappeared down the road, and on the way back to his room wondered how much it would cost to ship his belongings across the country.

《《—》》

It happened in the early evening. The prosecuting attorney, a close colleague of Maxwell Stevens, pushed to have the arraignment before the weekend. The family, according to Sheriff Tanner, declined to be present when he was notified that the court appearance was scheduled. Three miles was the distance between the Cheyenne Police Station, which housed the city jail, and the courthouse.

Ray's expression was solemn. His court-appointed attorney would meet him inside. Realizing Darla would tell all in order to save her own hide, his hope now was that he could make bail. He was good at deception, since he had years of practice. Crossing the state line, or several, would be no problem. Perhaps he could disappear so even Worthington wouldn't be able to locate him. What he couldn't do, is spend the rest of his life in prison.

Of Art and Air

The patrol car stopped in the designated area in front of the courthouse. Two officers exited the vehicle, then opened the back door so Ray could step out and onto the sidewalk. Shaking his head at the handful of protestors, he marveled at the speed with which news traveled. Signs were held that encouraged the death penalty, life without parole, and that the highest level of deception is the betrayal of a trusted friend. Someone on the police force had alerted the media to his arrest, and the whole story of Bear's life, and sudden end, had been splashed on TV and radio.

Partway up the courthouse steps, one of the officers dropped back in a show of keeping the demonstrators away from the one in custody. The silver sedan rolled down its window on the passenger side. People screamed, ducked, and scattered, the protesters abandoning their signs as the *pop-pop-pop* emanated from the car. In the moment of silence after the shots were fired, and before the squeal of tires, intense pain filled Ray's mind. Bullets had entered his left thigh, torso, and shoulder. As his knees crumpled, the concrete steps were unfelt as his body hit them in slow motion. There wasn't a chance for regret, sorrow, or anger. In a flash he understood that this was the end. Unconsciousness took him, then Death. The officers' automatic reaction was to call 911, draw their weapons, memorize the description of the car, verify that no one else had been hurt, and then finally felt for a pulse that steadily slowed, then stopped. Pools of blood spread out and covered the gray cement.

Miles away, the sedan was found abandoned. No prints or hair were left behind that could lead the police to who had driven the car. It was rented, and a false name and address led them to another dead end. The only evidence forensics was able to uncover was residue from the gunshots. No shells. When it was sorted out, the call was made.

"Tanner," Shaun spoke automatically into his phone, not immediately recognizing the number.

"It's Ben. Have you been watching the news?"

505

Shaun rocked forward in the chair, taking his feet from the railing of his porch to the wood slats beneath him. His body tensed, his fingers gripped the phone. "No. What happened?"

"Ray Foster was gunned down on the steps of the Cheyenne Courthouse before his arraignment. He's dead, Shaun."

Squeezing his eyes shut and rubbing his forehead, he attempted to recognize what he was feeling. First, there was nothing. Then shock, disbelief, and finally anger.

"Son of a bitch. Tell me they got the shooter."

"Sorry. The car was dumped. Cleaned," Ben hesitated, not sure how Shaun felt about his father's suspected murderer getting his own, he offered, "I'm sorry. Can I do anything?"

What was there to do? "Someone wanted him dead. Maybe he would have talked, said more about Darla's connection with Worthington. Homicide is handling the case?"

"I'll find out who it was assigned to and let you know."

"Keep an eye on Darla. It could be that whatever happened to Ray may also befall her. Someone wants this to go away."

"A call to the jailhouse will increase her protection. Will you be alright?"

Shaun sighed. "Yes. Thanks, Ben."

He set the phone on the railing next to the glass of whiskey. Since Ray had been killed, would Darla be next? And would it matter if she were? Even if she didn't pull the trigger herself, she was just as guilty for orchestrating the plan. Who would want Ray dead? Someone who thought he knew too much and might be tempted to share the information.

Picking up the whiskey, he drained the liquid in one swallow. He was sorry for another death, sorry they wouldn't be able to use Ray to make more connections with Darla and Worthington and anyone else that thought to gain by Bear Tanner's death. Carli and Samantha. They needed to know. Taking his phone and his glass, he made his way to his kitchen and another serving of fine liquor.

It really didn't amaze him that his sisters had a similar reaction. Sad for Ray's death, anxious to discover who might be behind it. Sam was vague in her answers as to any more unusual occurrences at Crystal Springs Farm. Either she didn't want to worry him, or she had yet to discern which ones were usual happenings on a ranch of that size, and which situations might have been manipulated. Not to be outdone, Carli was just as quiet regarding her whereabouts on the Preserve and what she had been doing, but assured him all was well.

Tomorrow would be Saturday. His official day off. Glancing at the sling, he realized the pain medication must be enhanced with the use of alcohol. An unwise shifting of his elbow told him that wasn't completely true. That would prevent him from doing much work around the house. Maybe he should drive to Cheyenne, see what the cops knew about the shooting. Ethan may have input, or theories. With a fuzzy head induced by the whiskey, he took himself to bed. He had finished the bottle. Perhaps in a sober moment he should consider the implications of that.

«« — »»

"Have you seen the news?" asked the voice around the toothpick held between lips that were partially hidden by a mustache and beard.

"Of course. Three clean shots. The remainder of the funds will be transferred to your account ... now," Worthington said, pressing the computer keys to complete the transaction.

"Nice doing business with you, Boss."

He hung up the phone and leaned back in his chair. Ray won't talk now. He wished he felt as sure about Darla. The attorney will do his part in representing her in court. Her acquittal or sentence was in the hands of the jury and judge. The Preserve was no longer an option. Darla failed to claim the property, and if he made an outright bid, his connection could possibly be linked to her, and he refused to jeopardize his campaign with a sour real estate deal. If it needed to be done, he was sure he could find a way to dispose of his imprisoned partner.

It was cocktail hour at the Club. He promised Rose he would meet her there. Flicking off the desk lamp, he locked his office door behind him. Shaking hands and presenting a pleasant face were the agenda for the evening, as it was never too early to begin collecting votes.

«« — »»

It was late when he stumbled up the steps, the gibbous moon on its descent towards the western horizon. Alyssa's car was parked in its usual place, but due to the hour she would be asleep. Jim wandered through the living room, paused as he passed the kitchen, contemplated having another beer, but continued down the hallway to his own room instead.

He thought about the money in the bank and the repairs that needed to be made to the truck and the house. Better spent there than a donation to the University of Wyoming. Sighing into his pillow, he remembered the gun he had won from Ray and the understanding he and Alyssa now had. He would talk to her in the morning about working full-time at the lodge. After all, the check from Bear Tanner wouldn't last long.

CHAPTER 48

As the sun rose, a slant of light fell across his face. Normally up in the early morning, Shaun's internal alarm clock rolled open his eyes, which resulted in a squint at the bright light, a muttered curse, and an attempt to escape the offending sunshine. He was immediately reminded of his injury as acute agony radiated from ear to knee. Either he had wounded himself during the night, or it was past four hours since his last pain pill. Swinging his legs over the side of the bed, he held his head in his hand while he waited for the room to right itself. Deciding he could navigate his way into the bathroom with little incident, he remembered the whiskey from the previous night, which offered an added incentive to get out of bed.

Thirty minutes later he emerged, ready to face the day. With nothing worth eating in his own fridge, he thought the lodge would be the next best place. Grabbing his keys, phone, badge, and weapon, he stepped outside.

The air was clear, crisp, and the winter chill was gone. Tiny drops of dew clung to pine needles and fern leaves. Birds chattered in the trees and squirrels chased each other up one trunk, jumped to the branch of a nearby tree, then down that trunk to scamper further into the woods that surrounded his home. He shook his head with amusement and climbed into the company van.

Readjusting the rearview mirror, he looked at himself. The slicked back, light blonde hair, clean-shaven face, and street clothes didn't quite cover the justice-searching man inside. Nor did the hours of sleep erase the lines of worry or the edge of pain. Sighing in annoyance, he turned the mirror and started down the drive. Before he reached the highway, his phone vibrated in his pocket. Carli. What did she want this early in the morning?

《《—》》

This had to be a dream, Alyssa thought. The dusting of dark hair on his chest, the growth of a night's beard, his lips relaxed in sleep instead of their easy smile or friendly chatter. She reached out a finger and softly traced his lean, muscled shoulder. What would his skin taste like first thing in the morning? Her curiosity had her leaning forward, placing an open-mouthed kiss on his chest. He tasted like Zach.

His arm curled around her to hold her to him. Without opening his eyes, he stretched, then breathed her in, his nose to the top of her head. She shifted, and when his gaze focused on her, incredibly blue, loving eyes looked back. He kissed her then, slow and thoroughly, his hand moving to brush the blonde stands away from her face. Shifting, he rolled Alyssa under him. With one hand in the drawer at the nightstand, the other holding his weight so he didn't crush her, he went about greeting her properly.

With the condom for protection, he settled between her thighs. "Good morning, Lys. I've been waiting for what seems like forever for you to be here, in this place, so I could say that to you."

She smiled and pulled Zach's lips down to hers while lifting her hips to meet his. Pleasant surprise fluttered through her that it was different than last night, both at William's Lake and when they arrived back at Zach's room. Wondering if it would always be different each time flashed in her mind before all thought burned away as the fire built between them.

Touches and kisses were slow. Sighs and words were whispered. They danced to the edge, and the second time they teetered close, they tumbled off, catching each other. The sun was over the trees by the time he checked the hallway, then took her hand as they descended the stairs.

《《—》》

Ethan's fingers played in her hair. Knowing he had fallen, and hard, it wasn't difficult to imagine waking up this way for the rest of his life. And that could be a problem. As the sun began to rise and the forest creatures initiated their daily routine, he marveled at his ability, only recently, to sleep in total darkness. There were no nightmares, though what he had seen and lived through was never far away. Deciding that the probability of the images fading, and being able to spend the remainder of his days in the presence of the woman lying next to him being equal, he shut the door on the thoughts that reminded him of the myriad ways humans had contrived to wound each other.

The temperature inside Cabin 4 wasn't as cold as it had been. When he tugged the sheet and comforter down, he enjoyed the sight of her shoulder, the curve of her breast, her waist as it dipped in just above her hipbone. Within moments, his sight wasn't the only sense that wanted to experience Carli, so he indulged them. It seemed being with her encouraged him to ... enjoy, whether it was lunch, the view from Wolf's Ridge, or the woman herself.

Fingertips and mouth joined in the exploration. Carli's languid movements, her fingers tunneling through his hair to hold him to her breast, her sighs signaling the release of inhibitions as he was focused solely on the landscape of her body. Feather-light caresses against her ribs, gentle nips along her thighs, the falling open of her knees to display herself before him pushed his senses to their limit. If he was to make this journey, to fly apart, he saw no reason to go alone. As he could have predicted, Carli was a willing traveler, and from the first touch they were both lost.

Pushing her up and over the edge was more heady than anything he had known. He was awarded great pleasure as she shattered around him. Not allowing her the opportunity to fully land on the ground, he covered her body with his and joined them completely. The queen-sized mattress afforded Carli the room to encourage him to his back, where he agreed to shift and relinquish the rhythm to the woman who now was astride his waist.

She took his hands from her hips and interlaced their fingers. Drawing them over his head, she kissed him. Realizing that for the moment she was in control, that her FBI agent allowed her to use him however she wished, brought a surge of gratitude. She took the lead, reveled in the safety she felt in being with him and the trust and love he must have for her, as she felt it in his touch, observed it in his gaze. Enjoying the slow movement of their bodies, the thought crept in that neither of them had said the words. She knew what she felt, and could see the same in Ethan's expressions and responses to her. How important was the phrase? If it was voiced, would it make their absence from each other more difficult? Perhaps it was her musings that enhanced their motions. Before she was ready, or could anticipate, the soft shuddering flowed from her center, out. Not cognizant of any words she might have whispered besides the name of the man that filled her, surrounded her, she rested her head on his shoulder.

Her sweet surrender was unexpected. Squeezing his fingers around her hand, he followed her, drifting, falling, landing softly in the emotions they stirred and sensations that had consumed them.

With some reluctance, she left Ethan and made her way to the bathroom. She thought to bring an extra pair of clothes or a toothbrush with her to Cabin 4, but then remembered he would be gone tomorrow. Fighting off irrational sadness, she stepped under the spray of the shower. Bargaining with herself to forego any tears until Ethan had left, she promised to enjoy their remaining time together.

So caught up in her own conversation, she hadn't heard Ethan open the door and place her clothes on the closed toilet lid. Pulling on her jeans, she paused as she heard his voice from the other room. He was speaking with a serious tone and she wondered if his boss at the FBI had called. Dressed, she finger-combed her hair and opened the bathroom door.

He looked up at her, and though she smiled at him, he recognized a shift from the woman in his bed to the one standing before him, and wondered at the change.

"Yes," he said, then ended the call.

"Am I interrupting?"

"No, but you do provide a very fine distraction," he smiled at her and held out his hand.

She crossed the room and placed her hand in his. He was sitting in one of the chairs, wearing unbuttoned jeans and nothing else. Rising to his feet to meet her, he searched her eyes. Whatever he saw before, was gone.

"Your boss?"

He nodded. "I may have to leave earlier than planned."

"While you're waiting, might as well have breakfast. I'll meet you in the dining room?"

And just like that, her guarded expression was back. He contemplated asking her if she was alright, but he knew she would reassure him that everything was fine.

"I'll meet you there in—" he was interrupted by a car horn.

The puzzled look on Carli's face told him this was not a typical occurrence. Moving to the window, he pushed aside the curtain to look out, his training and a lifetime of city living lending him caution. Carli, with her life experience being mostly here or in primitive villages around the world, simply opened the door and walked out to the small porch. He had pulled on his boots and was pushing his hands through the sleeves of a flannel shirt when the tone of Carli's voice saying his name had him extracting his gun from its holster and grabbing his phone from the table before quickly joining her on the veranda.

"Who is that?" he asked, clicking the safety off and keeping his weapon low by his thigh.

"Jim Lockhart. Alyssa's father. There has been some ..."

"Abuse? The scar over her left eyebrow," he told her when she glanced at him.

"Zach was concerned that Lys was hurt since she called in two days ago. Practically begged me to allow him and Alyssa to live in Cabin 9," she paused as Ethan lifted a brow. "They've been in love since Zach came to work at the lodge over a year ago. He even showed me the ring he was going to give her." She waved away the rest of the details and focused on the truck in front of the lodge. "Seems Jim has become upset since he woke up to find his daughter gone."

The horn continued to sound as Jim shouted, demanding that Zach come outside. Ethan handed her his cell as they began to make their way towards the angry visitor. A moment later, the lodge door opened and Zach stepped out onto the veranda. Within a breath's time, Jim moved to the front of his truck. Zach raised his hands to show that he was unarmed.

Ethan leveled his gun and stepped in front of Carli. "Jim Lockhart. Lower your weapon," he called out to the man holding a rifle aimed at Zach's chest. He heard Carli's voice behind him, and he realized she must be calling Shaun.

Jim shifted his focus from Zach to the man approaching him with gun raised. "Who the hell are you?" he demanded, his gaze bouncing between Ethan and Zach.

"Ethan Brooks, FBI. Now, lower your weapon." He continued to advance, keeping himself between Jim and Carli.

"FBI ain't got no business in this. I'm here to pick up my daughter. This *boy* seems to think he can have her. She needs to come home."

Zach was at the bottom of the steps. The rifle looked familiar. He wondered if that was the one Jim used to scare Alyssa. This was not going how he planned, hoped, the meeting would go with Lockhart.

"Jim, Lys isn't going home with you. We're engaged. She's eighteen and will be living with me here at the lodge."

"The hell she will. Alyssa!"

"She's not coming out—" he began, but was interrupted by the click of the door behind him.

"Seems your *engagement* means nothing," Jim smirked.

"I'll go with you," Alyssa's soft voice floated to everyone.

"No, you can't. Lys—" Zach started to turn, which gave Jim the opportunity to step closer to Zach and load a round in the barrel.

"Yes, I can," she answered.

"He'll hurt you—"

"Shut up, *boy*. You're in enough trouble."

"What?" Zach turned to look at Jim.

"Did you sleep with her?" Jim asked. By the hesitation and the redness that colored Zach's clenched jaw, he knew. "I believe that's rape. Alyssa would never do that."

"She's eighteen. You can't tell her what to do, and I won't let you leave here with her." Zach's anger was tangible.

"If I don't go with him, he'll kill you," Alyssa said, standing behind Zach, her hand on his shoulder.

"No one is going anywhere—" Ethan began, then cursed under his breath.

Jim grabbed Alyssa and shoved her behind him, toward the truck. Zach reacted by reaching out to catch her, but Jim jammed the rifle into Zach's belly. She regained her balance and grabbed her father's arm. Just before Ethan squeezed off a shot, Jim whirled around and knocked her aside with the butt of the rifle. Falling to the ground, she remained there.

So focused on the action playing out in front of him and trying to get a shot, he didn't realize that Carli had moved until she appeared at Alyssa's side. *Shit*, Ethan thought. This situation could end badly, with the parking lot of the lodge littered with bodies. He moved behind Jim, trying to get to Alyssa and Carli.

The crunch of gravel announced the arrival of Shaun. He drove the company van right up to where Jim held the rifle on Zach.

"Good thing you're here, Sheriff. You need to arrest this boy for raping my daughter," Jim began in a self-righteous tone.

Shaun, gun held on Jim, approached from the man's right side. He understood Ethan's intention and needed to keep Jim's attention on him, and away from Agent Brooks.

"Is that true, Zach?" Shaun asked. He would apologize later for the shocked, betrayed look on Zach's face.

"Hell no, Shaun."

"Then why don't we put our weapons down and talk this out," Shaun suggested.

"You should be arresting Jim. He just hit Alyssa with his rifle. And you know this isn't the first time," Zach glared at Shaun.

"Sometimes you have to teach kids right from wrong when they can't figure it out for themselves," Jim said.

"And how often have you had to 'teach' Alyssa, Jim?" Shaun asked, moving closer. He could see that Carli was fine and that Alyssa was cradled in his sister's arms.

Zach answered instead. "All the time. Every time Lys called in sick to work or couldn't go to school. Two days ago he shoved that rifle in her face. I brought her here last night, Shaun. She can't go back with him. She can't."

Shaun, standing in front of Jim and to Zach's left, watched as Carli helped Alyssa to her feet. "That true, Lys?"

With a shaking hand, Alyssa cleared her blonde hair from her face. She could feel the heat from the hit. Most of the stars in her head had cleared, and out of habit and reaction, her hand came to her cheek to test the tenderness. She winced. It was already swelling. This hurt more than his fist. She was aware of Carli's hand on her arm to help steady her, but the sight of her father with the rifle aimed at Zach, his finger on the trigger, stopped her breath. A knowing filled her. If she didn't do something, her father would kill him. Last night she agreed to marry Zach and to talk to Shaun about the abuse. The flood of anger, the years of lying and covering up, swamped her. She made a promise to Zach. His expression pleaded with her now to tell the truth. He wasn't concerned for himself, only that she stay away from her father.

"Yes." The word streamed from her with more force than she thought possible. Pride and love beamed from Zach's face a moment before her father began to turn.

Three shots were fired. Ethan's hit Jim in the back of the leg. That surprise caused Jim to squeeze the trigger, the rifle round embedding itself in the veranda, sending wood splinters in every direction. Shaun's gun, aimed at Jim's shoulder, took the weapon from Jim's hand.

Zach recovered from ducking amongst the flying wood and rushed to Alyssa. She buried her face in his chest, tears of relief streaming down her cheeks that the gun was no longer pointed at the person who meant the most to her.

"I'm alright," Zach continued to repeat as Alyssa held him, her hands roaming his torso and arms searching for a wound.

Shaun kept his gun pointed at Jim as he moved closer. Nudging the rifle further from Alyssa's father, he crouched and spoke quietly as Jim held his left hand to the blood oozing from his right shoulder.

"Of all the scenarios that could have played out on the day Alyssa steps up to admit the years of abuse, and I get to arrest your ass, I never imagined this. Perhaps it's just a little payback for how you've treated your daughter."

Jim stared at Shaun with gritted teeth.

"You have the right to remain silent," Shaun began.

Finishing the Miranda Rights, he glanced up to see Carli on the phone with the 911 dispatcher, and Ethan with the rifle in his hand. Behind him, with lights flashing, was Vince. He signaled his deputy to bring the first aid kit, then stepped aside as Vince packed gauze onto the wounds. Shaun joined Carli and Ethan, who seemed puzzled.

He gestured toward the rifle. "I'll have to take that."

"Shaun, this is Dad's rifle, the one missing from the gun safe in the basement," Carli stated. "Were we wrong about Ray killing Dad? Was it Jim?"

Though she struggled in understanding, and certainly not agreeing, with why Ray had confessed to at least conspiring with

Darla, it didn't make any more sense that Jim would kill Bear. Alyssa relied on the paychecks from the lodge, and Lockhart was dependent on his daughter to bring them home. Was there a burglary that her father didn't even share with Shaun? None of the rifles that were sent to Cheyenne for testing matched with the slug taken from her father's chest.

Shaun turned as more sirens and lights filled the parking lot of the lodge as Stan and the Centennial Ambulance arrived. Not wanting this mystery to complicate matters, he approached Alyssa's father.

"Where did you get the rifle, Jim?"

Stan and Brad worked on recording vitals, starting an IV, and getting Lockhart ready for transport by lifting him onto the gurney.

When Jim remained mute, Shaun threatened, "This is my father's hunting rifle. It's been missing from the lodge for over a week. Unless you tell me where you got it, I'm adding burglary to the charges."

"Ray Foster," was the terse reply. Shaun walked with Stan and Brad as they moved Jim towards the back of the ambulance. "When?"

"Wednesday night. Won it at the—" Lockhart stopped. The back room poker games were illegal.

"Poker table?" Shaun finished for him.

Jim nodded once then looked away.

"Vince, ride with him in the van. Keep me updated on his status," he held Vince's gaze and a whole conversation passed between them. The deputy would stay with the wounded man and call to inform him if Jim made it through surgery.

"Sheriff, Ivison Memorial is dispatching a helicopter to the Centennial Clinic. Two gunshot wounds tends to give a person a ride in a chopper," Stan said and held out a clipboard and pen to Shaun.

He signed and placed it on the gurney at Jim's feet. Stan climbed behind the wheel while he closed the back doors, glancing at Brad pressing cotton wads onto the seeping wounds. A moment later, the siren and lights retreated down the drive.

He returned to the four people that witnessed the shooting.

"You alright?" he asked Zach.

"I am now. And Lys will be, too," he answered, his arm around Alyssa.

Shaun noticed the swelling and discoloration of Alyssa's jaw. "Call Doc Miller," he began, then shifted his gaze to Carli who waved her cell phone.

"Already done. Just waiting for your okay to leave the scene," she said.

"You're pressing charges?" he asked Alyssa.

Without hesitation, she again assured him, "Yes."

He nodded. "Then ask Doc Miller to begin a full report. From the first time you went to see him for a broken bone or stitches, and ending today," he said, emphasizing the last two words.

She nodded and continued to cling to Zach.

Softening his voice, he said, "I'm sorry, Lys. Sorry that CPS from Laramie couldn't step in to do anything, whether from overwork and understaffed or losing the paper trail or ... and I'm sorry I didn't do something—"

"There was nothing for you to do, Shaun. Remember, it was me being clumsy. I ... I could have stopped it sooner if I had told someone," she shook her head. "I was too scared."

"It's over now," Zach told her and held her to his side, his hand caressing her soothingly. He steered Alyssa around Shaun and the blood stains on the gravel to his truck. After helping her in, he slid behind the wheel.

Shaun pushed his fingers through his hair and turned to face Ethan and Carli. "Jim said he won the rifle in the poker game at the bar. Said Ray had it."

Ethan handed it over. "That solves the mystery of the missing rifle. You have my cooperation in collaborating on the paperwork. The Bureau will want your statement of what happened here."

"Of course." Shaun knew it would be more complicated if Jim died from his wounds.

Ethan glanced at the display on his phone, then stepped away to answer it. The look of grave stoicism was familiar to Shaun. He guessed the call was from some director in the FBI and that the topic of conversation would not be a pleasant one. His gaze shifted to Carli as she watched Ethan's back, then turned to face him. She was worried, and sad.

"Will Jim make it?" she asked.

Shaun shrugged.

"I've seen more of Stan in the last week than I have the last six months. Maybe I should offer him a free room for the last four trips."

A ghost of a smile touched his lips. "Perhaps promise him a room if you *don't* have to call him."

"There isn't anyone left, Shaun. J.J. and Zach and Alyssa, they'll be staying here full-time. You have your house and your duties. Tim will be leaving for New York, and Ethan for Baltimore. Darla is locked up. I sincerely hope this is all past us. Murders, car wrecks, and gun-threatening drunks would be hell on business."

He chuckled. That was Carli. Taking a miserable situation and making a joke. He watched as Ethan returned to her side, and vowed to keep an eye on her humor when the agent left. It would be the gauge by which he would judge the depth of her love for Brooks.

"There's a … situation. In Georgia. Micah, my boss, has changed my flight. I leave tonight. Red-eye to the East Coast."

Carli's only hesitation was to wet her lips before pasting on a smile. "That leaves us time to get breakfast and check out William's Lake."

Ethan smiled enough to set off his dimples. "Yes. It does."

"Shaun?" she said his name as an invitation to join them.

Shaking his head, he answered, "I need to take pictures, fill out the paperwork."

"Alright. I'll leave some coffee and wrap up some breakfast for you."

He turned toward the deputy's vehicle to begin gathering items to process the scene, while Carli and Ethan retreated inside the lodge.

Tim was descending the stairs with his luggage. He smiled at Carli and Ethan as if he just confirmed a secret.

"Good morning," he greeted cheerfully.

"It was, then it wasn't," she said.

"What do you mean?" he asked, setting his bags on the floor.

"Didn't you hear the gunshots?" she raised her brows.

"What? No. I was working and wearing my ear buds. Gunshots? Was anyone hurt?"

"We'll tell you about it over breakfast. Where's J.J.?"

Tim shrugged. "We met earlier in the kitchen. He's probably out in the barn." He followed Carli and Ethan across the lobby to the dining room, saying, "With everything that has occurred this past week, no more comments regarding the 'fireworks' that occur with regularity in New York."

Carli tossed over her shoulder, "Bet you a hundred bucks another shooting will occur in the City before anything like these events happen here again."

Tim scowled. He knew the statistics and believed he just lost the hundred dollars.

CHAPTER 49

It was decided that the cases would be shipped to the *Views* instead of Tim handling them on his own. A company promising to overnight the crates to New York was on their way with a van. Shaun ate his breakfast, which was now lunch, standing in the kitchen. Taking his coffee in a travel mug, he was on his way to the office in town, then Laramie. The call from Vince told them that Jim Lockhart had entered the OR fifteen minutes ago. J.J., who was in the walk-in freezer in the corner to do inventory and retrieve some elk meat for a meal later in the week and therefore didn't hear the gunshots, was the one who volunteered to take Tim to the airport. There were no clients, and no immediate repairs that needed to be done on the Preserve. Zach had called to assure everyone that Alyssa was fine. They would be stopping at the house she shared with her father to gather her belongings before returning to the lodge.

"Have you talked with Scott?" Tim asked as he set his bags inside the back of the van and closed the doors.

"I keep putting him off," she answered with a shake of her head. "Tonight."

"Then he'll be even more pleased to see me on Monday morning," he said with slight sarcasm.

"I'll be sure to offer my opinion of your idea for the new feature in the *Views*."

Facing her, he refused to believe that this was a final goodbye. "I'll see you at the end of the month for the showing. Then you'll have to come to the office, clear out your desk."

She stepped up to him and wrapped her arms tightly about his body. He closed his eyes and returned the hug.

"I'm going to miss you," he whispered.

"I know," she said, blinking to keep her eyes dry.

"I love you."

"I know." She moved back, keeping her hands on his arms for a moment longer. "You won't be the only one with a broken, lonely heart."

He offered her a slight smile.

"But that gives me reason to call and text you at all hours of the day. Then maybe you won't miss me so much," she threatened good-naturedly.

He put on his sunglasses, then reached behind his head to straighten his ponytail. "And I'll answer every time, unless I'm occupied with someone else."

"Charlie?" she raised a brow.

He shrugged. "New York is a long way from the Bay. But you know I like surprises."

Climbing into the passenger seat, he waved once to Ethan. The gesture was returned from the agent who leaned a shoulder against a post on the veranda. He closed the van's door, then rolled down the window. Smiling fully, he removed the hundred-dollar bill, old, crumpled, and stained from his shirt pocket. The radio was on while they ate and the news reporter stated that the New York City Police had an upscale hotel building surrounded where shots were fired just an hour earlier. Placing the bill, and her hands, in her back pockets, she stepped away from the van and towards the veranda, and Ethan. She didn't say anything as she turned to watch the van disappear down the drive.

Though he appeared relaxed, casual, Ethan's entire awareness was focused on the woman in front of him. She had been through more in the last several days than most people experience in their lifetime. Yet here she stood, one hip slightly cocked, blonde hair ruffled by the breeze, a smile on her face, and powerful hazel eyes turned fully on him. She had laughed, cried, shot a gun, danced at her father's funeral, consumed copious amounts of alcohol to the man's memory, sat astride a horse as if it were second nature, recovered from two attempts on her life, had her mother arrested, a lifelong friend murdered, began the separation from a close colleague, took over her father's business ... and despite it all, gave her heart to him.

"Well, Mr. Brooks, seems we have the entire Preserve to ourselves. It could be that the fish are biting today."

"Does catching the fish require a boat?"

"Possibly. Generally, waders are used if trout from Little Shy River is what you would prefer." She climbed the steps slowly.

"And those keep you from getting wet?"

She nodded.

"Hmm. Ms. Tanner, I have no aversion to water. In fact, I rather like it ... wet."

"I'm sure we can arrange to accommodate you request," her voice dropped to a near whisper.

He unfolded his arms and brought his hands to her jaw. "Ms. Tanner, between your attributes and your offer to please, it makes it difficult for a man to leave."

With her lips close, her eyes on his, she breathed, "No one has to leave, and everyone is welcome to return."

He could make no promises, except to be here with her now, so he kissed her. The underlying heat was a welcome friend, and the quick passion that ignited within forced him to rein in his control. She pressed herself against him, and his attempt to keep the kiss from escalating and taking her against the railing of the veranda, even though he knew she wouldn't object, began to slip. Her hand was on its way to the front of his jeans when the sound of an engine had her pulling away. He was at first regretful that he hadn't acted and taken advantage of their time together, but relieved when he saw Zach's truck pull into the parking lot, Alyssa's Honda following. If they had arrived a few minutes later, it would have been awkward.

Carli left the veranda and met Zach at his truck. Ethan couldn't hear the words, but guessed she was inquiring after Alyssa's health, and discussing the move into Cabin 9. He resumed his stance against the post and enjoyed the view of not only Carli, but the nature surrounding the lodge that seemed to come alive just because she was here. The sun was high in a blue sky, broken only by the tops of trees and Wolf's Ridge, which he knew to be on the other side of the lodge. The green shades of the foliage, the differences in the browns of the pine needles, gravel, and boulders framed the people discussing their future.

There was satisfaction in knowing that Alyssa would no longer be the recipient of her father's rage and ineptitude, so he ignored the fact that Jim Lockhart was not the only, or the last, parent to inflict physical and emotional abuse on their child. The love, which was fresh and should have been naïve, was tainted by what they had experienced. He liked Zach and Alyssa, and hoped that their feelings for each other would surmount Alyssa's past.

Breathing deeply of the clean air, warmed by the sun and scented by pine, he acknowledged the tightness in his chest that told him he would miss this. 'No one has to leave, and everyone is welcome to return,' Carli had said. Would she welcome him if he returned? Could he? How could he not?

Booted feet at the end of long legs planted themselves confidently on the ground as Carli strode across the parking lot towards him. The easy sway of her hips and swinging arms was topped off by a mischievous smile.

"Zach and Alyssa will take care of the crates. That leaves us," she glanced at her watch, "about four hours before you need to … catch your flight." Her smile faltered slightly at the last three words.

"We better see about those fish, then," he grinned, allowing a spark of heat to light his eyes.

An ice chest was packed and loaded into the company truck, along with Ethan's backpack and Carli's camera case. As they drove to William's Lake, she recounted stories of her youth and how certain landforms came to have their name. He enjoyed the tales and the scenery that passed outside his passenger window.

Arriving at the lake's edge, he was impressed by the size. Picturing a pond, she informed him the surface area was actually three-hundred acres. Quite small on the map of a Preserve of several thousand acres.

"Dad installed the boathouse about ten years ago. When families visit, the wife and kids come here for the day, paddle around in a canoe, while the husband tries to bag big game."

She unlocked the padlock and opened the door of the boathouse. Both sides were lined with racks, which supported a dozen canoes. Eight kayaks were stacked against the back wall. Inside the front wall hung personal flotation devices.

"Grab that end," she directed.

He complied, and they carried a canoe to the edge of the lake, setting it down so one-third of the craft was in the water.

"I'll get the paddles if you'll bring the stuff from the truck," she said.

The quietness of the forest surrounding them added to the battle that raged in his mind. The case in Georgia could bust open anytime. The bodies of the missing children from the Atlanta area were being found and a profile of the killer was in the construction process. Pulling the ice chest out of the bed of the truck, setting his pack and Carli's case over one shoulder, his thoughts alternated between what Sloan had told him of the crimes and the beauty of the Preserve. As he approached the canoe and Carli, he felt a moment of guilt for soiling this time with her with what was happening in Atlanta.

Placing the cooler in the middle of the boat, he helped Carli step inside, then nudged the canoe further into the water. Pushing off with one foot, the boat rocked slightly as he stepped in and took the bench at the end of the craft. The gentle rolling caused laughter to bubble up from Carli who sat at the front of the boat. It was the sound of her enjoyment that closed the door, however temporarily, on the case unfolding in Georgia. He only had a few hours left in Wyoming, and being here with her would need to sustain him for what awaited on the East Coast.

After a couple tries, their strokes coordinated and the canoe cut smoothly through the water. She pointed out the beaver dam, a hawk's nest, and the edge of the lake that she knew was Zach's favorite.

"How do you know that?" He set his paddle across his knees and looked at Carli. They had decided to paddle and drift, giving him a chance to capture some of the wilderness with his sketches. She had taken several shots with a new digital camera. It rested now on the cooler that sat between them.

"Wildflowers grow in the glade on that end of the lake because it receives more sunshine. On days when Alyssa is scheduled to work the front desk, those flowers appear in a mug of water next to the phone."

The image of Carli receiving flowers, or wearing nothing but, flashed through his mind.

"Are you ever in the pictures you take?" he asked, abruptly changing the subject.

"No. Most of the pictures are for work."

"What about when you come home? Family photos at a holiday dinner? Shaun ever get one of you with Sam?"

She shrugged. "Sure. There were several albums of us growing up. Unfortunately, most were in the storage shed before it was torched."

He gestured toward the camera. "Mind if I take one of you?"

"What? Why?" Her scrunched up face reflected how some women felt when a camera was pointed in their direction.

"I think you're beautiful. Out here in the canoe, the lake water nearly still, the sun shining through the trees ... you belong here, Carli. There's nothing more natural than a picture of a woman where she loves to be."

Grateful for the sunglasses that hid her eyes and what she knew was her love for this man shining in them, she nodded and smiled. Her heart softened, and her expression became one of genuine pleasure and enjoyment when she saw him use the viewfinder instead of the screen. Bringing the camera close, utilizing the human eye to capture the picture instead of the computer readouts, showed an intimacy with the subject. She struck a few poses that had Ethan's chuckle rumbling in his chest.

They ate when they paused for pictures, the conversation easy between them. They had circumnavigated most of the lake, and a noticeable sadness settled around them as the shadows began to lengthen. With a few more strong strokes, they beached the canoe in front of the boathouse. She climbed out and steadied the craft while he gained his feet, then they pulled the canoe from the water. Items were quickly stashed and carried to the truck, the boat and accessories were placed in the shed.

He felt her tension, and hated that his plans, ones that he couldn't control and didn't make, had put it there.

After securing the padlock on the door, she turned and found herself nose to nose with her FBI agent. His jaw was clenched and his eyes burned with intensity. It was silly to ask why there was a change in their easy banter and comfortable silences as each was lost in their art during their paddle around the lake. He was leaving and apparently had several thoughts that he either couldn't make sense of or ones that were unpleasant. Any stream of chatter her mind tried to create was cut short by the desperation in his kiss. In the next heartbeat, she was riding the waves of emotion along with Ethan.

Warm palms cupped her jaw, but then one moved to tunnel in hair to keep her lips where he could brand them, while the other slid around her waist to bring her into full contact with the front of his body. Rewarded with her willingness to accept the brutal assault of his lips and tongue, she groaned at the evidence of his wanting her naked and beneath him. He secretly hoped that she was too swamped with his desire, and her own, to notice the shaking of his hands.

He stepped forward, causing Carli to walk backward. At the corner of the boathouse, he grasped her hands as they tugged his shirt from the waistband of his jeans. As he moved to kneel in front of her, he encouraged her to follow him down to the ground. Spring grass and newly sprouted ferns created a blanket of green in a patch of sunlight that wasn't blocked by the towering pines or the roof of the boathouse. The temperature had yet to cool in the late afternoon, and he refused to allow her skin to raise with anything that wasn't created by his need for her.

Sighing as his weight settled over her, she pushed the rush of time from her thoughts and forced herself to focus on every detail. The exact color of his hair, the length and surety of his fingers, the depth of his eyes where so many emotions swirled she doubted even Ethan could name them all. His clever tongue as it tasted and teased, exciting her beyond logic. She fought the haze that began to settle over her mind. If this was the last time they were together, the final opportunity for her to remember him, to take him further into her soul, then she wanted to be cognizant of it.

She was fighting herself. This was not how he wanted his memories of her to be. Free of inhibitions, her incredible spirit taking both of them higher was what he wanted, what he *needed*. He would just turn up the heat, leave her no choice but to burn with him in the attraction, the love, they had for each other. That acknowledgement had him increasing the intensity with which he pulled her after him.

Shoving her shirt up over her ribs to bunch between her breasts and her collarbones, he stretched the lace of her bra, releasing that which he sought. The 5 o'clock shadow on his chin and cheeks rasped against her delicate, sensitive skin. She arched up into him, her hands fisted in the material of his shirt over his back. Her button and zipper were undone to allow him room to slide his hand to her center. Breath coming in gasps, he knew she was losing the control she struggled to keep. Good. He wanted her saturated in pleasure, screaming his name. With fingers as relentless as his mouth, he sent her flying into space.

Did she miss it? What had escaped her notice as Ethan pushed her to completion? Barely becoming aware of his hands as he tugged her jeans the rest of the way off her legs, she struggled to come back to the slanted, afternoon sun on the patch of greenery beside the boathouse. Details. Her observations. The nuances of this man was what she needed to catalogue, what she would hold to her when he was thousands of miles away. But it appeared Ethan had no such agenda. Slightly numb from his determined attention, she had no time to hurry along her breath and blood to return to some semblance of normalcy before Ethan settled his weight between her thighs, and proceeded to fill every empty part of her.

This was what he wanted to haunt his dreams. Carli, blonde hair spilling around her face, tangled in the leaves of the ferns. Her lips, a perfect match to the hardened tips of her breasts, slightly swollen and glistening from his greedy mouth, served to fuel his desperation to have her completely. His heart had no concern for the logistics of him in a city, air clogged with smog and sky that was choked with concrete and steel, and her in the clear, fresh air surrounded by the wilderness that was so much a part of who she was. The rhythm of his hips was as unrelenting as his tongue as they both laid claim to her body and her soul.

Shattering around him, taking him with her as she exploded into a million brilliant colors, she knew all she needed to know of the man who possessed her. Through the rush of blood in his veins, the fierce pounding of his heart, the breath that seemed to still in his lungs as he gave himself to her, he had only her name on his lips.

The conversation on the way back to the lodge was quiet and stilted.

"So, whenever you're done in Georgia, you'll return to Baltimore?"

"Yes. I should be back in the City by Tuesday."

Interesting, she thought, that he referred to Baltimore as 'the City' instead of 'home'.

"And the art show at the end of the month ... you'll come?" She hated that desperation crept into her voice.

"If I can. Depends on ... work."

The sun was near the western edge of the valley when they pulled up in front of the lodge. He climbed down from the truck, his pack over one shoulder.

"I have my gear ready," he gestured with his head toward Cabin 4 and the rental vehicle at the far end of the parking lot.

She pocketed the keys and walked with Ethan.

"What do you plan to do with that?" he asked as a way to fill the silence when they passed the remains of the burned storage structure.

"A studio. Every artist needs one," she glanced up at him and saw the tightening in his jaw.

Within minutes, he had loaded his bag, laptop, and backpack into the back of the rental. He wasn't sure what to say. 'Goodbye' seemed too formal. 'See you later' was too casual. He couldn't tell her he loved her. Instead, he gathered her close, as if he could take some part of her with him. Realizing it was selfish and silly to bring something that Carli represented to the crime scene he would be investigating in seven hours, he placed his lips on hers. Everything that he felt, he poured into the kiss. And he took all that she offered. Knowing he had to stop, he rested his forehead on hers, his breath coming hard.

"Carli, I—"

She placed the tips of her fingers against his lips. "Shh. Don't make excuses or promises. I'll be at the gallery showing on the twenty-ninth. I would love to see you. Then I'll come home. Here, Ethan."

Moving away from him, one hand dropping from around his neck, the other tracing the outline of his mouth, she offered him a small smile. Tucking her hands inside her back pockets, she remained where she was. She wouldn't force him to stay, wouldn't make him feel anything different than what she had discerned from his kiss. Twice, he opened his mouth to say something, then closed it. Without another word, he got into the SUV and pulled away.

She crossed her arms under her chest and gave up any attempt to keep the smile on her face. The further away the vehicle drove, the deeper the fissure in her heart. She tried to blink back the tears, and was surprised when they fell anyway.

He looked in the rearview mirror. Though he couldn't see her eyes through the tinted windows and distance, he suspected they were tear-filled. For a moment his foot let off the accelerator.

With white knuckles he gripped the wheel, depressed the pedal, and turned the corner of the drive. Staring ahead, he ignored the thoughts of anything besides getting to the airport in Laramie. The tightness in his belly, the heaviness in his chest, was just a precursor to what he would feel when he arrived in Atlanta. He continued to delude himself on the plane when he tried to sleep, but pictures of Carli filled his mind.

Just before landing, he pulled his pad from his backpack and found her camera. He must have shoved it in there when they arrived back at the boathouse. Turning it on, he forwarded through the shots Carli had taken until he found the ones of her.

"Sir, can you bring your seat forward? We're approaching Atlanta."

He glanced at the flight attendant, then complied, his attention and gaze back on the woman smiling at him from the digital display of the camera.

Standing on the curb outside the terminal, his backpack over one shoulder, carryon in his hand, his bag at his feet, a man in a suit approached him.

"Agent Brooks?" The man awaited Ethan's nod. "We're here to take you to the crime scene. I'm Agent Tallson. Agent Goldman is in the vehicle," he gestured to a black SUV.

Ethan followed, loaded his bags, then climbed into the back seat. "Are there any updates?"

«« —»»

J.J. glanced at his watch, then decided there was time. It was Saturday afternoon, there were no clients at the lodge, and everyone who should be in jail was, or on their way. Shaking his head at the story retold in the kitchen about Jim Lockhart holding Zach at gunpoint with Bear's missing rifle, and then getting shot, twice, seemed like an incredible cap to the unbelievable previous week. He would have to make an effort to talk with Zach alone to ensure for himself that his friend was alright.

There weren't many cars in the dirt lot of the Rockin' R, but he knew that it would fill up over the next few hours. Parking by the corner of the building, he smiled a little at the Corvette out back. Sissy was working a double shift today. He was tempted a few times to ask Shaun why he didn't marry Sissy. They had been on and off in their relationship since high school. But then he figured that he and Shaun weren't that close and it really was none of his business.

Sissy was the only one working the floor and the bar. Either John was coming in later or he was in his office. The kitchen was closed off from the bar by a giant swinging door that had one window in it that prevented two people from going through the door in opposite directions at the same time. Those that worked in the kitchen weren't able to see what was happening on the other side of the door unless they stood next to it and peered through the window.

Two people occupied one of the pool tables and there were four others in the table area watching a game on the television that hung above them. The only person at the bar was Justin. J.J. knew him only because in this part of the country there weren't many people, or bars. He hadn't worked with Justin except a couple of weeks after Bear hired him and let Justin go, since the younger cowboy was a seasonal employee. That was the last time Justin worked for Tanner's Outdoor Adventures. He currently was a wrangler for one of the big ranches in this part of Wyoming. Justin had a reputation, from the days when he used to rodeo, as being tough. He was known around town for getting wild on Saturday nights and starting fights. The vehicles in parking lots that were vandalized after Justin was forcibly asked to leave an establishment, had never been connected to him, but folks in the area knew to watch the hotheaded kid, especially when he'd had a few.

J.J. took a stool on the opposite end of the bar and waited patiently for Sissy to make her way back from the customers at the table watching the game.

Rounding the corner of the bar, she smiled at J.J. He didn't come in often, and when he did he had one or two beers, told her a joke, and left a good tip.

"How are you?" she asked.

"Fine. On my return trip from the airport. Dropped off Carli's work partner. With no one out at the Preserve, thought I would stop in and see how things were going at the Rockin' R."

"Great. What can I get you?"

"Just a draft," he said, and set a ten-dollar bill on the bar.

"Things must be pretty quiet out at the lodge if the cabins are empty, huh?" She set the pint in front of him and left the money where it was.

"You would think so, but there has been more action since Bear's death—"

"Just a minute," she interrupted, and moved to where Justin sat, an empty beer in front of him.

"I'll take another," Justin said, his words just beginning to slur.

Without a word, she took the empty and replaced it in the case, then pulled a bottle from the ice, popped the cap, and set it down in front of him. When she reached for the dollar bills he had laid on the bar, he placed his hand over hers. She tried to pull away, but he gripped her fingers, the bills crumpling in her hand.

"How about you have dinner with me after your shift?"

"I don't think so."

"Why not? Cause I ain't Sheriff Tanner?" He leaned over the bar towards her, his half-smile full of sarcasm.

"Shaun and I are friends. I go home on Saturday nights, Justin. And I don't date customers." She tried to pull her hand away, but his hold only tightened.

"Think you're too good for me? Shaun comes in here, and you go out with him. Hell, I've seen you in town with one of the other employees from Willow Ranch. You got something against me, Sugar?"

"Let her go, Justin. It's a little early in your evening for me to ruin your night out by discussing this in the parking lot," J.J.

spoke quietly from behind Justin's left ear. The hand on Justin's shoulder squeezed considerably tighter with each word.

Justin looked at J.J.'s hand, then released Sissy's. She moved away and placed the money in the till. He shifted his gaze to the man who worked at the Preserve.

"Just having a little fun," Justin said and smiled into eyes that held no humor, only distaste.

"Sissy wasn't laughing." J.J. stayed a moment longer, then turned his back on Justin and returned to his seat.

"Thanks," she told him as she stood once more across from him. "He gets a little mean when he's drunk." She glanced at Justin, who was staring at her, tipped his bottle in her direction, then took a swallow. Turning her attention back to J.J., she said, "You were saying something about excitement?"

In between a trip to the table with food and two times to the pool table with drinks, she listened to J.J. recount the events at the lodge.

"Unbelievable. I'm so glad none of you were seriously hurt." She moved off to fill a drink order for a couple who just walked in and sat at the bar.

He noticed that Justin was stumbling back from the bathroom. The kid glared at him, then pushed through the front door. He shook his head. Justin was trouble. Taking out his cell, he called the sheriff's office. Whoever was on duty needed to know that there was a drunk driver on the road. He briefly wondered if a night in jail would improve Justin's attitude.

"Can I get you anything else?" Sissy's smiling face filled his field of vision.

She was pretty and had a knockout body. He figured she made a decent living working at the Rockin' R. She had a small house in town and kept her Corvette in top shape. Usually when she asked him that, the thoughts that floated through his mind were 'Yes. Dinner. A movie. A drink after work. A night out at the lake, under the stars'. He had always kept those to himself.

Perhaps it was seeing what Zach was planning with Alyssa, or observing the interactions between Carli and Ethan, but a surge of courage came from somewhere, and he asked, "Breakfast tomorrow morning at the diner?" When her smile faded and she blinked at him, he kicked himself mentally and tried to cover up what he shouldn't have asked. "I'm sorry. I didn't mean to imply that we should spend the night together. I'm sure you have plans." Once again realizing he was digging himself deeper he tried, "Not that you'll be spending it with someone else. I mean—"

She chuckled and placed her hand on his forearm. "J.J., stop. I know what you meant. I can't have breakfast with you—"

"Sure, it was stupid. I'm sorry."

"No. It wasn't stupid." She looked at him and recognized what she had often seen. A friendly man, handsome and kind. He didn't drink to excess and always had a ready smile. Why shouldn't she meet him for breakfast, or dinner, or anything else? She had decided not to wait for Shaun. There were dreams she held for her life, and if Sheriff Tanner wouldn't be a part of those dreams, there was no reason she shouldn't look for other ways to fulfill them.

"Sunday mornings are tough for me. I work doubles most Saturdays. How about lunch?"

He smiled.

"I'll meet you at the diner in town," she offered. It was a few blocks from her house and it would be good to go for a mid-morning walk somewhere besides from the bar to a table.

"Sounds great. Noon?"

"Noon," she nodded.

He left the ten dollars on the bar and drove back to the lodge. Maybe he would stay in Centennial a while longer. His employment at the Preserve wasn't much like what most people thought of as work. He enjoyed being outdoors and giving clients fond memories of their vacations, and he was excited about the direction in which Carli wanted to move. Tomorrow he had a lunch date with the prettiest girl in town. He smiled as he pulled into the driveway at the lodge.

CHAPTER 50

Carli forced herself to have dinner with J.J., Zach, and Alyssa that night instead of eating with the loneliness she knew would find her. She figured she would have to hire a few more employees and decided to enjoy the time she had with just these three. Their conversation drew her away from brooding. There was change coming, and if they hoped to ride it with any amount of success, they would need to begin planning. Tomorrow was Sunday and she thought it could be their only day off for a while. They agreed to meet for dinner with ideas about how to move forward with the Preserve.

It was an early night for each of them, and after J.J. looked in on the horses one more time, they all climbed the stairs and disappeared into their respective rooms. J.J. picked up the novel he had been reading and rested against the headboard of his bed. Zach and Alyssa talked of what they would need for Cabin 9, her plans to register for UW, and what they thought would happen at court and to the Lockhart house.

Calculating for the time difference, it was late, but not too late, and she knew the hours Scott kept. Telling him she was resigning was not something she wanted to send in an e-mail. She would prefer to do it in person, but it wasn't feasible to leave the lodge at this time. Her room looked sparse with the crates gone. Perhaps promising him that all the prints will be in his hands by Tuesday would be a good way to lead into, 'Sorry, Scott, but your award-winning photojournalist is quitting to run a photo safari in Wyoming'. When she got him on the phone, that's what actually came out of her mouth.

For the first time since his acquaintance with Carli, the editor of *International Views* was speechless. It didn't come as a total surprise. Tim had hedged a direct answer, and Scott hadn't heard from Carli as to her plans to return to New York before now. He supposed it was similar to caring for an ailing parent. They will die eventually, and even though the caretakers prepare for that, there is still some amount of shock. He knew from years of experience with Carli that once her mind had formed a decision, there was no moving her.

He pinched the bridge of his nose and sighed. "You realize this means I'll have to give up my yacht in Ft. Lauderdale."

"What are you talking about? I tell you that I'm resigning and you're thinking of selling your boat?"

"Without the top journalist in the country, and probably the Western Hemisphere, no longer at the *Views,* subscriptions will decrease, which will affect my paycheck, and therefore the maintenance on my boat."

There was only a slight bit of truth to the statement, but it was his attempt at not having Carli feel horrible about leaving. She shared with him the events of the past week, and even though his favorite *ex*-employee, would, could, normally handle whatever life tossed at her, had indeed dodged, and dealt with, more than her share.

"Look, I understand what you've been through. And I do appreciate all the awards that line my office. But, damn it girl, I'm going to miss you." He sighed again as another thought occurred to him. "And who the hell am I going to pair with Tim?"

That gave her the perfect opening for something she thought of during the conversation at dinner. "First, I would check with Tim to see if he demands another partner. I've taught him all I know. I think he's ready to go it alone. When you see him on Monday morning and he tells you his idea for a new feature in the *Views,* you could, I don't know, be ecstatic and give him the suggestion that informing the readership on where the 'most contributing photojournalist' resides now, is an awesome idea. A spread on the Preserve would help all three of us."

He chuckled. Just like the first time he sat her down in his office for an interview, Carli Tanner was still an innovative, pushy, bright woman.

"You no longer officially work for me, yet you continue to toss out original ideas." He quieted his voice. With all traces of humor gone, he told her, "I'm going to miss you. You ever need anything ..." he left the statement for her to complete.

"I know, Scott. Thanks for being the best overbearing, egocentric boss an independent, strong-willed girl could ask for. If you ever find the need to escape the city noise, I'll have a cabin waiting for you in Wyoming."

"You take care of yourself, Carli." He hung up before any more words of farewell made him feel something besides the push for the next deadline.

"Bye, Scott," she said, but knew she was speaking to herself.

《《—》》

On Monday morning, Shaun picked Carli up at the lodge and they drove to Cheyenne. Darla would be arraigned and they wanted to do what they could to convince the judge to deny bail. They met with the defense attorney before entering the courtroom. Thanks to the FBI, they had evidence of real estate fraud and several counts of trespassing. Apparently, Darla would list houses for wealthy clients who either weren't in California or the country, or didn't want to be bothered with the details of selling their estates. So, she would move into the houses that she was showing. The change of addresses listed through the post office showed that she had been doing this for years. When the clients who had hired Darla were informed, some of them decided to press charges.

There was enough circumstantial evidence for the arson charge to stick, but with Ray's death, no collaboration or plea bargain with the prosecutor for attempted murder or conspiracy of murder. The judge seemed mildly impressed that the petite, well-dressed woman in his courtroom could accumulate such a list of charges. Since Darla had no permanent address in California, no place to remand in Wyoming, and with the gravity and amount of complaints filed against her, the judge denied her bail and invited her to enjoy the accommodations of the Laramie County Jail.

The lodge was once again empty when everyone piled into the van to attend the hearing of Jim Lockhart on Friday of that same week. Judge Burns saw them all together, then dismissed everyone except Alyssa. It was an hour later that she emerged from the judge's chambers, eyes puffy and red, but dry, to announce that if she hired a lawyer to represent her in court, she would have to appear, as Jim Lockhart had a right to face his accuser, but she may not have to take the stand. During the celebratory dinner at the Rockin'R, Carli had received a call from Stevens confirming that he could recommend a family law attorney, and that it would be possible to place the house on the market if Jim was convicted.

Raising their glasses in a toast, J.J. smiled, especially at Sissy behind the bar. She smiled back and sent him a wink. Shaun paid her no extra attention. There wasn't the expected disappoint at that realization, and she was as friendly and efficient as always.

It was Carli and Shaun that dealt with the poachers. Dan, Bob, Paul, and Jerry were remanded to their respective homes. At the preliminary hearing, it was decided that retribution would be agreed upon at the pre-trial conference, scheduled for later in the summer. The evidence and confessions were enough to save the court's time, and the defendants' money in going to trial. The new owner of Tanner's Outdoor Adventures decided that many hours of community service at conservatories and preserves might alter the game thieves' further decisions on theft and hunting.

The next three weeks were filled with getting Carli's ideas prioritized and implemented. Reservations were being booked and ads were posted for seasonal employees. It was decided that if a new hire worked out, then a year-round position would be offered. Donna's mother had taken ill, so she resigned from the lodge, but accepted Carli's offer that the job was available should she be able, or want, to return. Carli, Zach, Alyssa, and J.J. met every afternoon to check on their progress and make revised lists for the following day. New contracts were written with the businesses that made regular deliveries to the lodge. The vet and BLM were informed of the change in direction of the Preserve, and she met so many times with Maxwell Stevens regarding the will and trust funds and accounts that she wondered if people thought they were dating. Sometimes they met for meals, and other times it was while she was in town at the feed store, the ranger station, or the post office. It would take some time to go through all the paperwork, and she decided that at least Max was pleasant company.

Contractors were interviewed, and a local company hired to complete the renovations on Cabin 9. When she couldn't find anyone in Wyoming that could take on the task of marketing and PR for Tanner's Outdoor Adventures, Sam encouraged her to do a national search. The portfolios and resumes that began to arrive daily were a task to which Carli dedicated her time. However, her first priority was always to the clients.

Her days, filled with managing the Preserve, left her little time to dwell on Ethan's absence. She sent him a few e-mails, updating him on the news of what was occurring in regards to construction, J.J., Zach, and Alyssa. She didn't have much opportunity to miss him. That was what she had convinced herself of when she dragged her weary body from bed in the early morning and lay down exhausted late at night. Ethan always replied, if a day or two, or three, later. He was polite and interested, always asking after her welfare, and often, like some of their verbal banter, writing something that could be taken a couple of different ways.

She knew she was in love with Ethan and recognized when the loneliness shifted to excitement at the prospect of seeing him at the gallery showing. One World Piece had already received what the gallery owner and Carli had decided on, as well as a few prints from her last trip to Africa and South America, thanks to Scott's permission. Her time in New York would be filled with releasing her rented apartment, selling or shipping her furniture and possessions, and cleaning out her space at the *Views*. She had packed her usual attire. There were a couple of formal dresses in her closet in New York that she wore to awards ceremonies and company dinners. One of them would work for the gallery showing.

Sleeping the first couple of hours on the flight, she then pulled out her laptop and worked for the next few. She had taken a red-eye mainly because she hated to waste a day traveling. To her surprise, Tim was waiting at the gate. The two of them talked nonstop from the airport to her apartment. They agreed to meet later in the afternoon, at the *Views*, where Tim would show her his new office.

"He loved the idea, by the way," Tim said as she turned to walk up the steps of her apartment building.

She gave him a puzzled look.

"For the first feature article by Tim Moore. 'From International Villages to Back Home, Photojournalist Carli Tanner Finds the Perfect Shot in the Wilderness of her Backyard'."

"I love it!" She enveloped him in a hug and laughed.

"Which means I'll be coming to visit before the end of summer."

She stepped back. "You're always welcome, Tim."

He left her to begin boxing up what she would ship back to the Preserve. One-of-a-kind gifts from tribes and villages that she had stayed with, artifacts, and even airport trinkets that represented a memory, were wrapped and situated to make a safe journey to their permanent home in Wyoming. Not caring much for her furniture, she placed an ad online and sold several pieces by the time she left at 4:05 p.m. to catch the subway to the office building that housed the desk from her previous life.

She was surprised when her colleagues had decorated her work space, hung a banner wishing her luck, and then placed a chocolate sheet cake amongst her stack of mail and pictures and collection of toy cameras. Encouraged by her friends to give a speech, which she kept short in an attempt to control any emotions of clinging to her life of the past years in this building, at this desk, she relented with comical tales of her travels and her first award she had won for Scott. Cake was eaten and toasts were made, stories were shared, and then they drifted back to their desks and phones, or home, once Scott announced that her picture would hang on their Wall of Fame and that she would receive a lifetime subscription to the *International Views*. A moment of appreciation and respect passed between her and Scott before he returned to his office to take up his editor's hat and bark out demands and barely veiled criticisms.

She gave away some of the things that had collected dust while she had been gone, and packed the rest. Accompanied by Tim, they left the office by way of the mailroom where she shipped her boxes to Wyoming. The dinner they enjoyed was punctuated by laughter. Each shared news of their lives the past weeks, and both recognized that it was the same between them, and yet something was different.

"I can see you're tired. I understand how hard you've been working on the Preserve, but that isn't it. I've seen you go thousands of miles and countless days with restless sleep and little food. That was all physical. That was the adventure of your life as a photojournalist for the *Views*. No, my Dear Love, this is something deeper. Heartfelt," he paused and sipped his wine.

She glanced down at her plate. *Damn him for seeing too much*, she thought.

"He loves you. Anyone who saw the two of you together would have known. I imagine your FBI agent has the same circles under his eyes, the same heartbroken expression."

She shrugged. "If he does or if he doesn't, there isn't much I can do about it. His life is in Baltimore. Mine is in Wyoming."

"And you're desperately hoping he shows at the gallery tomorrow night."

"With everything that I am," she answered immediately and honestly.

"I bet you a hundred bucks he shows—"

"He may be on a case—"

"Ethan Brooks will show," Tim stated with all the authority of a man used to winning his bets.

She wanted to believe him, but she also hated the feeling of disappointment. She shrugged, sipped her wine, and directed the conversation in a different direction.

«‹‹—››»

The moveable walls of the gallery were rearranged to accommodate the number and size of the prints they were showcasing from Carli's collection. Track lighting was adjusted to shine on, or shadow, the pieces. In the front, facing the windows that lined the street of populated Manhattan, were Ethan's sketches. A few were of the Preserve, Wolf's Ridge and Miner's Paradise and the fountain with the lodge and veranda in the background. The remaining sketches were of Carli. Riding Lady, laughing at the lake, another where her eyes reflected the concentration of what she was seeing while her camera was lowered below her hazel irises.

"I thought this would be the perfect introduction to your showing," explained Cecil Marks, the gallery owner, as he came to stand by Carli who had just stepped through the gallery doors.

The room was full of people and more continued to enter, brushing past her as they failed to recognize who she was. Any picture used for publicity or interviews shown on television, she was dressed casually, her hair down, and no make-up. The woman that stood there tonight was in an expensive pair of high-heeled shoes, a form fitting, floor-length gown of deep green, which, even though it was devoid of sequins, shimmered in the reflective lights of the gallery. Her dark blonde hair was piled atop her head, with wisps that gently framed her face. Hazel eyes were accented by black eyeliner, mascara, and glittery shadow, her lips, though, remained a soft, glossy pink.

"It's perfect," Carli agreed.

Cecil checked his watch. "Enjoy yourself for the next half-hour. You're due to give a little talk at 8:30."

She raised a brow at the retreating business-like gallery owner. Cecil had gotten his wish, which was to showcase the foremost photojournalist in America. The sketches done by Ethan were just gravy.

Lifting a glass of champagne from a passing server, she began greeting a few people she knew who lived in the City. Seeing that Charlie accompanied Tim was unexpected.

"I applied for a transfer. They often don't come through," he glanced at Tim, "This one did."

"And you kept this to yourself," she smiled and shook her head at her former partner.

His eyes looked past her shoulder. "Seems tonight is a night for the unexpected."

She turned to see Shaun and Samantha enter the gallery, then pause to gaze at Ethan's sketches. Excusing herself, she made her way towards them.

"Shaun, Sam—" she began.

Sam hugged Carli, and when she stepped back, Shaun draped his good arm around her shoulder. He wasn't wearing the sling, but kept his left arm guarded against his side.

"This is some show," he told her, his eyes traveling from the prints to the wait staff to the scantily clad groupies who hung out at gallery showings hoping to go home with the artist, or one of the artist's friends.

"No way we would have missed this," Sam said, taking two glasses of champagne and giving one to Shaun.

"It makes it more special that the two of you are here." Carli's excitement continued to bubble as Cecil appeared from nowhere to direct her to a podium and microphone.

Sam followed, chattering about Ethan's sketches and the press of people that turned out for the show. "What are you going to say?" she asked.

"Not sure. This 'talk' is impromptu. I was informed of it only thirty minutes ago."

"Tell them how you started in photography and what you look for in a shot," Sam suggested.

Carli relaxed a little as she realized the sound advice. Photography is a subject she rarely grew tired of discussing.

Asking for the attention of those in the part of the gallery that immediately surrounded her, she gave a brief history of her interest in art and her time at college. There was laughter as she recounted her interview with Scott, who caught her eye by raising his glass in a silent toast to the memory. Her smile brightened at seeing him. It seemed to follow naturally that she share some of what she learned on her first international assignment. The chuckles from the gallery attendees faded as her attention was caught by the opening of the front door. The brief, awkward moment of silence was covered quickly by her genuine smile. She conveyed to those present her passion for capturing on film the emotions of nature.

"These expressions are a reflection of the human soul," she explained. Speaking from her heart, she knew the words were true about photography, but they were also directed to the man who enhanced her life and filled her in ways she hadn't realized were empty.

Ethan, dressed appropriately in a black tux, his hair a little long and slicked back from his face, was drawn to her. It was as if no one else in the gallery existed. Her words, he knew, were spoken for him, to him. Making his way towards the front, he stood slightly to the side, completely captured by the woman who owned his heart and brightened his soul.

Shaun spotted Ethan and elbowed Sam. "I'll be damned," they said at the same time.

"Has the other artist shown up?" someone from the crowd called out.

"I'm not at liberty to say," she offered, unsure how much of Ethan's identity needed to be protected because of his employer. "Thank you all for your attendance. Enjoy the evening."

Applause followed her from the podium to the corner where Ethan stood. The air of the gallery was then filled with voices in conversation.

"I'm glad you were able to attend. Cecil, the owner, and Barbara, the manager, did a wonderful job to showcase your sketches," Carli said as a greeting, unsure how Ethan would respond.

"The sketches are fine. But I came here for you." His eyes held hers. Placing one hand against her cheek he whispered, "I've missed you, Carli. Your smile, your laugh, the way you smell, those beautiful hazel eyes that see the world as it is, that capture the true essence of everything ... that look at me as if I am all that matters."

He brought his lips to hers and it steadied him. The spinning of his world slowed, and he caught his breath. Her hand was on his heart and she kissed him just as reverently.

"I love you, Carli Tanner. If you agree, I won't live another day without you by my side, filling my life with your beauty." Half-amazed at himself for giving her the words he thought but unsure of how she would accept them, he pulled the ring from his pocket. Taking her hand in his and bringing the ring up so she could see it, he waited for her answer.

The instant she saw him, she felt complete. Heat and love and desire and joy all bounced and lengthened and twined together inside of her. A proposal of marriage was not something she had thought about. When she searched his eyes, she found resolute determination. Ethan had recognized what they had together and was putting his plans in place to have her. There was no fear, no teasing mischief, just a knowing that this was right. Looking inside herself, she was surprised that there was no second-guessing, no wondering if accepting his ring was appropriate. They belonged together. It was just that simple.

"Ethan Brooks, in all my travels I have never found a man of more courage, truer heart, or such giving of himself for the lives of others. Perhaps there has been some orchestration between letting go of my father and welcoming you into my life. Yes, I will be your wife."

He slipped the ring on her finger and kissed her. The sound of applause and whistles, the flashes of light from the media were temporarily ignored as two souls that had witnessed much, found comfort in each other.

Sam glanced at Shaun who wore a peculiar smile. "How did you know about this?"

Without halting in his careful applause, he answered, "A fax came into the office two days ago. Agent Ethan Brooks has been reassigned. The Director of the Northwest, Region 2, wanted to alert me that I would have high-level backup in my town."

EPILOGUE

Four Months Later

The chairs were filled and soft music floated over the guests' heads, carried on the ever-present breeze. Ethan briefly closed his eyes and inhaled. The air, warm and clean and fresh, reassured him that he was really here, that this was indeed happening.

"Are you alright?" Sam asked quietly across the aisle.

"I've never been more so," he whispered back.

The traditional song started, and this part of the ceremony, they decided, was all that would follow custom. Everyone in the chairs stood and looked behind them as Carli, dressed in a sleeveless, ankle-length, white dress covered with lace, was on the arm of the town sheriff. To Carli's left, were Sam and Tim. On her right was Ethan. Zach and Alyssa, Charlie and Micah Sloan sat in the front row, with Scott Banding at the far end.

"Who gives this woman to this man?" the judge asked.

"I do," Shaun answered. Taking her fingers from his arm, he kissed Carli's knuckles and placed her safely inside Ethan's hands, then stepped to the groom's side.

"Please be seated," the judge continued.

They shared vows they had written, exchanged rings, and were pronounced Mr. and Mrs. Brooks. As Ethan and Carli turned towards those who had gathered, they marveled at the distance they both had traveled individually to arrive at this place and time. Under a hail of bird seed and flower petals and cheers of well wishes, there remained the work to be done on the studio and Cabin 9 and converting her father's rooms to something more accommodating. Employees had been hired and the search for a marketing and PR person was narrowed to three possibilities.

Amid the revelry of the reception held at the lodge, was the concern for the trials of Darla and Jim. Sam had been in quiet conversation with Shaun while the band played a favorite country tune, over her concerns regarding Crystal Springs Farm and the threats she received. J.J. suggested they put that aside and enjoy the festivities.

Carli stuck her hand out. "Thank you, Micah, for helping Ethan."

He offered an easy smile and took her hand in his. "I should dislike you. You forced me to pull some strings and transfer my best field agent."

"I won't apologize," she chuckled.

"He's a good man, Carli. It means a lot to me to see him happy. I never thought he would allow himself to be. Take care of him, and yourself." Micah squeezed her hand, then released it and made his way to the bar.

Tim approached her and asked for a dance. Ethan's eyes, never far from his bride, looked with interest as Carli, held in Tim's embrace as they swayed on the dance floor, threw her head back and laughed.

《《—》》

Two Weeks Later

Charlie let himself into the apartment, dropped the mail on the kitchen counter, then reached for the ringing phone. He sighed and hung up when he realized it was a prank call.

Pulling the bottle of white wine from the refrigerator, he took two glasses from the cabinet and filled each half-full. Carrying them to the couch in the living room, he set them on the coffee table.

"Who was calling?" Tim asked, looking up from his laptop.

"No one. You have a letter from Wyoming," Charlie said and leaned back into the cushions.

Tim hesitated, but when Charlie wasn't forthcoming with more information he moved to the kitchen and searched through the stack. It was a brown, clasp envelope. The return address was the Preserve. Tim lifted a brow and broke the seal. Tipping it, two items fell out onto the counter. A hundred-dollar bill and a sonogram. He ignored the bill, but picked up the black and white picture and smiled. Turning to face the fridge, he used two magnets and centered it on the door.

Raising his voice to be heard in the other room, he asked, "How do you feel about being called 'Uncle Charlie'?"

Questions to Ponder

1)   What do you feel is the most appropriate consequences for those involved in child abduction, trafficking, and exploitation? What would be needed in order for a recovered child to overcome the trauma? Would it even be possible?

2)   What are your opinions on same-sex relationships and marriage?

3)   Do you side with animal activists in that every creature should be protected from being hunted and treated humanely when raised domestically for consumption, or do you ascribe to the belief that all of nature is available for human use?

4)   What contributes to abusive tendencies, and how can one halt the cycle of the mistreatment of others?

5)   Winning a war, contributing to the success of a business, and attaining goals and dreams require many things. When, if ever, does the end justify the means?

Turn the page for a brief introduction to

Of Hoof Prints and Heartbeats

the second book in The Tanner Trilogy

Stuffing his gloves into the back pocket of his well-worn jeans, he latched the gate linking the small pasture with the summer one, which sported grass that was knee-high. The first few hundred head of cattle would be taken through the gate next week. By October, and before the first snow coated the ground, they would round up the prime ones and ship them to market. Others would be taken to auction for breeding stock or the rodeo circuit.

Left foot in the stirrup, he swung up onto Racer's back. His keen eyes, despite their age, scanned the horizon and the line of trees. He had felt uncomfortable the last two stops, as breaches in the fence showed it was more than pushy cattle that had wandered this way. Nothing moved, but that didn't squelch the uneasiness. Nudging Racer in the direction of the barn, and his dinner, he urged the gelding into a canter.

The crack of the rifle was heard a second before it tore through Joe's back, piercing lung and heart. The jerking body fell to the side, then off the horse to hit the ground. Racer shied away from the rider now laying motionless in the tall grass. Two horses emerged from the line of trees, passed through the gate, and collected the spooked gelding. The body would be difficult to discover in the tall foliage. If things went well, Uncle Joe, ranch manager for Crystal Springs Farm, wouldn't be found for several days.

A short distance beyond the gate, the horses were loaded into a trailer and hauled several miles from the sight of the crime. They would be too busy pushing cows to spend the extra funds, given anonymously and in secret, to complete the deed. A guilty conscience was of no concern, else they wouldn't have accepted the job. They would keep the gelding for now. If they needed more cash, he could always be sold.

«««—»»»

She thanked Cole for the cup of coffee, then shook her head that she didn't need anything else. Her youngest son descended the front steps and moved in the direction of the barn. Confidence oozed from Cole, but so did the warning signs that nobody would get too close to him. She understood why he kept others at a distance, and hoped that time and experience would increase his trust and bring down the walls he had erected to protect his wounded heart.

She shook her head again at her own musings. Her fractured wrist was healed, but hurt occasionally when she overdid things. The medication prescribed to 'Alice Branson, in case of pain', by her doctor, remained unused. Brackets of discomfort around her mouth eased as the worry and anger for the real reason for her broken wrist and ribs and numerous bruises, all now healed, pushed its way to the front of her thoughts.

Four generations of Branson's had lived in this part of Colorado. Drought, blizzards, miners, and government workers had all tried to intimidate the family to give up their home. They not only refused to pull up stakes, but had acquired more acres, which allowed them to grow financially and in influence of local affairs. She hadn't told Cole anything other than she took a tumble off the porch steps. He was a smart man, a criminal lawyer for a big firm in Chicago, and she knew he didn't buy the story. For now, his life was in the Midwest. This was her problem, and she would deal with it the same way Jack, her late husband of thirty-five years, would have. She would dig in her heels, and if offered the chance, give as good as she got. This was Branson land, and no greedy son of a bitch was going to take it away from her.

《《—》》

'Fell off the porch steps,' my ass, Cole thought as he walked to the barn. Tacking up his favorite horse and doing a day's work in the saddle was the only thing he could think of to derail the confrontation he held on his tongue about the lies his mother muttered to explain her injuries. In the moments when he wasn't spinning scenarios about what really happened to land her in the

hospital, his mind turned to Samantha Tanner. And when he couldn't reconcile that issue, he occupied himself with the ramifications of resigning from the premier legal firm in the Midwest and returning home to the JAR-C, hence the reason for working cattle.

«« —»»»

"Welcome to Durango. Local time is 3:35 and the temperature is a warm 83 degrees. Thanks for flying with us. If you're lucky enough to live here, welcome home. Only visiting? We hope your trip is enjoyable."

She turned on her phone and called Matt. "We're at the gate. I should be outside the terminal in about ten minutes," Sam said.

She smiled and waved as her ranch manager pulled up in front of her in the red company truck. Setting her carryon in the bed, she climbed up into the passenger seat.

Clicking her seatbelt, she turned to him and asked, "How is everything?" believing that an open-ended question would elicit more information than several specific ones.

Matt didn't disappoint. He glanced at Sam, then back out the windshield, deciding that the news he hadn't shared with her on the phone while she was at the stock auction, could only be said plainly.

"Haven't seen Uncle Joe in three days. Don't think he was dumped, as Racer would have found his way back to the barn. We've searched the north pasture and the east and north fence line. Nothing. It's like he and the horse just disappeared."

Shit, Sam thought and closed her eyes, wondering if the trouble they had been having escalated to something happening to Uncle Joe. Something bad.

Made in the USA
San Bernardino, CA
27 May 2015